# THE WHOREHOUSE PAPERS

**ALSO BY LARRY L. KING**

NONFICTION

. . . And Other Dirty Stories

Confessions of a White Racist

The Old Man and Lesser Mortals

Wheeling and Dealing
*(with Bobby Baker)*

Of Outlaws, Con Men, Whores,
Politicians, and Other Artists

FICTION

The One-Eyed Man

PLAYS

The Best Little Whorehouse in Texas
*(with Peter Masterson and Carol Hall)*

The Kingfish
*(with Ben Z. Grant)*

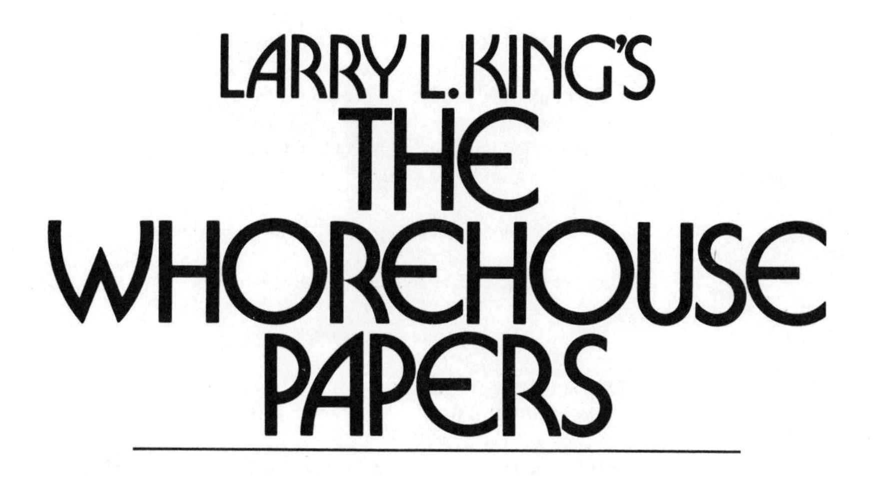

THE VIKING PRESS
NEW YORK

First published in 1982 by The Viking Press
625 Madison Avenue, New York, N.Y. 10022
Published simultaneously in Canada by
Penguin Books Canada Limited

An excerpt from this book originally appeared in *Playboy* Magazine.

**Library of Congress Cataloging in Publication Data**
King, Larry L.
The whorehouse papers.
I. Title.
PS3561.I48W4 818′.5403 [B] 79-56274
ISBN 0-670-15919-0 AACR2

Grateful acknowledgment is made to the following for permission to reprint copyrighted material:
*Field Newspaper Syndicate:* A selection from *It Happened Last Night* by Earl Wilson. Copyright © 1978 by Field Enterprises, Inc. Courtesy of Field Newspaper Syndicate.
*New York Magazine:* A selection from an article that appeared in the April 24, 1978, issue of *New York* magazine. Copyright © 1978 by News Group Publications, Inc.
*Michael Perlstein, Esq., for Combine Music:* Portions of lyrics from the Kris Kristofferson song "The Pilgrim—Chapter 33." Copyright © 1970 by Resaca Music Publishing Company. All rights reserved. Used by permission.
*Westward Productions Inc.:* Edna Milton's bio from *On Stage,* the program notes for Entermedia Theatre's Production of *The Best Little Whorehouse in Texas.*

Printed in the United States of America
Set in Fototronic Caledonia

This one is for my wife,
lawyer, and literary agent—
Barbara Sue Blaine

And for
our own first collaboration:
Lindsay Allison King

## IN MEMORIAM

Three friends who were members of our various stage companies have died since *The Best Little Whorehouse in Texas* originally opened on April 17, 1978. This page is to honor and remember them for their talents, friendships, and contributions.

*Cameron Burke*, twenty-five, one of the original dancing Texas Aggies in our Off Broadway production, was killed on May 30, 1978, by a drunk driver as he rode his bicycle to Long Island to watch the sunrise.

*Glenn Holtzman*, forty-nine, a former professional football player with the Los Angeles Rams, who played Sheriff Ed Earl Dodd in Houston and with the second national company, died in Reno on May 5, 1980, from a heart attack.

*Jo Rosner*, a thirty-year veteran of the show-business road, and general manager for our first national company, died of a ruptured spleen in Los Angeles in September of 1980.

Rest in peace.

# INTRODUCTION

Shortly after we began working on the play that is the subject of this book, I decided to keep a journal of the experience. The notion was not to chronicle the making of a Broadway hit but to gather material for a magazine article about how and why we had failed.

Failure, indeed, was my expectation. The simple mathematical odds against any play's getting to Broadway would seem to dictate that result. There are, after all, only forty-two Broadway houses and hundreds or possibly thousands of playwrights attempting to break into them on any given day. There were reasons beyond the statistical indicating a dismal end to our project: neither I nor my collaborators had ever written a show. No hard evidence existed to make me suspect that anything might come of our efforts other than hard work, experience, and perhaps a little comic relief along the way. I hoped to use the latter as grist for the journalistic mill I long had operated at my house. As luck would have it, that magazine article never got written.

I did not, I must confess, hew hard to my intention to record everything that happened every day. I did not even come close to that goal. When I knew I was privy to a vital meeting or encounter—our initial conference with Miss Edna Milton, the whorehouse madam, and Sheriff T. J. Flournoy; key disputes between the collaborators; audition or rehearsal highlights—I went to my desk to record it as quickly and completely as possible. But as I became caught up in working on *The Best Little Whorehouse in Texas* (and on other projects at the same time), to say nothing of living a disordered and sometimes rather desperate personal life, I too often contented myself with terse entries such as "Pissed at Masterson about Melvin's g.d. barking and growling" or "Aggie scene grows more miserable and hopeless each time we stage it." Often I neglected even to date these hurried scribblings.

Such skeletal records might appall the true historian, but my "Whorehouse papers" kicked off many memories when I went back to reconstruct the years they skimpily represent. I have jogged raw memory by consulting marginal jottings in the several script drafts we produced, a few memos passed among the participants, old clippings, random letters to my Texas cousin Lanvil Gilbert (for whom I named the mythical county and town in *Whorehouse*), and the occasional promptings of my wife and son.

I have not gone back to refresh my recollections by interviewing my collaborators or others connected with the show. I wanted this book to reflect what I personally experienced and felt during the creation of *Whorehouse* and afterward, rather than to be the winnowed truths of a committee with divergent points of view. My story is subjective, without apology.

It is a fair bet that numerous people who are part of this story, when reading a given page or scene, will shout or snarl that it didn't happen that way and will supply their own superior versions. So be it. This is the way *I* remember it. Let dissidents write their own books or tell their own versions as best as they can. *Rashomon,* you will recall, tells of the rape of a woman from the standpoint of the victim, her husband, the band of accused rapists, and random eyewitnesses; by the time all have told their stories, one is left to ponder whether any rape occurred at all. In this story, too, were many moments of passion, struggle, and dispute which I am certain each of us recorded in our minds from a special or selfish viewpoint. I hope those of my colleagues who occasionally feel abused or misused will consider that even in my biased version I could not always avoid giving instances of my own jackassery.

This is, I suppose, a kiss-and-tell book. People did and said things in the heat of the moment, and under terrific pressures, that they surely did not expect to see recorded for others to share. Were I not a writer, I would feel bad about that. "Everything goes by the board"—William Faulkner said—"honor, pride, decency . . . to get the book written. If a writer has to rob his mother, he will not hesitate; the *Ode on a Grecian Urn* is worth any number of old ladies."

If it appears to the reader that we collaborators often fought like tigers, or were guilty of greed, rudeness, back-stabbings, egotism, or worse, then the mitigating consideration is that collaboration is an unnatural act. Two or more people getting together to write something, Evelyn Waugh said, "is like three people getting together to make a baby." And as Agatha Christie put it, "I have always believed in writing without a collaborator, because when two people are writing the same book, each believes he gets all the worries and only half the royalties."

I identify with those sentiments; it would not surprise me to learn that my collaborators do, too—even though our "unnatural act" turned out far better than anyone might have dared dream. Yet it must be confessed that all during it, at various times, I most sincerely wanted to choke Peter Masterson, Carol Hall, or Tommy Tune—though not always in that order. One of the amazingly clear things, in retrospect, is how my villains changed from moment to moment. Simply put, I was always maddest at the unreasonable person or persons who in any given moment would not permit me to have my way.

The wounds have healed now; we collaborators are civil toward each other again, if not always the warmest of friends. Whether we like it or not we are—and forever shall remain—in each other's debt. Not one of us could have accomplished what we ultimately accomplished without the others. All other considerations aside, that is the bottom line. So here is a partial payment on that debt: thanks to Pete, Carol, and Tommy, and to Stevie Phillips, our producer, who saw the potential in *Whorehouse* when it was very raw, and acted on her instincts.

THE
WHOREHOUSE
PAPERS

CHAPTER

# 1

My great, improbable adventure began by accident and with two incoming telephone calls spaced roughly three years apart. The first came from a Texas lawyer, an old friend named Warren Burnett, during the long, hot summer of 1973. It was a time when I again was toying with the idea of moving back to my native state, simply because it seemed more and more that New York—that glittering dream city with nightmares lurking in every alley and doorway—was whipping me down. This normally happened in February, the cheerless month. Early darkness, ice, snow, slush, cold, a malaise of the spirit, a chill in the bones—these would overtake me each February and linger like a tedious guest. Increasingly, however, homesickness struck at random and without regard to the calendar. Then I would fantasize some rural Texas escape where the sun shone even at midnight, where green grasses grew and gentle rain cooled, and where I would find myself in harmony with nature and my work.

I remember I was a shade drunk, listening to country-western music whine and thump and whinny from an aging hi-fi in my modest apartment on Manhattan's East 32nd Street. If it was not exactly a bad neighborhood, neither was it a good one. Laced among the high-rise apartment buildings were X-rated moviehouses, pizza parlors, semi-Chinese restaurants, undistinguished bars, tiny newsstands and candy stores, sweaty laundries, Mom and Pop delis, the walk-up lairs of palm readers and call girls. Fruit stands in the summer months smelled like tropical islands gone to rot. Street derelicts sometimes pressed their dirty noses against the glass of the corner liquor store, the better to admire its display of half pints and cheap wines; some slept in doorways or nursed their stupors among mounds of dogshit, requiring the alert citizen to hopscotch down the sidewalk like a child at play. Street babble clearly floated up to my third-floor digs, unless erased by the roar of trucks or the wails of sirens blatting down Second Avenue. To combat these distractions, I turned up the sound on my hi-fi.

Periodically, as was their habit, the old couple in the adjoining apartment thumped on our mutual wall to protest the decibel level of my music—and, perhaps, its horse-country sentiments: laments about cheating husbands, honky-tonk angels, dead or drunk old daddies, born-to-lose convicts, lonesome truckers, sorry fuckers, and hard, mean jobs. Routinely, for it had become close to a ritual, I reached for an old military-police nightstick I once had liberated during an enlisted-man's-club melee at Fort Monmouth, New Jersey, and vigorously whacked the wall at the exact spot where I judged my neighbors to be more timidly thumping. This usually stilled them for a while, and it did that time. I mixed a fresh drink, added another layer of Waylon and Willie and Jerry Jeff offerings to the turntable, and dutifully prepared to get grass-grabbing, knee-walking, commode-hugging drunk. Along about then the telephone rang.

A deep, rich voice said, "Get your ass to Texas."

"Why, Lawyer? Did they get around to indicting me?"

Warren Edsel Burnett said, "There's a story breaking down here that's got your name on it." I may have groaned. I had grown tired of writing about Texas and Texans. Indeed, I had recently shoved aside a faltering biography of Lyndon B. Johnson with which I had struggled for several years, in favor of a painfully autobiographical novel about a middle-aged writer in New

York who drank too much, was ass-over-elbows in debt, and couldn't seem to get along with—or without—women. I had resolved that the novel would be confined to my New York period, that the word *Texas* would nowhere appear in it, that my protagonist would be a rootless urbanite with no personal history beyond the moment he lived in. In short, I had become weary of being labeled a Texas writer—though my soul knew that was pretty much what I had been.

But Burnett was saying, "There's a little town between Houston and Austin. LaGrange. There's been a little one-gallus whorehouse operating there for maybe a hundred years, as I get it, and now it's about to be closed. The governor's got his dumb ass all tangled up in it through pressures applied by some Houston TV man crusading to close the place. And there's a crusty old sheriff who sounds colorful. He's apparently permitted the whorehouse to operate for reasons of his own, and he's resisting the pressures."

"I dunno," I said. "I can't see much poetry in it."

"Well, I've got a feeling about this one," Burnett said. He had several times suggested stories to me and had a good track record. While I struggled with the notion that I should remain in New York to thump on my typewriter and not give in to the temptation of partying with a crowd of lively Austin renegades, Burnett said: "The damn story's starting to hit the Texas papers. You ought to get your ass in gear before Truman Capote or somebody beats you down here. Remember *In Cold Blood*?"

"Shit," I said. "You're talking about a magazine story. Nothing more."

"They pay the rent," Burnett said. "Get your ass down here."

Burnett was right. Magazine stories *did* pay the rent, and East Side rent was not cheap. There was a son in an expensive boarding school and other family responsibilities; Washington and Albany seemed insatiable in their demands for quarterly tax payments, and the City of New York wielded a third tax club; my personal habits were careless, wasteful, and costly.

For more than a decade I had produced books generally smiled on by critics and ignored by the masses. I had won a few minor plaques and scrolls but was a stranger to best-seller lists or big book-club money. Out of economic necessity I had produced magazine articles by the yard—for *Harper's, Life, True, Texas Monthly, Playboy, The Atlantic Monthly, Sport, Cosmopolitan, New Republic,* you name it. There was an unevenness in this work. Some of it was pretty good and some was simply terrible; writing the articles, however, had become tedious. I kept a chart on my writing-room wall, the better to herald the pressures of upcoming deadlines, and compulsively took on more assignments than I could realistically expect to accomplish, in a vain attempt to stay ahead of the financial hounds. Such work can come to seem debilitating and grow to be hated: one scrambles about putting fingers in the dike and feeling guilty because the "big work" never gets done, even though the advance royalty money has long been spent.

But, as I say, there *was* the rent. So the morning after Warren Burnett's call I telephoned an editor at *Playboy,* Geoffrey Norman, to describe this whorehouse story I claimed to be palpitating to do. "Sounds good to me," Norman said. "Let me check it out with Arthur Kretchmer and get back to you." Kretchmer, the magazine's editor in chief, gave the green light. We came to terms: $3,000 for the article and all expenses paid; *Playboy* would immediately wire $1,000 toward expenses. I stuck the dough in my faded blue jeans and headed toward home, where—sometimes—the heart was.

Though I had moved with atypical alacrity, the story had gone national by the time I got on the ground in LaGrange. Perhaps this would not have happened had I gone directly from the airport to the whorehouse city. I had larger plans, however, and the pause for a celebration with old Austin pals and gals lasted four or five days.

Before I planted a foot in LaGrange, jokes were being cracked on TV by Johnny Carson about the Chicken Ranch—the nickname the little bordello had earned when its girls began accepting poultry in trade during Herbert Hoover's Depression. Newspaper wire services had moved a few hundred words coast to coast; every sizable newspaper in Texas had sent in reporters and photographers. By the time I arrived as *Playboy*'s representative, these had done their mischief and had disappeared—as had the fifty-year-old madam of the Chicken Ranch, one Miss Edna Milton, and the working girls she demurely called her boarders.

The seventy-year-old sheriff, T. J. Flournoy—Mister Jim, in local parlance—had reluctantly (on orders from Governor Dolph Briscoe) padlocked the whorehouse. He and Miss Edna had been special friends; the salty old sheriff was stomping mad at all the meddling reporters, writers, and television men in the world. The little town of about four thousand people was in an uproar. Perhaps half the people resented the closing of the Chicken Ranch and half welcomed it; to the last in number, however, they resented the bad publicity their hometown had received. Most blamed Marvin Zindler, the flashy TV newsman-showman, who wore outlandish silver wigs and a huge ego, and who had pressured the governor and the state's attorney general to close the whorehouse. As Zindler had hied himself to the Caribbean for a vacation following his big triumph, townsfolk now focused their ire on me and on Al Reinert, another magazine man, on the scene for *Texas Monthly*.

I gingerly poked around town asking questions of touchy people, most of whom seemed to consider me their natural-born enemy and many of whom dressed me down. Tough old Sheriff Flournoy, a six-foot-six former Texas Ranger who wore a huge thumb-buster six-gun the record proved he knew how to use, cursed me every time he saw me; I soon became dedicated to his not seeing me. A few bold natives in beer joints or on the streets and a local newspaperman named Buddy Zapalac filled me in on Chicken Ranch lore.

The whorehouse allegedly had operated since 1844, each succeeding madam paying local taxes on the bordello as a boardinghouse. As the establishment was thought to be a boon to the local economy—and as Sheriff Flournoy insisted the place kept down sex crimes and aided him in solving other crimes because their perpetrators often grew boastfully garrulous in the presence of sweet scented womanhood—the law always had winked at its operations.

The old sheriff, indeed, was known to have been aggressively protective of the institution. Lieutenant Governor William Hobby recalls that when he made his original campaign appearance in LaGrange one of his supporters sidled up to whisper that Sheriff Flournoy wanted a signal as to how the candidate viewed the Chicken Ranch. "Go tell him I said I wish I had a credit card for it," Hobby joshed. Soon Sheriff Flournoy was around inquiring what he might do to help Hobby.

Candidate Hobby shipped a carload of his campaign literature to the sheriff, asking that it be addressed to all LaGrange voters. This was promptly done. "After the campaign," the lieutenant governor of Texas remembers, "my wife, Diane, was in charge of sending thank-you notes to all who had helped us. She telephoned the sheriff to ask who had addressed my campaign literature. He stuttered and stalled and wouldn't say. Diane persisted. Finally she told me of the situation, and I called Sheriff Flournoy. 'Well, Governor, I tell you,' the sheriff said. 'I give them pamphlets to Miss Edna. Her and her girls addressed 'em for you. But I think we ought to keep that between ourselves.' I agreed with him."

I walked the grounds and sifted through the trash cans of the padlocked farmhouse, which sat in a tree-guarded glade a few miles out of LaGrange, down a bumpy dirt road. Truth to tell, it was a pretty grubby dump. Miss Edna and her girls had gone into effective hiding—according to Sheriff Flournoy, "from such medium shitasses as you"—and definitely would not be available for comment. The old sheriff represented himself as "goddamn tard of answerin' goddamn questions"; one took him at his word. Other local officials scowled and dummied up. Governor Briscoe, who once called a press conference to disprove rumors that he might be dead or seriously ill because he had not been seen for weeks, was again holed up at his backwater ranch and would not return the many calls I left with his minions. Zindler, the story's villain as the town saw it, could not be located on his Caribbean holiday. I wanted to know *why* he had crusaded to close the little nine- or ten-girl operation while blithely ignoring the larger sins of Houston, but I had to return to New York without finding out. I frankly feared that I did not have much of a story.

Because I didn't know much about the girls or the madam as individuals, I decided to focus on the hypocrisy of the politicians who had panicked and closed the whorehouse under pressure ("Governor Briscoe and Attorney General Hill expressed their official astonishment that Texas had a whorehouse in it"), and on the media's talent for turning molehills into mountains while dealing with the trivial rather than the important or profound. It wasn't a bad piece, containing some funny history and a few good one-liners, but it was a far cry from being Faulkner. I wrote the article in about a week's time, at the last minute scrawling across the top page of the manuscript "The Best Little Whorehouse in Texas" because I couldn't think of a title that truly pleased me, and dropped it in the mail to Chicago.

In due course my $3,000 check arrived, sans ten percent agent's fee. A few months later—in April 1974—"The Best Little Whorehouse in Texas" appeared in *Playboy* as scheduled. Busy with other articles and trying to teach a writing course and a political science course one day each week at Princeton—a dismal chore I hated with much relish—I took little notice of the article's appearance. Nor, apparently, did anyone else—until more than two years later.

The second of the two telephone calls that would inch me toward Broadway came from Carol Hall, another displaced Texan in New York. Carol was a talented songwriter and singer I had known as a friend for several years; occasionally, between ongoing romances, I had dated her younger sister Ann. Carol and Ann's baby sister, Jane, once had written a lengthy paper about me as part of her work at the Columbia School of Journalism; she had been kind enough to leave out the parts where I got drunk and cried and slobbered late at night. I looked on the Hall girls almost as kin, though they came from Texas oil money and I came from Texas redneck hardscrabble.

I knew Carol Hall as a vivacious and charming woman who told funny stories and always seemed of good cheer—though not the first time I met her. That had been in the late spring of 1971. I was living in Washington then. One afternoon between sundown and dusk I entered the Cellar Door, a Georgetown bistro, in search of my friend Mickey Newbury's dressing room. Mickey had come to town to open at the club that night, playing guitar and singing his songs about pains and trains, and on arriving from Nashville he had telephoned to invite me over. As I walked through the empty club—chairs were still stacked on the tables—I heard someone loudly sobbing. There at a piano sat a slim woman wearing blue jeans, a hippie-type blouse, and a kerchief wrapped around her reddish-brown hair. As she sobbed she smote the piano keys with tiny fists, producing a most discordant sound. Prone to slight tantrums myself when frustrations stack up, I saw in the distressed lady a kindred spirit. I approached and asked, "May I help you?"

"Those sons of bitches," she sobbed. "I've got to open the show for Mickey Newbury in an hour and their damned piano is out of tune! Listen!" She again banged the keys in a series of angry downward jabs, flung her slight upper torso onto the piano top, and issued an accompanying melancholy wail. "Isn't that *horrible?*" she sobbed. "Have you ever *heard* worse?" Not wanting to admit to near tone-deafness, I agreed. *"And they can't even find a piano tuner!"* This dismal thought led the lady into new spasms of boo-hoos. I clucked, shuffled in place, and felt clumsy. Then I offered a characteristic solution: "Listen, lady, what you need is a stiff drink. Let's go find one." Over her wet protests that she didn't really drink and had to find a piano tuner and climb into her show clothes, I dragged Carol Hall away. It wasn't difficult: she was thin, almost frail; I was thick and hairy and macho and hell-bent on playing Good Samaritan.

Alas, Mickey Newbury had no liquor in his dressing room: he had freshly married a Christian Scientist and had gone straighter than straight. While Carol Hall cried her woes to Mickey, who was smiling uncertainly and shooting me what-the-hell-you-got-me-into looks, I ran off to liberate some bracing spirits. I returned with two stiff Scotches, one of which I administered to Carol Hall like an old aunt offering chicken soup. Word shortly came that a piano tuner had turned up; Carol's mood began to improve. Soon she was laughing at herself, and at my jokes. An hour later she came on stage cool, poised, and very cosmopolitan, and superbly entertained Cellar Door patrons with songs she'd written: "Nana," "Hello, My Old Friend," "Would You Be My Lady?", and many more. I cheered her on and became a true Carol Hall fan on the spot. She made me a gift of her two record albums. Thereafter, when I visited New York, I met Carol for drinks at P. J. Clarke's or was invited to small gatherings at her apartment. Once I'd moved to New York, following the death of my wife, Rosemarie, I got to know Carol better—and her sisters as well, and her fiancé, Leonard Majzlin, who later became her husband. So that was our history when Carol Hall telephoned in the spring of 1976 with a proposition that both amused and astonished me.

"You don't know Peter Masterson," she began.

"Guilty as charged."

"He's a Texas actor here in New York. I've known Pete since college. Anyhow, he read something you wrote about a whorehouse and he's got the craziest idea!"

"Yeah? What?"

"He says it would make a wonderful musical comedy!"

Wellsir, I laughed and laughed. "That's pretty crazy, all right."

"Pete wants to know if you'd be interested in collaborating on it with us."

"Carol, I don't know diddly-shit about musical comedy. And only a dime's worth about the theatre."

"You don't need to," she assured me. "I know music; Pete knows structure and staging. I'm sure he could help you with the libretto."

"I've heard of that," I said. "Dan Jenkins told me about it when that guy Merrick asked him to write the libretto for a musical of *Semi-Tough* that never got done. Libretto is the opposite of soprano, Dan says."

"Come on, King! Quit playing dumb Texan! The libretto is the *book.* The story line. The play proper."

"Aw, shit," I said.

"Be serious! May I see a copy of the whorehouse article?"

"Hell, Carol, I don't have one. That damn story came out two, three years ago."

"How about your carbon copy?"

"Well, see, I don't make carbons. They're messy and take too much time."

"I can't believe this," Carol said. "Who's your agent? He'll have a copy, won't he?"

I told her his name, adding, "But I don't know if he has one. I hate business details."

"I'll call him," Carol said. A few minutes later she phoned back: "Yes, your agent has a copy but he won't release it without your approval. Call him now. I'll take a cab straight to his office."

I made the call, though it seemed like much fuss about very little, and went back to my perusal of a highly personal letter from one of America's great corporations. The gentlemen of American Express courteously explained that although they had let me have one of their credit cards in good faith, they were rapidly losing that faith. And they might soon deprive me of their little green card unless, by God, I was prepared to pony up more than six hundred very tardy dollars. *Muy pronto.* I sighed and stared at the walls, then pawed an old stack of newspapers in hope of being smitten by a new magazine idea.

There are two versions of how Peter Masterson and Carol Hall came to ask me to collaborate on a musical. One is Masterson's and one is Hall's; in each case the teller of the tale, perhaps understandably, is more prominent in it than the nonteller thereof—a condition, the careful reader may very well notice in time, of this book also.

Anyway. In the Masterson version he was playing on Broadway in *That Championship Season.* "I was playing this drunk former basketball hotshot who lives in the past, lives in the memory of his old glories. Anyhow, I went out to eat at Joe Allen's between shows—it was a matinee day, I'm sure of that—and when I got back to my dressing room there was this dog-eared copy of *Playboy.* Don't know how it got there or who put it there. I started turning through it, like you'll do killing time, looking at the girlie pictures"—he laughs—"and ran across your whorehouse story. It cracked me up. I read along, enjoying it, laughing, and then it hit me: *Goddamn, this is a musical!* Well, I'd known your work for years but I didn't know you. I knew Carol knew you. So I called her and said, 'Hey, call this guy King.' And you know the rest."

"No, no, no," Carol Hall said when Masterson's version gained popular currency. "We were at a dinner party, I think at Bill and Ilene Goldman's, and Pete suggested we find material for a musical we'd work on together. He had something by Larry McMurtry in mind. Not *King: McMurtry.* I think he suggested *The Last Picture Show.* I told him I didn't see that as a musical, that it had already been done as a straight film—which he knew—and then I said, 'I like Larry *King's* work a lot. Do you know it?' And he said he'd read an old story by you in *Playboy,* about a whorehouse, and it might work. We talked about the prospects of a whorehouse musical making it big—we couldn't recall one that had—and the next day I called you."

Well, who knows? Anyhow, the call was made and now I got a rich baby, but that's leaping way ahead in the story.

Three or four days after the initial contact I met my would-be collaborators in Carol Hall's spacious, well-appointed apartment on Park Avenue in the East Seventies. As they say down home, it was up to snazzy. Oil never hurt nobody.

Peter Masterson proved to be a compact, athletic-looking man with a pleasant smile, good teeth, a ready laugh, and a low-key manner; despite a bald dome he appeared younger than his forty years. While Carol's maid brought drinks we got acquainted by talking Texas: people we knew in common, growing-up tales, biographical highlights. Masterson was from Angleton, a small town near Houston. He had graduated from Rice University, where he had played what he called "last man" on the basketball team: "When we got hopelessly behind or, infrequently, safely ahead, they stuck me in the game for a couple minutes." He had crewed on winning sailboats, jogged, didn't smoke, and by my measurements drank barely enough to stay alive.

For "not any specific reason," Masterson had declined to become a lawyer in the family tradition. Soon after college he began acting at the Alley Theatre in Houston. He came to New York, failed to stand Broadway on its ear; he gave Hollywood a shot and it, too, fizzled. He had been back in New York for about fifteen years, slowly gaining acting jobs and credits that would earn him a good reputation in professional circles. He did not have the problem, however, of being recognized on the street, except for a few months after he played the male lead in the movie *The Stepford Wives.* He also had movie roles in *Man on a Swing, The Exorcist,* and "some junk you've probably never heard of." His heart, he said, belonged to the stage. On Broadway he had played the title role in *The Trial of Lee Harvey Oswald*—which folded after nine performances, despite good notices for Masterson—and lesser roles in *The Poison Tree, The Great White*

*Hope,* and *That Championship Season.* He had acted, and sometimes directed, at Actors Studio, off Broadway, and in summer stock.

I told Masterson of growing up in Midland—deep in oil, cowboy, and desert-sands country—and of dropping out of Texas Tech in freshman year after being bounced from the football squad before the first game. The charge: drinking beer in the locker room while singing "Jesus on the Five-Yard Line." I spun a few yarns of my youthful Texas newspaper days and of living the rum life of the free-lance writer. Carol Hall suffered this Good Ol' Boy ritual for a decent interval before bringing up the proposed musical.

"Look," I said, "my ignorance of the subject is absolutely awesome. I've only seen three musicals in my life and didn't care for any of them." They laughed; Carol asked if I remembered their titles.

"One I saw when I was in the army over in Queens in the late nineteen-forties," I said, "was called *Oklahoma!* I understand it did quite well."

"Yes." Carol laughed. "I guess you could say that *Oklahoma!* did quite well. It had only about the ninth- or tenth-longest run in Broadway history."

I volunteered how I discovered the theatre in New York, as an eighteen-year-old soldier: "They had a U.S.O. around Broadway and Fortieth, along there, and I heard you could get free tickets to pro football and baseball games. You know, something for the boys in uniform. But when I went there all the ballgame tickets were gone. This woman hostess persuaded me to take a Broadway show ticket: they weren't in demand like sports tickets. I spent the evening seeing Marlon Brando in *Streetcar Named Desire.* Brando had a full head of hair and a flat belly then."

"My God," Masterson said.

"Yeah, and I liked the play. So I kept going back and getting tickets. Only had to pay the tax, as I recall. I saw a number of dramas, but I quit musicals after three. Not my cup of whiskey."

Carol Hall asked why I objected to musicals.

"Well, as a writer it irritates me when the story comes to a screeching halt so a bunch of bank clerks in candy-striped coats and carrying matching umbrellas can break into a silly tap dance while singing about the sidewalks of New York."

There was another burst of obligatory hilarity—after all, *they* were hustling *me*, and so carried the burden of proof; I wasn't after anything and didn't have to laugh unless sincerely amused.

"It wouldn't have to be a big, slick musical with trombones and a lot of dancing," Masterson assured me. "I had in mind more of a straight play with, you know, maybe a little incidental music."

"Now wait a minute, Pete," Carol Hall said. "That's not what I've been hearing from you."

"We can work it out," Masterson said soothingly. "We'll try it one way and, if that doesn't work for us, we'll try it another way." I would come to know that expression very well; if there's any justice, it will be on Masterson's tombstone. He quickly slid into another gear, asking how much of the show I would be willing to write.

"As little as possible," I said. "Why don't you people just go ahead and adapt my article as you like? If anything comes of it, you can cut me in for a piece."

"Well, no, you're the writer here," Pete said, graciously. "Oh, I won a college contest in play writing at Rice, but I'm really an actor and director. Looking at it with a director's eyes, I can help you with structure and theatrical bits and—"

"You're going to direct this?" Carol Hall seemed surprised.

"Well, yeah, thought I would. At first, anyway. While we're putting it together. If nobody objects."

"Hell," I said, "I don't care." Carol Hall saith not.

"But we really need you for the writing," Masterson finished.

"Look," I said, "I've got a couple of books to write. One of them is seriously overdue. Frankly, I can't afford to work on speculation. There's got to be money up front."

"You can go ahead with your books," Masterson said. "This wouldn't be a full-time deal. We'll work on it catch-as-catch-can and get together occasionally to see how we're doing. There's no hurry." Presently he looked at his watch, said he had an appointment to audition for a TV commercial, and asked how soon could we meet again.

I explained that I had just signed a collaboration agreement to write Bobby Baker's recollections of his wheeling-and-dealing days on Capitol Hill, which had ultimately landed him in Federal prison, and that I had to go to Washington to begin taping him. I figured it might take a working week to get enough on tape so that I could write a general summary or prospectus, which we hoped would attract bids from several publishing houses. The book itself, if we made a sale, might require a year or two to write: it would be a complicated story and I had a mountain of financial papers, trial transcripts, and other documents to wade through. So really, I said, I could give very little time to futzing around with some wild musical notion.

"Well, anyhow, call me when you get back from Washington in a week or so," Pete Masterson said. I agreed. As Carol's maid let me out I heard the lady of the manor say to Pete, "Now, about how much *music* this show's going to have . . ."

As it developed, the Baker tapings consumed about three weeks. First one and then the other of us would get drunk and wake up with a hangover that left the guilty party only marginally functional. Tapes would whir while one of us sat dumbly, unable to think of questions or answers, or stammered incoherently. In self-defense, we agreed to get drunk together on a set schedule so we'd be incapacitated at the same time and capable of working at the same time. Ground rules: not a drop before 5:00 p.m.; to bed no later than midnight. Drunkenness permitted only on *alternate* nights. Amazingly, it worked pretty well.

Still, Bobby Baker and his Boswell worked at cross purposes; he, consumed with proving he was an innocent man railroaded to jail because of dirty political expediency, wanted to use his book as a forum to vindicate himself; I, on the other hand, needed to extract confessions and untold secrets that would land a juicy contract from a publisher. It was something like a dentist pulling a hippo's teeth with a pair of pliers, the hippo not wanting his teeth pulled at all. Baker candidly admitted that if he didn't desperately need money, he would not live through his past misery again or risk the sneers of skeptics and critics when the book came out.

By the time I returned to New York, school had let out. I learned that Pete Masterson and his family, and Carol Hall and her children, had retired to a summer place they chummily shared. "We've been talking musical, musical, musical," Carol said on the phone. "When can you come to the country? It's only an hour plus by train." A few days later she came to the city and escorted me to the train station. We clattered toward Katonah, passing by wooded fields and little picture-postcard towns, on by the *Reader's Digest* publishing plant and the Gates of Heaven cemetery. Pete Masterson met us at the Katonah station and stuffed us into an old wagon that perfectly suited his role as a respectably shabby summer squire. I recall a festive mood and light banter.

Pete's wife, Carlin, a stately and attractive woman in her mid-thirties, gave us a warm greeting and a cool summer luncheon of melon, salad, light sandwiches, and iced tea.

"I want you to get to work, Larry King," Carlin said. "Write me a good part. I want to play the madam."

I laughed, not knowing the lady was an accomplished actress under her professional name of Carlin Glynn, and made a small joke: "Well, Carlin, I'm afraid I've put that role up for auction among five or six of my girl friends." There was one of those silences that scream something is amiss. Pete said, "Carlin, uh, is a pretty good actress. We met when we were acting together at the Alley Theatre. She's done some Off Broadway and movie stuff, too."

"Of course," I said, deeply studying my cucumber salad and wondering at my talent for foot-in-mouth disease. I would later learn that I had met Carlin Glynn at a couple of parties—indeed, had passed a few words with her—but I hadn't made the connection between *that* lady and the one sitting across from me on the airy, screened-in porch.

"Do you sing?" Carol suddenly asked.

"Only in bars late at night," I blurted.

"Not *you! Carlin!*"

"Oh," I said.

"Oh," Carlin said. She laughed a bit self-consciously. "Well, I'm starting lessons." All I heard for a while was silverware clinking on plates. I began to get a feeling that many complications awaited in ambush.

Later, we sat on the front veranda with cold beers. Pete said, "You mentioned the madam's operating rules in your article. Try writing a scene where a couple of girls come to the whorehouse to apply for jobs. And in the course of interviewing them, the madam explains her house rules."

"There could be a song in that," Carol said, enthusiastically.

"I dunno, Carol," I said. "Wouldn't it kinda get in the way of the story that early?"

She looked at once distressed, unbelieving, and perhaps the tiniest bit pissed: "The *song* could help *tell* the story."

"Oh," I said. I was getting pretty good at saying "Oh."

There was only the sound of the wind whispering in the trees. After a time Peter Masterson said, "We can work it out. We'll try it one way and, if that doesn't work for us, we'll try it another way."

I returned to the city and began attempting to organize the Baker tapes. This was like trying to teach a roomful of one-year-olds to dress themselves. There were all those false starts, silent gaps bringing back memories of the departed Richard Nixon, disjointed ramblings, incomprehensible drunken babble. We had hopped and jumped around the subject matter like two spastics playing hopscotch. If it had taken three weeks to fill the tapes, I realized, it might require six months to make any sense of them.

It is an old survival trick of writers to switch projects if one is going badly. Out of that desperation I sat down at the typewriter to turn myself into an instant playwright. And sat and sat and sat. After two hours I abandoned the blank paper leering at me and quit my place in favor of Harley Street, the neighborhood pub on Second Avenue, and there drank a hearty lunch. This instilled much more confidence than was becoming.

Back at the typewriter my fingers ultimately spasmed on the keyboard. In time I invented a tough, street-wise whore, April, and the no-nonsense madam, Miss Mona. I had in mind a short, brisk, efficient scene. Somehow it rambled on and on. The two characters gabbled more than had King and Baker on those miserable goddamned tangled tapes. I didn't know how to get my two characters off stage. So I simply brought a houseful of other whores *on* stage—impulsively, and perhaps perversely, naming several after former girl friends—which tactic, as might have been predicted, only added to the clutter. I began to think that perhaps I wouldn't mind if Carol Hall threw in a scene-ending song after all.

I mixed a fresh batch of eighty-proof smartjuice with grapefruit squeezings and read what I had written. It was the sorriest shit since Jacqueline Susann last sat at her typewriter. I cursed, ripped the pages to shreds, and took it from the top as we say in show biz. Peck a line. Think. Peck a Line. Stare. Peck a line. Groan.

Around midnight, I quite suddenly began warming to the form. My characters became people my mind's eye could see; they talked as they might in real life. I knew what they were going to say or do—what they *should* say or do—out of their shaping experiences. I fell impossibly in love with Miss Mona. This foolish feeling of euphoria came floating down from the heavens, gathered me in its arms, tenderly patted my head, blew in my ear. *Shit,* I exulted, *this ain't so fucking tough! I can do this! I'm a goddamn playwright!* I knew I would never again write another magazine article, novel, book of nonfiction, or worthless check. No, I would turn out more plays—and far better ones—than Neil Simon. The moving fingers wrote until about 3:00 a.m. and, having writ, moved on to bed. My head was full of happy fantasies outside the norm. I lay in bed cackling like a lunatic; you might have thought I was cuddled between Dyan Cannon and Farrah Fawcett and each was begging to be first. *Move over, Arthur Miller! Stand aside, Tennessee Williams, you old fart! Sissy on you, Eugene O'Neill! You boys ain't seen nothin' yet!*

By the dawn's early light my opening scene was not so proudly hailed. I tinkered like a mechanic under the hood; crossed out, rewrote, tightened. Late in the afternoon I sent the scene to Pete Masterson's apartment on the Upper West Side and repaired to Elaine's restaurant, the East Side gathering place of writers, politicians, and show folk who like to exhibit themselves. I knew of no place where I could better preen myself as a playwright.

I don't know why it is that when a writer is doing nothing but brooding over writer's block, every son of a buck he sees asks what work he is doing and how it goes. Conversely, if that writer is eager to talk of his newest enthusiasm, he suddenly finds himself in the company of deaf-mutes. The rule held that night at Elaine's, though I did receive satisfaction in telling three or four bewildered strangers in the men's room what a threat I had become to the American Theatre.

Pete Masterson's call the next day reinforced my good opinion of myself. He said he had read nothing so moving since the Holy Bible, that my lines made the scribblings of Chekhov and Ibsen appear as but the immature bleatings of ignorant goats, that monuments should be raised to me wherever box offices exist—or words, anyhow, to that effect. Then he said, "I've been playing with it a little. I'll get it to you when I'm finished."

What, playing with it?

"I'm just, you know, touching it up."

What, touching up? Would you touch up the "Mona Lisa"?

"It's nothing major," Masterson said soothingly. "Mainly it has to do with structure and staging."

When the script arrived I saw that Masterson's "touching up" also had to do with an entirely new character—a country-bumpkin would-be whore named Shy, who had joined my tough, street-wise April in seeking a job at the Chicken Ranch. I read on, bellowing as if punctured, snorting and emitting shrieks and wails until my aged neighbors thumped the wall and threatened to call the vice squad.

I got Masterson on the phone and roared, "Goddammit, Pete, this Shy creature just won't do!"

"Why?" he asked. Masterson is very good at asking why. He knows that *why*'s are much more difficult to answer than to ask.

"Well . . . she just won't, that's all. She . . . she . . . she's a goddamn *cartoon*! I mean, in real life no girl that innocent and dumb would *dare* go to a whorehouse looking for work! You're the silliest shit I ever met! And if she did, no madam in her right mind would hire her! Shit! Goddamn! Piss! Fuck and hellfire!"

You may not think Masterson had an answer for so reasoned an argument, but he's a sly one. "Well," he said, "in real life you might be correct. But the theatre, after all, is . . . well, it's *the theatre*! Audiences make allowances. You're permitted a certain poetic license to make the magic."

"No. No. Bullshit. Horseshit. It won't wash."

"I think Shy is a good contrast to April," Pete said calmly. "Her sweetness is good counterpoint to April's toughness. By using her we can set up great dramatic possibilities for later on."

"Her dialogue ain't worth crap," I said. "I don't believe a goddamn word she says."

He chuckled. "Well, touch it up. I didn't carve it in stone."

"Besides," I said, "we simply can't use that dumb part about her leaving home because her *daddy* was screwing her! That's unreal! Phony! Pure bullshit! We'd be laughed out of the goddamn theatre!"

"Well," Pete said, "we can work it out. We'll try it one way and . . ."

# CHAPTER 2

July, August, September, October—these months in 1976 passed in a vague blur. Looking back on them years later, I see them as a landscape is seen from a speeding train—quickly gone, slightly out of focus, here a mountain impossible to climb, there a valley too dark and deep to walk. Personally and professionally my life was becoming such a mess as to suggest the more garish soap operas. I climbed ever deeper into the jug, juggled two lady friends, neither of whom I was willing to give up or to commit myself to, and was spread thinner than boardinghouse butter in my work. I was involved in the presidential campaign of old friend Mo Udall, and to a lesser extent in the New York senatorial campaign of fellow Texan Ramsey Clark, both of whom ran as if their legs had been cut off at the knees. It seemed that I constantly changed gears, revved up engines—but my wheels only slid, spun, and smoked in place.

I had signed a contract with W. W. Norton Publishing Company, high bidder for the Bobby Baker book; this meant much commuting between New York and Washington. I was taping

Baker, reading his voluminous trial transcripts, financial records, personal correspondence, and talking with one of his former defense lawyers, Mike Tigar. As I got paid only when each chapter of the book was turned in—smart people, those W. W. Nortons—it might have made sense to stick with that project exclusively. Naturally, I did not. I galloped about writing magazine pieces for *Sport, True, Classic,* and other publications that did not demand Faulknerian prose but wanted a lot of it, and had the virtue of paying promptly. I also wrote a twice-monthly column, "Fulminations," for *New Times* magazine.

There existed what seemed to be compelling reasons for this chaotic madness. As a child of the Great Depression I was acquainted with economic bogeymen and feared to say no to any editor approaching me with a dollar in his hand. No matter the complications, I would somehow work his article in: had I found myself the guest of honor below the guillotine, hands bound, I might have agreed to dictate three thousand words on my emotional reaction for *Psychology Today.* (I worked for them, too, incidentally.) For, friends, 'tis sad but true—moneywise, my ass belonged more to the gypsies with each passing day. My Manhattan rent had risen to $750 per month, I paid $450 per month for a cubbyhole Washington apartment for Baker book work, and my son's boarding school in his senior year had hiked tuition by such an amount that it rivaled Princeton's. And, of course, there was that $100 per night often whoopeed away at Elaine's in New York or the Palm in Washington. *Now*—you say—*why didn't that boy quit all that drankin' and high-falutin' livin' and settle down and behave hisself?* The answer is I never had much practice at it. It was my wont to make merry until I dropped in my tracks; I required it as much as breathing. When I thought of overdue bills it so depressed me that I simply quit thinking about them. If you open your bills you are likely to think about them; I quit opening bills. When the creditors' calls came I made promises impossible to keep, sat in a dejected funk for a few minutes, mixed a few healing toddies, and rationalized: *What the hell, even if they kill me they can't eat me.* Buddy, them was dark days.

I worked on the *Whorehouse* play only when goaded or shamed by Peter Masterson. He was nothing if not dogged. Though we only infrequently saw each other—passing our work back and forth by mail, much of mine being posted from Washington or Indianapolis or wherever my sullen craft took me—he haunted me on the telephone. After each major cajoling I would draft the new scene we had discussed, he would touch it up, I would retouch it, he would reretouch it . . . on and on; sometimes it seemed as slow as playing chess by mail.

Every time the script changed hands we haggled by telephone, though generally in a good-natured manner. I had learned not to shout at Masterson because it did no good; he was simply unflappable and one's anger went to waste. Too, I was coming to appreciate his determination, energy, and suggestions. We would flounder, it seemed, interminably, and then—lo! presto!—we somehow had produced a new scene. Meanwhile, Carol Hall and Pete met often to talk about songs; I talked with her less frequently. "She's working," Pete would say. Then with a small laugh: "Though not as fast as I would like it." I sometimes thought Pete seemed in such a hurry he must have premonitions of a premature death.

We gathered at Carol's apartment one October evening for the first public reading of what we'd done—five scenes, with three songs. We brought along friends, spouses, and lovers to assist in the reading and a few to serve as the audience. Perhaps thirty-odd people met in Carol's comfortable living room (roomy enough for a basketball scrimmage), the focal point of which was her piano.

Reading parts were assigned while I gnawed my knuckles and nervously wondered why I'd let myself in for this. Writers of books and articles, I tardily recalled, did not face the dangers of seeing people who confronted their art laugh in the wrong places or frown in boredom or disgust. To make matters worse, I had the added responsibility of reading the role of Sheriff Ed Earl Dodd—and, to illustrate the tedium of collaborations, you should know that Pete had supplied the "Ed Earl" and I had supplied the "Dodd"—who cursed and stomped almost constantly. "Type casting," Pete Masterson said, laughing, when he assigned me the reading role.

I had not heard Carol's three songs—"Twenty Fans," "Pissant

Country Place," and "Girl, You're a Woman"—but already I resented them for taking up space I was certain more properly belonged to dialogue. I was powerless to stop her, however, as she sat at the piano to sing and play "Twenty Fans," which, she smilingly explained, would open the show and encapsulate the history of the Chicken Ranch. She sang about the house being located in a green Texas glade, surrounded by trees as soothing as fresh lemonade. And I felt chills, no kidding, and thought *My God, that's beautiful! This fucking thing may work!*

We began to read dialogue. People tittered and then laughed louder, and in all the right places. I was absolutely astonished. The more they laughed at Ed Earl's cussing and stomping, the more I permitted ol' Ed Earl to cuss and stomp. Maybe it didn't feel as good as soft warm hands, but it was a whole lot better than ice-cream. There were back-poundings and handshakes following the reading, and the kind of joyous, hopeful smiles I hadn't seen since Nixon quit.

I happily went off to Elaine's to celebrate and to spend some of the money I felt certain we would make. Man, I was higher than three miles over Denver. "It's gonna work," I kept saying to my date of the evening. "It's gonna by-God *work!*" I don't suppose I said it over three dozen times. Ultimately the lady said, "Well, sure, it has potential. But don't forget you were reading for friends and family." I never dated her again: who would want to go through life with a goddamn killjoy at his side?

One morning Pete Masterson called with as much excitement in his voice as I had ever heard him permit himself: "I've arranged to present those scenes on stage at Actors Studio as a workshop project."

"Good show! How much they paying us?"

He semilaughed. "Well, nothing. But it'll give us a chance to see how it plays. We'll have the benefit of the comments and criticism of a lot of good actors and directors. People like Ellen Burstyn, Frank Corsaro, Gadge Kazan, Lee Strasberg . . ."

"Ain't that the place with that Method-acting stuff? Where they teach people to pretend like they're tables or snakes or rocks and what not?"

"Something like that." He laughed. "It's a form of realism. The actor's supposed to react like he might be expected to in life. They do really fine work there. They've trained actors like—oh, Marlon Brando, Al Pacino, Pat Hingle, Steve McQueen, Shelley Winters. Marilyn Monroe enrolled there after she was a star, when she decided she didn't know enough about acting. Several Tennessee Williams plays started at the Studio. No kidding, it's a good place. Carlin and I have been working there for years."

"Sounds okay," I said, "but I can't help much. I'm up to my ass in that goddamn Baker book."

"We don't need to write anything more right now. We'll work to polish the scenes we have. But I hope you'll come to a few rehearsals and get acquainted at the Studio. It can be a big help to us."

So a few nights later I beat and threshed my way through the derelicts, winos, whores, pimps, and street crazies who populated the area around Eighth, Ninth, and Tenth avenues, with Masterson and Carlin Glynn at my side, to reach the famed Actors Studio on West 44th Street. A clot of thespians in faded jeans, dungarees, bulky sweaters, granny dresses, and similar garb waited outside in a chilling wind, which swirled small cyclones of street debris about them. While Masterson made introductions—"Clint Allmon . . . Gil Rogers . . . Elaine Rinehart . . . Joan Ellis . . . Barbara Burge . . . Mallory Jones"—I peered over shoulders, hunting for famous faces; apparently the Brandos, Burstyns, and Pacinos were otherwise occupied. We shivered in the wind while inquiries were made about a key—"Don't you have one?" "No, I thought you did"—until someone was dispatched to a telephone booth two blocks away to call around the city in a great search. "Typical." Pete laughed. "I hope it's not an omen," I said. We shuffled from foot to foot; I was thoroughly depressed. I thought it was the funkiest-looking bunch, and the funkiest-looking neighborhood, I'd encountered since the El Paso bus station.

The interior of Actors Studio failed to cheer me. I don't know what I expected. Not opulence, surely. But even a theatrical ignoramus like me had read or heard of the place and knew it to be hallowed ground among serious actors. Certainly I was not prepared for couches with sagging springs, overflowing ashtrays, scummy coffee abandoned in wax cups, battered trash cans tested beyond their capacities, floor litter, warped metal folding chairs—*surely* Marilyn Monroe wouldn't have sat her sweet ass in one of those!—and gloomy stacks of dingy stage flats. It looked like an indoor hobo jungle in there. Carlin Glynn read my face and said, "They operate on a shoestring here, but the Studio does more for working actors than any other place in America. *Thank God* for Actors Studio! All the years I've been raising children and existing on television commercials, it's helped me keep my sanity and my hope."

Masterson made the major assignments—Gil Rogers as Sheriff Dodd, Carlin as Miss Mona, Clint Allmon as the villainous TV man I'd named Melvin P. Thorpe, Joan Ellis as Shy; he made a little speech about our work in progress and the rehearsal schedule. I sat in one of the cold metal chairs, listening to a bunch of strangers read lines that suddenly sounded flat, uninspired, and about half silly. There was nothing for me to do; I felt friendless, very much the outsider, a stranger in a strange land. When nobody was looking I sneaked down the stairs to weave through the moaning wind and a covey of clutching, ware-calling, real-life street whores who looked as wretched as I felt. I found a bar where I might not be raped or poisoned and could sit with my back against the wall. Perhaps I had the thought—if not, I should have—that although Actors Studio was but a block or so away from Broadway, the two were, in measurable ways, a world apart.

I soon departed for Washington, where I costarred in a tense scene with Bobby Baker. Ol' Bobby obviously had consumed goodly portions of smartjuice and now divested himself of a lecture: "Goddammit, you dash in and out of town writing a bunch of other shit and nothing gets done on *my* book. I wouldn't have signed you to write the goddamn thing if I hadn't thought you'd give me a good effort. I tell you, pardner, I'm gonna pull out of our fucking deal if you don't get with it! I'll get another writer and you can sue my ass if you want to."

There was, of course, very much truth in what Baker said; for that reason, I didn't want to hear it. "Listen, you asshole," I said, "you're lucky I consented to write your piece of shit. You can't fire me, I quit!" I stomped off, hearing behind me Baker's threats and curses intermingled with the voice of his lady friend, Doris Myers, attempting the thankless role of peacemaker.

Doris brought the two pouting prima donnas together for lunch the next day; we had the decency to act contrite and subdued. "Let's face it," Doris said, "you need each other." It was true. We both were so desperate for money that only cowardice kept us from robbing banks. I agreed to concentrate on Baker's book and to an extended stay in Washington; he agreed to reveal more of himself and to strive for a sunnier disposition. We mutually vowed to work tirelessly. Whereupon we sealed the pact with a handshake and ordered a tubful of drinks. Soon we had thrown our arms across each other's collarbones and were singing hymns dear to the country churches of our youth. Poor Doris Myers sat shaking her head, uncertain whether to laugh or cry.

For two or three weeks we truly worked hard; I deviated only to write my *New Times* column and express it to New York. Then Peter Masterson called, only four days before the big showcase production would be offered at Actors Studio.

"We've got a problem," he said. "Gil Rogers had a chance to go into a paying show, so he can't play the sheriff. I don't know anybody I can get on short notice. How about you?"

"Shit, Pete, I don't know any actors."

"No, dammit, I mean how about *you* playing it? You already know the lines. All you'd have to do is brush up on them."

"Aw, Pete, I dunno . . ."

"Maybe fly up here and run through a couple of rehearsals."

"I can't do that, Pete! I'm really being pushed on this goddamn Baker book."

"You wouldn't have to be perfect," he said. "Just read the part over a few times between now and Thursday."

"I dunno . . ."

"See you Thursday," he said.

"Wait a minute, Pete. This is Monday!"

"Don't be late," he said. I heard the growl of a dial tone.

Surreptitiously, so Baker wouldn't know, I mumbled the sheriff's lines as we worked, and sneaked looks at the *Whorehouse* scenes. Soon I began secretly to envision a great personal triumph. Lee Strasberg would rush to sign me; Brando and Burstyn and Pacino would shove each other in the stampede to wring my hand; the audience—terribly moved—would at once applaud and cry in gratitude at being in the presence of such artistry. The more the fantasy was indulged, the more it seemed likely to come true. I telephoned a New York special friend, Diane Smook, to make certain she would be present when it did.

And, who knows, the fantasy *might* have come a little bit true if, on Wednesday, one of my special pals, Charles Wilson, had not invited me to lunch. Wilson was, and is, a Texas congressman known far and wide as Good Time Charlie; I will go with him anywhere he asks me, without I got a broke laig and am tied to a tree. We met at the Rotunda, then a favorite watering hole of Washington's statesmen, and warmed up with a few practice Scotches for the more serious partying we knew was bound to follow. Me and Good Time Charlie don't go out together unless it's understood nobody will poop the party until he faints.

For many hours I had a wonderful time, bragging to Good Time Charlie about how dead I would knock everybody in my debut at Actors Studio the following day. Wilson began to mull the shifting of affairs of state so as to accompany me to New York and bask in the fringes of glory. Different people dropped by our table, tired themselves out socially, cheerfully departed, and were replaced.

Long past dark, and then again about midnight, several things happened that kept us from going to New York. These things caused Good Time Charlie to think he was not having a very good time; he waved to me and weaved out the door toward home. I don't remember much of what happened, and don't wish to tell the parts I do remember. Suffice it to say that I wound up with a broken hand that had to put in a small cast and spent the remainder of the night in a room with a lock on it for which I had no suitable key.

About three hours before I was to make my show-biz debut—hand throbbing, garments rent, wino eyes aflame, and a session with a lawyer scheduled—I telephoned Pete Masterson to regret that I would not be present at Actors Studio that day. Mr. Masterson was far from amused. Though he did not berate me, his chilly disapproval could have been felt through a steel door. "I guess I'll have to read your goddamn part from the script," he grumbled. I attempted to make a funny story of my misadventures, the story flying about like a concrete airplane.

I spent the balance of the day trying to explain to a lawyer exactly who struck John, and two other fellows whose names I had failed to get. "I don't think they've got you on a felony," the lawyer said by way of comfort. Much bruised and chastened, I returned to my cubbyhole apartment on New Hampshire Avenue. There I sat cogitating how to inform Bobby Baker that his Boswell had lamed a typing hand.

I very much wanted to telephone Masterson, of course, to see how we'd fared at Actors Studio. Somehow that act seemed injudicious. Then I remembered that Diane Smook was to have been there, and dialed her Village apartment.

"What happened to you?" Diane said on hearing my voice. "Are you all right?"

"Uh, yeah. Fine."

"Well, what happened? Peter Masterson said you'd been in an accident!"

"Wish it hadda been."

"What?"

"Nothing, honey. Everything's fine. Pete must have misunderstood me. I just had a bunch of work down here and—listen, so how'd it go at Actors Studio today?"

"Larry," Miss Smook said, "do *not* permit that material to get away from you."

"Uh, wha—?"

"It's wonderful! Everyone loved it! They laughed at the lines, the songs are great, it's—listen, Larry, don't let that material get away. Protect it! I know a good property when I see one."

"Well, I'll be goddamned! Come on, Smooker, tell me what happened! Details, baby, details!"

"Well, some official of Actors Studio critiqued the play afterward. Actually, all he did was praise it. There was *no* criticism. Not a bad word. Don't let that property get away!"

I blew kisses, hung up, and promptly began to worry that my property would get away. Did *I* own the copyright to my *Playboy* article or did Hugh Hefner? Did we own it jointly, maybe? Would we flip a coin for it, or what? I knew that my agent normally would get such a copyright transferred to my name upon publication of the article—I'd noticed several deductions from my checks for that purpose—but was uncertain whether he *always* did this in the case of magazine articles. When Pete Masterson called, a few moments later, he only increased my anxiety in that regard.

Masterson was bubbling to overflowing. "Hey! Man, it really went well! The Studio people like it a lot! Tremendous! Carl Schaeffer—he runs the place for Strasberg—says if we'll finish the thing he'll give us the money to budget a full showcase production!"

"How much, and when can we get it?"

"We can't know what the show will cost until it's finished," Pete said, "but we talked in the area of ten thousand dollars."

"Three-way split, right?"

"Naw, dammit, we don't get any personal money! The money's for production costs."

"But we'll get a cut of the gate, right?"

"No, no! Christ, Larry! Actors' Equity rules won't permit us to charge admission to a showcase. We can accept donations at the door, but usually the door money goes to the actors. You can't ask actors to rehearse for weeks and then do a dozen performances for a total of one hundred dollars each. That's the Equity minimum for showcases."

"Then where's the advantage of doing it at all?"

Pete said, "Look, it's a great opportunity! Actors Studio has *never* produced a musical that I know of. The prestige and publicity could be tremendous! See, you mount a showcase production to attract potential producers. Producers put up, or raise, the money for a show—you *do* understand that?"

"Now I do."

"We'll invite every damn producer in New York. Potential investors, too. And people who *know* investors. A lot of shows are bought as a result of being showcased. Now, how soon can we get to work?"

"Soon as my hand heals," I said.

I had not told my agent I was writing a play. I knew he did not believe in work one might define as speculative. Most agents do not. Ten percent of nothing ain't much.

Yet, I had a need to know whether I might one day have to

wrestle Hugh Hefner and his boys in court. So I called my agent and chitchatted: about football, the weather, the Baker book, politics—everything but ladies' fashions. Then I casually said, "By the way, you remember that *Playboy* piece I wrote about a whorehouse a few years ago? The copyright is in my name, isn't it?"

I could feel his antenna go *zoom!* My agent was a cautious man. You would not catch him standing downwind of bad odors or playing in mud. "Why?" he asked, with great suspicion.

"Oh, I was just sitting around the house and got to wondering about it," I said. "No particular reason or anything . . ."

After a long pause that branded me a bad liar he said, "I'll call you back." When he called an hour or so later he said, "Uh, Larry, gee whiz, we normally transfer those copyrights to your name immediately. It's routine. But in this case, maybe we had somebody on vacation, nobody seems to have—"

"Do it," I said.

"Ah, surely. But what—"

"Just *do it,*" I said. "Do it quick and do it quietly. Move like you're trying to sneak up on a radar station. And let me know the minute it's been done."

Very, very shortly—he must have used Federal Express—I owned clear title to "The Best Little Whorehouse in Texas." My agent and I chortled and celebrated over the phone.

"God would have wanted it this way," I told him, "Hugh Hefner already being rich."

But I refused to tell him more. "Later," I promised. "Soon."

Now, for the first time, I felt a keen, sustaining interest in the play. I wanted to rush it to completion as quickly as possible, hold distractions to a minimum. I had appeased Bobby Baker by completing another chapter of his book. I now pled that I must return to New York to counsel about my overdue taxes—a dilemma I knew Baker would understand from his own I.R.S. problems—but, I swore, except when closeted with tax agents I would work on nothing save the Bobby Baker saga. With fresh money in his pocket from the recent chapter, Bobby magnanimously wished me Godspeed and good hunting

I went straightaway to my agent's office on Madison Avenue, took a deep breath, and said he should accept no magazine assignments for me until further notice.

"Oh, you've decided to spend all your time on the Baker book? Good. I think that makes sense."

"Uh, not exactly. I'm, uh, writing a play."

He stared at me as if I had farted during chamber music. Loudly.

"Let me see if I heard right," he said. "You are writing a play. I would guess no one has bought that play. Have I got it right that far?"

"Uh, yes. That's . . . pretty much right."

"While you are writing this unsold play, you will not be making money from it. You also will not be making money from magazine articles you refuse to write. *And* you will not be making money from the Baker book unless you honor the terms of the contract. The contract says that when you send them a new chapter, they send you money. So how will you live?"

"Well," I said confidently, "there's my *New Times* column. And . . . uh. Yes, there . . . certainly is . . . the . . . *New* . . . *Times* . . . column."

"A big fat nine hundred dollars per month," he scoffed. "You owe—name somebody you don't owe."

He peered at me like a well-fed owl, adjusting his horn-rims as if maybe he might understand if only he could see me better.

I said, "Well, uh, I don't think I owe any money to, uh, the Confederate States of America. I'm, uh, almost positive about that."

"Larry, Larry, Larry," my agent said softly and sadly. "Do you know the odds against getting a play to Broadway? A million to one. Perhaps more." He sat and gently rocked, shaking his head as if palsied, a man in pain. When he could speak again he said, "Plays come to me by the dozen. Not one in a roomful is ever produced anywhere in the world. Any agent in this city will tell you. And of those few that *are* produced"—he shuddered—"a tiny, tiny, *tiny* percentage return one thin dime."

I said, "I am growing old and burdened writing articles for chicken feed and books which sell like chicken guts. I am tired and discouraged and often would jump off something tall if I but had the strength to climb. I *got* to dream about chasing my rainbow. Let me chase it, please."

"But the Baker book—"

"Is his," I said. "Not mine."

My agent sighed and slumped in his chair. "Promise me you'll split your time between the play and the Baker book. Otherwise . . ." He shrugged, showing me empty hands.

"Swear to God," I said.

He shook his head and said, "I must assume this is what that copyright business was about. With *Playboy.*"

"Right."

Whinnying, pitiful little sounds bubbled up from deep in his throat. He said, "You are writing a play about a whorehouse? That's what you are telling me?"

"Ah, a, a, ah. Yes. A musical."

He dropped his head in his hands and softly said, "Dear God. A musical. A musical. A musical. *A musical!*" He moaned and looked stricken and raised his head to regard me with wounded eyes: "Do you know how many musicals about whorehouses—"

I held up a traffic cop's restraining hand: "Let me chase my rainbow," I said.

I was raised in a Fundamentalist religion. We devoutly believed that God tests His children for reasons of His own. I believed it then, and I believe it now. I offer in evidence poor old Job and me.

Job, though seemingly a fine fellow who went about working hard and minding his own business—much like myself—saw his vast herds of sheep, oxen, and other cattle stolen by robbers and his many field and body servants killed; wanting a little variety, apparently, God next permitted a cyclone to kill Job's wife and ten precious children. Poor old Job had no more than planted his loved ones than God sent him a batch of painful boils to plague his body the rest of his days. Me, He sent a letter from Jon Larsen.

I had spent a productive day at the typewriter, working on the play, and was preparing to meet the writer Tommy Thompson

*(Blood and Money)* for rest and relaxation at Elaine's. God obviously did not want me so happy. As I left my apartment building the doorman handed me a special-delivery letter bearing a *New Times* return address and the initials—J.L.—of that magazine's editor.

I thought this peculiar. The *New Times* office reposed on Park Avenue between 32nd and 33rd streets, only three blocks from my apartment. Jon Larsen had been in my home, and I in his—both in Manhattan and his weekend retreat in Vermont. We had shared jokes, wine, smokes, and work. Why, then, a letter? And a special-delivery one?

Standing under a street lamp on Second Avenue, I ripped open the envelope to see if good old Jon had maybe sent me a bonus for good work. He had not. He had, however, sent a letter the opening paragraph of which spoke highly of me as a human being and as a writer. Unfortunately, it went on from there. In short, I was fired as a *New Times* columnist. But—the letter said—I need suffer no embarrassment: Jon Larsen himself, good pal that he was, would personally see that the magazine's next issue explained to its readers that I had taken "a sabbatical to go to Washington to write a book." This abrupt message ended with effusive low-grade bullshit culminating in the odd hope that the new turn of events would not damage our "personal relationship."

Standing under that street light, tugged by chill winds, I literally was stunned. Jon Larsen couldn't have done a more effective job had he sneaked up behind me with a baseball bat. I knew that my column drew more mail from readers than any other feature in *New Times*—and *I* hadn't made the count, Larsen's office had. I knew, too, that in addition to the column, I had written more feature-length articles for the magazine than any other writer—and *I* hadn't advertised that, Publisher George Hirsch had in one of his recent columns. I knew that I was the sole remaining founding contributing editor at the magazine—Jimmy Breslin, Pete Hamill, Mike Royko, Murray Kempton, Dick Schaap, Joe McGinnis, Nicholas von Hoffman, and others had long moved on, while I had stayed hitched. Goddammit, I had helped George Hirsch raise money to *found* the goddamn magazine! I had put him in touch with Steve Gelman and Berry Stainback, whom he had hired as his top two editors when *New Times* came into being. On my recommendation he had hired Frank Rich—now chief theatre critic for *The New York Times* but then freshly out of Harvard—as his first film critic. Jon Larsen, damn him to hot coals, had been around during exactly none of that. Now, apparently, Jonny-come-lately and God did not want me at the magazine anymore, for reasons of Their own.

In the cab bouncing over potholes to Elaine's, I got mad enough to chew iron and spit nails. I was also scared. Pitiful stipend my $900 monthly *New Times* check may have been, but it remained the only guaranteed salary I had. *Had* had, correction! Now I was totally at the mercy of the fates, skating on the thin ice of the free-lance pond.

Tommy Thompson was relaxing at a table with Liz Smith, the *Daily News* gossip columnist, when I rushed into Elaine's, agitated and trembling like a street prophet. Surely they were startled by my greeting: "I've just been fired, special delivery, by a goddamn rich kid who'd probably be working in a pickle factory if his old daddy didn't own a huge hunk of *Time*. Here, goddammit, see for yourself."

I thrust the crumpled Larsen letter at the bewildered pair, bellowed for a double Scotch, and sat snorting like a rodeo bull. I poked a finger at Liz Smith: "Put it in your column! That son of a bitch posed as my friend, may the worms work his sorry flesh, and fired me by a goddamn *letter* rather than face me down! *Elaine, goddammit! Where's my goddamn drink?*" I went on fuming, cursing, and generally deporting myself like the rowdiest guest at the hod carriers' ball. Tommy and Liz looked perplexed and as if they wished to be elsewhere.

About midnight I arrived home, walking in a slanting gait, called Western Union, and dictated a telegram to one Jonathan Z. Larsen: IF YOU WRITE THAT I HAVE GONE ON A SABBATICAL, KNOWING THAT IT IS A LIE, I WILL WHIP YOUR ASS. BELIEVE ME. LARRY L. KING.

The lady clerk gasped and said, "Oh, I can't send a telegram saying *that!*"

"It's *my* telegram, lady, and I'm paying! Send it!"

"That is against company rules, sir. I am sorry. I cannot send that telegram."

I hung up, thought a moment, redialed Western Union, and had the good luck to reach a different clerk. I dictated the exact same message—except for changing "whip your ass" to "flog your tokas."

"Sir," the second clerk asked, "how do you spell 'tokas'?"

For the next few days I did my wild-man act, hooting and dancing in a frenzy against *New Times* and all its fools and fixtures, and attempting to persuade writer friends to boycott the magazine by withholding their products. In retrospect I know that was terribly selfish, as well as wasteful of my energies. In my relatively brief writing career I had seen *Life, Saturday Evening Post, Show, The Reporter, Audience,* and a number of little literary magazines crash and burn; in such a shrinking market, no working writer should have been asked to honor the personal feuds of another. This did not stop me, however.

Most of my writer friends wisely ignored my tirade, or wrote damn-shame, keep-your-chin-up notes failing to pledge support of my boycott. I alternated between wallowing in righteous self-pity and working up homicidal rages. I am sincerely thankful, now, that I did not then own a gun. It might have been too tempting to walk over to the *New Times* offices and play a scene from *High Noon.* Especially after liquid lunches in bars in close proximity.

Two writers, however, did respond in ways that proved meaningful to me. David Halberstam said, "Just go ahead and do such fine work that Jon Larsen will have the dubious distinction of being remembered as the editor who fired Larry L. King." Norman Mailer wrote, "I thought the columns were not your meat right now. You didn't have the room to move that big bears need . . . you'll be five times as big as you've ever been once you decide you're either going to be a big writer or die, and that little stuff was killing you. Come out swinging 'cause I'll be ducking." Though I'm certain a great deal of kind flattery was involved—I have always found Mailer kind and supportive, despite his rakehellion's reputation—those words did something for my resolve. I gave myself a lecture: *Get off your duff and quit whinning. Fuck the "little" work. Gamble, take risks. Sink or swim, ol' buddy. Ain't nobody's ass but your own.*

So I would do "big work," as Norman said. The problem was, I couldn't decide whether a musical about a whorehouse made the weight.

## CHAPTER

# 3

In early December 1976, I visited my agent to say that I needed a collaboration agreement prepared: would he please contact the agents representing Pete Masterson and Carol Hall? The look he gave me might have withered an acre of hardy ragweeds. *You mean*—it said—*that in the unlikely event your foolish pauper's scheme produces a solitary dollar, you must split it with others?* It is difficult for a fat man who was born awkward to surreptitiously tiptoe away from anybody, but I tried.

But, alas, no agreement could be produced among the agents. Carol Hall balked at the across-the-board split Masterson and I proposed: one third of the creators'—or "talents' "—share of earnings to each of us. Ultimately, after much wrangling, the agents threw up their hands and recommended a meeting of the three principals. We met, several times, and soon the dialogue began to sound like a broken record:

HALL: I cannot and will not accept it. I'm writing music *and* lyrics. It's standard for the composer to receive a share and for the lyricist to receive a share. I am both. I want two shares. Period.

MASTERSON: But this one's different. Larry and I are contributing song ideas. You're taking some lyrics and song titles directly from his original article. I conceived the idea of the show, I got everyone together, and I'm pretty much shaping it. I don't feel I should take a penny less than anyone else.

KING: If we can't agree to a one-third split, ain't gonna be no musical. *I* own the underlying material, and I'm writing the lion's share of the dialogue and inventing most of the characters. Nobody's gonna get a bigger slice of my pie than I am.

We played that variation on a tired theme for days running into weeks. Just before Christmas, when it became necessary to return to Washington for more Baker-book tortures, the issue remained unresolved. Nor was the *Whorehouse* script growing: I had gone on a sit-down strike until Carol Hall would agree to the one-third split and sign a document so signifying. And I no longer considered her "almost as kin."

Despite brave words and defiant vows not to take on work outside the Baker project and the now fallow *Whorehouse* script, the harsh realities soon demanded that I eat crow. With my *New Times* base gone, that $10,800 annual guarantee cried to be replaced. I accepted an offer from Jim Bellows, editor in chief of the Washington *Star,* to become a visiting writer in residence at that newspaper, as had Willie Morris, Jimmy Breslin, Michael Novak, and Jane O'Reilly before me. It was honorable work and I was in good company—but, face it, it also was an offer I had summarily rejected a year earlier, and so made me dwell on recent slippage. That is not a productive exercise for a forty-six-year-old man who wakes in the night to wonder where his bloom has gone.

The *Star* assignment required three columns weekly of about 1,700 words each. If that sounds easy to you, try it sometime. Try even to think of three subjects each week worthy of a column. Russell Baker and Art Buchwald have no trouble, but they obviously are not normal people and know a secret they refuse to share. Early on I learned I could not write effectively in the noisy, clattering *Star* newsroom, as I had done in the Texas newspaper offices of my youth. I had been spoiled by thirteen years of solitude, locked away in a private writing room with only a drink and a cigarette for company.

There were problems, too, writing in the Washington cubbyhole apartment. My eighteen-year-old son, Brad, had abandoned Texas after graduating from boarding school and had joined me in Washington to seek his fortune as a musician and entertainer. He was in my temporary home at my invitation, and was warmly welcome, but his presence did complicate the space problem. When we unfolded the couch at night into a rickety bed, it lay side by side with my own. To get to my tiny writing table each morning I had to step across Brad's bed and sleeping form—he sang and played guitar late in a small club—then wedge a chair against his thin mattress and hope I hadn't gained the pound that might prevent my sliding in to the writing table. Around and about the tiny room, and in a kitchen built for midgets, sat boxes of Baker trial transcripts, clippings, correspondence, tape machines, Brad's guitars and his books and backpacking outfit. We had everything in there but a motorcycle. Brad is considerably over six feet tall, and I am disgustingly bulky; we did not fit naturally into minimal space.

Three mornings each week I banged out a column to the sound of Brad's snores, my groans, and Bobby Baker's telephone calls demanding to know when I would arrive for work. The columns, with rare exceptions, were mediocre in the extreme. As each one was completed perilously close to deadline, I would dash downstairs, hail a cab on New Hampshire Avenue, and study the driver's face to determine whether he had character enough to make timely delivery of my copy to the *Star* offices across town. Then I would chase back upstairs, struggle with the heavy tape recorder, and puff a couple of blocks to Bobby Baker's apartment. There I would sit, gasping and panting, while he patted his foot. This circus went on for weeks.

As 1977 began and Jimmy Carter took up local residence, there was yet another distraction, though I cannot truthfully say I minded it. Her name was Barbara Blaine and I found her to be as attractively packaged as any young lawyer who ever drew a brief. Miss Blaine not being the type one might casually have one's way with—on a promise to call again soon, as one skipped off to the nearest bar—I quickly found myself dancing a jig of serious courtship. The lady had much to recommend her in addition to charm, grace, beauty, youth, wit, and intelligence: she, too, was a displaced Texan and she had more money than I did. She would not learn the latter until it was too late, however. I wined and dined Barbara in Washington's best restaurants in a manner to indicate that I might be on the way to a stock exchange seat rather than to the poorhouse. Each time I handed the waiter my credit card at the end of our romantic dinners, I flinched against the possibility that he might insert it into a machine that would go crazy with flashing red lights, beepers, honks, and flags signaling that the abused card should be captured and destroyed on the spot. That, I knew, would rob me of all remaining pride and such few illusions as one had managed to retain.

When I returned to New York in April, the Baker tapes mercifully completed, the cold war with Carol Hall had not thawed even though spring was just around the corner. "She won't budge an inch on the collaboration agreement," Masterson gloomed. I said that made two of us. Looking agonized, he inquired whether I'd be willing to suffer yet another three-way meeting. "I don't think so, Pete," I said. "I'm afraid I might choke her." He laughed and said, "Well, if you do, squeeze her once for me." Then he sobered himself and said, "I would hate for this project to come to nothing. I just have this gut feeling we'd be making a terrible mistake to throw the thing away. It—it just wants to be *done.* It's there *for* us." And so on. Finally I sighed and said, "Okay, okay. Call the witch."

As usual, we met on Carol Hall's turf. Pete telephoned me before the meeting, humming and hawing, so that I knew sticky matters were on his mind. "Uh, Larry, I know Carol's being difficult but let's try not to get mad and cause an explosion. We've got to get this project back on track. Let me ease into the deal. If she backs off the business part, then at least we can go on and have a creative meeting. Just try not to get in a dog and cat fight with her." I grumpily agreed.

Carol received us graciously, smiling and chatting and taking drink orders as if we had met to plan our wedding and no differences existed. Pete made chitchat; I frowned and fidgeted.

Then Carol said, "Well, have you guys got some new scenes for me?"

"I ain't done squat and ain't going to," I said, "until we comes to terms." Masterson looked stricken. Carol coolly said, "I believe I've made my position clear. There's nothing more I can say."

"Well, good luck to you wee folk," I said, rising to leave.

"Now wait a minute," Pete said, attempting a laugh that never would have played at Actors Studio. "We can work that out later. What we've got to do is push on with our project. Let the agents do all the business hassling."

"They don't have anything to talk about if Carol refuses to budge from square one," I said.

Pete ignored the remark and quickly said, "Now, I think the play wants a romance—no, a *suggestion* of a romance—between Ed Earl and Mona. Carol, have you thought about a song to help that idea along?"

"Matter of fact I have," she said. "I haven't written it yet, but the other day I thought, Gee, wouldn't it be nice if the sheriff and the madam sang a duet."

"Hold it right there," I said. "That's the dumbest idea I've heard. The sheriff is an old, mean, macho bastard. I won't consent to his singing a goddamn love song. It's off the wall."

Carol sighed and said, "Larry, just one time when a song is suggested I'd appreciate if you didn't treat us as idiots."

"If I agree to Ed Earl singing a sissy love song," I said, "then you'll want him to do a goddamn tap dance. Look, the man is Slim Pickens not Fred Astaire."

"No, no," Pete said. "We don't intend any dancing."

"No *dancing?*" Carol said. "Pardon me, Pete, but whoever heard of a musical without dancing?"

"I mean *the sheriff* won't dance," Pete said, looking harassed.

"I don't see why anybody's got to dance." I sulked. "How you gonna tell a story when people tap-dance all over the lines or stop the action to sing about moonlight and roses? Dammit, we're not talking *Romeo and Juliet* here. We're dealing with a story about a bunch of whores!"

"Larry," Carol said, "if you don't want a musical, why are you here?"

"Good goddamn question," I said.

"Larry," Pete said, "we're not trying to stop the action or dance on your lines. A musical is always a compromise—a blending of techniques. Songs serve two purposes. One, they complement the story—help carry it along. Two, they'll develop the characters in a way that will permit the audience to know them better. That's all we're trying to do."

"If you'd see a few musicals," Carol said, "you'd understand. Have you gone to any, like you promised?"

"I've been too busy," I said.

"Now you've just got to *do* that! See *Chicago.* See *Pippin.* See *Grease.* There's a new one called *Annie* that is so cute!"

Abruptly, I said, "I think we've got the wrong title for our play." My collaborators stared at me. "It just hit me, when Carol named those musicals I should see. They are all one-word titles. So is *Oklahoma!*"

They looked at each other and broke into laughter.

"No," Pete chuckled, "believe me, that's just an accident. Carol probably named half the one-word titles in history."

"There's a book you should read," Carol said. "A wonderful book called *Words With Music,* by Lehman Engel. It's the best I know on musical theatre. You definitely must read it."

"Sure. Okay."

"Will you pick up a copy?"

"Yeah. Damn right."

"What's the name of it?" she asked.

"What? Oh, *the book!* Uh, it's, uh, *Writing Musicals.* By, uh, Eghardt . . . uh . . ."

"Oh, Lord help us," Carol said. She rose, crossed the room, and returned with a book. "Take my copy. But promise, please, you'll read it?"

"Swear to God," I said. "Just show me the page where it recommends singing sheriffs."

* *

Pete persuaded me not to wait for Carol to sign the collaboration agreement before pushing on with my script work. I settled down in the Manhattan apartment among familiar books and artifacts, the place echoing the sounds of a typewriter happily chattering. I had decided to divide time equally between the bean-and-rent project—Baker's book—and the *Whorehouse* roll of the dice.

I spent some weekends in Washington squiring Barbara Blaine, though increasingly she came to New York. We gladdened Carol Hall's life by taking in a number of musicals. I studied the uses of songs, dances, and sets but overall was not greatly cheered. It seemed that the "book" portions of most musicals—the story line—got short shrift. The story was something of a stepchild. Indeed, all too often the story was told in brief sketches jammed and crammed here and there; it seemed to exist largely as a device for the stringing together of songs and dances. This worried me.

I went to Pete Masterson to express my concern. "Well," he said, "we can do it our way. All along I've thought of *Whorehouse* as a play with music, not the other way around."

"The last time you said that," I reminded him, "Carol replied that you talk altogether another way to her."

He winked. "The best way to get along with Carol is tell her what she wants to hear."

I laughed conspiratorially. Not once did it enter my vain, birdbrained head that Pete Masterson might be using that same technique on me.

Our playscript grew rapidly. Pete occasionally fretted that Carol seemed to have lost interest. "I can't find that she's working on new songs. I show her where we need them in the script, discuss what they should say, but nothing happens."

One day he called to say, "I've found what Carol's trouble is. She apparently isn't gonna push ahead unless the sheriff and the madam sing a duet."

"Goddammit, Pete, that's been settled! No!"

"Well, she makes the point that no musical she knows refuses a song to one of the two leading characters. I've thought about it and she's right. She really is."

"So now," I said accusingly, "*you* want the sheriff to sing."

"Well, it seems to me the play wants a subplot. The only conflict is between the people who want the Chicken Ranch closed and those who don't. The most natural and obvious subplot would be a little something going on between the sheriff and the madam."

"No problem, Pete. I'm increasingly showing a long-time affection between them. But it's a subtle thing—a residue of what once was, of something between them in an earlier time. But I can't see a cussing old lawman and a woman who peddles pussy for a living yowling love songs at each other like Nelson Eddy and Jeanette MacDonald. That'd be goddamn ridiculous."

"I sat down a few nights ago," he said, "and went over the plots of a lot of Broadway shows. And not many smash hits failed to have an ongoing romance weaving through the plot."

"Fine. We've got that young boy who loses his cherry to Shy. Let *them* fall in love."

"I've already thought of that," Masterson said. "In fact, I was thinking he can be one of the Texas Aggies celebrating their football victory over the Texas Longhorns at the Chicken Ranch. That would be an easy way to return the kid to the whorehouse after he's originally met Shy."

"Good! Them being young, we can let 'em sing a whole damn medley of lovey-dovey songs. If that's what you and Carol want."

"I'm not sure that will satisfy her," he said. "She's pretty set on having a romance between the sheriff and Miss Mona."

"Dammit, Pete, we can't have *all* the whores involved in misty-eyed romances. How many subplot love stories can a show carry?"

"*Fiddler on the Roof* carried four," he said. "And guess how many *Seven Brides for Seven Brothers* carried?"

"Oh," I said. "Well. Shit. Anyhow, I bet they weren't whores." I thought I heard Masterson smothering a laugh. "Look, Pete, the only way I'll consent to the sheriff singing is if the song is *in character.* He can sing of how he hates his political enemies, the TV man that's bugging him, the—hell, if he's just *gotta* sing, if nothing else will do—he can sing that his hair hurts or he's of a mind to kill somebody. And if Carol Hall can't live with that, then I vote we find another composer-lyricist who can. Surely there are other people who can write rhyming words and la-de-dah-de-dums."

"Okay," Masterson said, perhaps a bit wearily. "I'll talk to her and get back to you. But damn if I'm not starting to feel like somebody refereeing a tennis match."

I had enjoyed a big night on the town. One of those nights that leaves frog hair growing on the tongue and a cadre of tiny sadists beating on the brain with very large hammers. Hair-of-the-dog being a time-honored cure, I was mixing a breakfast batch of Bloody Marys when Brad entered the kitchen: "Into the breakfast of champions again, huh, Dad?" I hurt too much to engage in a repartee with a young smartass who had no respect for his elders. I concentrated on pouring from the pitcher. A fair amount of the healing juices somehow missed the highball glass and formed a small red lake on the counter top. "Hands shaking a little," I said, making an affirmation of the obvious, and flashing what surely was a ghastly grin. Brad nodded. "Ever think about plunging your hands in the pitcher about wrist deep?"

I was trying to decide whether to turn him out on the street or throw the pitcher when the telephone rang. Somebody sounding like an exwife was making a terrible bunch of screeching sounds at the other end.

"Uh, what?"

*"They don't have to rhyme!"* a voice instructed in a high soprano.

"Mornin', Carol. What don't have to rhyme?"

"Those song memos you keep sending. *I'm* the songwriter! Why do you keep making them rhyme?"

"Hell, I dunno. It just seems easier."

"I am *not* putting any of your lyrics to music, Larry King."

"You don't seem to object to lifting lyrics from my article and script," I snapped.

"I don't 'lift' them. I fold them in. That's standard practice. And I'm doing far less of it than most lyricists. I take one of your lines and then write two dozen of mine and you make it sound as if I'm stealing from you!"

"I guess I don't see the precious difference, Carol. Why is it okay to 'fold in' lines from my article or script, but it's such a goddamn sin for me to write a rhyming memo?"

*"Because you are trying to write the songs!* That's my job! Either I'm going to be the composer-lyricist or I'm not. Now, I'm not trying to write your play. You *are* trying to write my songs."

"Carol, the end product is what counts. If I write a good line or a verse in my rhyming memos, then what's wrong with folding *that* material in?"

"Uh-uh. No way. If I use a single verse of yours, Larry King, you'll be telling everyone I didn't really write the songs."

"Oh, hell, Carol, this could go on forever. My health is delicate. Good-bye."

I was damning Carol for an unreasonable shrew when the doorbell rang.

Pepe, my building superintendent, stood in the hall, looking melancholy and aggrieved.

"Now Pepe, dammit, if that old couple is bitching about my music again—"

"Ain't them," he said. "Read this." He thrust a sheet of paper into my clammy hands. The signature revealed it came from a neighbor in 15-D, who had the bad luck to share my last name. I read:

> Dear Mr. King:
> My Patience and sense of Humor have worn thin. I am a Businessman living in this building several years with normal business hours and I would appreciate if you would make an effort to (1) Inform your friends of your correct apartment #—especially when they call at 2-3 or 4 in the morning. (2) Make an effort to inform the desk downstairs of your correct apartment #—so they will not call me at 2-3 or 4 in the morning. (3) Inform your friends of your correct phone #—so they will not call me at 2-3 or 4 in the morning, many of which are Women which upsets my Wife. Your co-operation in this matter is appreciated and I am sick of it.

"Pepe," I said, "tell this poor sumbitch he has my deepest sympathy. I wouldn't want to deal with most of my friends at two to three or four in the morning myself."

"Geeze, I don't know how much longa I can stall the guy, ya

know?" Pepe said. "He could go ovah my head any day, ya know? He's really pissed, ya know? On top of the old couple next door complaining to me and calling the police, ya know?"

"Pepe, we've been through the old-couple story a dozen times—"

"Ya don't help things, ya know? Like the old bird next door, he tells me he knocked on your door the other morning when you're partying, it's five o'clock in the a.m., ya know? And he asks ya if ya know what time it is. And ya say, 'No, but if you'll wait a minute I'll find out.' Now come on, ya know?"

Pepe sighed deeply, put on a mournful expression. I sighed deeply, put on a mournful expression. I handed Pepe a $20 bill. His mood and expression improved considerably. Mine did not.

Pepe handed over the rest of my mail. I stood in the hall debating whether to open an envelope clearly from my dear friends at Internal Revenue Service. Such a message could only deepen my depression. I was curious, however, about how much I now owed in back taxes; it was the sort of curiosity a loser might have at the gaming tables when he's lost track of his play.

The I.R.S. letter said my original unpaid tax bill had taken a giant leap forward to more than $9,000, what with interest and penalties. It threatened to "seize and sell" my personal property to satisfy the debt. I momentarily felt like wiring my acceptance; certainly it was the best offer I'd had. But, alas, the fine print announced that should my personal goods prove to be worth less than $9,000, my tax account would be credited only with the amount those goods actually sold for; I would remain liable for the balance.

Head pounding, mouth dry, pockets empty, hands tremulous, I uncertainly marched into the kitchen, where Brad was rummaging my bachelor's refrigerator in search of breakfast foods. He settled for a Popsicle, one of daddy's home remedies against morning dehydration.

"You were right, kid," I said.

"What?"

I held my shaking hands in the air, turning them like a surgeon who's just been scrubbed and sanitized, and then plunged them—wrist deep—into the Bloody Mary pitcher.

* *

I took my trusty portable typewriter to Nantucket Island, off the Massachusetts coast, when Barbara Blaine and I slipped away just before Memorial Day as guests of David Halberstam. My machine was not always in use. We idled on a windblown beach, watching the chilly Atlantic Ocean pound a shore soon to be invaded by summer people; we sat before crackling fireplace flames in the brisk evenings, consuming wines and steaks and salads, playing Scrabble and some other games ain't none of your damn business. Mornings, we strolled the cobbled streets of the island's main village, visited a whaling museum, watched local artists readying their wares for the seasonal tourist influx, drove Halberstam's vintage jeep down-island to Siasconset; in the morning mist and fog on lonely, narrow roads one could imagine something of Ireland. Most days I stole time to sit at Halberstam's dining-room table writing the final scenes of *Whorehouse.* I had promised my collaborators I would return from Nantucket with the play completed.

Just before our trip, Carol Hall had delivered a surprise. She'd called her collaborators to her apartment to hear new songs she'd written for the show. One was "No Lies," a duet between the madam and her black maid, then called Pearl. I liked "No Lies" then, as now, better than any other song in Carol's fine score. There were a couple of other new songs, though my notes fail to name them. I recall, however, that we were pleased. After appropriate congratulatory tidings and more easy smiles between us than there had been in months, Carol said, "Ah-hem. Now I take my life in my hands. Here's a duet for the sheriff and the madam."

I gathered myself on the ege of my chair, ready to pounce like an attack dog, until Pete Masterson shook his head at me. Carol had been outgoing and friendly; Masterson obviously did not want me to spoil the promising mood. *What the hell,* I thought, *it won't hurt to hear the song.*

As I heard it, it was not so much a duet as two songs—Mona singing "Have a Memory on Me" to crusty old Ed Earl, who responded in the negative by singing, in "Sissy Wishing Well," how he didn't want to hear her sentimental hogwash. I am afraid I was not pleased, though I trust this confession will not shock the reader.

At the conclusion of the song, Carol hanging expectantly, Pete said, "Yeah, that's interesting. Nice melody in Mona's song . . ."

I said, "Uh, I hate to be the meanie—"

"Since when?" Carol asked with a laugh that didn't have a lot of bells in it.

"Naw, Carol. I *like* Mona's song. Really. But the sheriff's . . . well, it doesn't say all that much to me."

"It is *in character*," she said. "That is what you've been demanding and demanding and demanding and that is what I have given you!"

"Now, don't get mad," I said. "I like everything else I've heard, especially that 'No Lies.' But I don't think—"

"You don't think the sheriff should sing. Anything. Ever. Period."

"No, now, be fair. I've backed off on that a bit. I'm just having trouble seeing where that double song, or duet or whatever you call it, fits the script. We've only three or four scenes to go, I've got them in my mind, and that number doesn't seem to fit."

"Well, talk to me about those scenes," she said, "and we'll see."

"Okay. There's got to be a scene in the sheriff's office. Pete and I have talked about it. Angry citizens shouting at the sheriff, jumping through their asses, demanding action, and so on. He realizes he has no choice other than to close the whorehouse. I don't yet know the action that will make him come to that decision, but—"

"Simple," Pete said. "He can get a telephone call from the governor ordering him to close the place. I've thought about that conversation, and I'd like to write it."

"That seems a little contrived," I said.

"*Contrived?* Christ, Larry, how do people communicate these days? You want him to get a *singing* telegram?"

"Maybe a Texas ranger could show up with a court order," I said.

"No, that would call for a big macho confrontation between the two lawmen and we're too late in the play. The governor has to *personally* order the whorehouse closed. Ed Earl's too goddamned stubborn to obey anyone else."

"Okay," I said, "but in any case it's no scene for a love song. Then in the next scene we must show the sheriff acting on the governor's order. We see him actually close the place."

"Might do that with a song," Carol said.

"Oh, shit, Carol!" I said. "We don't want the sheriff singing so much we'll have to resurrect Mario Lanza to play him. What's he gonna sing, 'Padlocking My Baby'?"

"We can settle the doing of it later," Masterson hastily said. "But the play wants a good-bye scene between the sheriff and the madam, to bring down the curtain."

"Got one in mind," I said. "It's about half-written in my head. I'll bring it back from Nantucket. But it won't hold a love song. It goes in another direction."

"Do you goddamn guys mean to tell me," Carol said, "that you're going to close a musical—*a musical*—without a musical finale?"

Pete and I stared at each other. With a sheepish little laugh he said, "Well, now that you mention it . . .'

I said, "I don't see how we can stick music in there. How do you perform what is essentially a sad act—closing the whorehouse and saying good-bye forever—with a big, sunny, whoopee number?"

"Maybe with a sad song," Pete said.

"No!" Carol said emphatically. "If we get everyone sympathetic to Mona, her girls, and the sheriff and *then* end on a sad note—whether with music or without—the audience will chase us out of the theatre! It's *got* to be upbeat."

"Let's don't worry about the song this minute," Pete interposed. "Larry, you just come back from Nantucket with those final scenes—"

"That's begging the question," Carol said. "I think we should clear it up here and now."

"How can we?" Pete said, spreading his hands and looking hurt. He could be very good at looking hurt. "I don't see how we can judge our final musical requirements until we've got the complete text. Then we can tell better what music goes where."

"Let me give you a clue," Carol said. "The musical finale *always* goes at the end of the show."

Pete laughed and slid into a smooth transition full of buttery praise for Carol's new work. I was gathering my manuscript and a light wrap when Masterson hissed in my ear, "Say something nice to her." Perhaps I looked at him as if he'd asked to borrow serious money. *"Come on!"* he whispered.

"Ah, Carol," I said. "Way to go and stuff." Behind her, Masterson shook his head in disbelief at my pallid effort. So I said, "Yeah, team. Ah, fight! fight! fight! Team fight!" Masterson rolled his eyes. I said, "Uh, ah, we've had some differences and stuff, Carol, but I do respect your talent and all."

Carol smiled a nonsmile and said, "Larry, don't worry about it. Rodgers and Hart worked together for years, and half the time they didn't speak except through their agents or in writing."

"Did anybody send rhyming memos?" I asked.

After several days in Nantucket I told Barbara that while I realized it surely would work a personal hardship on her, she must leave my sweet body be so I might finish my play. While the poor girl sat in a corner sulking over her law briefs, I wrote the sheriff's office scene. In New York, Pete Masterson was writing his version. We later would meld them, choosing the stronger lines from each effort. Pete had his way on the telephone call from the governor to the sheriff. Ed Earl agrees with a minimal amount of grace, and the requisite amount of cussing, to close the Chicken Ranch.

Now it got sticky. I was determined to avoid the sheriff singing the bad tidings to Miss Mona. I just didn't have the imagination to see the possibility of a song that might make it work. How do you *sing* terrible news? I envisioned something like: *Well, baby, I'm sorry/The news ain't so good/Guess the old horny menfolks/Must now pull their puds/Governor's done told me/That nookie for sale/Ain't constitutional/And could land us in jail.*

On the other hand, I couldn't find a way to write the scene in dialogue. Everything I attempted was overly sentimental, or too abrupt, or too self-righteous, or too . . . something. Unable to solve the problem, I avoided it.

I next opened on the whores, packing to abandon the Chicken Ranch amidst the litter, clutter, and debris of such leave-takings. Obviously, Miss Mona already has received the bad news from Sheriff Dodd—though we don't know how. The girls talk of their future plans and of their past lives, revealing themselves to be cynical, foolish, practical, or romantic according to personality traits earlier established. One of the whores, April, sings "Bus from Amarillo." The song tells the story of how she got in the flesh trade, of her youthful dreams, of life's compromises, of its unexpected turns, random selections, and attritions.

Though the sheriff and the madam had shown an easy, friendly informality with each other through the play, I stubbornly had permitted no romance; Pete finally had come around to this point of view. Now, as she packs, Miss Mona discovers an old gown, which leads her into a reverie about a day and a night she spent in the long ago with the sheriff in a Galveston waterfront motel; at the conclusion of their fling together the sheriff had given her the gown. In her words, "He poked it at me, kinda like it might bite him, and said, 'Here, Cakes. This here's for you.' He never was worth a damn at grammar." The one-time tryst obviously meant much to her; she has carried a torch through the years, but knows the impossibility of an ongoing romance with a man who represents the establishment, while she is an outcast. The black maid, Pearl, and the girls are enthralled and astonished by Mona's story.

I had chosen to have Mona say that during their Galveston assignation they watched President John F. Kennedy's inaugural address on television in their motel room. I wanted to select an event neither of the lovers would be likely to forget, an event that would put their fling into a time frame—and also lay the groundwork for the good-bye scene between the sheriff and the madam at final curtain.

In that curtain scene the sheriff is apologetic toward Mona about the turn of events and, as always, is bordering on the apoplectic as he goddamns his enemies, turncoat friends, and the screws of fate. He is an angry and prideful man, one who surrenders hard, one who has difficulty realizing that while he has been a one-man ruler in his small domain, he is helpless and impotent before larger authority. This is a strange, painful, and humiliating lesson for him. Mona, more practical, advises Ed Earl to put recent events behind him as quickly as he can; as a specialist in the underside of life, she knows that life will grind inexorably on without pausing to mourn them.

Mona then asks whether Ed Earl remembers President Kennedy's inaugural speech—and where he heard it. We think he knows; as the action plays out we are *certain* he knows. But there is so much emotion bubbling in him he cannot handle more; he will not permit himself to recall the moments Mona desperately wants him to recall. Instead, the sheriff filibusters with detailed memories of where he was when Lee Harvey Oswald shot JFK: "I'd just picked up three Meskin kids, they'd stole a goat from old man W. B. Starr and was throwin' theirselves a barbercue. I was just out on routine patrol, don't you see, when I seen this smoke comin' up out of old man Starr's pasture . . ." He goes on and on, making something of a hero of himself in his own eyes—perhaps repairing his psyche in the face of current humiliations—while avoiding her real question. Mona regards him wordlessly, sadly, perhaps accusingly: she is on to his game. Trying to cover his discomfort, he extends the filibuster by regretting having missed Jack Ruby's murder of Oswald: "Only live killin' they ever put on TV—hail, just about the only *decent* thing ever was *on* TV in all history. And I asseled around and missed that, damn sure did." On and on. Mona ultimately surrenders when she sees that Ed Earl is incapable of remembering; she tells him, not unkindly, that she guesses he'd better run along. He exits slowly—one feels he wants to go back for a longer and better good-bye but knows no beginning—a sort of ride-off-into-the-sunset-without-a-horse ending.

I wanted that scene to say how difficult it often is for men and women to communicate; how tough it can be to commit oneself in meaningful ways; how role-playing and conditioning to role-playing can trap one in a frozen script, limit one's actions, one's possibilities. I think it did say that. Though I was pleased with the scene on completion, the curtain simply didn't work. Something else had to happen. But what? The story was over, done, finished.

While I mulled this, David Halberstam and television newsman Fred Graham arrived in Nantucket for the Memorial Day weekend. They fished in rough waters off the island while I walked the streets and piers with Barbara, feeling distant and remote, my head searching for a workable curtain. As our host and other guests ate, drank, talked politics and books and bullshit, laughed and joked and seemed carefree, I was mentally rutting around in an old, abandoned whorehouse searching for something I could neither name nor find. Late in the evening I had a flash: *Bingo!*

My *Playboy* article had brought down the curtain, so to speak, by juxtaposing against the innocent crimes of the Chicken Ranch many true outrages and injustices of recent vintage in Texas. The torture-murders of twenty-seven young boys in Marvin Zindler's spotless and sinless Houston. Mafia violence and gang wars in Galveston, Fort Worth, Dallas, Beaumont—none of which had excited the governor or the state's attorney general. Dope wars in Austin and El Paso. A fifteen-hundred-year sentence in Midland to a young man who'd sold modest measurements of dope to a narc, followed by a twenty-two-hundred-year sentence shortly thereafter, for the same offense, in rival and neighboring Odessa. Industrial blight and pollution. Business swindles. Crooked political deals. Against those crimes I had counterpointed the words of the official state song, "Texas, Our Texas":

> Texas, our Texas,
> All hail the mighty state.
> Texas, our Texas,
> So wonderful, so great.
> Boldest and grandest
> Withstanding every test
> O, Empire wide and glorious,
> You stand Supremely blessed.
> God Bless you, Texas,
> And keep you brave and strong
> That you may grow
> In Power and Worth
> Throughout the Ages long.

*Hell,* I thought, *that song can give us our curtain!* As Ed Earl exits after his long good-bye to Miss Mona, we could come up with some sort of stage business—maybe the play's villains coming on stage in shadowy lights, grinning like so many jackasses eating briars, pounding backs, shaking hands, trading awards or trophies—while an offstage choir sings an ironic interpretation of that idealized, candy-assed state song. Probably Pete Masterson could take that idea and stage some theatrical business we would be proud of. Beautiful! Bingo! Hot stuff!

I hurried across the room to drag Barbara away from a circle of admirers and said, "Lawyer, Lord love us, I just finished that sumbitch in my head! It's done!" We hugged and babbled and I leaped joyously for the wine. Nobody had told me, you see, that when a playwright reaches the end of a play he has only arrived at a small beginning.

## CHAPTER 4

Flying back from Nantucket I was atypically quiet, if typically morose. I recognized the early symptoms of them ol' postcreative glums. Never have I finished a book, or even some magazine article I cared about, without a flash of elation soon to be trailed by blue and heavy vapors. One feels drained, vaguely sorrowful, a general torpidity. These are reactions to a reluctance to let go of something that for so long has lived in one's mind and occupied one's energies. I always think in such moments of the lost, dispirited feeling that overtook me as a child the day following Christmas: *Okay, Lawrence, the fun's over. Now let's go jump in the shit again.*

I rattled the ice in my Bloody Mary glass, gloomed, sighed, and thought I was going to have to cry to attract Lawyer Blaine's attention. She looked up from a book and dutifully asked what was bothering me.

"Carol Hall," I said. "Damn if I don't worry about her more than taxes. She's gonna throw a screaming, running fit when she sees I've ended the play by using a curtain song other than her own."

Barbara said maybe she wouldn't blame her. I muttered something about women always sticking together.

"To the contrary," Barbara said. "I think you and Pete Masterson are treating Carol differently because she's a woman."

"Please," I said. "Do not hand me that Betty Friedan bullshit."

"See what I mean?" my favorite lawyer said.

"You haven't even met Pete Masterson. How can you know what's in his head?"

"I've met you," she said.

"Pete's as straight and steady a dude as I know. If you don't like him, you don't like mankind."

"*Man*kind?" she asked, sweetly. She serenely returned to her book, which probably was a goddamn raving silly unreasonable feminist tract.

"Come on, Barbara! Look at the facts. Carol refuses to sign a collaborators' agreement that's fair and equal—one-third to everybody. If we don't like that, is it because she's a woman? She's trying to dictate the relationship between the sheriff and the madam, even though the story line is outside her purview. If we don't like that, is it because she's a woman?"

"You'd give her more leeway if she happened to be a man."

"Gimme a break! If anybody's using sex or gender in this thing, it's probably Carol. Who puddles up and cries if she fails to get her way?"

"No wonder, with you two ganging up on her and you cursing her all the time."

I wanted to tell the sweet lawyer to go to the hot place and take Gloria Steinem with her, but that seemed poor tactics of courtship.

The collaborators pooled resources to order fifty copies of the finished playscript professionally bound at Studio Duplicating Service on West 44th, near the theatrical district. The afternoon Pete and I picked them up we stood fondling the maroon covers with their spiffy brass studs, permitting our eyes to feast on gold lettering wondrously proclaiming: *The Best Little Whorehouse in Texas.*

I grinned at Pete and said, "Damn, it feels good. I'm about to start believing."

We laughed, shook hands, and then impulsively hugged like two clumsy bears. It seemed a good idea to walk over to Joe Allen's, on West 46th, to toast our show with a drink. Joe Allen's is a show-folk hangout. Its walls are decorated with posters from Broadway shows. Looking them over I said, "Damn, I hope our poster is up there one day."

Peter spewed beer and choked. *"Oh, hell no!"* I was puzzled. "They only put posters of miserable flops on the wall here," he said. "It's an inside joke. See, there's *Breakfast at Tiffany's,* which cost a ton and closed nearly overnight. They're all that way. Bombs!" He merrily laughed. I felt a foolish new awareness of my show-biz ignorance.

Pete said he would drop a copy of the play off at Carol's that evening. "You better fling it in the door and run," I said, "before she discovers that curtain song ain't hers."

Carol did not cry or throw a running or screaming fit when she made the discovery. She simply looked at us with flinty eyes, raised her chin to a determined angle, and said, "No. Never in the history of the theatre has a composer had to suffer another composer's song at final curtain. It has not happened before, it will not happen now. Period."

"But Carol, hunny," I said, "don't you see the irony of the lyrics to 'Texas, Our Texas'—"

"No," she said.

"—juxtaposed against the politicians and—"

"No. Absolutely not."

"Well," Pete said, "we can try it one way—"

"No," Carol said. "Anytime you say that, Pete Masterson, it means things will get done the way Pete Masterson wants them done. You will *not* do this to me. No."

Later, when we were alone, Pete said, "I think she really means it."

"Yep. Ain't a inch of give there."

"Goddamn," Pete said softly.

"What do we do now?"

"I guess we do something different," he said. "I just wish I knew what it was."

° °

I went with Masterson to present a copy of the play, and his estimated budget, to Carl Schaeffer of Actors Studio. Pete had cautioned me not to mention Carol Hall's rejection of our curtain song.

Schaeffer, a tiny, bearded man in his sixties, smiled us into his office, shook hands, and muttered pleasantries. On the walls were posters of past Actors Studio productions and several Broadway plays Schaeffer had invested in or been connected with.

Pete proudly placed the spanking-new script on the desk. Schaeffer beamed, riffling through it and speaking congratulations. Pete then placed the proposed budget on the desk. Schaeffer rapidly flipped pages until he reached the bottom line and jumped from his chair, screaming, as if his hemorrhoids had suddenly gone back on him: "*Thirteen thousand? Whatta you, kidding?*"

"We maybe could trim it here and there," Pete said calmly.

"Here and there, he says. *Thirteen thousand,* he says. What are we, Chase Manhattan? We're a soup kitchen! My mother I couldn't get thirteen thousand! Eight! Eight! Eight tops! Seven, maybe. No more."

"Carl, Carl! You promised me *ten* last winter!"

"Ten thousand I promised him," Schaeffer said, slapping his forehead. "Ya hear that? I'm running a soup kitchen that I should go promising ten thousand, right?"

"Doubling and tripling the actors in their roles, Carl, we'll have a cast of about forty. And a five-, six-piece band. And all the Equity people have gotta receive a minimum of a hundred dollars each. You know that, Carl."

"*Forty,* he says to me. *Musicians,* he says to me." Schaeffer thumped our pristine script and looked down on it as if it might be a long-dead herring. "Whatta ya got here, *The King and I*? You're bringing me *Fiddler,* maybe? *Dolly*?" He turned to me, pointing a finger: "Did I promise ten thousand? Did I?"

"Uh, I wasn't here, Carl. Pete told me—"

"I don't promise ten thousand. Never in my life. I run a soup kitchen. I got—"

"Eleven thousand, five hundred," Pete Masterson said.

"Eight! Eight! No more!"

"Carl, I can't stretch it. Eleven thousand is bottom line."

"Cut ten characters. I give you eight five."

"Ten five," Masterson responded. I began to feel like a spectator at an auction.

"Nine," Schaeffer said. "Not a penny."

"Ten," Pete countered.

"Nine I guarantee. Ten I *try*, with no promises."

"Done," Pete said.

They grinned and clasped hands. I sat bewildered, since matters seemed to have ended pretty much where they'd started in the winter, until it dawned on me I'd perhaps witnessed a ritual as obligatory as a mating dance.

"Now the payback," Schaeffer said, briskly.

"Right."

"You pay back the budget to the penny. The Studio takes one, maybe one and some fraction percent of future productions. The Studio also—"

"Gee, Carl," Masterson said. "I don't think so. Not a full percentage point. Some fraction, sure, but—"

"Wait a goddamn minute!" I said.

Schaeffer looked at me, looked back at Pete, jerked a thumb in my direction: "Who's he?"

"What's this payback jazz, Pete? Nobody mentioned anything like that to me," I said.

"What, I should operate a charity?" Schaeffer bellowed. "You sell your show, we take a piece. A return on our investment. Simple. It's business. You don't know from business?"

"But suppose we *don't* sell the show? I'm supposed to go in hock, personally, so Actors Studio can put on a play? What is this Mickey Mouse crap?"

"Where'd you get this guy?" Schaeffer asked Pete. To me he said, "You don't sell your show"—an elaborate shrug—"poor Carl Schaeffer takes a bath. The poor Studio takes a bath. You *sell* your show—okay, we take a tiny piece. Tiny! You hit the biggest number since *Grease*, we're still a soup kitchen here. You get rich and forget us. That's life. That's the business."

"Pete?" I said. "Shit, man, I dunno. You know I dunno."

"It's a standard deal more or less," Masterson assured me. "I mean, we'll have to work out the figures. Carl's a little high in his first demand, but basically—"

"High, he says." Schaeffer threw his diminutive arms skyward and spoke toward the heavens. "I offer the boy a shot, I'm a robber. I give him money I don't got, I'm a robber."

Masterson ignored him. "In a showcase, see, whoever bankrolls it normally gets a piece of the action if the show sells and goes into a professional production."

"*Such* a tiny piece," Schaeffer said. "You wouldn't believe."

"Okay, I guess," I said. "But I don't sign anything until I talk to my agent. If he's still talking to me."

Schaeffer said. "You two boys sign. The girl, the skinny one—she writes your music? She signs. Everybody signs. Talk to your agent all day, but everybody signs."

"Lotsa luck, Carl," I said. "We haven't even been able to get her to sign a collaboration agreement."

"Oh, shit!" Masterson said, reddening and glaring at me.

Carl Schaeffer's little eyes widened. "Pete, Pete, Pete," he said. "Don't tell me, Pete! No collaboration agreement? There's trouble? There's trouble!"

"No, no," Pete said. "We're making headway, Carl. Larry's been away. He doesn't know what's been going on."

"Larry? Who's Larry?"

"We're ironing out details," Pete said. "She'll sign any day. I guarantee it."

"He guarantees it! He guarantees trouble, that's what he guarantees! I shoulda got in furs. Stocks and bonds I shoulda got in. A nice resort in the Catskills." He closed his eyes and dramatically suffered. Brando couldn't have done it better.

"Uh, we'll need a thousand or so pretty soon for set designs, materials, and so on," Masterson said.

"So take the money," Schaeffer said, mournfully. "So rob a soup kitchen."

While Pete Masterson went about his mysterious magic involving set design, costuming, lighting, and other production details, I shifted gears to pound out a couple of chapters of Bobby Baker's book. There were many encouraging this: agent, creditors, editors, and Baker himself. During the time I had been sprinting toward a *Whorehouse* finish, Baker again had become restive. Each time he called I had shamelessly lied about the promptness with which I expected to finish a chapter not yet started. Writers understand that such lies are permissible and do not count against them in Heaven's ledgers. Nonwriters have trouble grasping this. Bobby Baker could not fathom why his partner and pal would repeatedly deceive him; he saw this as a character defect and divested himelf of morality lectures. Soon I began to insist that Brad answer my telephone. He shortly grew weary of absorbing Baker's ire and began to pressure me in Bobby's behalf. "Dammit, son," his loving father snarled, "if everybody pushing me about that goddamn book buys just one copy, I'll have my first best-seller." I eked out the two new chapters, however, and turned my thoughts back to the theatre adventure.

One night as Pete Masterson and I dined on bacon-cheeseburgers and beer at Joe Allen's, he talked of budget troubles. Equity actors—in the principal roles—would probably cost $2,000; he would have to cast non-Equity people in the lesser ones. "By the time you figure in musicians, a musical director, lighting technicians, sound technicians, a choreographer, publicity costs—well, even with everybody working cheap we're knocking a big hole in our budget. And I haven't mentioned set design, the set itself, costumes, props. Plus all the backstage and backup people."

"Damn, what will we do?"

"We'll make it,' he said. "The Studio's reputation will attract volunteers, a lot of dedicated people who love the theatre and being around it. Manpower's not the problem—it's *things.* We'll ask the actors to furnish their own costumes where possible. The rest we'll scrounge at the Studio and elsewhere. Same with props. The set's gonna have to be real bare bones. The audience will have to use its imagination."

"Like how?"

"We'll improvise. Make a couch out of three or four folding chairs placed side by side. A table or desk in one scene can be a café counter in another. An old tree stump could suggest the out-of-doors. That kind of stuff."

"Sounds pretty crappy," I said. I had innocently envisioned

spiffy painted flats showing barbershops, small stores, the exterior of the Texas Twinkle Café, parking meters, and so on. My concept of Sheriff Dodd's office had included filing cabinets, a police radio lashup, F.B.I. posters on the walls, a suggestion of jail cells. Pete laughed at these expectations: "Forget it."

I said I couldn't understand why actors would work free, as non-Equity people would be expected to do, or why Equity members—*professionals,* now—would rehearse for weeks, then sweat through fifteen or more performances, for a miserly $100 each.

"Actors exist to act," Pete said. "Paying jobs are available to only a fraction." He nodded toward the crowded bar across the room in Joe Allen's: "Probably half of those people are unemployed actors, nursing beers. They hope to hear of something they can audition for—*anything.* They hope to make a contact, talk to other actors for the pleasure of it, learn something. There are thousands and thousands like 'em in this city. They work as waiters, waitresses, bartenders, cabdrivers, dog-walkers—shit, anything! But they think of themselves as actors. Everything else is just marking time until they find the big break."

"Jesus! I thought writers had it tough."

"I've been getting calls for months just on the rumor I'm directing a play," he said. "See, in a showcase—especially one at a prestigious place like Actors Studio—they'll have a chance to be seen by the right people. That could lead to future work. Or if our show's bought, they dream of moving with it. Even if they don't get to go with us, they'll be entitled to two weeks' salary at the Off Broadway or Broadway level. Depending on where we go."

"Pete," I said, "why do you drop these goddamn financial surprises on me?"

"What?" he said, himself looking surprised.

"Well, you've just told me we're on the hook to pay a bunch of folks money I didn't know about. The ones we'll leave behind."

"No getting around it," he said. "Equity rule. You don't fuck with Equity rules. What we'll do is negotiate with whoever buys our play so they'll pay the actors."

"But are *we* legally accountable if they refuse?"

"We wouldn't want to sell to anybody on such a stingy budget they'd even think of refusing. Besides, they wouldn't dare buck

Equity on it. They'd be shut down. Anyway, when you're talking about a first-class production of a show as big as ours, you're talking an investment cost of . . . oh, seven hundred thousand to a million bucks."

I was aghast: "Tell me you're kidding me."

"Not a nickel's worth, man. Musicals are expensive."

"Nobody's got that much money but the Arabs," I said. "We don't have a chance of a sale."

"Yeah, we do," he said, with such conviction that I at once grinned happily and lifted a skeptic's eyebrow. "I'm serious. We've got a real solid shot."

"Wish you could prove it to me, Pete."

"I'm going to," he said.

The first order of business was to cast the leading man and leading lady.

I wanted a fellow Texan, Pat Hingle, to play the sheriff. He was of an age and size and look. I had seen him in any number of movies and considered him one of our finest character actors. Masterson knew Hingle from Actors Studio and took him a script. "He likes it," Pete reported, "but he's too busy working for pay."

I suggested yet another Texan and Actors Studio member, Rip Torn. Not only did I like his work, I'd enjoyed a few nights drinking with him in the distant past. "Yeah, Rip's a great talent," Pete said. "Some people say he can be hard to work with, though." Yes, I said. I remembered when Torn—working in a movie produced by, directed by, and starring Norman Mailer—had taken his assassin's role so seriously that he had, from ambush, assaulted Mailer (who had modestly cast himself as President of the United States) with a hammer. Not a rubber hammer, not a prop or trick or breakaway hammer, but the kind of hard iron hammer that could kill. Rip had leaped from the bushes and knocked the pure-dee crap out of poor ol' Nawmin. In the fight that followed, Mailer had chewed up a big hunk of Rip's ear; both men had emerged bloody and with an old friendship shattered. "That's it," Masterson chuckled. "You never know what Rip's likely to do. But hell, I'd like to have him in the role. Damn right." He took Rip Torn the script. Again, our choice for sheriff claimed to like the role—but said he couldn't afford to work several weeks for a hundred dollars.

One day Pete said, "I think I've found the guy. Henderson Forsythe."

"Never heard of him," I said. "And he sounds British."

"No." He laughed. "He comes from some little town in the Missouri Ozarks. Henderson's an old-timer. He's done some really fine work off Broadway and on Broadway. Did you see the Preston Jones plays—the Texas Trilogy?"

"All three. Loved 'em. Nobody once sang a song or danced."

"Anyhow, Henderson played the head honcho of the lodge in *The Last Meeting of the Knights of the White Magnolia.* And in *The Oldest Living Graduate* he was the real-estate partner of the son."

"Yeah, yeah. I remember him."

"What did you think?"

"I remember thinking his Texas accent sounded a little phony. I liked him otherwise, though."

"The only reservation I have," Masterson said, "is that he may not look exactly right. His face seems a little . . . soft. For a guy supposed to be as goddamn mean as Ed Earl."

"If you can get an experienced old dude like that for a hundred bucks," I said, "don't worry about him looking mean. I'll find ways to piss him off and *make* him mean."

Pete laughed. "Oh, I can get him. He's crazy about the role. That's how you get good, seasoned actors for showcases—dangle a juice roly."

So Henderson Forsythe was cast as Sheriff Ed Earl Dodd.

There never had been any doubt in my mind that Carlin Glynn would play Miss Mona. Sure, you say—she was the director's wife. Well, yes, but that's only part of the story.

I had been so impressed with what Carlin Glynn brought to the reading of Miss Mona's early scenes—a sort of tough, earthy compassion—that in writing later scenes I had tailored the part to her. Each time I was around Carlin, during the writing, I studied her mannerisms, speech patterns, and expressions. She superimposed herself on that character without knowing it. I knew that despite her limited recent professional experience, while raising children,

Carlin was a fine actress: she had been admitted to membership at Actors Studio (where far more aspirants are rejected than accepted) by the normal route of impressing a tough panel of judges in a thirty-minute audition. She had worked in a number of Studio projects, off Broadway in *Waltz of the Toreadors,* and in the movie *Three Days of the Condor.* Though her single scene in that movie had been a brief three- or four-minute stint as the wife of a man who has just been murdered, she gave a powerful one-on-one performance opposite Robert Redford. There was a warmth, spark, and intelligence about the woman that convinced me she couldn't miss as Mona.

In retrospect, I am amazed I didn't worry about Carlin Glynn's lack of training and experience as a singer—after all, she would be expected to carry the vocal burden of a big musical. Perhaps it was my infatuation with Carlin as a person, but for whatever reason, this handicap didn't bother me. It understandably bothered Carol Hall. What composer-lyricist wants to see the leading singing role in his or her opus go to an untested vocalist?

"Don't misunderstand," Carol Hall told me. "I like Carlin as a person. I think she's a fine, fine actress. But *sing?* She does not sing. She never has. How can we cast her as the singing lead?"

I mumbled, shuffled, and changed the subject. All I knew was that I was bent on casting her, come hell or Ethel Merman. Carol urged me to raise the singing question with Pete. She, after all, was the couple's long-time friend. I was new to the group and could express reservations, whereas Pete and Carlin would certainly be hurt if Carol did. I reluctantly made a halfhearted stab at it. Pete, turning red on his bald dome, said, "Carlin will be fine. Just fine. She's taking singing lessons and I know she'll come through. I know what she's made of."

Eventually, Carol's reservations about Carlin's ability to carry her musical score led to tensions that made it impossible for the old friends to continue sharing a summer home. Soon the Mastersons became sole occupants. That could not have done much for Carol Hall's morale or disposition.

So Carlin Glynn was cast opposite Henderson Forsythe. Pete Masterson and I had now accomplished the seemingly impossible: we had cast, in both leading roles in a big musical, two people who never had sung a note in public.

* *

We held auditions for the remaining roles at Actors Studio in August of 1977. The place looked as bummy and decrepit as I remembered from my first exposure. I told my collaborators that I intended to play the tiniest role in casting decisions: "I can't tell a good singer from a bad one, and I think you two should be able to choose the people you'll be working with." Pete and Carol lightly protested, though I felt they received the news with ill-suppressed glee and may have hugged each other once I left the room. Young Jay S. Cohen, engaged by Carl Schaeffer as working producer, assisted in the casting.

My contribution was to organize a clean-up brigade from among Actors Studio volunteers. No way to prettify the place—could you undent chairs, ungrime the work of years?—but we hauled out garbage cans of debris, stacked unsightly stage flats and hid them, coiled and stored tangles of ropes and cables. We announced that company members, after each rehearsal, would be expected to police the place for cigarette butts, coffee containers, soft-drink bottles, candy wrappers, and half-eaten sandwiches. (Fat lot of good that did, as it proved.) Another of my important jobs was to round up empty beer cans and cart them off each night; the Studio had a no-drinking rule, which I failed to honor as flagrantly as the company failed to police its daily litter. Live and let live.

Most actors and actresses who auditioned were people Pete Masterson had worked with or whose work he knew from fifteen years of theatrical knockabout. In its final statistics our original *Whorehouse* company comprised nineteen Equity members—a $1,900 bite from our budget—and fifteen non-Equity types, counting the band. One of these amateurs was my son, Brad, freshly nineteen, who played guitar and harmonica in the little four-piece show band; he also doubled as a singing Texas Aggie football player. Yet another amateur was your present hero. I played a nameless town hangabout and ne'er-do-well—the Old Nester—given to gossip and baiting wisecracks.

Henderson Forsythe was the nearest thing we had to a big name or star. Most of our players were youngsters with few credits, or old heads who had not had much good happen to them in a tough and uncertain business. That implies not a lack of talent so much as a lack of luck or opportunity. Being in the right place at the right time, maybe. Perhaps the following were typical:

*Clint Allmon:* An Oklahoman in his mid-thirties, he was cast as the villainous TV crusader, Melvin P. Thorpe. He had worked in a number of Actors Studio plays and some off Broadway. He'd had a bit part in the movie *Dog Day Afternoon,* once appeared on Broadway in *Indians,* and had made fleeting appearances on TV. His paying job at the time he was cast in *Whorehouse* was to water Rip Torn's roof-garden plants and vegetables twice a week; the remainder of his time he spent in pursuit of acting jobs. In casting him, the unfailing King-Masterson duo struck again: Allmon hadn't sung a note, either. His role, of course, called for songs.

*Joan Ellis:* A New Jersey product, twenty-two, she was cast as the young whore, Shy. A new addition to membership at Actors Studio, she was tabbed as an actress with great potential. She had few credits other than workshop productions, however.

*Susan Mansur:* A native of Wichita Falls, Texas, in her early thirties. She was an excellent comedienne and—surprise!—had a truly fine singing voice. She had toured with USO shows, made many television commercials, and had starred at Abilene Christian College in *The Unsinkable Molly Brown* and *Kiss Me, Kate.* We cast her as the waitress, Doatsey Mae.

*Pamela Reed:* A graduate of the drama school at the University of Washington, she was then twenty-six years old. She had worked extensively in television soaps, had done some summer stock, and later would receive good to rave notices on Broadway for her work in *The November People* (short-lived) and *The Curse of the Starving Class.* In 1980 she would be featured as a prostitute in the movie *The Long Riders* with Keith Carradine. Those credits were in the future, however, when we cast her as the tough, mischievous whore, Linda Lou.

In short, the majority of our cast had little—sometimes no—experience on or off Broadway, in major touring companies, in movies, or in television. They were people hunting a break, chasing dreams, and willing to give prodigious energies. Probably we made only two obvious mistakes in casting: we turned down a young woman named Alma Cuervo, fresh out of Yale's drama school, who went on to excellent Broadway notices in *Once in a*

*Lifetime* and *Bedroom Farce*. And we failed to turn down a confused fellow—whom I shall call Dakota—who had a bad bottle problem we didn't know about.

Little in the theatre is quite as exciting as the first day of rehearsal. Nothing has gone wrong up to that point; an improbable optimism insists that nothing can. It is like that first day of football practice when all teams are unbeaten, untied, and unscored on; when Podunk Tech can imagine itself the equal of Ohio State or Notre Dame.

Our cast gathered in a circle, perched on those dismal folding chairs, and after a little pep talk by Director Masterson, read through the play. There were first-time laughs larger than some lines deserved, a sparkle in all eyes, and for a brief period no tensions, even among the three collaborators.

When Carol Hall played piano and sang her songs, the cast pressed in close around her, I found myself about half misty-eyed and leading the cheers. Such was the spirit of hope and cooperation that a potentially ugly scene between Carol and myself was averted: I had wanted a bartender friend from my neighborhood pub, Marci Maullar, to play the role of a whore named Ruby Rae; Carol was pushing a nightclub singer, Marta Sanders, for that role. I had received the impression from Pete that Marci had the job. On that first day, however, Director Masterson asserted himself and ruled in Carol Hall's favor. I was miffed. Shortly, however, Marta Sanders opened her mouth to sing and this huge, wonderful voice came out and filled the room. Even I could tell that Miss Sanders was exceptional. Marci Maullar and I looked at each other and shrugged; she graciously consented to accept a lesser role.

At the end of that first-day reading, Pete Masterson—looking like a small-town football coach in an old letter-jacket, faded dungarees, and sneakers—told the company we would open our Actors Studio production on October 20th and give a dozen performances, concluding November 6th. "That's the maximum number of showcase performances Equity allows. But"—a small laugh—"there are ways of dodging the rule. We hope to add three to five performances by calling them dress rehearsals. I'm working on that now. Ed"—he nodded to Ed Setrakian, who had been elected Equity deputy for the company—"I hope you and the other Equity people will back me on that. If you guys say it's okay, then I'm sure the union will." General murmurs of assent.

"Now let's mill around for a while and get to know each other," Pete said. "You're gonna be working and playing together for a couple months—if we get lucky, maybe a hell of a lot longer." Applause. Masterson grins, bows. "Larry King, our refreshment producer, has sent out for beer. Maybe he'll share some with you." General laughter.

High spirits prevailed in the mixer that followed. People said, "The music is just super," and "I just love your lines," and "We're all so excited about working with you." The three collaborators preened themselves as if Walter Kerr had praised them.

I met a striking blonde, Liz Kemp, cast as the whore April; a saucy brunette, Mallory Jones, playing the whore Ginger; a perky little lady, Elaine Rinehart, cast as the whore Durla, who had the kind of figure to make good men leave home. "Damn if this show-biz stuff ain't all right," I said to my son. Brad had little time for me, however, as he bowed, aw-shucksed, shuffled bashfully in his cowboy boots, and removed his cowboy hat while calling all the ladies ma'am in a Texas accent that seemed to grow by the moment. I found myself hugging Carol Hall, laughing with her, and flashing on the thought that perhaps all our troubles were behind us.

Sure they were.

# CHAPTER 5

Peter Masterson was putting a group of actors through their onstage paces. Now and again he stopped the action, draped a friendly arm over the shoulder of one or another individual, led the actor off a few paces, and spoke softly, intently. His voice did not carry to the rows of folding chairs where I sat, scribbling some new notion in the margin of my script.

"Hi!" a breathy voice said. "Is it okay if I laugh during orgasm?"

I looked up, astonished, into the face of a pretty young actress. Then I glanced around to see whom she might be so intimately addressing. Incredibly, I appeared to be her target.

"Uh, wah," I said.

We stared into each other's eyes. Hers were brown and deep. Mine were wide and popped. She smiled a dazzler.

"Peg bardon?" I said.

"Laugh." She laughed. "When I have an orgasm. Do you mind?"

"Uh, wah-wah. Certainly not."

She placed one slim round bare knee in the chair where I had propped my booted feet and, smiling, leaned forward. I reluctantly looked away from two perfect cones, seeking objects of interest on the Actors Studio ceiling. Lights. Ropes. Pulleys. Girders.

"Sometimes when I'm making it?" she said. "Well, I laugh at the moment of climax. Know what I mean?"

"Uh wah," I said. "Wah."

"Not always." She smiled. "Just *some*times." She delicately nibbled a fingernail: a blood-red patch on a lean, tan sausage. Hoo, boy! I got a thang about sexy hands, momma, and I be durn if I can heppit.

I gazed again at the lights, ropes, pulleys, and girders. Yep. Still up there, all right.

"In the Act One curtain scene?" she said. "When the Texas Aggie football boys take us whores upstairs and are making out with us in the dark?"

"Uh, wah," I said. "Yes." Fine, light beads of moisture rested on her twin cones and made me thirsty.

"Well, I thought it might be real neat if I laugh there. When I reach orgasm?"

"Uh, wah. Wah."

"Is that all right with you?" Serious round clear eyes looking into mine. Nibble nibble nibble at the red-on-tan fingernail.

"Uh, wah. Sure. Right. Be my finger—uh, be my *guest!*"

"Thanks!" She flashed the dazzler again, about ten thousand watts, before twitching and jiggling away. *Jesus Christ, you boys open them windows! Ain't it hot in here?*

I never did recall what I had started to scribble in my script.

Henderson Forsythe appeared to be a nice, low-key guy. Indeed, such was his role in the soap opera *As the World Turns,* in which Forsythe for seventeen years had played Dr. David Stewart. Dr. Stewart was a warm, thoughtful, humane, generous, wise, too-good-to-be-true type—what the American Medical Association would like us to believe all doctors are, and some might actually have been before they gave up house calls for golf and Neanderthal politics.

One afternoon Forsythe called me aside, "to go over a few of my lines." I did not realize he meant all of them. Two hours later he was still asking what the sheriff meant here, how he felt there, what some down-home expression meant. His professional quest for perfection and understanding was near to exhausting. I would learn this dedication was typical of Forsythe. He was a whirlwind: he did TV commercials, his soap opera, benefit dinners, personal appearances, stage work, directing, teaching acting. He kept a small appointments book so crowded with entries that if you asked him out for a beer, he had to whip it out and check whether he might spare the fifteen minutes.

Near the end of running over his lines he said, "Ah, I've got a problem with one thing in your script." He pointed silently to a passage. I read: "Goddamn goddamn television anyhow! It ain't nothin' on it but meddlers and pryers and a buncha niggers jitterbuggin' in the end zones!"

"I don't want to say that word," he said.

"Well, now, Henderson—it wouldn't be *you* saying it. It would be an old red-neck Texas sheriff. And it would be the most natural word in the world for him."

"How about changing it to 'college boys'?" he asked.

"Damn, don't you think it loses something in the translation? 'College boys' just . . . well, it doesn't *say* the same thing as 'niggers.' "

"But that's a shock word," he said. "You'll lose your audience. They'll recoil against it. It'll take a while to get them back. It could spoil the whole scene."

"I disagree," I said. "The word's in character. I think it's vital. It's another way of showing what a rough-hewn old Texas bastard Ed Earl is."

Forsythe shook his distinguished gray head and said, "I hope you'll reconsider."

"And I hope you will."

"Well, in all honesty, I want you to know I'll take it up with Pete. I just don't believe I can play the scene like it's written."

That sounded to my ears like gentle blackmail, but I didn't want to lose Forsythe or be accused of having run off our star. "Let me talk to Pete first," I said, "and see what we might work out."

After several sessions with Forsythe, Masterson came to me

and said, "Henderson just won't say it! He claims it will spoil the mood, upset the audience . . ."

"Oh, bullshit! I'm tired of hearing that. His role calls for him to use every obscene word in the language except *cocksucker* and now he balks at this."

"Well, see, Henderson is trying to make the sheriff a little more lovable than we've written him. And maybe that's good. He's bringing a new dimension to the character, new comic overtones. And he's afraid the audience won't love Ed Earl if Ed Earl runs around saying 'nigger.' "

"Is he threatening to quit?"

"Naw, not directly, but he's hanging-in real stubborn. And if we try to force him to say it—assuming he stays in the play—and he's unhappy with it, it just won't work. He'll be worrying about the word all through the scene and throw it out of kilter."

"Goddamn goddamn actors anyhow," I said, parodying Ed Earl.

Pete chuckled. "Okay to change it, then?"

"Okay. But damn, see if you can persuade him to say 'football boys.' It'll still play weaker than a popcorn fart, but it's a little better than 'college boys.' "

"Thanks," Pete said, relieved.

"But if we sell this show, Pete, I'm gonna insist on going back to the original word. And I don't care if Henderson Forsythe or Laurence Olivier is playing the role. Who the hell ever heard of a Texas sheriff that wouldn't say 'nigger'?"

"Nobody but us." Pete laughed.

We had been in rehearsals for about ten days, and the grind was setting in. Now it was close to midnight; under Equity rules we could not hold the cast beyond that hour save in special circumstances. The company was exhausted after a long and chaotic rehearsal. It had been one of those terrible evenings when the players had seemed to regress—they blew lines, exited at the wrong place or the wrong time, bumped into other actors or caromed off furniture, dropped things, cut another player's lines. Now a weary, dispirited group slouched or huddled in the sorry folding chairs or sprawled on the floor, yawning or yapping and sweating. Cigarette smoke used up the air. Everyone was hot, sticky, touchy. Director Masterson was giving the cast notes on everything that had gone wrong—and very much had.

"Pete," Pamela Reed interrupted. "I'm not going to say that line 'Let go your twats and grab your socks.' "

Master frowned. "Why?"

"It sucks," she said.

"Pam, I don't find that real helpful. Can you be more specific?"

"It makes no sense! What the hell does it mean?"

Pete said, "Uh, Larry . . . ?"

"In the army," I said, "I woke to the sound of a sergeant screaming before daybreak, 'Let go your cocks and grab your socks.' It was irritating, it started your day on the wrong foot, and you began the day hating somebody. In the scene we're talking about, Pam—or her character, Linda Lou—is waking the other girls. She's full of piss and vinegar and she's a smartass. So . . . well, I just adapted the old sergeant's line."

Long silence.

PAM: That's all? That's *it?*

KING: What more do you want?

PAM: (*flashing hot anger*): I want some fucking *help,* man! Gimme some fucking help!

MASTERSON: Uh, okay, this ain't cutting it. Let's call it a night. Everybody get some rest and we'll see you tomorrow at four-thirty. And, uh, Pam—we'll try to work on the line.

KING: *You* work on the fucking line, Pete. I don't see a goddamn thing wrong with it.

PAM: All I'm asking is for *help,* man! That's your fucking *job!*

KING: Goddammit, Pam, if you wanta be a goddamn playwright, then get off the goddamn stage and behind a goddamn typewriter.

She glowered at me. I glowered back.

"Good night, people," Peter said, flushing and trying to laugh.

The actors trailed out as if they were about to board trucks that would haul them to their appointed place of execution. Masterson slapped me lightly on the arm, did a soft-shoe shuffle, and mock-sang: "Ain't *no* bidness like *show* bidness . . ."

"Piss on her wrist," I said. "That girl's bitchier in real life than Linda Lou is in the script."

"Just getting in character, maybe." Pete grinned. "A lot of actors do that, you know. They adapt the mannerisms or personalities of the roles they play."

"Actors are a bunch of goddamn children," I said.

"Come on," Pete said, "let's walk up the street and cool off with a couple beers."

I steered Masterson into Rudy's, a decrepit Ninth Avenue joint with booths whose leather seats sagged and groaned as if they ought to belong to Actors Studio. Whiskered or tangle-haired derelicts sat at the bar over straight shots or tap beers, waving their hands, agitatedly discoursing to themselves. It was like watching a troop of mad mimes. The place smelled of stale beer, senior piss, and a mangy dog that slept in the middle of the floor, sometimes rousing himself to emit sneaky sour farts.

"Damn," Pete said, "can't we do better than this?"

"Rudy's has two advantages," I told him. "It's the bar handiest to the Studio and I ain't likely to run into Pam Reed in here."

With the arrival of our second beers Pete shifted on the cracked leather and said, "Larry, we need to talk. Hear me out, now. Don't get mad."

I took a swig of beer, nodded, and tensed, the better to get mad.

"You've got to quit cursing the actors," he said. "If the Equity members report you . . . well, we're in trouble. They could close us down or demand that you be barred from rehearsals."

"Now dammit, Pete—"

"Please! Let me finish. I know you don't mean to, but you're making my job more difficult. See, you're not supposed to say anything to the actors. That's—"

"They say all manner of shit to me!"

"I know, I know! But tomorrow I'm gonna instruct 'em to quit it. They shouldn't approach you with their problems or ask your interpretations or quibble over lines—anything. There can only be one voice instructing the company and that's the director's voice. It's not a matter of my ego, see, it's simply the only way a show can work."

"So I'm supposed to stand around with my thumb up my ass?"

"I'm not saying that! I need you for changes, cuts, consultations. If there's anything you don't like—come to me. I'll take it up with the actor. That's my job, Larry, and you've got to let me do my job. Any more cursing people and they might file a complaint against you."

"I yelled at Elaine Rinehart once," I said, "when she ad-libbed so much in one scene I thought a page was missing from my script. That's all I recall . . . except the Pam thing tonight."

"Didn't you call Dakota a 'dumb turd'?"

"He *is* a dumb turd! Grab-assing the girls when someone else is delivering a line. Missing cues. Going out to his car to hit the bottle. Always creating a goddamn commotion."

"I talked straight with him today," Pete said, "but no matter what he does, you can't curse him in front of the cast and crew!"

"Fine. Next time I'll call him out back and privately kick his ass."

"No, no, now," Pete said. "Goddammit, Larry . . ."

"Don't curse the writer," I said.

We mooned and gawked and yawned over our beers and I looked out on the hubbub and squalor and dirt of Ninth Avenue. I felt weary to the bone, uncertain whether the game was worth the candle. Maybe I should go up to Broadway and attack George M. Cohan's statue with a hatchet. I had truly been astonished by Masterson's rebuke. Damn, would I get the reputation of being as big a prick as David Merrick?

"I dunno, Pete," I said. "I've worked in oil-field gangs . . . the army . . . the rough and tumble of politics . . . newspapers. None of those places are finishing schools. We yelled at each other when it seemed that circumstances warranted it. It was . . . hell, it seemed natural to me. You get the red ass—*boom!*—you lay it out on the table and deal with it. I guess I haven't thought about . . . well, other people's sensibilities, all that much."

"Do me a favor," Pete said. "Think about it."

* *

I don't suppose anybody likes issuing those most difficult words, "I'm sorry." Me, I'd druther eat a bucket of hairy wigglies. Apologies stick in my craw even when I know I'm as guilty as Charles Manson.

The day after my talk with Pete at Rudy's, however, I concluded I must attempt to convey something healing to Pam Reed. As soon as I arrived at Actors Studio I would rush directly to her and blurt, stammer, or stutter something—before I got cold feet. I stopped for a couple of bracers at the Edison Hotel bar, hoping to think of some clever, charming, painless way to approach the task. No luck.

When I walked upstairs to the stage area, I saw Pam Reed talking with a group of other stage whores. She looked at me, looked away, looked quickly back. I started directly for her. She came to meet me.

I wouldn't want you to get visions, now, of two lovers rushing across a misty meadow in slow motion, their arms outstretched, glows on their faces, beautiful heads of hair streaming behind them in the wind, like they show in the shampoo ads. No, we were rushing toward each other like two fighters at the bell.

"Sorry about last night," I said.

"Okay. Forget it."

"Well, I didn't want to leave it hanging."

"I don't suppose either of us deserves a medal," she said. Her eyes were cool and impersonal. I gawked and shuffled and vainly sought an exit line. "I really do hope you'll do something about that goddamn line," she said. "It truly sucks."

I bit my tongue, nodded, and walked away. *Piss on her! Goddamn her!* Morosely, I banged among the folding chairs, resenting that she'd robbed me of my fantasy. The scene was supposed to have played like this:

KING: Pam, I'm terribly sorry about last night.

PAM: No, darlin'. It was all my fault. Don't worry your wonderful head about it.

KING: Well, I didn't want to leave it hanging between us. I respect you too much for that.

PAM (*tenderly placing her soft hand on his muscular, throbbing arm*): Baby, *I* was wrong. It's a beautiful line! How will I ever make it up to you?

KING: You could start by letting me buy you a drink tonight.

PAM (*squeezing his muscular, throbbing arm*): Not just *one,* sweet darlin'. And not just tonight . . .

(*Music soars up and out as she gazes worshipfully into his bright and burning eyes. BLACKOUT.*)

See, I've never had any trouble conceiving that Walter Mitty stuff; the difficult part is in the execution.

Here is why ain't no bizness like show bizness: after all that flapdoodle, we cut not only the offending line but the entire scene that spawned it. And now I can't even recall why.

By the time we'd been in rehearsal three weeks I felt like a zombie held together by wax and wire. Normally I met Pete about noon; we haggled over changes and cuts; we perhaps met with Carol, or talked with her by phone, about song repairs or new requirements as we shifted and changed the script. Or we talked with Janie Rosenthal, who was handling publicity. Carl Schaeffer, meanwhile, was wringing his hands and wailing because we hadn't signed the agreement with Actors Studio; Pete clucked and promised and stalled him, because Carol Hall still wasn't studying no signing of no kind. Period. We talked with the set designer, and any number of technicians, and I still have little understanding of what was said. Always there was something: meetings or errands or taking scenes back to the typewriter.

Around three o'clock I would bolt a chicken leg or a pickup sandwich, shower, and run lines with Brad. Or we'd talk of the show's needs, relate the latest cast gossip or stories. Always it was The Show. Nothing else intruded. World War III might have raged for a week before we would have taken notice.

At four or four-thirty, burdened with Brad's guitar, music sheets, our scripts, and assorted other paraphernalia, we entered the citywide competition for rush-hour cabs. Normally we arrived at Actors Studio in a sweat and a jangle. We rehearsed until midnight. Too wound up and wired to retire sensibly, we stopped for a relaxing drink, which more often than not ended with a predawn sing-along in some wretched bar. "The only rest I get is when I faint," Brad said one night. I appropriated the line and stuck it in the mouth of the stage whore named Ginger.

It was at this dizzy and fatigued point that Director Masterson ran out on us. Abandoned ship. Flew like a goose.

Well, not exactly, though it certainly seemed so at the time. Pete was apologetic when he broke the news: "See, I owe this production company a film and they're calling in the debt. I can't get out of the contract."

In short, he must fly off to Hollywood to film a made-for-TV movie, *A Question of Guilt,* in which he would play the lead: a Chicago detective faced with solving some heinous crime or other.

I blanched and snorted: "Goddamn, what'll we do? I can't direct this sumbitch!"

"No problem, really," Pete said. "I'm going to stay in real close touch with you and Carlin and Spider Duncan by phone. And I can probably fly back for a couple weekend rehearsals."

Christopher (Spider) Duncan was a dancer who was listed as choreographer in a show that then had very little dancing in it; he also wore the title assistant director, but until that point it had been strictly honorary.

"I dunno, Pete! Has Spider ever directed anything?"

"Oh, yeah."

I waited. And waited. "Goddammit, what's he directed?"

"Lots of stuff," Pete said vaguely. "He teaches in the drama department down at Rutgers, you know."

"Yeah," I said, "and I taught political science at Princeton but it doesn't mean I could run the country."

"He'll do fine," Pete assured me.

"I'm not so sure. Spider's not real assertive. Some of the toughies in this cast might chew him up and spit him out."

I had looked at Spider Duncan slightly askance since the first day he showed up at Actors Studio. His first act of business had been to solicit and write down the birth dates of everyone remotely connected with our show. He went home, consulted his astrological charts, and came back to announce we could not possibly open on October 20th as planned because the stars wouldn't be in their proper places. The stars promised all manner of mischief, he insisted: physical injuries, financial reversals, and maybe a fire. He stood sincere and sweating, earnestly explaining how Jupiter would be at cross purposes with Saturn and this somehow would surely agitate Mars or some such, I dunno. Others may have laughed him off, but I failed to suffer Spider's preachment with either humor or grace. Only after I'd barked three or four times did he cease and desist.

And now Pete Masterson was telling me he was placing our show in the hands of a goddamn stargazer.

For the first time I began to look at Masterson through beady, suspicious eyes. "You know what I suspect?" I confided to Brad. "I suspect Pete has put all his time and energies into this show, starving to death in the process like I am, and now he's picking up a payday he can't refuse. I don't buy that crap about an old contract being called in."

The cast was demoralized—nay, devastated—when Masterson announced his abdication. Some seemed on the verge of tears and others in shock. Pete sprinted to catch a taxi to the airport, Hollywood bound. I moved with Carlin among the numbed survivors, helping to soothe the spooked: *There, there, kiddies; Big Daddy will come back soon to kiss it and make it well.* When the cast had reeled away, Carlin and I retired to a bar for therapeutic liquids. "King," she said, "I'm scared to death. You're going to have to give me a lot of help and support, honey. This thing could fall apart without Pete." When I put her in a cab we clutched each other as if one of us might be off to die at war.

The first two nights of Pete's absence, little attention was paid to anything but a dance number called "Two Blocks from the Capitol Building." I hated the thing and had begged Pete—who had conceived it—not to put it in the show. This freak-scene number, as it was popularly called, featured assorted perversions: flashers, suggestions of bestiality, all manner of kinkiness. From a line she'd discovered in my magazine article and the script, Carol Hall had fashioned a song preaching that while the poor little

Chicken Ranch was being closed, you could get any sexual gratification known to man within two blocks of the Capitol. The song, to me, sounded like an Indian chant gone wrong.

Spider Duncan was the featured artist in the number. He got to wear an Uncle Sam suit or Captain U.S.A. or some damn improbable thing—anyhow, it was red, white, and blue and absolutely gaudy with stars, wouldn't you know it? Spider wore it to each rehearsal. He got to prance and pirouette and leap and slink and wildly fling himself about while twirling a baton with one hand and suggestively running the other up and down his leg, and he was apeshit crazy about it. The rest of us would sit bitching and groaning while Spider took it from the top again and again and again. So, after consulting with Carlin, I beckoned Spider aside and suggested that we get on with the show and quit fiddle-farting around with all this leaping and bellowing. By now, I said, everybody not in the number was ready to hang him. Spider was hurt, surprised, and felt picked on.

Shortly, Spider attempted to change some stage business Pamela Reed was doing. Better he had chosen to correct Muhammad Ali when Ali was reciting his own poetry.

"I'm not taking that direction," Pam snapped. "You're not my director."

"Well," Spider said, looking stricken, "I'm the assistant director."

"Whatever you are," Pam said, "I'm doing this scene as I worked it out with Pete."

Spider tried gamely to go on. Too late. The remainder of the evening was a shambles of querulous whining, bitching, pouting.

"You've go to do something," Carlin whispered.

"I don't know what to do," I said.

"I'm caught in the middle," she said. "Director's wife *and* cast member. What can I do?"

"You can tell *me* what to do," I whispered back.

"Stop the rehearsal. Until we can think of something."

I sneaked around and persuaded Spider Duncan to ring an early gong. At two or three in the morning Carlin telephoned. She was near tears and had not slept. "You've got to call Pete," she said. "This can't go on."

I located Masterson at his Los Angeles hotel. "The cast is acting like a bunch of kindergarten kids when the teacher's left the room," I began my report, "and Spider Duncan is lost in the stars." Masterson took the news with great equanimity. "I'll call Frank Corsaro and have him take a look tomorrow night."

Who he?

"Frank's a friend, we've worked together. He's directed from Broadway on down and has done some good work at the Studio. I'll ask him to stick around and give Spider a hand until I can come back."

I was calmed and reassured, and telephoned Carlin to pass it on. *That's that,* I thought, and smugly slept.

Little did I know, ol' buddy. Little did I know.

Corsaro's appearance the following night perked up the cast; many knew his work and spoke him well. I was as glad to see him as anyone. To a reporter on the scene for *The New York Texan*—a small newspaper keeping several thousand displaced Lone Star sons and daughters posted on matters of common interest in Gotham—I said, "I feel as if a truck hit me a couple days ago, but I'm on the road to recovery."

Corsaro watched Spider direct a scene in which Mona and her girls sing "Little Bitty Pissant Country Place." Halfway through the dance number, which suggested a miniature Radio City Music Hall Rockettes routine—girls dancing with extended arm, hand on the shoulder of the girl in front; kick, reverse direction, change hands; repeat—Corsaro called a halt. He asked everyone to gather around a table in the stage area. I watched as he prepared to offer his first comments—a middle-aged man with 1960s long hair, black turtleneck sweater, old slacks and low-top boots—and thought he'd wasted little time stepping in. Good.

"I don't think you know what you're doing," he said. Uneasy movement and darting eyes among the cast. "Why imitate cliché-ridden Broadway musicals? That's not what Actors Studio is all about! I don't believe that's what your show is all about. Let's try to discover what it *is* about." He went around the table, asking actors to describe their characters, motives, purposes. Answers came slowly and incoherently. Frankly, it amounted only to loose jabber. Corsaro listened intently, sagely nodding during speeches I found totally incomprehensible, as if they might contain the wisdom of the ages. At long, long last he said, "Here's what you do: throw away your scripts. Forget your scripts."

I wanted to shout, "Just a goddamn minute there, Frank," but held my tongue to see what might happen next. Corsaro said, "I believe in improvisation. You people seem not to know your own characters or how to relate with the other characters. I want the characters to get acquainted. We'll do it by improvising. What would happen at the start of the day at a whorehouse? Can anyone tell me? Huh?"

A long wait. Shuffling. Silence. *"Breakfast!"* Corsaro said, triumphantly. "Don't you think they'd start with breakfast?" The cast murmured and nodded heads that, yes, whores might start their day with breakfast.

"Okay," Corsaro said, "let's pull some tables or benches together and that's our long breakfast table." Much scurrying about and moving of furniture; someone was sent to Props to seek useful objects: coffee pot, cups, plates, a tablecloth, and so on. When all the goodies were in place Corsaro pointed to Lorrie Davis, playing the black maid, Pearl. "You be the cook. Now, some of you girls—you, you, you, you—sit down at the table. You and you enter yawning or scratching. You've just waked up. Now, eat breakfast."

Everyone ate breakfast. Corsaro beamed and nodded as if overjoyed at their eating techniques. After the whores had put on maybe three theoretical pounds each he said, "Now what happens during breakfast? *Talk* happens. There's table talk. Come on, talk to each other." The whores talked about getting appointments at the beauty shop. "Good, good!" our new director exulted. "Miss Mona, enter the kitchen. Girls, speak to her. Remember, she's the boss!"

"Hi, Miss Mona," April said.

"Hi, Miss Mona," Ginger said.

"Hi, Miss Mona," Durla said.

"Hi, Miss Mona," Ruby Rae said.

"Hi, Miss Mona," everybody else said.

Corsaro smiled and called encouragement, almost jumping in place and clapping his hands, as if the whores were writing better than O'Neill times Williams multiplied by Miller. "Now you girls talk about your weird dates last night," he said.

Again, I wanted to interpose an objection: the story and a song made it clear that Miss Mona brooked no "smutty talk." But Corsaro's suggestion had let down the barriers; all the frustrated playwrights began to make long speeches inventing the wilder sexual adventures, everyone talking at once, until it sounded like the Democrats trying to hold a convention in a porno store. Carlin sat with a smile on her face that seemed to grow more strained by the moment. Corsaro was almost beside himself, hopping about and cackling over how good it all was.

I got up and left the rehearsal hall as our new director was setting up an ironing board and instructing other whores to start making up their faces or their beds. Henderson Forsythe sat in the back of the room, arms folded; I thought his lips made a rather grim line. Henderson had not worked at the Studio before and I got the notion he was not real partial to the Method exercises Corsaro was directing. I marched up to Rudy's, stepped across the farting dog, drank feverishly for an hour, and didn't know whether to laugh, cry, shit, or suck a lemon. When I returned an hour later Corsaro was still in the improvisation stage: now the girls were quarreling over whose turn it was to empty the garbage or some such. The next night it was more of the same. By now some cast members had developed the jitters and crept around as if they expected to be attacked from ambush. I couldn't blame them. I went out back with several Texas Aggies—J. J. Quinn, Eric Cowley, Elliott Swift, John Kegley, Brad—and we smoked, guzzled beer, and wondered what might become of us. Periodically, cast members popped outside to express bewilderment, outrage, or fear. I decided I had to face Corsaro down.

I asked him out for a drink. He declined with thanks and cited the late hour. "Well, then," I said. "Sit down. We need to talk." Corsaro looked at his watch rather pointedly, perched on the edge of a table, and frowned.

"Frank," I said, "I appreciate your coming in to help us but I'm afraid matters are taking a disturbing turn. This improvisation stuff wasn't what we had in mind. We've got a short time to get the cast ready and I think it's time to get back to the play as it's written. And I'm speaking for a number of cast members as well as myself."

Corsaro said he thought two or three more days of improvisation would familiarize the cast with their roles: give them the feel of the interpersonal relationships in the play, and put the actors in touch with their individual feelings. I bit my tongue and said as gently as I could that Pete, Carol, and I hadn't spent fourteen months writing a play so that he could instruct the cast to throw it in the trash can and make up their own lines. He interrupted, rather stiffly, to say that he was in touch with Pete daily and Pete approved of what he was doing. And quite abruptly he walked away.

I grabbed Carlin before she left the Studio and told her I was on my way to telephone Pete and tell him that if he didn't return forthwith to straighten out the damned mess, then I was withdrawing the play. Poor Carlin looked fatigued and ready to cry. "I can't tell you what to do," she said. "Frank is Pete's friend and I'm in the worst possible position."

I got Masterson on the phone and threw a nine-dollar conniption, and he walked into Actors Studio fresh from Kennedy Airport about mid-rehearsal the following night. There sat Corsaro, yukking and slapping his leg at the wonderful improvisations going on. Pete told him to go ahead, sat down, and watched about twenty minutes' worth. Occasionally he chuckled as if in approval; I threw him murderous looks and was tempted to take a hatchet to him. When Corsaro called a break I heard him tell Pete, "I see a real difference." *You can say that again, Frank,* I grimly thought.

Shortly, Masterson and Corsaro disappeared into a small office downstairs. A half hour later Pete returned alone to a fidgety cast. He announced that we would go back to the script, that he would give Spider Duncan a strict scene schedule to follow day by day until he could return full time himself, and that, meanwhile, he would come back for all weekend rehearsals. I hadn't heard such cheering or seen such hugging since the Watergate gang got indicted. I never saw Frank Corsaro again, though presumably he's somewhere out there improvising his ass off.

Slowly, we hammered the show together and began to see it take on promising shape. True to his word, Pete Masterson bounced between California and New York like a yo-yo until his film, mercifully, was done.

One came to know and appreciate special talents in the cast. Henderson Forsythe and Carlin Glynn worked together in a way beautiful to watch. Susan Mansur as the waitress, Doatsey Mae, was a marvelous comic actress and made the most of a mediocre song, "Doin' It and Sayin' It Are Two Different Things." Pam Reed, Liz Kemp, and Joan Ellis were outstanding among the whores.

Ellis in particular was impressive as Shy. Each time she rehearsed the scene in which she confessed a hard past to Miss Mona and was reluctantly taken on as a Chicken Ranch "boarder," she cried real tears and appeared to be in true agony as Carlin sang to her "Girl, You're a Woman." Poor old soused Dakota, witnessing this scene one night, himself sobbed and boo-hooed so loudly he damn near drowned out the vocalist. Joan Ellis was intent; she truly believed in Method acting and each night worked herself up to *become* Shy: awkward rolling walk, slouching posture, timid soul. Though neither ugly nor beautiful, she *looked* ugly when she was supposed to and became absolutely radiant in the transformation scene, in which the other girls repair her hairdo, introduce her to cosmetics, and dress her better than she has dressed before. I never understood how she did it. It was not easy to ask. The offstage Joan Ellis was a loner who appeared spacy and distant. I had three or four conversations with her in my life, that I can remember, and each of them was somehow unpleasant.

We finally had solved—though not to everyone's satisfaction—the problem of the singing sheriff. Yes, Ed Earl would be permitted to sing, but not a duet or love song. This was a decision Henderson Forsythe did not approve. As is the case with many nonsingers, he thirsted to warble and perhaps secretly judged himself better at it than he was. Ultimately, he was stuck with a mediocre solo number, "Goddamn Everthang," which said nothing he had not said in the dialogue over and again. (It would be among the first songs to go when we moved the show.)

The first-act curtain problem never was solved during the Actors Studio production, though we tried everything but hanging Frank Corsaro in effigy. We had written a scene in which the Texas Aggie football seniors are at the Chicken Ranch celebrating their victory over their arch-rivals, the Texas Longhorns; they whoop, hoo-haw, drink; the girls make Aggie jokes; eventually the boys and girls go off to make commercial love. At this point the villainous newsman, Melvin P. Thorpe, arrives with a raiding party of cameramen and catches a state senator and Sheriff Dodd red-handed on the premises, along with the college boys. It was a long and confusing scene—my God, it ran an unconscionable twenty-seven minutes—which read like a dream on the page and translated to a nightmare in action. It required timing that never was found, an understanding of Aggie jokes—they're based on dumbness, like Polish jokes—and sustained whoopee. Sustained whoopee should not be tried on the stage. Ever. I did not know that in 1977.

When the Aggies arrive at the whorehouse, Lone Star beers in their fists and carnal mischief on their minds, they are to whoop and ad-lib until a given Aggie—J. J. Quinn—shouts the scene's first scripted line. The problem was that J. J., whom we might describe as having a concentrated mind, would get carried away whooping and grab-assing and forget to yell his line. All you heard, until somebody prodded J. J. or kicked him, was this goddamn awful racket and clamor that went on forever plus a day.

There was a fight that required a chair to fall just so and a second chair to be pulled from behind an actress just as she starts to sit in it, and the timing for *those* little bits ain't been found till yet. You kiddies who aspire to stagecraft, remember, now, that nice Uncle Larry advises you not to try complicated fights on stage. The movies, fine. You can stop and start the action when you want, and even patch it in the cutting room. Not so on stage.

Carol Hall contributed a song—I liked it—in which the Aggies lined up in T formation and ran a pass play while singing "Pussy." The chorus, repeated several times, ran as follows:

Pussy Pussy Pussy Pussy
Pussy Pussy
Pusss-eeee.

In that number—in performance as well as rehearsal—Quarterback Spider Duncan invariably threw the ball away or Receiver J. J. Quinn, sprinting down an aisle into the audience, somehow managed to muff it and fall into a tangle—people in the audience shrieking as the ball bounced off their noggins—so that the alleged champion Aggies looked worse than the New York Giants.

I thought "Pussy" was a clever song cleverly staged—or would have been, had we been able to get it right—though it only served to embarrass the audience into a frozen, stricken silence; it was a show-stopper, all right, but that kind you don't need. (The night Ellen Burstyn saw the show, "Pussy" so offended her that she rose from her front-row seat and stalked from the theatre in a mother huff. Not an eye missed her regal passage; were I of a suspicious nature I would suspect she knew it. Ms. Burstyn will be happy to know that "Pussy" did not survive past Actors Studio.)

It is easy to see, now, that the scene should have been scrapped and rewritten from scratch early on. Somehow we could not see that when it counted. We blundered along trying to repair the unrepairable. That Aggie scene was so bad—seriously—that I spent each intermission during the Actors Studio run cowering in the wings, afraid my friends might see me while it was fresh on their minds, and a couple of times I hid behind flats and props stashed in the darkest corner.

A few days before our opening, Carl Schaeffer announced there would be no opening unless and until the three collaborators had signed the agreement with Actors Studio.

The three of us met at my East 32nd Street digs, Carol Hall plopping down on a couch, crossing her arms, and telling us by body language she intended to budge not. Very much shouting went on. Everything that had been said dozens of times was said again, only louder.

After perhaps an hour I said, "Enough. I'm joining Carl Schaeffer in his threat. If that goddamn collaboration agreement is not signed within twenty-four hours, it's all over. Done. Finished. Kaput! Carol, it's up to you. I'm not discussing it one more time, now or ever." I held the door wide open and she left without a word.

"Pete," I said, when Carol was gone, "let me tell you about the first time I met Carol Hall." I told him the story related earlier in this book, and then the rest of it:

"During her first set at the Cellar Door that night, Carol introduced one song by saying, 'My favorite writer is in the audience tonight. We have in common that we are Texans, and good friends. His work always is an inspiration to me. I read a story he wrote a few years ago that so touched me I sat down and wrote the following song as a result. And I would like to dedicate that song to my friend Larry King.' And she asked me to stand and take a bow, which I happily did. The song was about an old house in Texas, the history it had known, the human drama it had witnessed. I was flattered and touched, and got sentimental and wept in my beer.

"Willie Morris, my buddy who edited *Harper's,* came to Washington the next day. I'd been quite smitten with Carol and her work, and I prevailed on Willie to go with me to see her act again. It was tough: Willie probably couldn't tell the difference between the *William Tell* Overture and "Old Black Joe"; he simply has less interest in music than anyone else I know. We go to Carol's dressing room before the show, I introduce them; they get along famously. Now we're in the audience and Carol's at her piano again. And at a given point she begins 'My favorite writer is in the audience tonight,' and goes on with the same spiel as she'd made the previous night. I'm thinking, *Aw, she didn't have to do it again!* though, of course, I'm secretly pleased. And I begin to arrange myself to take my bow, when she finishes: 'And I would like to dedicate that song to my friend *Willie Morris.*' Willie, of course, the sucker, falls for the deal as hard as I had. He takes his bow, he weeps through the rest of her show, he keeps saying she's the most original talent since Kate Smith or Peggy Lee or somebody."

Pete Masterson was howling.

"Now," I said, "get this, Pete: later that night, Carol asks me if I know the writer Larry McMurtry. I say, 'Sure, we're buddies. McMurtry has a book store about three streets over from here.' So Carol asks me to bring him to the show the next night."

"Don't tell me." Pete laughed. "Not a *third* time with the name changed!"

"We'll never know," I said. "I begged McMurtry to go with me to the Cellar Door, but he hardly drinks at all and never hangs out in clubs. So I can only guess. But I'm guessing, yes, that the song would have been dedicated to the third man to have 'inspired' it in as many nights."

"My God." Pete laughed again. "So that's what we're negotiating with!"

" 'Fraid so," I said.

A bit later in the day my agent called. "What the hell did you and Peter Masterson do to Carol Hall?"

"Not nearly as much as she deserved. Why?"

"Her agent just called me screaming that Carol refuses to ever again be in the same room with you and Masterson—"

"Promise?"

"—unless others are present. He said Carol's half hysterical. She says that you two pulled the drapes, berated her, and she actually was in fear of being physically attacked."

"Very curious," I said. "I have no drapes. Come over and check if you wish, and bring Carol's agent with you."

My agent chuckled for the first time in almost two years.

"Agent," I said, "I am chock plumb full of this shit. You tell Carol's agent that if his broom-riding client hasn't signed the collaboration agreement *and* the paper with Actors Studio by the close of business today, I am pulling out of this project. And do impress upon him, please, that I goddamn sure ain't kidding. And tell him to tell her she won't have the satisfaction of killing the project, if she thinks that is what will happen. Pete and I are quite prepared to hire someone else."

A few hours later my agent called back: "She's signed," he said.

# CHAPTER

# 6

I guess Opening Night jitters are about the same on Broadway, at Actors Studio, or back in Pocatello when the junior class interprets one of those wholesome family comedies where everything turns out hunky-dory by final curtain, as everyone knows going in that it will. Certainly I had the jitters, and reasons enough for them.

We had postponed our opening a full week from October 20th—delighting only Spider Duncan, who found the stars more favorable—in search of two decent curtains. Nothing had worked. The first act still ended in the tiresome confusions of the Aggie scene, culminating in Melvin P. Thorpe's raid on the whorehouse. I had attempted to resurrect "Texas, Our Texas" at final curtain—figuring that in desperation even Carol Hall might agree—but our composer successfully caterwauled, bared her teeth, and flashed her fingernails. We settled for the play's newspaper editor coming on to moralize and philosophize our curtain down with a dull thud. Carol continued to complain that we'd deprived a musical of a musical finale, though Masterson countered that he couldn't stage a musical finale she had not gotten around to writing. There was a wrangle over whether we'd agreed she could—Pete said yes, Carol said no; there'd been so damn many disputes, abandoned plans, and changes I honestly couldn't remember.

Two old friends, Roy Bode of the Dallas *Times-Herald* and Steve Daley of the Washington *Star,* came to New York to write feature stories on our opening. I now regretted that I had invited them in a time when optimism had been higher. As we lunched at Harley Street, I carefully sticking to beer, I warned them the show could turn out something of a shambles. I liked many of the scenes and individual lines and much of Carol Hall's fourteen-song score, and I knew a number of the actors would acquit themselves well. But my friends should be prepared to witness the longest and most convoluted scene in the history of the American theatre—the Aggie misfortune—and two of the most dismal curtains to be found outside a fire sale.

I desperately wished I had not invited so many writer friends and a smattering from politics and television. I cringed when I realized that my public disgrace might be witnessed by Norman Mailer, Kurt Vonnegut, Tom Wicker, Dan Jenkins, Carl Bernstein, Nora Ephron, Gay Talese, David Halberstam, Michael Arlen, Frank Rich, Roy Blount, Russell Baker, Phyllis George, Pat Collins, Bobby Zarem, Bill Moyers, Sander Vanocur, Dick Tuck, Bobby Baker, Elaine Kaufman, and congressmen including Good Time Charlie Wilson, Jim Wright, and Mo Udall. They would not all be present at once—Actors Studio could seat only 99 at each performance because of the fire laws (though we later stuffed in up to 125 or 130) and so we were limited in the number of guests we might ask each night—but this would only prolong the misery. I had groaned anew on seeing the guest lists of my two collaborators and Carl Schaeffer. Now add: Tennessee Williams, Eli Wallach, Lynn Redgrave, William Goldman, Al Pacino, Gadge Kazan, June Havoc, Robert Redford, Ellen Burstyn—*bye, hunny*—Robert Duvall, Tommy Tune, Mama Gabor, Joey and Cindy Adams, Budd Schulberg, Sissy Spacek—on and on. To say nothing of many producers, directors, and theatre-money-men whose names I would not have recognized on a well-lighted marquee.

Damn, what madness, what puffed egos, to set ourselves up for so grand a public failure! Well, I rationalized, if we crashed and burned, we'd certainly do so in spectacular fashion.

Ten minutes until opening curtain. In my rustic gear as the town ne'er-do-well, feeling strange in greasepaint, I sat on the ledge of a tall window near stairs leading to the upstairs balcony. I could hear the buzz and hum of our invited audience. About 120 had assembled, well over the fire marshal's ideal; extra folding chairs were being unstacked and placed in all remaining spaces.

In the men's cramped dressing room a few moments earlier I had shaken my son's hand and said, "Go get 'em, Brad." He had grinned and we gawked for a moment. "Damn," I said, "seems like we ought to have something colorful or historic to say at a moment like this."

Brad wrinkled his brow. "I can't think of anything."

"I think," I said, "it's traditional to say 'Break a leg.' "

"Okay," he said. "Break a leg. I sure feel silly saying it, though."

I had perched on the windowsill seeking a place for introspection: some moment to remember, some inventory of emotions after almost a year and a half of sweat and toil on something that now might blow up in a couple of hours or . . . do *what?* Who knew? I was having small luck working up significant sentiments, however—mainly I just felt tired and jagged—and then someone screamed at me.

*"I hope to God you don't intend to sit there!"* Startled, I looked down to see Joan Ellis—Shy—face contorted, trembling as if she'd been ridden hard and put up wet.

"Ah, what?" I said, brightly.

*"This is where I make my entrance. You can't sit there! Go! Go away!"*

"Jesus, I'm four feet above your head. How can—"

*"Just go! Go, dammit, go!"* She began sobbing. I scuttled up the stairs, startling patrons in the balcony, thinking I'd heard of first-night jitters but this was ridiculous: the playwright put to rout by a cratering neophyte actress.

I wedged against the wall behind balcony patrons. Below, Pete Masterson came on stage in his letterman's jacket and sneakers.

He proceeded to chew out our guests as if they'd returned to the locker room down 0–27 at halftime. "What you're about to see is a work in progress. It's not a finished play and is not intended to be"—news to me. He went on to remark that nobody had paid to get in; if they didn't like it, they were free to leave. *Jesus,* I thought. *All the warmth and compassion of H. R. Haldeman. What's that all about? Intimidate the audience so it'll fear to boo?* Masterson scowled at everyone and disappeared.

The opening strains of "Twenty Fans" began as the lights dimmed. And bouncing up the stairs came three couples spiffed out in evening clothes, carrying an assortment of rattling, rustling paper sacks. They clomped and shoved to folding chairs near the balcony rail and—I kid you not—began to rip their sacks open and distribute Chinese food. Talking as loudly, now, as if they were at home:

"Sadie, want some sweet and sour?"

"Morrie, how about a nice egg roll?"

"Duh mustaard! Who's got da mustaard?"

*"Ssssshhh!"* I hissed.

"Ribs, maybe? Anybody got rice?"

*"Shush, goddammit!"*

Patrons on the main floor were twisting to look up at the commotion, some frowning, some smiling half-expectantly, as if they thought this crazy scene might be part of the show.

"Here's the mustard, Ralph. Nice and hot!"

I banged and bolted my way to these barbarians and shouted, "Out! Out! Out, goddammit, out! Get your goddamned Chinese food out of here!" In a frenzy I grabbed their egg rolls, ribs, little cartons of rice, and began chucking them back into their split sacks. People all over the house were standing up, gawking to see what the fuss was about.

I shoved the three men toward the stairs, cursing steadily; their women followed, nattering. The party sputtered, dropping and trailing Chinese food, while loudly declaiming they were guests of Carl Schaeffer.

"I don't give a shit! You ill-mannered bastards! Get down those stairs, goddammit! Out! Out!"

Pushing and pulling, I herded them down the stairs and out the door, leaving them stranded in disarray—though very well dressed for it—on the outdoor steps. Then I slammed the door and bolted it.

Several members of the cast—including Joan Ellis, still standing by to make her entrance—gaped at me as if I had gone mad. I flashed a grimace of a smile and said, "Break a leg, babies." Then I reclaimed my prior perch on the tall window ledge, and nobody suggested I should move.

Things went splendidly on stage. Henderson and Carlin worked together as if they'd been teamed for a lifetime; Liz Kemp received a roaring ovation when she sang "Bus from Amarillo"; Joan Ellis was poignant, vulnerable, and funny as Shy; Pam Reed's Linda Lou was tough and brassy as intended; Clint Allmon was properly self-righteous as the crusading TV man; Susan Mansur drew laughs every time she opened her mouth, except when she sang. I got through my three scenes and twenty-odd lines without fainting or falling down. Oh, the Aggie scene was the usual embarrassing shambles, and the curtains predictably dismal, but the applause was warm and enthusiastic at the end. I knew we were playing largely to friends and relatives, but I headed for the cast party feeling about a million dollars better than I had expected.

The cast party was at my neighborhood pub, Harley Street, courtesy of the owners, Malcolm and Frank. I stood at the bar with one arm around Barbara Blaine, drinking heartily with the other, grinning and yelling as each cast member came in. As Pete Masterson and I embraced he said in my ear, "Whoee, shit, am *I* relieved!"; we laughed the laughs of winners who'd jumped in the lifeboat in the nick of time. Carol Hall and I hugged and kissed so passionately we should have been X-rated. "Beautiful score," I said to her—meaning it—"beautiful, beautiful goddamn score!" Soon she was at the Harley Street piano playing her score, with cast members taking their solos to huzzahs and applause. I babbled to my newspaper buddies, Daley and Bode, squeezed my favorite lawyer, and wished the moment would never end. I became so carried away I wanted to tell a secret—that Barbara and I in September had decided to get married—but she wasn't ready to go public and shushed me.

Henderson Forsythe, quietly sipping a beer, accepted congratulations and said, "This is the best cast party I've been to in years. Know why? We don't have to sweat out the reviews."

"We will soon," I said, feeling my oats. "We will soon."

•

Not everybody, of course, was nuts about *Whorehouse.* One night my guests were Gay Talese and his wife, Nan, the book editor, and Kurt Vonnegut and photographer Jill Krementz. Talese obviously hated the show. I watched him during the performance—by then I had written my small part out of the show, the better to concentrate as a writer—while he squirmed, crossed and uncrossed his legs, sighed, tugged his underwear, and generally looked to be in hell with his back broken.

Unfortunately, Barbara Blaine and I had arranged to go to dinner with our guests. It was about as cheerful as an open-casket funeral. Our guests apparently had little good to say about *Whorehouse,* but were too polite to knock it, and so said nothing. Nan Talese tried, remarking on good performances by several cast members, but the drift was very much toward choppy waters.

Kurt Vonnegut, a private man who seldom flowers in the presence of strangers—and he didn't know Barbara—pushed at the food on his plate and appeared morose enough to require a good dose of lithium.

Barbara's hair, at the time, was of a striking auburn hue. Vonnegut, in an effort to carry his end of the evening socially, attempted small talk. "Did you know," he said to Barbara, out of the blue, "that redheads, statistically, are as rare as albinos?"

Barbara merrily roared: "Tell me, Kurt, do you know any fake albinos?"

After that it was back to the scraping of silver on china.

Good friends gave conflicting advice.

David Halberstam grabbed me and said, "It has potential, it can be something with work, but get that goddamn faggoty number out!"

"You mean 'Two Blocks from the Capitol Building'?"

"Yes, yes! Horrible! It's like something from another show. You've got all that wonderful, earthy Texas dialogue and humor and then that number comes along as if it had been dropped in by a couple of fags! That goddamn number belongs in a Greenwich Village play, not yours. Get it out of your show!"

"I agree," I said. "I've hated it from scratch."

A night or two later Norman Mailer and his lady, Norris Church, joined me for a postshow drink. "You've got a shot," Mailer said. "You could make it to Broadway. You might have an outside shot, I'd say, of becoming a modest hit. But let me tell you—move that marvelous freaky number up front."

"You mean 'Two Blocks from the Capitol Building'?"

"That's the one. It's strong, it's unique. It has a flavor of its own. It's a great contrast with the Texas macho stuff. There's raw meat in that number. Lead the show with it—let the audience see and smell all that good funky sex. . . ."

"Hmmmmm," I said. "That's interesting."

Mailer seemed to sense my reluctance. "Other people may tell you something else," he said. "When I made a play of *The Deer Park* all my friends gave conflicting advice. The truth is, nobody knows. The writer has to learn to listen to himself." He took another hit from his drink: "But I say move that number up front. Lead with it."

My agent came to the show, sat through it, and said not a mumbling word.

Old writing buddy Roy Blount looked as glum through the proceedings as had Gay Talese; he left the theatre by a circuitous route, and when I caught his eye he smiled as if I'd caught him picking my pocket, before skittering away sideways, like a crab.

My pal Dan Jenkins didn't show at all. When I caught him redhanded drinking at Elaine's, a few minutes after the performance he had been scheduled to attend, he blushed, put the wrong end of his cigarette in his mouth, and stammered complex excuses. As Jenkins worked with Roy Blount at *Sports Illustrated,* I was convinced he'd had his mind poisoned at the office. I imagined the following scene in the Time-Life Building, high above Sixth Avenue, and as close to Broadway as I then felt I was likely to come:

JENKINS: Hey, Elroy, how was ol' King's whore show last night?

BLOUNT: Oh, man, don't ask!

JENKINS: That bad, huh?

BLOUNT: Embarrassing. It's just a piece of shit.

JENKINS: Don't tell me that! I'm supposed to go see the damn thing tomorrow night!

BLOUNT: Play sick or something. I ran off like a sneak thief to keep from facing him.

JENKINS: But June wants to go, and if we don't show up King will be mad for five years. He thinks it's the greatest thing since G. B. Shaw died.

BLOUNT: Ain't no way I can tell you how pisspoor it is, Dan. And ain't no way *you* can tell *him* anything he'll want to hear. I'm warning you: don't go, and don't let June go.

JENKINS: Oh, shit! *(He buzzes his secretary.)* Pauline, hunny, get my wife on the phone . . .

There was, of course, the other side of the reaction coin. Bobby Baker walked up at the conclusion of the show, grinning, stuck his hand out, and said, "Pardner, you gonna make a million dollars. I used to book dinner-theatre shows at the Carousel and yours is better than any of them."

Elaine Kaufman met me at the door of her East Side drinkery and said, "I'm telling everybody that comes in, 'Buy a piece of *Whorehouse* if you can.' And I want to put in thirty thousand of my own. I mean it."

Bobby Zarem, the P.R. king: "I'll break your bones if I don't get to handle publicity for your show. And Bobby Zarem has turned down a lot of shows. . . ."

Bill Moyers wrote a detailed, encouraging letter of reaction. Writer Michael Arlen and wife, Alice, attended a second time to bring Mike Nichols; Nichols, over postshow drinks, was also encouraging. Since he was coproducer of *Annie*—rapidly becoming the biggest show on Broadway—I had to be impressed. Liz Smith's column in the *Daily News* said Gotham was buzzing over *Whorehouse* and predicted the show would be "a real corker if it ever gets to Broadway." Our only formal review, in a trade paper called *Show Business*, recommended the play as "excellent theatre." Soon we were turning away customers at the tiny Studio.

I tried, truly, not to be overly influenced by these tides and tugs of opinion. Friends were unsteady barometers, I knew; attempting to make sense of the present or read the future, based on the mishmash verdicts of what Marshall Frady once called "New York's estate of assessors, appraisers, traffickers in reactions and responses," could easily send me round the bend. But I couldn't seem to help myself. Each word of praise or encouragement lifted me higher than a double pop of amyl nitrite, each critical comment or suspect avoidance slammed me down below Quāālude depths. "After all," I told Brad one night as we tried to relax over beer at Harley Street, "ain't nothin' riding on this but my life and future. And maybe yours."

A week before our run would end—Pete somehow had persuaded Actors' Equity to let us add five more performances—I was at the typewriter vainly attempting to repair the two curtains when Masterson called.

"Don't go out of the house today," he said. "Don't drink. Avoid bars and fistfights."

"What the hell are you talking about?"

"You're playing Sheriff Ed Earl Dodd tonight," he said. "Congratulations."

"*What?*"

"That's right. Henderson Forsythe has to shoot a night scene in a Woody Allen movie, and you're elected. Nobody else knows the lines."

"Jesus, Pete, I ain't at all sure I know 'em!"

"Run 'em all day with Brad," he said. "You'll be fine."

"Why the hell didn't Henderson give us more notice?" I demanded.

"He did," Pete said. "But I was afraid if I told you before now you'd find some way to screw up. I'm counting on you. See you at the Studio. Break a leg." And he was gone, leaving me sputtering into the phone.

All day long, Brad fed me cue lines and corrected me when I blew. I particularly had trouble with a scene in which the sheriff faces down his tormentor, Melvin P. Thorpe, on the steps of the local courthouse. The sheriff curses Thorpe at great length and in the culmination of the scene chases him away by firing his six-gun into the air three times—in concert with music cues.

"I'll *never* get that scene right," I wailed to Brad.

"Run it again," he said, enjoying ordering Daddy around.

I would get a scene down during one run-through—letter-perfect—and then blow it sky high the next.

Pete telephoned in midafternoon to check on my progress, caution once more against booze, and ask that I be at Actors Studio early to run through the sheriff's key scenes. I appeared at the Studio feeling gaunt and jangly. Carlin Glynn hugged me, joked, laughed, and attempted to put me at ease. I appreciated her efforts but felt that a fifth of Cutty Sark might have been more effective.

Members of the cast came to offer hugs, handshakes, and warm wishes. It seemed they were treating me differently—more warmly, more as one of the group—than when I had played a bit role or had functioned only as coauthor. Even Pam Reed and poor old confused Dakota, whom I had berated during an earlier performance when he had missed an entire scene and showed up for the next one dressed in the wrong costume, offered the fraternal handclasp.

I was in the men's dressing room, getting into costume and makeup, when Gil Rogers—playing the town mayor, Rufus Poindexter—said, "I don't see why Pete picked you to play the sheriff."

I thought he was kidding and turned to banter. But he was serious and scowling.

"What's your beef, Gil?"

"I just think the job should go to an Equity actor," he said.

I was angry. "Gil, goddammit, you had first shot at playing the sheriff and left us for a paying job. So don't be giving me that shit now."

"I'm not talking about myself," he snapped. "I just think an Equity man—*a professional*—should get the job."

"If you think it's professional," I said, "to bring this shit up with me *now,* then God deliver me from professionals."

Nothing else was said as we tensely continued dressing. When I left the dressing room with Brad I said, "That son of a bitch!

Bringing that crap up when I'm already scared shitless. Look, my goddamn hands are shaking."

"Don't blame that on him," Brad said. "I noticed 'em shaking in the cab coming over here."

I was fidgeting in the wings, buckling and rebuckling my gun belt, when Pete Masterson walked up, grinning, as if he didn't have a care in the world.

"Pete," I said in a panic, "goddammit, I forgot to test-fire this gun!"

"It'll be all right," he said.

"But I don't *know* that. I'm gonna run out back and fire it now!"

"You can't do that, Larry! I'm gonna make my spiel and start the show in a couple minutes. Besides, we're down to three cartridges. You'll need 'em all in the scene."

"What do I do if the sumbitch misfires, Pete?"

"Yell 'Bang bang bang!' " He grinned and sauntered out to start the show.

*Jesus Christ, how'd I get in this fix?* Though I had not wanted to know who might be in the audience that night, I could not avoid hearing the cast react with squeals of delight as they called out famous names from the evening's guest list: "Robert *Duvall!*" . . . "Oh, my God, *Robert Redford!*" . . . I walked rapidly away and out back, smoking one cigarette after another.

Pacing in the darkened hall from where I would make my first entrance, I started to run my lines . . . and drew an absolute blank on the first one. Not a clue. I remembered it had profanity in it. I was to run on stage yelling . . . what? Shit? Hellfire? Goddamn and hell? *What, dammit, what?* Then I heard my cue and burst out of the darkness into astonishing, blindingly bright light, opened my mouth, and somehow yelled, "Goddammit, Mona, I gotta talk to you! I'm so goddamn mad my hair hurts!"

I got through the scene, stumbled back, sweating, into the welcome darkness of the wings, and felt people pounding my back, whispering "Way to go, Sheriff" and such. Then somebody said, "Your hat! Your hat!" I felt my head. Bare. Bare as a baby's ass. *Goddamn.*

I whirled, looked on stage, and there my ten-gallon hat lay on the folding chairs pushed together to suggest a couch. The scene was ending. The lights went down—save for a single spot, which lingered and lingered and lingered on that goddamn hat. I sagged against a wall, sweating and sighing.

Pete Masterson soon walked up, chuckling. "Here's your hat, Sheriff. Good thing you didn't take off your gun belt."

"How'd you get it back?"

"I saw what you'd done. As soon as the spot went out I grabbed it."

"Thank God," I said. "But why'd the spotlight stay on the goddamn hat?"

"Damn if I know." He laughed. "If anybody asks, we'll claim it was symbolism."

"Pete," I said, "I ain't sure I can get through this shit."

"Sure you can." He grinned. "You *got* to. And it's all downhill now that you got your feet wet."

Afterward, of course, I was on a happier high than you could get from a mixture of morphine and codeine. I almost bruised my cheekbones by grinning as the cast and visitors swarmed around to offer shameless flattery. If they were a little slow, I primed the pump: "Was I okay? Did I do all right?" Secretly, after a rocky beginning, I thought I had been sensational and assumed everyone else did.

Robert Redford pushed through the crowd, calling my name, and said a generous thing: "If you don't quit acting, I'm going to take up writing."

Next, Gil Rogers was gracious. Shaking my hand he said, "I see now why Pete picked you. You can play the sheriff any goddamn time you want." Waves of love flooded me. I wanted to hug and kiss this man whose throat I might have cheerfully cut a couple of hours earlier.

Carlin Glynn embraced me, tears in her eyes, spouting effusive compliments. Brad and I waltzed in a bearhug. Then Pete and I. That we had performed the show without my contributing a major boo-boo had obviously led to this great group emotional release—and probably had been something of a surprise to all hands.

I went swinging off to Joe Allen's with Brad, Pete, Carlin, Clint

Allmon, and others in the cast—determined to get as sweetly drunk as I had in my life.

"Brad," I said, after everyone had joined a toast to my performance, "here's the house key. It's up to you to get us home tonight and roll my carcass into bed. I got one coming to me!"

Carlin laughed and quoted one of her lines from the show: "A-men to that, Ed Earl."

On an evening in mid-November 1977, either the writer William Goldman or his wife, the photographer Ilene Jones, telephoned one of their friends named Stephanie (Stevie) Phillips, and thereby had a lot to do with changing my life.

Stevie Phillips, who only recently had joined Universal Pictures to acquire movie properties for that company, accepted Bill or Ilene's invitation to join them at Actors Studio that night.

"They said they were going to see a play about a Texas whorehouse and that some of their friends were involved in it," Stevie later would recall. "I had intended to curl up reading screenplays that evening, but on impulse I accepted. Not that I went to Actors Studio *expecting* anything, you understand. I had seen far too many showcases to become excited about another one. Truthfully, I guess I just felt like getting out of the house."

Bill Goldman was a prolific and highly successful writer. I knew his novels *Boys and Girls Together* and *Soldier in the Rain,* and a fine book he had written about Broadway show business, *The Season,* and I had seen and liked two movies for which he had written the screenplays: *Butch Cassidy and the Sundance Kid* and *All the President's Men.* Though I had met Bill and Ilene at a couple of Carol Hall's parties a few years earlier, I didn't know them well. They were, however, close friends of Pete Masterson and Carlin Glynn's. That connection had prompted them to attend *Whorehouse* and had inspired them to invite Stevie Phillips to come along.

After that performance, Pete Masterson sought me out backstage. "We're going over to Bill Goldman's house," he said. "There's a woman with him I want you to meet. She's a producer for Universal Pictures and she's really high on the show."

"She's seen it?"

"Saw it tonight. And she grabbed me right away and started talking about buying it. Carol's gonna join us."

It somehow didn't register. By then there had been rumors of several groups who were "interested" in raising money to produce the show—Mike Nichols, a combine headed by comedian Alan King, friends of Carl Schaeffer's—but no concrete offer. I went to Goldman's posh East 71st Street apartment, off Fifth Avenue, grabbed a drink, and got into a conversation with former New York Knicks basketball star Dave DeBusschere about whether his old teammate Bill Bradley might be successful in politics. Masterson dragged me away to meet Stevie Phillips. Ms. Phillips said she was eager to buy *Whorehouse* and when could we meet to discuss details? "Oh, a day or two," I said vaguely. "Work it out with Pete Masterson. He handles business, meetings and stuff."

My careless attitude was traceable to some knowledge of Hollywood history, and to the fact I thought we were talking of a movie option only. Many properties are optioned for small-beer sums; after the option expires—six months, a year, whatever—nothing is ever again heard of the project. People who originally claimed they would devote their lives to the property disappear without a trace. I had heard too many Hollywood horror stories from friends—and had experienced one with my first book, *The One-Eyed Man*—to expect anything good to come of Stevie Phillips's party talk. Of course, I did not then have the benefit of knowing what she would tell a reporter a year later: "I fell in love with *Whorehouse* from the first moment. Oh, sure, the costumes were out of a ragbag. The score was uneven. The play was far too wordy. The choreography was practically nonexistent. But the show had heart, it had warmth. I saw a real musical inside it, waiting to get out."

Anyway, I waved to Stevie Phillips and wandered away in search of Dave DeBusschere.

Soon Bill Goldman found me. "You should get together with that woman," he said. "She's serious about this."

"Goddamn movie option," I said. "Okay, I could use a few bucks, but . . ."

"No, she's talking about stage rights."

"The hell she is!" I blurted. And made a beeline back to her side. "How rich you promise to make me?" I began, always the serious artist.

"Well, that's to be seen." She smiled. "With the proper budgeting I'm convinced we'd have a chance at a tremendous hit."

"It's true, then? You want it for the stage? Not just some little pissant movie option?"

"I most certainly do want it for the stage!"

"Ah . . . *Broadway?*"

"I thought we'd try it off Broadway first. And if that works we'll move to Broadway. And if *that* works there's no reason not to expect the possibility of a big fat movie."

"Lady," I said to the dark-haired and attractive Ms. Phillips, "I do not know you very well, but would you like to get married?"

She laughed. "Business first. Would you like me to talk to your agent about a meeting?"

"No," I said. *"Oh, no!* I want the pleasure of talking to *that* gentleman myself."

For months I had heard from my agent only when he inquired how I was doing on the Bobby Baker book, and when he occasionally cajoled me into taking a magazine job. The night he had seen *Whorehouse* he had said not a word; not "Kiss my foot" or "Better luck next time." Nothing.

Now I savored the opportunity to bring glad tidings he never had expected to hear.

The morning after talking with Stevie Phillips I called him. We exchanged pleasantries. He played it as I would have written it, given the choice: "Are you about through at Actors Studio?"

"Yes," I said. "We're about through over there. Little less than a week to go." I paused for effect, trying to time it like Jack Benny. "Of course, if you're not too busy, some people with Universal Pictures would like to meet with you to work out arrangements to buy it."

Sweet, stunned silence.

Then: *"For a movie?"*

"Yeah," I said, ever so casually. "After it's been on Broadway awhile."

"Ah—yes. Yes! Of course! Congratulations! Gee, that's marvelous! Tell me the details . . ."

"It gives me great pleasure," I said.

Carl Schaeffer, on hearing of Universal's interest, sent for the three collaborators. We went to his East Side law office. You might have thought he'd caught us filching from the Old Actors' Fund.

"What do I hear about Universal Pic-chahs?" he demanded, waving his little arms. "You kids got no show! You got nothing to sell. You got a *showcase,* for God's sake."

"Universal thinks we have a show," I said.

"You kids got the *makings* of a show. That's all you kids got!"

"Carl," Carol Hall said, "we're not kids. Larry is pushing fifty, Pete's not far behind, and I'm of a certain age."

"She's sixty-two, Carl," I said, grinning at Carol; she did not grin back.

"You sell to a big pic-chah company," Schaeffer said, "you lose control. They couldn't care less about your show. *We* care. *The Studio* cares! Nobody else cares a nickel!"

"They're certainly talking as if they do," Carol said.

"What are they offering? Come on!"

"I don't think we want to say right now," Pete Masterson said. "It's still in the negotiation stage."

"You can do better!" Schaeffer assured us. "What does Universal Pic-chahs know from the theatre? Universal Pic-chahs knows *shit* from the theatre! You should pardon my expression. I got friends—*the Studio's* got friends—*in the theatre!*"

"Fine," Carol said. "Tell them to make us an offer."

"Sure," Pete said. "The more the merrier. If we like their offer better than Universal's, it's a deal."

"Hal Prince," Schaeffer said. "Alex Cohen. The Shuberts. Merrick. Alan King. Jimmy Nederlander. Everybody, anybody. They produce shows, they put money in shows—the Studio knows them. *Connections* we got! *Contacts* we got!"

"An offer *we* got," I said.

"Yeah, Carl," Pete said. "We're open to all offers. I've heard some loose talk from other people, but Universal is the only outfit to name figures."

"How much?" Schaeffer said. "Not enough. You can do better. Believe me. Much, *much* better! You kids leave the show at the Studio. We work on it. We shape it. We get the bugs out. When it's ready"—he opened his arms wide, expansively, smiled—"we connect you with people *we* know. Money people! *Theatre* people! Not some Hollywood unknowns, for God's sake."

"Well, Carl," Pete said, "we'll think it over and get back to you. But unless you know somebody ready to offer a deal . . ."

"Kids, don't sign papers! No papers! Not with Hollywood. Believe me. Promise me!"

Schaeffer followed us to the door, then to the elevator, shrugging and showing us empty palms, a sad face, a shaking head.

The elevator door shut. We grinned at each other and burst into laughter.

"You believe this shit?" Pete said.

"No," Carol said, "but my! Isn't it *nice* to be wanted?"

With a few days remaining of our Actors Studio run, and while agents hammered out contractual agreements with Universal Pictures, I left for Texas and a couple of campus lecture obligations.

In Dallas, I heard that a group of lawyers had purchased the original Chicken Ranch building outside LaGrange and had moved part of it to the city to serve as a restaurant specializing in chicken: Italian chicken, Mexican chicken, Swiss chicken, Spanish chicken, chicken pops, chicken livers, and a LaGrange Special featuring only breasts and thighs. Alice Love, a Dallas newspaperwoman, told me the lawyers had hired Miss Edna Milton—the last madam of the infamous brothel—to act as the restaurant's hostess. "Ain't no way I can miss that," I said.

I went to the restaurant on Greenville Avenue—called, natch, the Chicken Ranch—with my daughter, Kerri, and her husband, John Grandey, who lived in nearby Mesquite. The bar, featuring stools supported by wood-carved replicas of women's legs, was doing a land-office business; on a color TV set the Washington Redskins were giving the Green Bay Packers their *Monday Night Football* lumps. Not many customers seemed to be eating chicken.

I had read that Miss Edna Milton had been born and raised in Oklahoma, one of eleven children; her parents had been poor dirt farmers and raised their brood strictly: "No smoking, no drinking, no nothing. Church three times a week." Edna had skipped home at sixteen, had a baby that died within a year, and at nineteen—"after getting educated at the University of the World"—had gone to work at the Chicken Ranch. By the time it was shut down in 1973 she had spent twenty-eight years in that brothel, the last dozen as the owner and madam. She had been married four times and divorced three. At fifty, when she was not wearing her hostess gown, Miss Edna affected polyester pants suits and light makeup. She might have been a matronly Avon Lady.

My party was seated by a waitress in the skimpiest of costumes; I asked to see Miss Edna. When she arrived at our table I introduced myself and asked her to join us. She did, carefully waiting for me to pull a chair out for her.

"Oh, yeah," she said. "You're the one wrote that play about my place. I read about it." I admitted this was true. "You makin' good money off it?" she asked. I hastened to say we had not made a nickel.

"Be damn if I can understand that," Edna said, suspiciously. "I've read about it in Houston papers and here in Dallas and heard of it on TV."

"True," I said. "But we're doing it in a tiny theatre in New York and we don't charge admission for it. It's what's called a showcase production."

Miss Edna's look said I was the biggest liar to hit Texas since the Galveston flood. "Don't *charge*? Why in hell you doing it, then?"

I explained that we hoped to attract investors and sell the play later, carefully failing to mention negotiations then under way with Universal.

"Well, I know one thing," she said. "*I* ain't made a penny off of it. And if anybody's gonna make money off the story of my place, seems like it ought to be me. I've done talked to a lawyer about it."

I said if we got a sale we'd certainly get in touch, and how could I reach her or her lawyer?

"Try me here," she said. Then she leaned in close, placed a hand on mine, and said, "But this sumbitch's likely to fold any day. People come out and drink whiskey but the food's not worth a shit. I don't like the job nohow. I'll probably quit in a week or two."

Then how would I reach her?

"I ain't saying. Too damn many people after me. Newspaper idiots. Damn tax finks. I got a few enemies, too."

Then would she give me the name of her lawyer?

"Naw, sport," Edna said. "You found me this time without any help. Just try it again."

A couple of drinks later I went to the men's room. The walls were made of the huge signs Edna had painted, listing her house operating rules back at the bordello; in those days they had been posted in the kitchen–dining-room area. I took a few moments to read them:

1. Absolutely no narcotics are permitted on these premises . . . if any are found, the Law will be called Immediately.
2. Drinking is not permitted during visiting hours and anyone doing so will be asked or ordered to leave. In short, DOPE-HEADS, PILL-HEADS and DRUNKS are not permitted to live here, regardless of who they are.
3. Thieves, liars or robbers are not wanted or needed here.
4. Beds are not to be wallowed in—that's what hogs do.
5. I don't want any Boarder to receive more than one phone call per day—and that is from home. Three (3) minutes is sufficient time for anyone to talk concerning family or their business. MONEY is not to be discussed on the phone at any time.
6. As I have said this is not a "white slavery place" and it never will be, as long as I have anything to do with it. Therefore I will not have a Boarder in my house with an excess amount of bruises and a lot of tattoos on their body. Cattle are branded for identification, tattoos are much the same as brands. I can remember my name without them. Can you?????
7. Boarders are permitted to see their lover or pimp only one night a week. Phone calls are subject to be Monitored. Remember—don't let your mouths overload your capabilities.
8. Long, sad faces look like hell to me, and I don't like them

in my parlor. A smile doesn't cost anything but it could prove expensive not to smile.

9. When you go to town dresses worn should not be shorter than two inches above the knees. Pants or shorts prohibited in town.
10. Filthy talk can wait forever.

When I arrived back at the table Miss Edna said, "I hope that play you've wrote don't make a hero out of Marvin Zindler."

"Oh, no, Miss Edna. He's pretty much a figure of fun."

"I didn't find nothing funny about the sumbitch," Edna said. "Drove up to my place with his television cameras running and my picture went out all over the whole United States. And my family never had knew how I made a living until then."

Had it caused her embarrassment?

"Well, shit yes! Or it would have if my mama had seen it. Thank goodness my picture went out during them Watergate hearings, which my mama wasn't watching. If the soap operas had been on, her TV would have been on and she would have seen me. She died later without knowing it. One of my sisters in Oklahoma saw it, though. But she and my other brothers and sisters kept the news hid from Mama."

As we talked, three or four customers approached and asked to have their pictures taken with Miss Edna. She consented, but without any warmth. When the last one left Edna said, "A few nights ago a man was doing that and the people with him went to sniggering. I looked up and he was holding a five-dollar bill over my head.

"I snatched it out of that sumbitch's hand and run him off this place. He asked for his five dollars back. I told him, 'Hell, no, Mister. That's your bad-manners tax.' " Miss Edna swirled the dregs of a drink in the bottom of her glass and studied it: "That's why I won't stay on this damn job long. I'm tired of people treating me like some monkey in a circus."

I had difficulty adjusting to reentry into the Real World. In Fort Worth and Dallas nobody talked show biz all the time. Nobody screamed at me about line changes, songs, billing, Equity rules, percentages, house lights, or sound systems. People went to their jobs, performed their duties nine to five, and forgot about them. They played with their children, took in movies, visited the neighbors, watched television; they talked football, kinfolks, politics, news of the day; they told funny stories. No one subject obsessed or haunted them. I felt like a man from Mars dropped into an alien culture.

At the Dallas airport, awaiting my flight back to New York, I bought a copy of the new *Texas Observer* and caught up on my home state's political news. Then I turned the page to discover a story by Nathan Fain about the Actors Studio production of *Whorehouse.*

"Carol Hall was there," I read, "tired and cross: 'Please don't call it Larry King's musical. I wrote the songs, you know' . . ."

I grinned, and began to feel at home again.

# CHAPTER

# 7

I now could forget *Whorehouse* on a day-to-day basis. The Actors Studio run was behind us; a corporal's guard of agents and a battery of legal eagles were bargaining over fine print in the contract negotiations. I devoted full time to Bobby Baker's book and made good progress.

Barbara Blaine and I flew to her hometown, Corpus Christi, for the Thanksgiving holidays with her family and repeated the trip at Christmas. We were having difficulty agreeing on a wedding date. Barbara was deeply involved in the Alaska Pipeline case—as I understood it, big oil companies were squabbling over the rich spoils, and it was Barbara's job to see that Amerada Hess got its share—while I was awaiting word as to when we might begin reshaping our play, hold casting auditions, and go into rehearsal for the Off Broadway production. We finally threw up our hands and said, vaguely, that we would get married when we had time.

One morning Stevie Phillips telephoned my Manhattan apartment: "Larry, we must go to Texas. Our lawyers say we need release forms signed by Sheriff Flournoy and Edna Milton before we proceed."

"Oh, shit," I said, my heart sinking. "That goddamned old sheriff won't likely be inclined to sign."

"We'll deal with Miss Edna first," Stevie said. "From all you've told me I'm sure she could use a tidy sum of money. We'll make the offer contingent on her delivering the sheriff's signature, too."

"Smooth," I said. "Slick."

"How do I reach Edna?"

"Beats hell out of me," I said. "That chicken restaurant has gone out of business and is padlocked. I hear there's a lawsuit over it. Miss Edna's in hiding again."

"Find her," Stevie said. "We can't do another thing until we get those release forms signed."

I telephoned Alice Love at the Dallas *News;* no, she didn't know Edna's whereabouts, but she would make some contacts. I next called Kirk Purcell, a friend who was an assistant district attorney in Dallas. The young crime-fighter, too, pledged to do what he could to find my whorehouse queen.

For two or three days I heard nothing, except from Stevie Phillips, who grew increasingly impatient and alarmed.

"How much will you offer Edna?" I asked.

"Well, leave that to me. I don't want you talking money with her."

"Goddammit, Stevie, I won't talk money with her, but I was born curious. How much?"

Stevie said she hoped to obtain the signatures of Miss Edna and the sheriff for $25,000 each. "Damn," I complained, "you're offering them more front money than you've offered me and my collaborators."

"But they won't get sustaining royalties," she said.

A night or so later my telephone rang. "This is Edna Milton," a voice said.

"Hey, Miss Edna! How you?"

"I'm fine," she said. "Is that all you wanted to ask me?"

"Well, no. I want to come to Texas to see you as quick as I can. And I'll have a lady with me, Stephanie Phillips, of Universal Pictures. She wants to offer you money."

"How much money?"

"Hell, Edna, I don't know. I can't even make an educated guess."

"Then make an ignorant guess," she said.

I laughed. "Well, say, maybe fifteen thousand."

"That don't sound like enough to me."

"I'm sure it's negotiable," I said. "When can we see you?"

It was arranged that we would meet Edna and her husband in a cocktail lounge at a hotel near the Southern Methodist University campus—sweet little irony, that—at 4:00 p.m. the following afternoon.

"Don't bring no newspaper people with you," Miss Edna instructed. "I want this to be private." Agreed.

Stevie Phillips fretted and frequently checked her watch the next afternoon in Dallas: Edna and hubby, Glenn, turned up almost an hour late. He was a big, rawboned man with huge hands and a giant spit curl, who had been a truck driver, gas station attendant, cattle trader, soldier, and oil field supply house manager, among other things.

Stevie made her pitch, culminating in an offer of $25,000, which Miss Edna was quick to accept. "Of course," Stevie said, "that will be contingent on your delivering the sheriff's signature, too. Do you think you'll have any trouble with that?"

Miss Edna shot a glance at her husband. "Let's me and you go to the rest room," she said to Stevie. I stayed behind and talked football with hubby. Within a few moments I saw Edna go into a hall telephone booth just outside the cocktail lounge; Stevie Phillips waited by it. In a few moments Edna came out of the phone booth, said something to Stevie Phillips, and they laughed. They came back to our table.

"Hon," Edna said to her husband, "you just as well to go on home. I'm flying to Austin with these people tomorrow and then we're going on to LaGrange to see about Mr. Jim signing that paper."

"Won't you come with us?" I said to hubby, merely honoring form.

"Oh, hail no," he said. "That old sumbitch don't like me. It made him hotter'n hell when I married Edna."

The plan was to fly from old Love Field in Dallas to Austin—about a one-hour hop. In Austin we would rent a car and motor another hour to LaGrange. Sheriff Flournoy was to meet us at the

Cottonwood Inn, owned by one of his and the Chicken Ranch's most vocal supporters, at 11:00 a.m.

We learned at Love Field, however, that the Austin airport was socked in by fog. An hour or so later that condition had not improved. It was decided to drive from Dallas to LaGrange in Miss Edna's Cadillac—a trip that might require four hours.

"Miss Edna," Stevie Phillips said, "perhaps you'd better call the sheriff and tell him we won't be there until about three in the afternoon."

"Naw," Edna said. "Mr. Jim'll wait for me."

"I don't want him angry," Stevie said. "If he's there waiting three or four hours . . ."

"He'd wait a week for me," Edna boasted, and pointed her Caddy toward LaGrange.

I sat in the back seat, alternately reading *Texas Monthly* and watching the landscape through a foggy drizzle, listening to the two women make conversation. They made quite a contrast: dowdy Edna, the Oklahoma poor girl who'd fled home at sixteen, and whose entire existence had been one sorry saga of life's seamy underside; Stevie, who had graduated from Columbia University, skied at Aspen, lived in a rich apartment on Fifth Avenue, and dressed to the nines in the latest chic fashions. Each, I knew, was tough in her own way. If Edna Milton had clawed her way up from whoredom to owning her own cathouse, then Stevie Phillips had also fought her battles: from mundane jobs with motion picture companies to writing low-budget film scripts to agenting for the likes of Liza Minnelli, Bob Fosse, and Robert Redford; now she was an executive with her own staff, a posh office on Park Avenue, generous expense account, and a chauffeur-driven limousine complete with a beribboned lapdog.

Stevie obviously was more curious about Edna Milton than Miss Edna was about Stevie. The questions all were one way. "Naw," Edna said in response to one, "I never did marry nobody I met on the job. It didn't seem smart to get my emotions involved with a paying customer—same thing I taught my girls. That ol' boy I'm married to now, he asked me to marry him nearly twenty years ago but I married somebody else. Then a couple years back he—Glenn—come around and popped the question again. I figured if he'd waited eighteen years for me it might work. And so far it has.

"When a woman's been in my business she's got to be careful who she marries. Most men, they'll throw the past up to a woman's face anytime they get mad about the least little thing. I had a couple like that and I just *adiosed* 'em. Told 'em, 'You knew I wasn't no blushing girl when you married me,' and I booted their tails out the door."

Stevie asked if Edna and "other women in your business" had maintained any social contact.

"Sorta. When Hattie Valdez operated over here at Austin, we exchanged information on girls that was sorry. And we might tip each other off if either one of us had a troublemaking customer that made a habit of it. You might say we blackballed such people.

"The problem with whores is that most of 'em is lazy. They don't want to work. They won't save their money. I never could see peddlin' my ass and then giving the proceeds to some damn man, which is what way too many of my girls did. I saved my money so I could own my own place and not have to screw anybody I didn't want to."

"I see," Stevie said. I wondered if she did.

"I always run a straight place," Miss Edna volunteered. "We didn't roll nobody, we didn't give our customers diseases, and I never allowed kinky stuff. I expected my customers to treat my girls right—not be talking rough or trying to hurt 'em—and if anybody got out of line, I telephoned Mr. Jim. He'd be there before you could say scat. And I made sure my girls didn't hang around town. When they had a reason to be in town they was to get their business done like a lady and move on. And I think that's one of the reasons our place was let to run so long."

Stevie asked how Miss Edna had been treated by the townsfolk.

"Pretty damn good. I made lots of friends in LaGrange. It was my home. Most people looked on me as a businesswoman. Oh, maybe they didn't invite me home for supper and stuff—though a few did. But they knew I donated money to charity. I'll take you by the hospital—it's got a plaque in the lobby thanking me for ten thousand dollars I put up for it. I give money to a lot of causes and word got around. I paid my taxes. I think most people thought of me as a good citizen of the town."

We pulled into LaGrange around 2:30 p.m.—more than three hours later than Sheriff Flournoy had been led to expect us.

He sat at the counter drinking a cup of coffee, decked out in a three-piece, western-cut suit and a tie; the moment he spotted Miss Edna he rose, swept the big cowboy hat off his head in a gallant gesture, and gave her a big hug with a bonus peck on the cheek. I was relieved to see he wore no side arm.

Miss Edna made introductions. The sheriff shook my hand, inspected me closely, and said, "Do I know you?"

Not wanting him to recall me as the *Playboy* writer who had incensed him, I quickly said, "Sheriff, I was a police reporter in Texas for years. Probably met you at some Peace Officers Association meeting."

"I expect that's it," he said.

The sheriff acknowledged his introduction to Stevie Phillips by nodding and saying, "Miss Stevie, we're proud to have you visit."

"Thank you, Sheriff," Stevie said, smiling a dazzler. "Miss Edna has told me many wonderful things about you."

The old sheriff looked bashful, ducked his head, and mumbled.

Sheriff Flournoy led us into the Cottonwood Inn's large rear dining room; I noticed management had arranged for complete privacy by confining all other customers to the counter and several booths up front. A lone waitress had been assigned. The sheriff supervised the ordering of iced tea and coffee.

By prearrangement with Stevie Phillips, I led the sheriff into a discussion of many Texas lawmen I had known. "I guess you knew my friend Slim Gabrel in Ector County?"

"Oh, yeah. Slim was a good un. Damn shame—excuse me, Miss Stevie—a Republican beat him."

"And Ed Darnell in Midland?"

"Big Ed and me has served longer than any other sheriffs in Texas. He's about got fifty years in. I aim to catch him before I quit."

We attributed many virtues to Gene Eckols in Reagan County, Blackie McNerlin in Ward County, Pete Ten Eycke in Pecos County, Morris Lear in Crane County. I failed to mention that two of the four had once found reasons to put me in jail in my wayward youth.

"Ol' A. B. Nail in Reeves County," I said. "*There's* a tough case."

"Oh, Lordy." The sheriff grinned. "You know, A.B., he got to stopping hippie fellers passing through his territory and cutting their hair short and delousing 'em. He had to quit it, though. They sicced them civil liberties fellers on him." The old sheriff laughed, and Stevie—knowing the ice had been broken—began her pitch.

The sheriff listened carefully, occasionally darting a look at Miss Edna, rubbing the backs of his hands, pulling his considerable nose. "Our play is very sympathetic to the sheriff," Stevie Phillips finished. "You might say, in fact, he's the hero."

"He *is* the hero," I said. "The only one in the play."

"Except Miss Mona," Stevie reminded me, with a glance at Edna.

"Oh, yes. That, too."

The sheriff appeared in a thoughtful study. He traced invisible patterns on a checked tablecloth with his big, rough thumbnail. "Well, Miss Stevie, I just don't know," he said. "This little town, it's been lied about and run down plumb across Texas and past. I sure wouldn't want to do anythang would embarrass these people again. I wouldn't want my name used, or my town's name, or my county's name."

"Oh, we've changed all that," Stevie assured him. "The sheriff is named Ed Earl Dodd. The town is Gilbert, and the county is Lanvil."

The sheriff nodded. "Well, I'd want your word on that."

"You've got it," Stevie said. "Should I put it in writing?"

"Naw, naw," he said. "Your word's good enough." He looked at Miss Edna. "Edna, what you think about all this?"

"Well, Mr. Jim, it sure would help me. If you can see your way clear to do it."

"Of course, Sheriff," Stevie said, "we'd expect to offer you a consideration to sign."

He stared at her. "You mean money?"

"Yes," Stevie said. She hesitated. "I had in mind . . . fifteen thousand dollars."

*Ah-hah,* I thought. *Miss Stevie's sensed she can trim the budget a mite.*

"Give it to her," the sheriff said, jerking a thumb toward Miss Edna.

Stevie appeared taken aback. Hell, I was too. "Ah," Stevie said, "of course, if you feel you couldn't accept the money *personally,* we'd be happy to donate it to any charity of your designation."

"Goddamn it," Miss Edna blurted, "didn't you hear him? He said give it to *me!*"

"Of course, of course!" Stevie said, rapidly.

"I'd want to study it," the sheriff said. "You got a copy of that play I can read?"

"Not with us, Sheriff. But I'll express one to you from New York tomorrow."

"I wish you would," the sheriff said. "You know, been several outfits come through here begging to make a movie on this thang. I run 'em all off. That's another thing—if you wind up making a movie, like you mentioned, I sure wouldn't want it made here in LaGrange. It'd just stir people up again and we'd be eat up by goddamn newspapermen. Excuse me."

"We would certainly honor that request," Stevie said.

"Further away from here the better," the sheriff pressed.

"We'd like to do it out around Alpine," I said, lying through my teeth but carefully choosing a site several hundred miles to the west. "That's cowboy-looking country, you know. Ranches and mountains and so on."

"Good idea," the sheriff said, nodding. "Well, send me your play and the paper to study. Could I buy ya'll some supper?"

"Thanks, Sheriff," Stevie said, "but we've got to move on to Austin. I certainly thank you for your cooperation. And I'll get those items in the mail tomorrow."

Sheriff Flournoy proudly led us to the west wall of the dining room to display a large mural of himself and his ranch, accomplished by a local artist who perhaps had worked with more enthusiasm than talent. We praised it as if it were a collaboration between Monet and Matisse, with Renoir standing by, calling out the colors. Local people, seeing that our conference was finished, began to drift into the room to hug Miss Edna or shake her hand.

In a private moment I said, "Sheriff, I don't want to touch a sore spot—but whatever happened to those lawsuits Marvin Zindler filed against you?"

Zindler had perhaps unwisely returned to LaGrange, about a year after his crusade to close the Chicken Ranch had been successful, this time to film a report on the economic difficulties—if any—the closing had forced on the town. Sheriff Flournoy apparently thought that was the last straw. Anyway, Zindler later told it this way: "I was sitting in my car outside the courthouse while my camera crew was shooting people in the square. Sheriff Flournoy came up and started cussing me and ordered me out of the car. I said there was *no way* I was getting out. He tried to pull me out—banged me against the door, and that's when I broke three ribs. He pulled my hairpiece off my head, threw it in the street, and ran around whooping like a wild Indian. That man just went completely wild." Wild enough—Marvin thought—to be sued (1) for physical damages and (2) for violation of Zindler's civil rights.

Now, as I privately asked the sheriff the disposition of those cases, he reddened and said, "Aw, that shitass, I didn't want to give him a goddamn dime but my lawyers insisted on it. They settled some money on him in one suit so he'd drop the other un. The sorry son of a bitch." He thought a moment and perked up: "But you know, my people here in this town raised the money to pay him down to the penny. He never got one goddamn nickel out of my pocket, by God!"

Stevie and I waited in Miss Edna's car while Edna held a long, private conversation with the sheriff in front of the Cottonwood Inn.

"You almost blew it," I joshed Stevie.

"How so?"

"Suggesting giving his money to charity after he'd said give it to Edna."

"Jesus!" she said. "I was so startled!"

"Think the old fart will sign?"

"I believe so. Did you notice I took pains to shake hands on the deal as I said good-bye? You Texans put great store in handshaking on deals, don't you?"

"You've seen too many of your own movies," I said.

Miss Edna climbed into her Cadillac. We drove away, waving like mad to the sheriff and grinning our best.

"So, Edna," Stevie said. "Did you deliver him?"

"He'll sign," Edna said, confidently. "Ain't no way Mr. Jim's gonna stand in the way of me gettin' forty thousand dollars."

I was in a hurry to reach Austin and party with old friends. Miss Edna, however, had other plans. She wanted to take a nostalgic tour of the town.

We stopped first at the county hospital, where Edna pointed with great pride to the brass marker attesting to her $10,000 donation in the long ago. We slowly drove past the sheriff's town house—though Miss Edna reported that Mr. Jim spent most of his free time at his ranch—and I asked whether Edna had ever made the acquaintance of Mrs. Flournoy. "I seen her on the streets," Edna said, "but she never once spoke to me."

At the courthouse, Edna pointed to an outdoor, open-air jail. Stevie Phillips was horrified. "But that's *barbaric,*" she protested. "By God, it works," Edna said. "Mr. Jim throws a badass in there in the summer, the sun'll bake the fight out of him. In the winter, with the wind howling in, he'll be too busy hugging hisself to think up trouble." Stevie was rolling her eyes, shaking her head, clucking her tongue, the personification of the American Civil Liberties Union in action. Edna grinned. "Actually, I don't think Mr. Jim's used that thing for years. It's just for show."

"Bet he'd stick Marvin Zindler in it," I said.

"I wish to fuck he would," Miss Edna offered. "I'd stand outside them bars and poke the bastard with a sharp stick."

Miss Edna saved the best for last: "Ya'll want to see my old place?"

"Sure," Stevie said. "I had intended to ask."

We stopped first by a wretched rural hovel in the woods. Miss Edna honked her horn. A fat, short black woman peered out, threw her hands heavenward, screamed as if she'd seen sweet Jesus, and waddled at high speed toward the car. Edna jumped out; they embraced and babbled. Three small children crept out of the shack and solemnly judged us from the tiny front porch.

"Lawdy God, Lawdy God," the black woman said. "Where you come from, Miss Edna? My eyes don't hardly believe theirselves!"

"This was my sidekick at the Chicken Ranch." Edna smiled. "How long was we together, honey?"

"Nine, ten, maybe lebben years, Miss Edna. My, them was good times."

"This girl could run my place good as me," Edna said. "If she hadn't been the wrong color I might have been workin' for her." She turned to the black woman. "We're going over to my old place. Want to go?"

"Oh, me, I sho' do. Lemme tell my man to watch after them chilrens." She waddled back toward the house, calling her man's name.

We bumped down a dirt-road approach and saw, in an open clearing beginning to be retaken by scrubby growths and weeds, what remained of the Chicken Ranch. "Bastard lawyers," Edna said. "They cut the goddamn house right half in two to open their fucking restaurant."

"Oh, that don't be looking right," the black woman said. "It make me sad."

A mongrel dog rushed from the wreckage, barking, trailed by a hollow-chested and bewhiskered old fellow in dirty rumpled khakis. "Why, there's Spud," Edna said, surprised.

"Yessum," the black woman said. "I hear it said he stays out here."

We climbed from the Cadillac and crunched over yard debris—chipped bricks, boards, rain-soaked cardboard boxes, shingles, piles of dirt and crumpled masonry, a filthy mattress, an abandoned icebox. Stevie Phillips was an incongruous sight in her designer jeans, Gucci boots, and gold jewelry. Coughing a harsh, ragged symphony, Spud led the way to a sagging back door, opened it for us, and kicked the dog so that it ran away yelping.

"This makes me sick," Miss Edna said. "This was a nice place, once. I had it fixed up real nice."

"I'm sure you did," Stevie said, with an uncertain smile.

We huddled in what had been the combined dining room and rec room. Miss Edna pointed to three bookshelves on the walls. "I kept reading materials there for the girls. You can see some books are still here." They were largely paperback romances and westerns, a few Reader's Digest condensed books, and such.

The long dining table remained, now an ungodly clutter: Spud's hot plate, assorted canned goods, dirty socks, worn paperback books, cracker and cookie boxes. Roaches darted about.

"How's your wife, Spud?" Edna asked.

"She died," he said, offering no more.

"Well, bless her heart," Edna said, absently. "Stevie, you and Larry want to see one of the girls' rooms?"

"Certainly. Yes."

We moved through debris and under a single, dangling bare light bulb into a small hall. Edna opened a door and said, "Oh, my God! Look at that shit!"

We peered inside. A wet mattress–soiled, musty–lay on bare springs, which themselves were on the floor. There was a small table, a battered chest of drawers; old newspapers and hunks of wet-looking gunk littered the floor.

"How'd everything get wet, Spud?"

He coughed and pointed to a sizable hole in the ceiling. "Kids done that."

"Shit, I wish I hadn't come out here," Edna said. "This makes me ashamed. Let's go, ya'll."

We retreated from the violated house like a ragged, defeated army.

"Well, that's too bad," Stevie said as we reached the car. Edna said nothing. She didn't look back at the place or mention it again.

A week or ten days after we returned to New York, Stevie Phillips received a handwritten letter from Sheriff Flournoy. He had read the play and the release, it said, and while he'd rather not sign any formal paper, his letter could be taken as giving his consent. Universal's attorneys agreed that was good enough.

Miss Edna proved that not for nothing had she haggled with Johns over the years. To ensure her cooperation, Stevie had sweetened her $40,000 deal (plus $50,000 more in the event of a movie) by offering her a small role in the show at Off Broadway Equity rates–something like $280 weekly, as I recall. ("Edna will be absolutely perfect in helping our preopening publicity," Stevie said.) Now Miss Edna asked for additional sugar: $150 weekly living expenses while in New York, a first-class airplane ticket to New York and another when she returned to Texas, the same for hubby Glenn when he came East for opening night, and a job for him "helping in the work crew" if and when a movie of *Whorehouse* was made.

She got what she asked.

"How about Marvin Zindler?" I said to Stevie one evening as we had a postwork drink near her office.

"What about him?"

"Why don't we need to pay him to sign a release?"

"Our lawyers say it isn't necessary," she said. "He's a public figure, he's had a book written about himself, he constantly promotes himself. He's got no privacy, in short, that we could be accused of invading."

"Here's to Marvin," I said, raising my glass.

"No," she said, raising hers. "Here's to our lawyers."

"Boy, do I have great news for you!" Stevie Phillips exulted over the telephone. "I've signed Tommy Tune! Isn't that *marvelous?*"

"Wonderful," I said. "Smashing. Who the hell is Tommy Tune, and what is his real name?"

Tommy Tune's real name turned out to be Tommy Tune. He proved to be a six-foot-seven-inch Texan out of Houston who weighed about ninety-one pounds and spoke in a soft, wispy voice that could have used help from a body mike. He had been signed to choreograph *Whorehouse* and codirect it with Peter Masterson.

"Tommy's very talented and right now he's very hot," Stevie assured me. "He won a Tony for his dancing in *Seesaw* and he's just won an Obie for his Off Broadway direction of *The Club.* I want you to see his work."

Stevie picked me up in the big limo and took me to a small theatre in the Village. *The Club* was an alleged comedy set in an exclusive British men's club in the nineteenth century, I think. All the men's roles were played by women in top hats, tuxedo jackets, white ties, fishnet stockings and high heels. They spoke in these teddibly, teddibly upper-class accents and I couldn't understand a clench-jawed word, don't you know? Periodically these men-women sallied forth to tap-dance for about twenty minutes before resuming their incomprehensible dialogue, most of which seemed to break them up. With Stevie increasingly tense by my side, I squirmed, muttered, yawned; twice I went to smoke.

When the house lights came up and everyone madly cheered I jumped to my feet. "Stevie, I ain't going to the second act. I'll be in that bar across the street."

"There *is* no second act," she said, astonished. "Why do you think the cast is taking curtain calls?"

I gloomed over my drink in the bar across the street and said, "Jesus, Stevie, what *was* that shit?"

She told me the plot, which I had not for a moment suspected. "Oh, I wish I hadn't brought you," she fretted. "I see now it wasn't destined to be your cup of tea. Please, *please* don't hold it against Tommy Tune!"

"I won't tell anybody about it if he won't," I said.

A few days later I met Tommy Tune when the collaborators gathered at his West Side apartment. Tommy had a huge living room I originally thought he hadn't gotten around to furnishing; later I learned he meant to keep it that way. Everyone sat on bright pillows. There were no ashtrays or tables to hold them.

"Tommy," I said, "you got any whiskey?"

"No," he said. "How about some herb tea?"

"No," I said. "Now we're even."

Tommy, it developed, had gone to Lamar High School in Houston at the same time as Carlin Glynn. During our Actors Studio production they had met by chance on a city bus, and Carlin had invited him to the show.

"I loved it," he said to me. "It's so earthy, so real, it's got so much heart! All those marvelous Texas expressions! Well, I told Carlin, 'If this show goes anywhere, I want to be part of it.' So the other day Stevie Phillips called me and I'm just walking on air!"

The rest of them talked about dance numbers. I smoked, knocking the ashes into my cupped hand, until Tommy Tune took notice and fetched what maybe was a hollowed-out dried gourd.

"Get rid of that demented-villagers scene," I heard Tommy say.

"Wait a minute," I said. "Are you talking about the townspeople? The scene where the sheriff confronts Melvin P. Thorpe on the courthouse lawn?"

Yes, that was the one.

"In a pig's ass," I said. "That confrontation is vital to the play. Pete, don't you guys go fucking around with that."

Tommy Tune recoiled as if I had slapped him.

Pete Masterson laughed and said, "Larry's bark is worse than his bite, Tommy. What I'd like to talk about is the Aggie scene. We need a dance there . . ."

I left, went out for a few beers, and returned to more dance talk. As the meeting broke up, Tommy Tune seemed to make an effort to seek me out; I had the impression perhaps Masterson had suggested it.

"I'm looking forward to working with you," he said. "Tell me a little about your Texas background."

In so doing, I mentioned that I had once worked in the oil fields.

"Oh, my father was in oil, too," Tommy said.

"Tommy, see, I wasn't exactly *in* oil. I was a roustabout and roughneck."

"You worked on those horrible rigs?" he asked.

"Right."

"Oh, when I was about twelve my father took me out to one. One of those off-shore rigs? We stayed all night and it was horrible! Bugs and things bit me, and everything stank! It was wretched!"

"It was that, all right," I said.

In the elevator I looked at Masterson: "Man, I don't know! I think that dude grew up on a different planet."

"He'll be fine," Masterson laughed. "I know his work and he's great. You two just have a little adjusting to do. . . ."

The three collaborators, Tommy Tune, and Stevie Phillips flew to Nashville in search of a western swing band. Tommy Alsup, an old-timer in the Music City, had recommended several groups.

We went to see one such group, the Rio Grande Band, which

was playing a peeling beer joint called the Pickin' Parlor in one of the scabbier sections of Nashville. The sparse crowd, working folks in rough garb, drank their beers straight from the bottle. My companions looked about uncertainly. I had grown up in such "fightin' and dancin' " clubs and felt perfectly at home.

"Don't let the cheesy surroundings mislead you," I said. "There are so many, many excellent musicians in Nashville looking for a break we'd probably have trouble finding a truly bad band."

The Rio Grande Band worked hard and sounded good. Within an hour lanky Tommy Tune was dancing an impromptu solo and repeating, "I love them! I love them!" Carol Hall clapped along, concurring. The consensus was that we wanted the band for our show.

We approached the leader, Craig Chambers—who would prove to be yet another Houstonite—and invited him to our table to talk. He listened to Stevie Phillips rap, staring as if he didn't believe her: were we putting him on? *New York?* Talk of show business? *Broadway?* Chambers arranged to see us the following morning at his Nashville home and returned to the bandstand. He spoke excitedly to the band members, who turned toward us as one, gawking and yammering.

God chose the next morning to bring the winter's largest storm to the entire Eastern seaboard. We mushed through deep snow to Chambers's home, where he had assembled his group. We met fiddler Ernie Reed, bassman Ben Brogdon, steel-guitar artist Lynn Frazier, Carol Chambers—backup vocalist to her husband—and a piano player and drummer who soon would be replaced. They ran through a number of the songs in Carol Hall's score, thumbed through the script. We sent out for pizza and worked well into the afternoon before fighting through snowdrifts to the airport.

Let that fiddling fool Ernie Reed tell it from his perspective a few years later: "I didn't like the play. Thought it didn't have a chance. Going to New York on the word of a bunch of strangers seemed like a hell of a gamble. But after you guys left, the band talked late into the night, drinking, arguing. It kept going back and forth. Finally I said, 'Well, I'm tired of playing for the door at these joints.' You see, we had no guarantee on most of our jobs: just the door money, which usually amounted to a cover charge of one dollar a head. 'What did we take in at the door last night, Craig?' Craig said it had been sixty-something dollars, I believe. I said, 'Damn right. And we had to split it a half dozen ways to boot. What have we got to lose? Nobody here is up-to-date on his house payment or car payment. We can't do worse in New York than we're doing in Nashville. If we're gonna starve, let's do it someplace we haven't ever seen.' So we voted to take a flyer."

As for the collaborators, who now included Tommy Tune as a working partner, it was back to the old drawing board. My bones were weary at the thought of walking through the same plowed ground again and again. There would be new fights, I knew, and resumptions of old ones. I wasn't certain I had the energy to go through it again.

Obviously, my indifference to dancing—nay, my *distaste* for it—no longer would suffice to keep it out of the show. I had managed to confine it to the hated "Two Blocks from the Capitol Building" to date. No more. "Dancing," Stevie Phillips lectured while I sulked and groused, "adds a new and necessary dimension. You must accommodate yourself to that reality."

"The bastards are trying to take my play away from me," I complained to Barbara. "It won't be a play when they're finished. It'll be a goddamn musical review, with a bunch of fags leaping and smirking all over the stage." Privately, I determined not to go down without a fight.

I drew Pete Masterson aside. "Tommy's gonna try to have a dance in every goddamn scene. If we had a funeral scene, he'd probably want the pallbearers to tap-dance and maybe the corpse to jump out of the casket to take a solo. I thought fourteen songs were too many at Actors Studio, and every time I hear Carol and Tommy talking they're mentioning *new* ones."

"Most of them are substitute songs," Pete said. "We'll scrap 'Goddamn Everthang,' 'Doin' It and Sayin' It,' 'The Memory Song,' and 'Pussy.' I'm certain of those as cuts. Maybe more."

"You're gonna have to take care of the play," I said. "You were my partner in that, and now it's up to you to protect it. I'll be damned if I'll let the story be chopped up just to string singing and dancing scenes together."

"Well, we'll have to find the proper balance," he said.

"I don't like the sound of that, Pete. It says nothing."

"Look," he said, "I'm as interested in a strong book as you are. It's mine, too, you know. But we've got to go in a more musical direction—that's why Universal bought the show, it's what they want. You've got to remember I don't have the autonomy I had at the Studio. I'm *co*director now. And we've got a producer, who controls the purse strings, with ideas of her own."

"You remember, this, Pete: if you don't fight the bastards to preserve the play's integrity, then *I'll* step in. And that could get goddamn messy."

"Give me a chance, dammit," Masterson said, flushing. "We haven't even started yet."

I was not comforted. Pete had seemed ill at ease, almost furtive. I suspected he might have made commitments or reached decisions he was reluctant to reveal. For the second time—the first had been when he fled to Hollywood—I wondered if he was all that he appeared.

I had my eye on Masterson when we met to determine which cast members from our Actors Studio production would be retained. Henderson Forsythe, Carlin Glynn, Joan Ellis (Shy), and Susan Mansur (the waitress, Doatsey Mae) were foregone conclusions: unanimous choices. I figured there would be a battle over one actress for sure: Liz Kemp, who had played April. I'd earlier asked Pete to fight for her.

Carol Hall had never liked Liz's singing. We had battled over it several times. "You like her because she's blond and beautiful," Carol once had blurted. "And you dislike her for the same reasons," I'd fired back.

Now I brought her name up again.

"Nope," Carol said. "She can't sing, Larry. *Still* can't sing."

"Bullshit, Carol. She sings like a dream."

"To *you* she sings like a dream. To me, she doesn't sing well enough to star in a Broadway musical."

"Carol," Pete said, "I've got to have some goddamn people who can *act*. And Liz is a damn good actress. We'll get you plenty of people who can sing. But I've got to have some people to work with, too. I want Liz Kemp." Her name went on the list; I silently cheered Pete's stand.

Masterson then nominated Clint Allmon as Melvin P. Thorpe.

Carol again pointed out a lack of singing talent. I agreed in my heart.

"Does he dance?" Tommy Tune said.

"No," Pete said. "But I want this one, Tommy."

I liked Clint, and I owed Pete one, so I voted with him.

We added my son, Brad, as a musician to play with the Rio Grande Band, and Carol Hall's friend Marta Sanders of the great voice. All told, a grand total of eight original cast members would make the jump from showcase to Off Broadway . . . and perhaps beyond. I recall feeling saddened that we couldn't take more of those hard-working people who had given so much of themselves, their time, their energies—people like Mallory Jones, J. J. Quinn, Elaine Rinehart, Eric Cowley, John Kegley, Thom Kuhl, Jane Ives, Marci Maullar; hell, *all* of them. Some would be angry, no doubt. Some would be hurt. I couldn't blame them in either case.

"Do any of those eight people dance?" Tommy Tune inquired.

Nobody answered him. Tommy read our faces, put his head in his hands, and groaned.

"You'll get your dancers," Pete said crisply. "We've got about twenty-five more people to cast. You can find dancers at the auditions. Singers, too. But I'm not going into this thing without a few good actors I trust."

I winked at Pete and gave him the thumbs-up signal: good man!

## CHAPTER

# 8

Almost three thousand actors and actresses appeared to audition for *Whorehouse*—a veritable army of hopefuls panting after fewer than twenty roles. When I learned that, it stunned me.

By doubling and tripling the players in roles, in a bow to the gods of economics, we had pared our cast to twenty-six persons, not including the band. Of these slots, eight had been locked up by transferees from our Actors Studio cast. The across-the-board odds for all others who auditioned, therefore, were something like 163 to 1 against being hired. How often have you seen racehorses win against those odds? Yet actors "go to the post" against similar odds time and again.

I fortunately missed the open call (or cattle call as it is brutally, if accurately, known in the trade), where aspirants are herded on stage in groups of fifty or sixty at a time, briefly checked for dancing abilities and for a certain "look" or "type." Talented people may be shunted aside because they do not "look right" or "feel right"—victims of an author's private vision, a director's concept, or a show's need for a certain mix.

Those beckoned from this initial dance line are merely beginning their ordeals. Next they are given brief singing trials and perhaps asked a few questions so their speaking voices may be heard and their movements and manners observed. They also might be asked to read a part "cold"—that is, without having seen it previously. The winnowed survivors then are invited to compete at an Equity call, where they are given longer and harder looks as dancers, singers, and actors. Some may be asked back as many as three times more—and they must be paid a day's rehearsal pay under Equity rules—before being hired or, heart-breakingly, rejected.

Tune, Hall, and Masterson had culled the best from the cattle call before I appeared at the final, Equity auditions. Thus a mere three hundred actors were in the running for eighteen slots when I arrived at a theatre in the West Fifties that did not then have a show on the boards and had been leased as our audition site.

Brad had been hired to assist Paul Phillips, a show-business veteran of thirty years who had been signed as our stage manager, in the mechanics of auditioning. Armed with a clipboard, he double-checked the players' names, agencies, and phone numbers, extracted their résumés and photographs, and helped Paul Phillips sort out the order in which the hopefuls would audition. This was a new and startling experience for my son. He called me aside that first morning and said, "Jesus, Dad, it's a circus backstage. You ought to see what some of them do."

"Like what?"

"All sorts of weird stuff. Some pray. Some beat their heads against the wall. Really, I'm not kidding! Some make pep talks to themselves. Some walk around mumbling or clenching their fists or staring straight ahead. It's spooky!"

Early on I hated those auditions. I felt much the coward as our small group huddled in the darkened theatre, calling out directions or questions to the players as they went through their paces like so many trained dogs jumping through hoops. There they were, their asses on the line, sweating under klieg lights, desperately smiling and attempting to make good impressions in a few pitifully short and precious minutes. They wanted work, *needed* work, and too often their attitudes, to put it bluntly, were fawning and obsequious.

I felt reduced as a human being by becoming a part of so cold, brutal, and final a process. Not that anyone was treated badly—on the contrary. The more hapless the actor or actress, the louder and more cheerful were our dismissing thank-yous from out there in the fat, safe dark. That was the death knell and the actors knew it. You could see them slump, smile too brightly, scurry away in haste as if to hide themselves. Brad later told me that some cried as they left the theatre, or punched inanimate objects, or otherwise raged.

I don't know whether I felt sorrier for those good talents who happened not to have the right "look" or "feel," or for those who couldn't dance a step or sounded as if they were being slowly strangled when they tried to sing. We had more of those than I would have imagined; I wondered how they'd survived the earlier cattle call. Pete Masterson would later say "Well, some had a certain look we were reluctant to pass up. You hope the guy can make it, so you give him another chance. Others, I guess, just slipped through the net somehow."

An occasional actor or actress who felt he or she had flubbed the big opportunity begged another chance. "I'm just getting over a cold," or "I couldn't find the music to the song I *really* had prepared for this audition," or "I'm much better than I performed today, I don't know what was wrong with me . . ." A few cried onstage; others rushed to the wings so they wouldn't. If you are ascribing such conduct merely to artistic temperament, then consider these hard facts: two-thirds of Actors' Equity members are unemployed in any given moment, and thirty percent work less than sixty days each year. It is a rough business.

My stomach began to knot earlier each day. I carried home indelible visions of those who had stumbled, wept, begged for another shot, or had simply staggered off stage as if shell-shocked. I could imagine them hungry in East Village lofts or Chelsea hovels, doomed to return to "straight" jobs they hated, wishing they had not told their friends they were auditioning because now humiliating explanations might be required.

On about the fourth day I said, "Pete, I'm sorry, I just can't do this anymore. Maybe it's the coward's way out, but I'm leaving the auditioning and casting decisions to you guys. It just makes me too damned unhappy."

"Well, yeah, it's tough," he said. "Hell, *I* see 'em bleed up there. And as an actor I know what it feels like to be knocked down and have to get up again. Over and over. It's a necessary process, though."

"Maybe so," I said, "but it ain't in my contract I got to watch it."

I walked down Broadway feeling a great surge of relief and hailed a cab, anxious to get back to my typewriter. The typewriter's virtue is that you don't have to look into the faces of those you are harshly judging while the process goes on.

Pete asked me out for a drink. He chuckled nervously, squirmed, seemed preoccupied. His manner hinted he might be the bearer of bad tidings.

"Ah, Larry, we've got a problem about Brad."

"Oh?"

"Yeah. See, Stevie has signed the Rio Grande Band as a unit. And now that the contract's been signed, Craig Chambers refuses to accept any outside musicians. I think the problem is that Brad plays guitar and is a soloist, and that's Craig's role with the band. So he refuses to accept Brad."

"Oh, goddamn. That's final?"

"It's final about him being in the band," Pete said. "He can audition to be a Texas Aggie and for the role as the kid, Leroy Sliney."

"Won't that mean dancing?"

"Damn sure will. All the Aggies gotta dance. Brad's young and supple, though. Tommy Tune can probably teach him."

"I don't know. The kid's got a bum knee he injured playing soccer at Selwyn School. I put him in a small private school so he wouldn't get crippled up playing football, and guess what?"

"How bad is it?"

"The knee swells on him sometimes. I doubt whether it would hold up, dancing eight shows a week."

"If he wants a crack at being in the show," Pete said, "he'll have to try. Tell him to report to Tommy and if Tommy thinks he can do the dance work, then he can audition for the Leroy Sliney role."

Bradley Clayton King received this news about like he would

have welcomed his draft notice. He was a musician, he said, not a goddamned dancer. Piss on the Rio Grande Band! Piss on the show! To hell with all of us! He stomped and threw things, leading me to wonder from whom he had inherited such bombastic genes.

I permitted his storm to blow out and said, "Brad, that's the reality. Now, you can get your young ass over to audition for Tommy Tune and Pete or you can sit here sulking and have a wonderful career as a busboy. Dammit, son, haven't you seen how desperate actors are for work in this city? And it's even worse for musicians! You know that! You've canvassed every club in New York where they permit guitars."

"I wouldn't have a chance," he said. "I can't dance and I'd be going up against professionals." Soon, however, he pulled on his cowboy hat and went off, grumbling, to see Tommy Tune.

Tune told Brad he had size going for him—"We need big, husky football-types"—and was lucky in that the Aggie dance wouldn't require the finesse of a ballet dancer. He put him through some steps and then asked if Brad played any musical instruments other than the guitar.

"I thought he meant I was so bad my only hope was the band," my son later would say. "But I named several instruments I could play. When I mentioned banjo he said, 'Good! You might be able to dance with the Aggies up to a point, then drop out and stand by the bandstand picking the banjo.' I thought, *Fat chance,* but I didn't say it."

The morning Brad went to audition for the role of Leroy Sliney, the virgin kid making his first visit to a cathouse, he was cross and morose. "I can't win," he gloomed over coffee. "I'll be competing against friends from Actors Studio—Eric Cowley, K. C. Kelly, Elliott Swift. If I get the part I'm gonna feel real bad for them. And everybody will say I got it because I'm your son. And if I *don't* get it . . ."

"Brad, there's nothing we can do about what people say or think. And it's a little late to change the fact that I'm your father. You'll just have to do your best work and let the chips fall. You've been playing guitar eleven years, you've studied music, you sing very well. Your acting was fine at Actors Studio and Tommy says he can teach you to dance. You'll just have to take your shot."

"Maybe I ought to try to get a job backstage with Paul Phillips."

"Would you be satisfied with that?"

"No," he admitted. "I'm an entertainer. I've been heading that way since I was four years old."

"Well, then?"

"I don't want you pressuring Pete or Tommy to take me," he said, proudly. "I want to make it on my own, or not at all."

"So sink or swim," I said. "So break a leg."

I carefully stayed away from my son's audition and avoided asking management how he had done. Brad was tense and silent for three or four days while awaiting the casting decision.

One night I was dozing on the couch when the telephone woke me. I heard Brad answer it, mumble a few words, and hang up. Then there was an ear-splitting "*Yee—hawwwwwww!*" He came running into the living room, a giant smile splitting his face, and it wasn't necessary to ask what the whoopee was all about.

Rehearsals were to begin in late February at City Center, on West 56th, with our Off Broadway opening booked for April 9th at the Entermedia Theatre in the Village. Stevie Phillips had budgeted $300,000, which gossip columnists reported to be an Off Broadway record; eventually, the Off Broadway cost would surpass $400,000. Such sums made a poor boy dizzy. They also made me feel more pressure. Who wants it said he was given a record amount of money to mount a show, and *still* failed?

On a bitter day when snow was thick on the ground, less than twenty-four hours before rehearsals would kick off, I accompanied Stevie, her lapdog, Petey, and her chauffeur, John, to the wilds of Staten Island. There we awaited the Rio Grande Band, motoring up from Nashville, at a frozen house that had been rented for them.

I use the words "frozen house" advisedly: we discovered that the heat had not been connected. Icicles had formed on the kitchen and bathroom faucets. Vandals had tossed a rock into the living room through a window; snow had swirled in to freeze on the carpet. The telephones and lights had not been hooked up.

Stevie began to hoot and dance in rage. She dispatched her chauffeur to telephone the rental agency with hot orders to get their asses in gear immediately.

"Those kids are going to arrive from down South half-frozen and exhausted," she said. "When they see this goddamn mess they might just turn around and go back. And I couldn't blame them."

The house was furnished with what I thought of as Early Fake Pretentious: shoddy imitation stuff, running to plastics and vinyls and cheap woods, gaudy bathroom fixtures and tinny chandeliers that looked as if they might crumble when touched. We waited and waited for assistance, and for the Rio Grande Band to arrive, stomping our feet and hugging ourselves in an effort to get warm. Periodically we retreated to the limousine and its warming heater, but this was difficult in my case because the little dog, Petey, had fallen in love with my right leg and kept trying to romance it.

The band members, country boys all, none of whom had laid eyes on New York City before, had become lost in the snarls and traffic circles of the metropolitan tangle and appeared hours past schedule. They were a rumpled, weary lot, their vehicles lashed round and about with musical instruments, suitcases, and personal effects, so that they faintly resembled the Joad family heading for citrus-picking opportunities in California.

Despite their tardiness, the band boys and their wives and girl friends arrived long before anyone appeared to turn on the heat or other utilities. While Stevie was driven off in her warm limousine to abuse the real-estate culprits, I attempted to soothe the new arrivals. We cut a temporary pane from a cardboard box to patch the broken window, resulting only in the tiniest improvement. Most of the time we stomped our feet, shivered, and shook.

"I knew New York wouldn't work," Arkansan Ben Brogdon said, shivering in a sheepskin coat and jamming his cowboy hat down over his ears. "We had to be proud crazy to come up here to this big icebox."

"No, no," I said, "we'll get this squared away . . ."

Carol Chambers said, "If we built a bonfire in here this minute it wouldn't thaw out for three days. *No way* we can sleep in this house tonight."

"What's that song about New York being such a wonderful damn town?" said Ernie Reed, the fiddler.

"Damn my soul," Brogdon said, "I'd give three dollars for a shot of whiskey."

"Sold," I said, producing a pint of undisturbed Scotch from my greatcoat. Soon I was the most popular man in the room.

Stevie Phillips returned with profuse apologies for the arctic conditions, and announced plans to stash the bandfolk in a nearby Holiday Inn. Our new arrivals climbed back into their burdened vehicles and followed the limousine away.

"Larry, those kids will sneak off tonight and go back South," Stevie said, worried.

Months later Craig Chambers said, "She'll never know how close she was to right. It was days before that sorry damned house was put in working shape. We had people crashing in every room—on couches, pallets, mattresses on the floor. Ernie Reed and Lynn Frazier slept in a basement full of cold water.

"None of us wanted to risk renting our own place until we knew if the show would make it. It was specially hard on the women, trying to keep house with a bunch of hairy-assed old boys layin' around. People got on each other's nerves, crowded up like a pack of rats. Not a bit of privacy. Ben Brogdon and Pete Blue, the piano player, were always getting into it. Blue, no matter what you said to him, he had to analyze it and question it and quarrel with it. And that drove ol' Brogdon crazy.

"We'd leave early of a morning, freezing our asses off, and get lost going to the city. Couldn't find a parking place when we got there. Got tickets, got our cars towed; had to run all over New York bailing 'em out. We went down to join the local musicians' union. Had cash money in hand and everything, but those suckers wanted our life stories and acted like they were doing us a big damn favor to take it. Seemed like everybody gave us a lot of unnecessary lip—toll-bridge clerks, cops, the union, goddamn phone company. Somebody was always lying to us or snarling at us. We'd just been accustomed to better treatment than that down home.

"Several times we felt like chucking it to these New York Yankees. We'd come in dead tired at night to a cold house and likely a cold supper, eat a few bites, fuss awhile, and tumble into bed. We'd hear rumors of you people running the show fighting over all kinds of shit, and we didn't know but what the deal might blow up in our faces any minute. And I'm telling you true, New York would be a hard mother to get stranded in!

"I believe if a single one of us had ever stood up and said, 'Fuck it, boys, let's go home,' then the whole shebang would have lit out of here like something was chasing us. We got on the edge of it several times, damn right. Somehow, though, nobody ever said the words."

Miss Edna Milton arrived at Kennedy Airport in a respectable cloth coat and accompanied by a small mountain of luggage—a dozen suitcases, assorted hatboxes, suit bags, carrying cases. Stevie's chauffeur crammed and jammed her goods into the limo's roomy trunk, storing the spillover items in the jump-seat area. For that reason I rode into Manhattan in the front seat, beside the driver.

It was Edna Milton's first trip to New York and she was full of questions and observations.

"How about the niggers?" she asked.

"Ah, I don't think you'll have any difficulties, Miss Edna," Stevie said.

"I'd of went back in business if it hadn't been for nigger trade. Went out to Nevada after they closed me down. Out there in certain places prostitution's legal, some little prick like Marvin Zindler can't close you down. But they told me I had to take nigger trade and I wouldn't do it."

Stevie chose to point to some matchless roadside attraction she thought Miss Edna should see. "Not that I got nothing against niggers," Edna said.

A few miles more and she was inspired to lecture on the clergy. "Preachers, politicians that's about as lowdown as you can get. Lots of 'em, anyway. We had Catholic priests come to my place late at night, and since they'd took a vow not to screw they'd ask to eat us and jackoff and stuff."

The limousine careened alarmingly as Stevie's chauffeur, who had an Irish name and a face like downtown Dublin, muttered and crossed himself. "Ah, is that right?" Stevie said, sounding wispy and faint.

"Damn sure is. Not that I got nothing against Catholics. But one time this priest—"

"Look, Miss Edna!" Stevie interrupted. "Look at the city lights! They're welcoming you to New York!"

"Be just my luck for a goddamn mugger to get me," Edna said.

I waited for her to say not that she had nothing against muggers, but she began to ask Stevie Phillips where she bought her clothes and got her hair fixed.

We arrived at a scabby apartment-hotel in the West Forties, a certified fleabagger with dim watts in the lobby and a dimmer still desk clerk. While Miss Edna signed in I whispered, "Jesus, all that Universal money and you're stuffing Edna's poor ass in this rat trap?"

"I'm embarrassed!" Stevie whispered back. "I sent someone to locate accommodations and suggested a decent price range. I don't know how this happened."

On the way up to Edna's apartment, in the tiny elevator, Stevie apologized and promised better quarters. "Don't worry about it," Edna said. "I bet I've lived in worser than this." *No doubt,* I thought. We helped Edna store her gear in the awful place, and escaped to the limo.

"Larry, what I shall *do?*" Stevie said, laughing. "If that wild woman says those things to the New York press . . ." Another fit of giggles.

"Aw, hell, let her talk. They won't print half of it in their 'family newspapers' and the other half should alert everybody to our show."

"I hope I've done the right thing bringing her here," Stevie said, worrying.

I liked the look and the feel of the cast when it assembled at City Center on a frigid February morning. We rattled around in a huge basement room reminiscent of a basketball court; the acoustics were absolutely horrible, but certainly we had room enough to caper. Tape had been placed on the floor, marking sections to serve as the whorehouse interior, courthouse lawn, town café, and so on. There was a happy reunion among members of the original Actors Studio cast, and a get-acquainted session with the new people. The cast read through the play, laughing excessively in an old tradition. When Pete Masterson and Tommy Tune split the players for individual work, and Carol Hall assembled the stage whores around a piano to teach them the opening song, I retired to my typewriter feeling good about many of our newcomers.

Among the new talents:

*Jay Garner:* A Tennesseean and a Broadway veteran, he seemed to specialize in playing politicians. Lester Maddox in *Red, White and Maddox;* Benjamin Franklin in the smash hit *1776;* the Lyndon Johnson figure in *MacBird.* In *Whorehouse* he became the state's nameless governor and doubled as a small-town insurance man, C. J. Scruggs. A marvelous song-and-dance man with a true comic flair, Garner was a loner who headed for home the moment he had taken his curtain calls. A consummate professional.

*Delores Hall:* We cast her as the black maid, Pearl—soon to be changed to Jewel. She had won a Tony in 1977 as featured actress in the musical *Your Arms Too Short to Box With God* and had been in *Hair, Godspell,* and other Broadway offerings; she had toured as a songstress with Harry Belafonte, worked with comedian Bill Cosby, recorded with Ike and Tina Turner, Frankie Avalon, and Dory Previn. She had a huge voice, amazing energy, a mischievous personality, and danced up a storm. Delores liked to talk what she called "trash and shit"; I soon was crazy about her.

*Pamela Blair:* The first thing I noticed was her great body, but there was more. She had created the role of Val Clark in the original Broadway cast of *A Chorus Line*—introducing the song "Tits and Ass." An accomplished singer, hoofer, actress, she had appeared on Broadway in *Of Mice and Men, Seesaw, Sugar,* and *Promises, Promises.* For reasons soon to become apparent, she opened in *Whorehouse* as the whore Amber—originally known as April. More about that little change soon.

*J. Frank Lucas:* A dour-looking Texan, he had a perfect country face and a tall, round-shouldered, pot-bellied frame and big feet, all of which made him look like the world's number-one rube. Cast as the small-town mayor, Rufus Poindexter, he doubled as the oily state senator, J. T. Wingwoah. His Broadway credits included *Bad Habits* and *Scapino.* Lucas had toured with many shows, worked almost every regional theatre in the country, and played comic bits in movies. You've doubtless seen him in many television commercials. Elected the Equity representative in the cast, he was a stickler for rules, regulations, and details. Though one admired his talents, one learned to avoid Lucas if one couldn't spare two hours for impromptu lectures. I once complimented him on a pair of shoes; he took it from there to discourse on those particular shoes, shoes in general, and the history of shoes.

Overall, our cast members had appeared in forty-two Broadway productions, thirteen Off Broadway shows, and countless touring, regional, and summer-stock productions. The cast also included what I considered a couple of oddities—the 1973 winner of the U.S. Irish step-dancing championship (Tom Cashin) and an opera singer (now cast as a whore) who had sung with the New York City Opera and at the Met (Jan Merchant).

There was, of course, another oddity—Miss Edna Milton. Edna was cast in two nonspeaking roles. As a long-ago Chicken Ranch madam, "Miss Wulla Jean," she briefly was pushed around the stage in a wheelchair in a single scene; as a townswoman she witnessed the confrontation between Sheriff Ed Earl Dodd and Melvin P. Thorpe. Occasionally, however, Miss Edna perhaps was transported to the past and forgot she was play-acting. *"Get that sorry son of a bitch,"* she sang out to the sheriff one night. Brad, who stood beside Miss Edna in the confrontation scene, said she almost constantly cursed the Zindler-like character under her breath during each performance.

Here is what Miss Edna wrote about herself in *On Stage,* the program distributed to theatregoers:

> EDNA MILTON. She was born in Caddo County, Oklahoma. She was one of eleven children in a family, part Cherokee, English and Dutch, living on a farm. As a youngster she appeared in school and church plays. She worked at the Chicken Ranch as many females did. She purchased The Ranch in 1961 and operated the legendary Texan brothel until 1973. This is her first time in New York and she is really enjoying it!

We soon would learn that Miss Edna did not enjoy New York every minute, or approve of everything she found there. I got my first clue when Brad burst into my apartment at the end of that first day of rehearsal and shouted, "Dad, they've changed April's name to Amber and Pearl's name to Jewel!"

"Did *what?* Why?"

" 'Cause Miss Edna pitched a bitch! Not long after you left City Center, she cornered Pete and said her mother had been named Pearl and she wouldn't stand for a 'nigger' named Pearl in the show."

"Oh, Christ on a stickhorse," I said.

"That's not all. She said her favorite working girl at the Chicken Ranch was named April, and she wouldn't tolerate using *that* name in the show."

"I think that woman's gonna be much more trouble than she's worth," I sighed. "You mean Pete went along with her demands?"

"Yeah, everybody had to scratch out the old names in their scripts and write in the new."

I went to Masterson the next morning, simmering like something that had been left on the stove all night. Frankly, my ass was as red as the trey-ball.

"Pete, what's all this about name changes in the script?"

"Yeah," he said with a small laugh. "Miss Edna got all upset. It seemed easier to change the names than haggle over them."

"I don't like it," I said. "You didn't consult with me. That's a dangerous precedent."

"Christ, it didn't occur to me to check a couple of name changes! We hadn't frozen them, you know."

"Good. Then they're not frozen now, and you can change 'em back."

That flush started on Masterson's bald head again—a sure sign of his irritation, betraying his emotions exactly as President Eisenhower's dome had betrayed his. "No," he said, "I'm not gonna change them back. That would just lead to more confusion."

"So you're making an arbitrary decision, one I disagree with as coauthor, to tamper with the script just to accommodate some old whore?"

"Well, Pearl *was* Edna's mother's name. I understand her feelings, even if I don't agree, and I'm gonna respect her feelings."

"Pete," I said, "if you change, slash, or cut one more goddamn thing without consulting me, then we're gonna have a long hard winter together."

"Dammit, I'll consult with you when I think it's important! This didn't seem like that big a deal to me."

"It's a big deal to me, Pete, because I fear what it might portend. And let me tell you about Edna: she's run her own tough shop, and she'll run this one if you let her. Unless you put your foot down, she'll walk all over you."

"No," he said. "Edna's not gonna walk on me. Nobody is."

We stiffly walked away from each other.

That second day of rehearsal contained another unwelcome surprise.

I was about to leave City Center for my typewriter (still trying to repair those miserable curtain scenes), when I saw Liz Kemp, wrapped and scarfed for the cold outdoors, heading rapidly for an exit. I ran after her. "Hey, Liz, where you going? You already mastered your part?"

She turned, and I saw tears in her eyes. She bit her lip. "I'm quitting the show," she said.

"You're . . . *what?* And *why?*"

"Carol doesn't want me," she said.

"What did she say to you? *What,* dammit?"

"She didn't say a word to me," Liz said. "But she's told other people I can't sing, and it got back to me."

"Well . . . goddamn! You gonna just *quit?* Just cave in?"

"Larry, it's not worth it," she said. "I don't want to work under that pressure. I'd feel Carol Hall looking over my shoulder every day. That I don't need."

"Wait, Liz! Come back here!" She halted in flight. "What the hell did Pete say? Didn't he do anything?"

"He was very sweet," she said, blinking. "He tried to talk me into staying. I just can't. I'm sorry."

And she walked away.

So that is how Pamela Blair was promoted from a lesser role to star as April. Er, I mean Amber. No, what I really mean is *Angel.*

You see, after April had been Amber for about six months, Pete Masterson changed her name to Angel.

No, he didn't consult me. I dropped into the theatre about

midplay one night to discover my favorite whore had again been renamed.

I still don't know why the second change.

Perhaps it was Pete Masterson's training at Actors Studio—that eternal quest for dirty-T-shirt realism—that led him to conclude it might be helpful for our stage whores to meet with Miss Edna, "to learn what whoring is really like."

The young women, almost all in their twenties and one as young as nineteen, giggled and joked about the handy tips they might pick up. But when they gathered round Miss Edna—Pamela Blair, Joan Ellis, Donna King, Lisa Brown, Louise Quick-Bowen, Jan Merchant, Carol Chambers, Becky Gelke, Marta Sanders, and Debra Zalkind—it appeared they had been stricken mute. There was a great deal of fidgeting, nervous lighting of cigarettes, inspections of fingernails.

"Don't you girls be bashful," Edna Milton said to encourage them. "I ain't ashamed of a damn thing I ever did."

"Miss Edna," Donna King said, "excuse me, but how did you—well, you know, get started in the business?"

"Hunny," Edna said, "I'm gonna give you the same answer I tell everbody that asks me that: I had a habit."

"Oh, I'm sorry," the young woman said.

"Yeah," Edna deadpanned, "a habit of eatin' three times a day."

Masterson laughed and said, "Uh, Edna, that's real funny. But it might help them understand their roles if you'd give a straight answer."

"That *is* a straight answer," Edna said. "If you're a teenage girl with not much education and no trade, it don't take long to learn you can make more on your back than you can on your feet. How many waitresses you know that drives Cadillacs?"

"Yeah." Pete chuckled.

"I learned early the world is run by the Golden Rule," Edna said, and waited in vain for someone to set up her punch line. When no one did, she finished, "Them that has gold . . . well, *they* rule."

"Did all your girls . . . do . . . everything?" Pam Blair asked hesitantly.

"No, hunny. Some girls wouldn't French for no amount of money. Oh, maybe they'd do half-and-half, but that was it."

After a pause Pam said, "And half-and-half is . . . ?"

"Hunny," Edna said, "don't take this personal, but did you ever put a man's penis in your mouth?"

The young actress rivaled the most colorful rainbow ever seen, red being her predominant hue, while the other stage girls gasped or tittered. Pam mumbled something about being married.

"Well, anyway, if you ever done that," Miss Edna said, "and then finished him off the old-fashioned way, then you done half-and-half."

None of the other girls seemed to want to risk questions after that exchange. Pete prodded them by saying, "You mean that's it? You know everything now?"

Becky Gelke said, "Miss Edna, how involved did your girls get in their . . . work?"

"I warned 'em against getting involved," Edna said. "Worst damn thing a working girl can do is fall in love with some John."

"No, that's not what I mean," Gelke said. "I wasn't talking about love. I mean, okay, if they're . . . entertaining . . . oh, several customers *a night,* then how do they—?"

"Oh, I see what you mean," Edna said. "I always told my girls to turn their minds off: 'Just grease and slide, hunny, just grease and slide' . . ."

I wandered into the rehearsal hall one midday to discover Carlin Glynn singing a song I had not heard before, "You Tell Me Your Dream." It was a beautiful song. She appeared to be singing it at the top of the show, however, and I was puzzled how it would fit there. When the number was over I made inquiries of Masterson.

"That's the opener," he said. "Then Carlin goes into the narration, giving the history of the Chicken Ranch."

I hoped to pose my objection softly. Carlin was, after all, Pete's wife. "Ah, Pete, I don't see that song there. It's a nice song, I like it, but 'Twenty Fans' aids the narration by describing the whorehouse, the girls, and so on. This new song does not. As I heard it, it's about sitting in a bar, drinking, seeing a stranger, and dreaming of romance with that stranger. Fine. But what the hell does that have to do with our play?"

"Well, see, we've decided to set up a flashback. We open with Mona in this bar scene. She sings the song and starts talking to the stranger at the bar. She's telling him the history of the Chicken Ranch, see, and then we flashback to the time when the troubles begin."

"Who decided that?"

"Well, I did. And Tommy."

"And Carol, obviously, since she had to know to write the song. In other words, everybody but me."

"No, now, dammit. It didn't happen that way. Carol brought the song in yesterday, we liked it, and *then* we decided to use it to set up a flashback."

"You mean you're scrapping 'Twenty Fans'?"

"No, no. 'Twenty Fans' stays. It follows the new song."

"In other words, the new song has just been dropped in willy-nilly."

"No, it sets up the flashback. Like I said."

"We don't *need* a goddamn flashback, Pete! 'Twenty Fans' opens with as direct a narration as you'll ever find. I don't know how you could improve on it."

"But if we don't use the new song, how will Carlin—Mona—get into the narration? She just walk out cold?"

"Well, that's another thing. Mona isn't supposed to do the narration. It works well with the bandleader doing it. The band's already there, already onstage, singing the song and interspersing it with the narration. What's the problem? That's worked before."

"We think we're waiting too long to bring on the leading actors," he said. "Mona doesn't come on for about twelve minutes the way we had it, and the sheriff doesn't show up for forty minutes."

"Look, we can push Mona on stage a little quicker. But damn, not this way! Not just dropping in a song and a scene to set up something that we already know will work without being set up."

"Well, we'll try it this way awhile. If we come to that conclusion, we'll go back to the old way." He excused himself to get back to the actors.

I stewed for a couple of days as the new scene was rehearsed again and again. Once more I approached Pete: "Don't get upset, now. I love Carlin and her work. But you've got her in the middle of the stage doing this and I can't hear her narration. When the bandleader does it, at the mike, he's clear as a bell."

"She'll be body-miked," Pete said. "Besides, the acoustics in this hall are terrible. It won't be like that in a theatre." I noticed Pete was not looking at me when he talked to me, and I realized that had been happening for several days.

"Pete," I said, "I think you're putting too much of a burden on Carlin."

"She can handle it."

"But she's already got the lion's share of the lines and songs! I just don't think we ought to put any more rocks in her sack. That aside, I'll just be damned if I see why you're insisting on that new song and scene. It does not add one goddamn thing to the show. All it does is blunt a sharp opening."

"I'll think about it," he said, walking away.

A day or two later I discovered the new song was gone, the new scene was gone, and the narration was back in the hands of the bandleader. Not a word was said about the change, then or ever.

They were singing the "Watchdog Theme Song" when I walked into the hall. Clint Allmon was barking and growling.

Allmon was playing Melvin P. Thorpe, who was, of course, something of a fool in our script. But he was a believable fool: a self-righteous prig, an egomaniac, a newsman out to create a story rather than merely report one, a public figure making naked use of his power and enjoying it. Such people exist. I did not believe, however, that they went around barking and growling like dogs.

I waited until a break in the rehearsal and called Masterson aside. "Whose idea is the barking and growling?"

"Well, Tommy and I agree on it," he said.

I shook my head. "I think it goes far beyond satire. It becomes . . . well, it's just goddamned silly."

"No, man! It's been breaking the cast up! Everybody loves it!"

"Pete, if you caricature Melvin Thorpe and some of these people too much—if they become goddamn cartoon figures—we won't have any credibility left for the sheriff and Mona. We've got to make the audience care about them, care about their real problems. If it's all a comic-strip joke, that won't happen."

"Well, I just think you're wrong about that. I gotta get back to work."

Getting madder by the moment, I watched Melvin Thorpe bark and growl for two or three more run-throughs of the scene. At the conclusion of rehearsal I asked Clint Allmon out for a drink. I thought he had not looked happy during rehearsal, and I thought I knew why.

"Clint, what do you think of the way they're having you play it?"

"I just work here," he said.

"No, come on. Tell me."

"Pete and Tommy are the directors. It's my job to do what they tell me."

"Fair enough. But here's what I think: I think it goes too goddamn far, I think it stinks, I think they've turned your character into a goddamn cartoon."

"Yes," Clint said quietly. "I can't argue with that."

"I'll talk to Pete again," I said, sighing.

The next morning I approached Pete and restated my objections, ending, "Clint agrees, by the way."

Masterson glared at me. "Yes," he said, "I've already heard you bypassed me and went directly to the actor. You told Clint I'd turned his part into a goddamn cartoon, and it got him unhappy. That's unprofessional! You're making trouble for me and for the show with that shit."

I was taken aback. I had not imagined that Clint Allmon wouldn't let his shirttail hit his behind before running to Masterson to further muddle the matter.

"I wouldn't find it necessary to go around you, Pete, if you'd check some of this shit with me. I'll remind you that you promised me—*promised* me—you would, when you asked me to back you for your job."

"Dammit, Larry, we can't direct this thing by committee! I can't conduct a poll or a vote on every bit of stage business that comes to mind. Directors have to make decisions, and Tommy and I have made this one. The barking and growling stay."

We next fought over the "freak scene" and its song, "Two Blocks from the Capitol Building." I'd never liked it, agreed with David Halberstam it was foreign to the rest of our show, and thirsted to see it replaced with a dialogue scene that might add new dimensions to our plot or to the play's characters. As far as I was concerned, Tommy Tune had taken a bad number and made it worse.

After he'd watched the scene several times, while reluctantly playing music for it, Craig Chambers came off the bandstand during a break, edged up to me, and said, "King, you're a Texan, like I am. What do you think of those freaks dragging the Texas flag on the ground?"

"I'm not too crazy about the whole number, Craig."

"Me either, but that flag thing chaps my ass. I just don't think they ought to drag the Texas flag in the dirt. Men died for that flag, by God, and there are some that'd still do it."

"Yeah," I said. "Don't believe I'd want to take that number to Dallas."

"Nowhere in Texas!" Chambers said. "Shit, that could be dangerous! You know, if this sumbitch ever opens, you're gonna have Texans come to see it in New York. And one night some damn old Texas boy, about three sheets to the wind, he just might strangle one of your he-she boys twitching around, dragging that flag or walking on it."

The funny thing is that I, too, had felt a resentful twinge when I saw the Texas flag being dragged and walked on. I had pushed the thought away, had actually been embarrassed at having it. It seemed too parochial a sentiment, too corny, too old-fashioned, too . . . well, too goddamned *Texan!* Had I not been refurbished and sophisticated by the years, by the East, by exposure to other cultures, so as to be beyond such gut reactions?

Buoyed by Craig Chambers's kindred feelings, I again sought

Masterson out to complain. I was getting weary of complaining; Pete's demeanor of late had clearly signaled he was equally tired of hearing from me. Sometimes he would turn icy, other times mumble and look away, or—his most maddening technique—pretend not to understand my complaint or the basis of my wrath. Pete was very good at playing dumb or puzzled. It bought him time and postponed shouting showdowns. He knew that every day he could stall me he was that much closer to having his way. I was reminded of a basketball team freezing the ball to protect a lead.

We went into the production office, just off the main rehearsal hall. "Pete," I said, "that freak scene gets worse and worse."

"How do you mean?"

"Well . . . it's just getting freakier and freakier. It's alien to our show, I've thought that all along, and it doesn't say a damn thing that hasn't been said shorter and more effectively in the dialogue."

"I kinda like it," he said. "I think Tommy's really bringing it to life."

"Of course you like it," I said. "You conceived it. I understand your reluctance to chop the head off your own baby. But it's hurting the show. And that business with dragging the Texas flags just ain't gonna sail."

"Well, I admit I'm not crazy about the flag thing. Let me talk to Tommy and see what we can work out about the flags."

"But you still insist on the goddamn number?"

"Well, Christ, at least until we can see what we have! Tommy's still working on it. I don't want to scrap the number until we see how well it might work. If it doesn't work . . ." He shrugged.

Obviously, that was the best I would be able to get out of him. I shook my head and walked away. As I was leaving the rehearsal hall, during a cast break, I saw legs poking out of a huge cardboard box resting on its side in a stairwell. Men's legs. Four of them. Instinctively, I stooped and looked inside. Two male dancers were embracing and nuzzling.

"Hi!" one said. "Come on in!"

"Ah, no, thank you," I said, retreating in some haste and confusion.

I heard a whoop of laughter. Ben Brogdon, the bass player, had witnessed the scene and was slapping a leg in delight. "Don't that beat all?" he said. "I wrote a note home this morning and told 'em I hadn't been in New York but two weeks and had already seen three or four heterosexuals."

# CHAPTER 9

The longer the *Whorehouse* rehearsals continued, the more disenchanted, belligerent, and impossible I became. There were reasons for this beyond the fact that I have what an old friend once described as an "erratic" personality and, perhaps, a natural tendency to bully and bluster in hopes of getting my way: while I believe in democracy in the abstract, there is nothing quite so satisfying to my soul as being able to dictate to all and sundry.

As the author of books and articles, I had largely dealt with gentlemanly editors—those at *New Times* aside—and had grown accustomed pretty much to calling the shots or, at bottom, to meeting only minimal resistance in the matter of how I would approach a story and the language to be employed. This near-autonomy is common in publishing. Such is not the case in show business. With Tommy Tune's arrival, I had what amounted to three collaborators, a producer, two codirectors, and a musical director to work with. This strained my diplomatic abilities.

As a musical is shaped, the book writer becomes a relatively useless appendage. Oh, sure, he's called in for rewrites; they beckon him for new scenes, a line here, a transition speech there;

but he really is little more than a glorified spectator, save for such patchwork. The work that was the writer's alone, or nearly so, now becomes community property. It is cut, changed, modified, put asunder. The writer's visions are shaped anew by a director's stage concept; his lines are changed by actors' interpretations even if they mouth his words as written. The writer begins to feel that strangers are raising the baby he has birthed—indeed, that his baby has been kidnapped and is beyond ransoming. As it is made increasingly clear by events that he is the low man on the totem pole, the writer feels neglected, superfluous, unwanted. It is but a short leap from frustration and self-pity to anger that, carelessly stirred, may soon border on the homicidal. At the root of my problem, too, was an unsurpassed ignorance of how a show was properly put together—especially a musical.

I shouted at Pete Masterson because it seemed that nine-tenths of the rehearsal time was being spent on songs and dances. "*I* still care about the book," I huffed, "even if you don't."

In weary exasperation he said, "Larry, we pretty well know what we've got in the book. I know my actors, and know they can be whipped into shape without much trouble. But we're culling songs, trying to find new ones—Carol's writing and rewriting constantly—and don't forget Tommy had to start from scratch with the choreography. The toughest part of a musical is getting the songs and dances to work. When they start coming together we'll spend more time on the acting."

I was not appeased. I sat grim-faced, fidgeting and muttering, while dancers worked until they dropped and songs were repeated until even I learned them. Barbara Blaine was foremost among those who urged me not to spend so much time at the rehearsal hall, feeding my frustrations. We were increasingly at loggerheads over the way the show consumed me, my time, and my thoughts, to the exclusion of all other pursuits. Indeed, on the first day of Equity auditions we had hissed and snapped at each other, in angry whispers and from the eighth row, for more than an hour, while players onstage desperately tried to catch everyone's attention. "I *hate* this show," Barbara had whispered. "You don't care about a thing in the world but this goddamn show." I had cracked back that my future depended on it, and that perhaps hers did—a comment that only increased her fury. Barbara had not yet been let in on the secret of my abject poverty (though I knew an accounting soon must be made) and therefore could have little understanding of how desperately I counted on *Whorehouse* to deliver me from the snares of many fowlers.

Despite her many entreaties that I retire from the rehearsal scene, I stubbornly insisted on my need to be there: "If I leave, and stay gone three days, I won't recognize my play when I get back. Pete and Tommy and Carol will turn it into a goddamned vaudeville act. They'll have the sheriff juggling, Mona walking a high wire in baggy pants, and probably bring in a dog act."

One afternoon Masterson beckoned me aside. "Uh, Larry, you're gonna have to ease off Tommy. He tells me he's afraid you might 'strike' him."

I was amazed. "*What?* I've said very little to the guy! Hell, I'd no more hit Tommy Tune than I'd kick an old lady!"

"I know that," Pete chuckled, "but Tommy's not certain of it. He's real upset. Maybe you can say a good word to him."

At the end of the day I approached Tune. He looked down from his lofty six-foot-seven-inch advantage in what I read as a glacial manner. "Look, Tommy, Pete says you're upset about me. I really don't know what it's all about, but—"

"Oh, you don't?" he said.

"Well. Naw. I guess—"

"How do you think I feel, working my ass off, and then looking up to see you staring at me and cursing? How do you think my *dancers* feel? They're sweating, they're sore, they're exhausted—they're giving their all to learn new routines, *difficult* routines, and all you give them is negative feedback!"

"I haven't said a word to the goddamn dancers!"

"They can see your face! I wish *you* could see it, I truly do. You look as if you *hate* us. And as if you could *kill* us!"

"Oh, come on—"

"You haven't approved one thing I've tried to do," Tommy Tune said accusingly. "You're trying to kill 'Capitol Building.' You killed Carol's new opening song. You won't let the sheriff dance and will hardly let him sing. You made a nasty scene about the staging of the Melvin P. Thorpe number. You stormed out of the room when you saw the 'Sidestep' number. You—"

"Tommy, I've got a right to my opinions. If I think something's not good for this show, then, by God, I'll say so!"

"Well if you *happen* ever to approve of something, would you say *that,* too? All my life the theatre has been great fun. Hard work, yes, but great fun. Your negative attitude has taken all the fun out of it. Whatever we do, you jump us. I go home exhausted and all I can see when I close my eyes is your angry face!"

"Tommy, I guess when I'm displeased, I look displeased. And when I'm mad enough to curse, I curse. To me that's normal. I haven't meant to hurt your feelings, and certainly I don't hate you."

"I can only judge by what I see," he said.

"I *do* hate some of the things I see being superimposed on my play, yes. Damn right. But what you're doing with the Aggie number, with the Angelette marching number, and—despite what you say—the governor's sidestep dance, I like. I know those are your original ideas and I really *like* them. I'm sorry I haven't said so."

"Thanks for that much," he sniffed. "I certainly couldn't have known it."

Tune was working to improve the confrontation scene on the Lanvil County courthouse steps, when Sheriff Dodd faces down Melvin P. Thorpe in a comic version of a *High Noon* shootout.

"Larry," he said, "the villagers just stand around with their mouths open. We've got all these people in the scene and we're not using them. Will you write a few lines for them? Especially for the church ladies, as they encourage Melvin?"

I retired to a corner alcove and was scratching out the dialogue on a yellow legal pad when someone touched my wrist. I looked up to see Miss Edna thrusting a folded sheet of paper at me: "Here's some lines them people can say to Marvin Zindler." Miss Edna never would refer to Melvin Thorpe by his stage name: to her, he would forever remain Marvin Zindler.

I unfolded the paper and read:

FIRST PERSON: Go on back to Houston, you queer-looking son of a bitch.

SECOND PERSON: What a Person does is a Person's own business, you asshole.

THIRD PERSON: When you fuck with our fucking you are really fucking up.

"Ah, thank you, Miss Edna," I said with a straight face. "I'll be happy to submit these lines to Pete and Tommy."

Miss Edna's debut as a playwright served a good and useful purpose: it provided the warring collaborators their first belly laugh together in days.

At long last we solved—correction, my collaborators solved—the problem of Sheriff Dodd's breaking the news to Miss Mona that he has no choice but to padlock the Chicken Ranch.

It began with Carol Hall's song "Good Old Girl," which the sheriff sings while onstage, alone, following the fatal telephone call from the governor. In a moment of private reverie Ed Earl recalls his easy friendship with Mona and comes as close as he ever will to sounding sentimental.

At the conclusion of the song, the sheriff sits at his desk and dials Mona's number. Upstairs, on a second-level stage, we see Mona as she answers the telephone. We see her happy look turn to concern and then to consternation as the impact of the bad news sinks in. We do not hear their words: as the sheriff starts dialing her number, lights go up on a previously darkened corner of the stage, where a lounging cowboy chorus unfreezes and picks up the singing of "Good Old Girl." They continue to sing as we see Mona approach her girls on the second-level stage: they are gossiping, primping, playing cards, and smoking pot, spraying vast amounts of perfume or hair spray to cover the odor. Mona breaks the bad news and the girls react, in mime, with alarm, shock, anger, or sadness according to their varied dispositions. Downstairs, the sheriff rises wearily from his desk and sings the tag line of the song, which indicates a tender and sentimental feeling for Miss Mona. He exits.

When my colleagues hammered all that together, I hugged and praised everyone in sight—Carol, Pete, Tommy, and Bob Billig, the musical director. For the first time I had some appreciation of what might be conveyed by songs and music with little or no dialogue. Hope began to rise anew.

I was sitting at the back of the rehearsal hall when Miss Edna approached and asked to speak to me privately. We walked out to a deserted hallway in the sprawling, cheerless City Center subbasement, pausing on gray concrete dotted by trash cans.

Edna grabbed my elbow. "I don't like the way that bitch is playing me, and I ain't putting up with it."

"What?" I said, startled.

"Carlin. She ain't playing me worth a shit. She couldn't run a cathouse if her life depended on it."

"Well, Miss Edna, it isn't necessary for her to run a cathouse. This is all make-believe."

"The bitch treats me shitty, too," Edna said. "Anytime I give her advice she ignores it."

"Edna, she has to take her suggestions from the directors. That's how this business works."

"Shit," Edna said. "They don't know any more about running a whorehouse than she does."

"There may be a certain logic in what you say, Miss Edna, but we're putting on a show. Reality gives way to illusion."

"I ought to get to play myself," Edna said. "I didn't come all the way from Texas to New York to do this shitty stuff they're forcing on me. If I'd thought I'd be treated this way, I'd of told you and Stevie to stick it up your asses. I want you to talk to her about me playing myself."

"Jesus, Edna, that won't work! You aren't a professional actress. You can't sing. It's—impossible."

"I had to do a lot of acting in my other profession," she said, "and I can sing good as that bitch can. Want me to prove it?"

"Well, naw, that's not—"

But I had spoken too late. Miss Edna had launched, a capella, into "You Are My Sunshine." Now, friends, I have earlier admitted sometimes having difficulty distinguishing good singers from bad ones. But I can tell the difference between the pealings of bells, say, and cats fighting, or between those same bells and the noises made by bus wrecks. Miss Edna in full solo was strictly catfights and bus wrecks. I had never heard, and fancy that I never shall, such a terrible, God-awful racket in my life. I stood shuffling among the trash cans, gazing at the ceiling, nodding, pulling my nose, not knowing whether to choke her or call for an ambulance. Edna, apparently wanting to be assured an adequate audition, sang all three verses.

When she mercifully ran down, and stood waiting expectantly, I said, "Uh, Edna, that . . . certainly . . . is unusual. Yes, I can safely say that is . . . unusual in the extreme."

"You gonna talk to Stevie for me?"

I took a deep breath. "No, Miss Edna, I'm not. I don't want to hurt your feelings, but there's no way you can handle that role."

"So-and-so says I can," she spat.

*Ah-hah!* Had I been in a cartoon, an electric light bulb would have flashed over my head. "So-and-so" was a middling member of the cast; I had heard rumors he palpitated to bum a little romance off Miss Edna. Now I thought I had some clue as to his tools of courtship.

"Oh?" I said. "How did he come to tell you that?"

"Well, he come over to my place Sunday and brought his guitar. I told him I didn't like Carlin playing me, that I could do it good as her. And I sung 'You Are My Sunshine' for him, and 'Rock of Ages,' and he said I ought to talk to Stevie about playing myself."

"Edna," I said, gently, "you can talk to her if you wish, but it won't do any good. For one thing"—sudden inspiration—"Carlin's already signed her contract as the leading lady. As Miss Mona."

"Never was a contract couldn't be broke," Edna said.

"Well, that's just not true, Edna. I really think you're spinning your wheels on this deal."

"If you won't talk to Stevie, I'm damn sure going to," Edna said.

After she'd walked away I wished there might have been some comfort to be bestowed. I truly felt sorry for Edna and, more, a certain empathy. As I felt frustrated, impotent, and angry while watching my script undergo radical surgery, so Miss Edna obviously had experienced strange and rebellious tugs watching her life being reshaped and changed for the stage—and worse, someone else literally standing in her shoes. It was all too clear that her problem wasn't really Carlin Glynn—who, I had noticed, had gone out of her way to be nice to Edna—but *anyone* playing the role.

As soon as I could get the actor "So-and-so" aside, I said, "You ought to have your ass kicked for the cruel thing you did to Miss Edna."

"What?" he said, feigning surprise.

"Don't hand me that bullshit. I'm talking about last Sunday. At her place."

"Oh, hell, Larry," he said, trying to grin, "I was just kidding the old gal along! Didn't you ever tell a woman what she wanted to hear?"

It was all I could do not to hit the bastard. I said, "You are making trouble for a show already up to its ass in trouble. If you encourage that poor woman in the slightest way to persist in her folly, you crummy shitass, I intend to run you out of this show. And I mean it, you sorry son of a bitch. Go tell *that* to your Equity representative."

Edna apparently reconsidered—or perhaps "So-and-so," fearful of the consequences, told her to cool it. At any rate, she never approached Stevie Phillips with a demand to play herself.

The first-act curtain continued to bedevil us. Nothing worked. We had the mad scramble as Melvin P. Thorpe discovers the Texas A&M football players, the sheriff, and the state senator at the Chicken Ranch on Thanksgiving night. The sheriff, who has dozed off in Miss Mona's parlor, awakes as he hears the girls screaming and the Aggies yelling while camera flashes light the darkened upper-level stage; the maid, Jewel, rings an alarm bell. The sheriff chases Melvin and his photographers off stage, firing his gun at the sky. Fine. As far as it went. But for months we'd been unable to find a line, a song—anything—to act as an effective button.

One afternoon as dancers danced and singers sang while I idly doodled, feeling used up and excluded—*Bingo! Eureka!* Lyrics and a half-assed tune seemed to jump from nowhere into my head. I rapidly scrawled words that my dear friend Carol Hall will not permit me to use here, they being copyrighted in her name. I bear Ms. Hall absolutely no malice. It is her legal and inalienable right and perhaps her duty to make a sorry bastard such as myself suffer. This detracts not one whit from whatever degree of admiration I feel for Ms. Hall, and I shall defend her against any slanders spoken against her name. She is a real sweetheart.

Anyhow, I ran to Pete Masterson in great excitement, waving my doggerel in his face as if I had found a formula for turning lead into gold. He read it and laughed: "Damn, that's it! We've found the first-act curtain!"

"I've even got a tune for it," I blurted.

"Hey, Tommy!" Pete shouted. "Come over here!"

Tune read the verse and he, too, broke into laughter. "I like it!" he said. "Somebody call Carol and read this to her. Tell her we need music."

"Oh, shit! Carol. Forget it," I said. "We're dead."

"No, wait," Pete said. "Sing the tune for us, Larry." Feeling a little foolish, I did so. The codirectors exchanged glances and laughed again. "So it ain't Cole Porter," Masterson said.

We got together with our musical director at the piano. I sang my little ditty while Bob Billig, grinning, picked it out. Then he played it through, adding a fancy musical curlicue at the end. "That's good," Pete said. "Keep that musical flourish at the end. Now, here's how we'll work it: as the actors scramble off stage in the half dark, we'll throw a spot on the bandleader. He'll sing King's Opus Number One"—general laughter—"and boom! That's it! House lights up! Intermission!" There was a small, friendly celebration. I felt much like the scrub who had come off the bench to score the winning touchdown as time ran out. That it seemed to be my first contribution to the show since Actors Studio made it all the sweeter.

"But what about Carol?" I asked. "She's refused every lyric I've given her. Why will this be different?"

"Unless she can top it," Pete said, "I'm going with it. It's funny, it gets us off, it's what we've been looking for." He thought a moment. "The only problem, Larry, might be if you insist on being credited or holding the copyright. Then, my God, I don't know what the legal complications might be."

"Forget that," I said. "It's not likely to make the top-forty charts. I just want the material used."

If Carol Hall was not wildly ecstatic, neither did she put up a fight. She made one condition: "I don't want Larry King running around bragging that he wrote that."

Carol, hunny, I swear this on a stack of Bibles—except for a few friends and loved ones, and maybe an occasional stranger late at night—I haven't told a soul. Honest.

Marjorie Kellogg delivered a scale model of the set she had designed for the show. She had worked out a two-level stage so that action could occur simultaneously on both levels. It featured red carpet and drapes and brass poles, and was an "open," airy set to accommodate a large cast, complicated action, and myriad scene changes. I thought the set was a very practical one. Almost everyone thought so.

Not Joan (Shy) Ellis.

"I don't like it," she said, turning up her nose. "That's not the way a country whorehouse looks!"

"This one does," I said, hoping that would be the end of the conversation.

"There's not one bit of realism in that set!"

"Joan," I said, "we've left Actors Studio. No more burping and scratching. We're slicking up for the Great White Way."

"Yes," she said, "and that's the trouble with our show."

This effectively cut the ground from under me, it being the same argument I had been advancing to my collaborators about any number of things.

A couple of weeks before our scheduled April 9th opening, we moved into the Entermedia Theatre, at Second Avenue and 12th Street, to acclimate the actors to their actual working stage and the set. It seemed a significant step in our progression, momentarily giving all hands a mental lift, though a close examination of the realities might have dampened optimism.

The show was running more than three hours long—at least forty minutes in excess of the permissible. We had "solved" the problem of extraordinarily long acts by creating three acts instead of two. This solution, of course, was no solution at all: the second intermission added another twelve minutes of captivity to the theatre patron's life, and gave us a bonus of an additional curtain problem.

Songs continued to fly in and out of the show like drunken birds, falling with a thud or zooming off never to be heard from again. I wrote new scenes, which failed to survive the day. Others appeared to be plopped in, willy-nilly, serving only to aggravate our length problem. Frankly, I thought the whole mess a shambles somewhat on a par with the Vietnam war. "This goddamn thing's gonna close quicker than a switchblade," I remarked gloomily to Barbara.

We had reached that point of exhaustion where numbness takes over without the numbed even realizing it: you *think* you are functioning and making rational decisions, when in fact you are coming unglued. All early exhilarations had fled, all optimisms had been driven away by repetition, fatigue, tensions, changes, quarrels, uncertainties, pressures.

Stevie Phillips, quite understandably, felt those pressures more than anyone. Universal Pictures never had produced a stage show. Stevie's superiors, fearing the unknown, grew jittery and dubious as the budget went up and hopes went down. Hollywood is not known for courage, except in its hokey scripts; it is a save-your-ass town, a cut-your-losses town, a pin-the-tail-on-the-scapegoat town; if the ship starts going down in Hollywood's turbulent seas, it is up to women and children to save themselves. "Don't embarrass us," Stevie was told by her bosses. She was bright enough to know that the unspoken part of that admonition was, "or you are out on your sweet ass." Stevie began to look haunted.

So many memos from our producer were hand-delivered to us that we joked of hiring a secretary to open them. They said things like: "Three times I have asked the collaborators to find a workable button for 'Pissant Country Place' and it still is not done. May I hear from you *soon*, Tommy?" . . . "Why have I heard no more about dropping the three-act concept? We *must* get back to two acts immediately!" . . . "Larry, days and days ago Pete told me you were working on a dialogue scene outside the whorehouse between Shy and Leroy. Where is it???????" . . . "Carol: what is the latest, please, on the song changes we discussed three days ago? Time is running out!" . . . "Why do we need the café scene *and* the sheriff's office scene? Is this not a duplication of effort? The same characters are in both scenes; they say basically the same things. We have discussed this numerous times, yet I see no change to date. Will you please communicate with me?"

"Goddammit," Pete Masterson grumbled, "we can't get any work done for answering goddamned memos. I think it must be this way in the bureaucracy. I think this is why government doesn't work any better. Everybody trying to *do* something has to stop and answer a goddamned memo!" The rest of us were equally hacked, and equally vociferous. We called an early-morning meeting in the downstairs lobby of the Entermedia, near the concessions bar, the better to shout at our producer to leave us the hell alone. "We can't put a show together if we are constantly harassed," Pete said, tight-lipped. Stevie Phillips left in a huff and wasn't seen for three days. "I guess she thinks she's punishing us," we told each other.

If it appeared to the addled and exhausted collaborators that Stevie Phillips had gone a bit bonkers, certainly she had sufficient reasons. She probably felt as if she presided over a kindergarten playground where the kiddies frequently attacked each other with knives, or had signed up the greatest collection of incompetent prima donnas since Congress last met. She knew other problems, too. One morning she walked into the Entermedia so chalk-faced I thought she might be in training to become a ghoul.

"What's wrong that we don't already know about?" I asked.

"No one will sell me ads for the show," she said. "Unless you're willing to walk around wearing a sandwich board, we may open in secret. *The New York Times,* among others, refuses to use the word *whorehouse.*"

"That's ridiculous," I snorted. "John Corry has used it there in his Broadway column. The *Times* will have to use the name when they review the show."

"Give me credit for having pointed that out," she said. "None—I repeat, *none*—of the New York anchor stations for the three television networks will consent to use *whorehouse.* ABC-

TV might—just *might*—permit us to show the title visually, but not speak it."

"Well," I said, in a misguided attempt at levity, "there goes the blind-folks trade."

"My only hope," Stevie said, "is the independent station here. Metromedia. If it comes around, perhaps that may influence the others. I've also thought of capitalizing on our misfortune, as best I can, by feeding the gossip columnists stories of our ads being rejected."

"Good idea. How about radio?"

"Radio is iffy and spotty. Some will, some won't, some are waffling."

"This is the silliest godamn thing, Stevie! It's 1978, not 1789."

"Twenty years ago," Stevie Phillips said, "when this theatre put up a marquee advertising *'Tis Pity She's a Whore,* which is a seventeenth-century play, there were such demonstrations in this neighborhood that the theatre's management changed *Whore* to *Blank.* Only twenty years ago."

"God bless America," I said. "All these uptight bastards are affirming the moral of our show. If we have one left."

Stevie got to the gossip columnists. Liz Smith in the *Daily News,* Diane Judge and Earl Wilson in the *New York Post,* and Nathan Fain in the short-lived and now defunct tabloid *Tribune* ridiculed television for its timidity. They did not, however, mention the sister *New York Times*—newspaper folks stick together like the proverbial thieves. All that this publicity seemed to do was to excite Stevie's superiors in a way that wasn't helpful. Every time an airplane landed from the West Coast, it seemed, here came some crusading Universal executive to predict disaster unless we cleaned up our title. Though I had originally dashed off the title because I couldn't think of a good one, I now became convinced that only after much thought, prayer, and pain had I conceived the most valuable title in history.

Fixing each new Universal crusader with my meanest beer-joint glare, I would snarl, "Are *you* willing to be the guy who throws away a million-dollar title? Would *you* like to tell that to Lew Wasserman face to face?" Invoking Lew Wasserman's name was much the same as invoking God's at the Pearly Gates, Lew being the stud duck of the parent Music Corporation of America, which is only about twice as rich as Japan, Italy, West Germany, Albania, Ohio, and Wyoming combined.

This ploy stopped the timid cold and visibly slowed the bold. To the waverers I said, "Go ahead. Go tell Lew Wasserman that you, *personally,* want to scrap a million-dollar title he owns and has paid for. Then come back and tell me what Lew said." Then I would grin, evilly, like a Pancho Villa *pistolero.* If this act implied that perhaps I knew something the crusader did not, or that perhaps my old buddy "Lew" met me for drinks each night following rehearsal, so be it—never mind that I had not, at that point, met Lew Wasserman or that when I would eventually encounter him in an elevator, while dressed like a buffalo hunter and weaving in invisible breezes, he shied away as if from a pox-carrier. At any rate, no one returned from such a mission to good old "Lew." This leads to the assumption that no such mission was risked.

Shortly, Metromedia Television decided to accept our ads. The three network anchor stations reluctantly followed suit, though two of them originally consented to use the dread word *whorehouse* only visually. The *Village Voice, Daily News, New York Post,* and any number of trade or neighborhood papers accepted our promotionals; the good gray *New York Times* held out. There are those in Gotham, especially in show business, who believe that should Manhattan be leveled by an earthquake, it wouldn't count in the standings unless the *New York Times* took notice. (Among those who believe this are certain *Times*men themselves. When I finally had finished my accursed Baker book, it astonished me by making the best-seller lists of *Time, Publishers Weekly, The Washington Post, Los Angeles Times,* and other publications. My agent suggested to Herbert Mitgang that I might be worth a squib in the *N.Y.T.*'s Sunday Book Review section as the only writer who simultaneously had a best-seller and a Broadway hit. Mr. Mitgang said I failed to qualify because I had not made the *New York Times'* best-seller list. "How could he?" my agent not unreasonably asked. "*The New York Times* was out on strike then!" Didn't make any difference. the *Times*man said.) Anyhow, jitters prevailed in Universal's countinghouse until the Gray Lady of Times Square herself capitulated, about ten days before we opened.

* *

Rumors reached me that Pete Masterson was considering taking the song "Bus from Amarillo" away from Amber (Pamela Blair) and giving it to Mona (Carlin Glynn). This disturbed me. I thought the song one of the better numbers in Carol Hall's score—had it been properly named "One-way Ticket to Nowhere," I am convinced it might have become a hit—and I was uncertain whether Carlin Glynn could handle it. It was a ballad, tender and haunting, different from anything Carlin had attempted.

At that point, I thought Carlin had regressed as a singer. Perhaps she had been affected by the fights, confusions, and general chaos attending so much of our rehearsal period. Living at home with Pete, himself under tremendous pressures, she certainly had to be aware of each dispute, uncertainty, or controversial decision involving him. Obviously, as the leading lady of a big musical with Broadway hopes, she had first-time butterflies of her own. I thought she appeared much less confident than at Actors Studio, and I didn't think it wise to subject her to more pressures by assigning a song that might give her difficulty. For once, Carol Hall and I were in agreement.

I sought out Masterson to make a gingerly inquiry as to whether the "Bus from Amarillo" rumor was valid.

"Yeah," he said. "See, that song tells how a certain type of young woman could slide into prostitution. In a way, you could say it's the show's theme song. I think the madam of the whorehouse should sing it, not just one of her girls."

"Pete, Pam Blair's doing a fine job with that song. I don't think it's fair to take it away from her."

"Nothing against Pam," he said. "The song's just been put in the mouth of the wrong character."

"You didn't think that at Actors Studio."

I saw the warning signal: a slow creep of red into Masterson's face. "I think it now," he snapped.

"Pete, Carlin already has—what?—two big solo numbers and a duet with Jewel. With all the lines she has, I think that's burden enough."

"Carlin can carry it," he said. "You always seem to be downgrading her. Listen, if I had to put my money on the one person in the cast who'll come through in the clutch, I'd bet on Carlin."

"I understand that, Pete. She's your wife—"

"Goddammit," he shouted, flushing the color of a fire engine, "that has nothing to do with it! I'm looking at Carlin from a professional standpoint. And I'm getting damn tired of you bastards saying 'She's Pete's wife' every time I make a decision about her. She's also a hell of an actress, goddammit! That girl is carrying this show on her back and you people don't appreciate it."

"Now hold it, Pete. I appreciate Carlin's talents but she's not out there alone or unarmed. We stuck some pretty good lines in her mouth, you know. I don't want to hear that she's carrying the whole show. She shouldn't have to carry it—that's my point! Why load her up with more?"

"If the codirectors think she should have that song," he said, "she'll damn sure sing it." He turned and walked back to a group of actors.

For the next few days Masterson and I tangled over everything but politics and the end result of infant baptism: Clint Allmon's barking, snarling, and growling as the "watchdog man"; that hated freak-scene number; more cuts in the book. When not standing toe-to-toe shouting, we rarely spoke. I began to avoid Carlin and nodded to her only in passing. One afternoon when Pete and Carlin's three children—Lexie, Mary Stewart, and Peter—visited rehearsal, I fancied that even these small Mastersons looked at me with gimlet eyes.

That evening, as Masterson started out of the theatre with his family, I beckoned him aside. He quickly said a word or two to Carlin; she and the children left the theatre. Masterson and I stood in the back of the house where, in about a week, we were scheduled to pace nervously on opening night.

"I guess it's too late to do any good," I said, "but for the record I want you to know you haven't done one goddamn thing you promised me."

Masterson looked at me with cold, flat eyes. I read them as saying he was not concerned with how I felt, though his lips said something else: "I'm sorry you feel that way. I just wish I knew why you do."

"*Oh, fuck that!* You know goddamned well what I'm talking about! You've frozen me out of decisions, you've excluded my participation, you've gone behind my back making changes."

"If you can give me specifics," he said, "maybe I can understand what you're so upset about."

I was so full of anger I became inarticulate. I issued a choked stream of profanity as all of our disputes and differences flashed through my head like a movie running at high speed. "Piss on it," I managed. "You haven't listened to a word I've said since February, and you damn well know it." I stomped away in such a murderous rage I literally feared a stroke.

That evening, talking to Barbara in Washington, I said, "I have never so misjudged a guy in my life. I really *believed* that bastard's Goody Two-Shoes act! Now it makes me feel foolish. But I'll tell you one thing: I'll never work with him again."

# CHAPTER 10

In early April, with about a week remaining before our scheduled opening, New York gossip columnists and theatre writers began to print a spate of items saying that *Whorehouse* was "in trouble." These reports made Stevie Phillips nervous: she knew the deadly effect such words might have on advance ticket sales, and that they might make it easier for critics to come down on the negative side, should they find our show marginal. As for me, such items almost restored my faith in the accuracy and integrity of newspapers. For the truth, dear hearts, is that we were in more trouble than a pregnant teenager.

The "talent team" held a tense meeting with our producer. The message was blunt: we can't come close to delivering a decent show by April 9th; we need more time.

Although this distress call could not have surprised Stevie Phillips, she looked as if we had collectively kicked her lapdog. "How much time?"

We gazed at the ceiling, popped our knuckles, hemmed and

hawed. Tommy Tune finally said, "I'd say a week. Yes, a week should do it."

"Do you know what a week will cost?" Stevie said, looking ill. We ducked our heads in guilt and shame. "Fifty thousand dollars," she informed us. "And we're already over budget by about that amount."

"What's the difference in losing three hundred and fifty thousand or four hundred thousand?" asked I, who of course did not have six bits to call his own, and surely would go to debtors' prison if his creditors could locate him. I had taken to marking "Unknown at this address" on any envelope with a window in it and dropping it into the handiest mailbox. I wanted to ask Lawyer Blaine whether this might be breaking the law, but feared to shake her belief in my supposed fiscal integrity.

"What's the *difference?*" Stevie asked. "Fifty thousand dollars is the difference."

"Stevie," I said, "if we go under now, we're all ruined anyhow. Think of this new fifty thou as a final, desperate roll of the dice. If we don't make our point"—a shrug—"then we all walk home from Las Vegas, so to speak."

Stevie sighed. "They're already very skeptical in California. And if we postpone our opening by a week there will be more bad publicity."

"All that may be true," Pete said, "but if we have to open April ninth, forget it. We're dead. Another week's work and we've got a good shot."

Stevie sat twisting her fingers and possibly thinking on suicide. "What can I tell California we will deliver on April sixteenth that we can't deliver on April ninth?"

"Well, hell . . . the whole thing," Masterson said. "We're making headway. We've compressed the thing, we've cut the running time down to—oh, some. We're still working on that. We've got to decide about a few scenes, what to cut and what to keep. We need to smooth out a couple dance numbers. It's—hell, you know, just a general tightening and screwing down."

We smoked, drank tepid coffee, and drummed our fingers while our producer decided our fate—or as much of it as she could control. Ultimately she tried a smile and said, "I'm going to recommend it to California. I believed in this show's potential when

I first saw it, I believe in it now, and I believe you people can do the job." I wanted to ask what had transpired to make her believe such foolishness, but held my tongue. "Let me go to the telephone," she said. We waited in the concessions lobby of the Entermedia, a bunch of strangers who had nothing to say to each other, until Stevie returned. "Jennings Lang is flying in today," she said. "He wants to see a run-through tonight. Tomorrow he'll give us a decision. That's the best I can do."

I didn't go to that night's run-through. I was exhausted and felt I might better my health by getting drunk. This theory proved, the following morning, not to have been entirely accurate, though several times during the night in question I had congratulated myself on my prognosis and successful treatment. Indeed, I recall I was so much improved at one point that I forced a one-hundred-dollar loan on another impecunious writer, who had been singing of how the wolf was at his door. One of whiskey's more marvelous qualities is that it somehow always makes me feel rich.

Stevie Phillips came to the Entermedia Theatre at midmorning. Tommy Tune stopped whatever dance number was being worked on, and we all gathered with the producer at the back of the house.

"Jennings Lang wants to talk with the talent," Stevie said. "We're all to meet him uptown for lunch."

"Can't he come down here?" Pete asked.

"Oh, I don't know. He's accustomed to people coming to him."

"If we have to put on coats and neckties and cab halfway across the city," Pete said, "we'll lose half the afternoon. I don't think he'd want that."

"Right," I said. "Besides, we might gain the psychological edge if we make the sumbitch come to us."

"Don't start playing power games, Larry," Stevie said. She next fretted that the neighborhood had no restaurant grand enough to feed the Universal bigwig. "The Second Avenue Deli," Pete said. "Hell, it's as good or better than the Stage Deli. And all the show-biz biggies eat there."

All I knew about Jennings Lang, other than that he obviously was a power with a hand on the purse strings, was that years earlier he'd been shot in a parking lot by a man who was married to, had been married to, or was about to marry the actress Joan Bennett. As we waited in front of the Entermedia for Lang to arrive I said, "Say, Stevie, what was that sumbitch's name that shot Jennings Lang over Joan Bennett? Was he married to her then, or what?"

"Oh, my God!" Stevie said, paling. "Don't you *dare* bring that up to him!"

"I always wondered what it felt like to get shot," I said, keeping a sober face.

"You'll find out if you even *hint* at that," my producer promised.

Lang's cab stopped in front of the Entermedia. Someone sprang forward like a doorman and flung open the door. I saw a big, bulky man in a war correspondent's raincoat crouched awkwardly in midexit from the cab.

On impulse I shouted, "Don't step in that dogshit, Jennings!" and merrily roared as he performed a desperate midair dance. Stevie Phillips threw me a totally unbelieving look that said, *I've thought all along you were a bit tilted and now I have evidence you are mad-dog crazy.* I stepped past the official greeting committee, grabbed Lang's hand, sang out my name, and said, "Come on, Jennings, let's go get a beer to celebrate that fifty thou you're gonna lay on us. Got it in that satchel?" Jennings Lang laughed heartily, shook hands all around, and we marched in a group to the Second Avenue Deli.

My theory, which very well may have been all wet, was that we should not appear to be beaten, imploring, or obsequious. Men of power grow accustomed to ass-kissery, and develop a contempt for those who practice it, even if they may secretly enjoy their roles as kissees. I wanted to keep everything loose and a little crazy so that Lang wouldn't be able to fall back on well-conditioned reflexes. If we could keep him slightly off balance, I felt we might have a slight edge; it somehow might make it more difficult for Lang to issue an automatic "No." To this moment I don't know whether that theory was correct. Events might—probably would—have turned out as they did in any case. However, such was my mind-set at the time, which accounts for conduct my colleagues thought slightly insane.

Lang wanted to talk about the run-through he had seen the

previous night. He felt the café scene and the sheriff's scene said the same things: "They even have the same people in them." I shot Stevie Phillips a murderous look; the wording was the same as her recent memo on the subject.

"You're wrong and maybe crazy," I said, as Peter Masterson kicked me under the table.

"Oh?" Lang said, surprised.

"The same people are in those two scenes for a reason," I lectured. "In the café scene, in Act One, the mayor and the townspeople are initially upset over the sheriff's handling of the Chicken Ranch—*but* he manages to joke and jolly them out of it. They think perhaps the sheriff, the whorehouse, and they themselves can survive the storm. In the sheriff's office scene—Act Two, now—the mayor, the sheriff, and the others are beside themselves. *That* scene clearly says the situation has deteriorated beyond hope, that all is lost. Both of those scenes are necessary to show the progression of the central crisis, to show the changing attitudes of the townspeople, and to signal to the audience—in the second case—that the end is near." Lang had nodded his head throughout my explanation. I decided to try to nail it down. "Did you count the laugh lines in each of those scenes?"

"Ah, no," he said. "No, I didn't."

"I know from Actors Studio," I said—making up the numbers—"there are exactly thirteen laugh lines in each of those scenes. That, too, was a matter of careful planning." *You a lying sumbitch,* my inner voice said, *but you purty good at it.*

"Oh, they're good scenes," Lang assured us.

"They are very, very carefully counterweighted," I said, inventing the jargon as I went along, "and I presume *most* theatre people would understand and applaud that. I know of no two scenes that have been more carefully calibrated, counterweighted, and synched than those scenes, Jennings."

"I had in mind the overall length problem," Lang said.

"We're aware of that," Peter Masterson said. He went on to enumerate the scenes under discussion for cuts while Lang nodded and chewed roast beef. The conversation back-and-forthed for about a half hour: Carol talked music, Tommy talked dance, Stevie played the role of the host of a panel show. When the talk began to wind down I said, "Jennings, you the stud duck in this deal? Have you got authority to say yes or no or do you have to check with somebody else we'll have to take to lunch?" Masterson kicked me again; I kicked him back.

Lang said, ah, yes, he would need to make one call to California. After we sat in silence for a spell I said, "Stevie, goddammit, give the man a dime!" Jennings Lang burst into laughter, in which we all gratefully joined.

"Keep your fingers crossed," Stevie whispered as Lang went to a pay telephone across the room. "I didn't sleep a wink last night."

We sat tensely while, across the room, the Universal executive droned on and on. "What the hell is he doing?" I asked. "Telling them the whole plot?"

"*Shhhh!*" Stevie said.

"Larry, sometimes I think you have a death wish," Carol Hall said. I stuck my tongue out at her, just as Lang returned to our table. "The money's yours," he said.

There followed a smattering of applause and happy babble. On the sidewalk we shook our benefactor's hand and hailed him a cab. Walking back in the group to the Entermedia, Masterson and I caught each other's eyes and exchanged real grins for the first time in days. "Sorry I kicked you," he said, "but I thought you were blowing it for sure."

"Come on, Pete," I said with a grin, "you've been wanting to kick me for days."

We did not remain a happy band of brothers. Carol and Pete soon had a fierce encounter over his plan to shift "Bus from Amarillo" to Carlin Glynn. I walked up near the end of the dispute and butted in to side with Carol—much, I think, to her surprise. Pete reluctantly agreed to permit Pam Blair to keep the song during the early shows we would play as previews to paying audiences. But he warned, "Even if Pam knocks 'em out—and she may, she's damn good; hell, I hired her, didn't I?—that still won't change my belief the damn song ought to be sung by the madam."

Though united on that issue, Carol and I soon boxed a few spirited rounds because I had resurrected my assault on "Two

Blocks from the Capitol Building." This was after Masterson had told me that either that song or a dialogue scene between Shy and Leroy Sliney must go. One or the other.

As that comment had been made shortly after an acrimonious exchange about whether or not Carlin would get the "Bus from Amarillo" number, I saw it as blackmail.

"Don't think I'm oblivious to what you're doing," I said.

"Tell me and we'll both know," Pete said, apparently surprised.

"You're telling me that unless your wife gets to sing that song, my son won't get to play his big scene as an actor in the bit with Shy."

"Look, dammit, I really *like* that Shy-Leroy scene! It says something! It's sweet, too, and we don't have much sweetness in this show. I want to keep it if we can. But all I'm telling you is we've got to cut *something*! For Christ's sake, man, we're still running three hours! So either the 'Capitol Building' number goes or the Shy-Leroy scene goes. That's all in the world I'm saying!"

Unless mercilessly pressured, I felt, Masterson would choose to retain the freak scene simply because it had been his concept. So I set out with a vengeance to kill it, attempting to enlist Stevie Phillips on my side. When Carol Hall learned of this she had twin reasons for fresh anger: not only was I trying to kill another of her songs, but also her friend Marta Sanders was the star soloist in that number and without it would be reduced to playing only a minor whore.

Brad's presence in the Shy-Leroy scene made it precious to me, no doubt about it. That personal consideration aside, however, I felt my book had been so chopped and mutilated to make way for songs and dances that the Shy-Leroy scene was needed to restore some semblance of balance.

In that scene, Leroy has taken Shy to a country dance on her night off. As they walk up the lane to the Chicken Ranch afterward, bantering, he—obviously smitten—attempts to kiss her. Shy turns her face away. The young man is put off by this rejection. He lights a cigarette and sulks while she comments on the night, the stars; prattles on about when she was a little girl. Then:

LEROY: You mind if I ask you somethin'?

SHY: A boy can get in trouble asking a girl the wrong question. *(She sees that he is serious.)* Well . . . okay. Sure.

LEROY: Well—*dang it,* how come you to go to work out here?

SHY: Did you ever pick cotton?

LEROY *(shaking his head)*: Uh, naw.

SHY: You walk on your knees till they're rubbed raw. When you can't stand that no more you bend over till your back breaks. Then you get on your knees again. *(A beat)* And hot? Sweet Jesus! And all the time, that cotton sack is getting heavier and heavier and the strap cuts into your shoulder like it's hungry for bone.

*(Leroy looks at her, nodding; we think he understands more than he has before.)*

SHY: No matter what you might think about me . . . it does beat pickin' cotton.

*(He reaches for her hand. BLACKOUT.)*

I thought that scene might bring home to those who had never done mule work something of the desperation to be found in a hardscrabble life. I believed it might hint at how certain young women could slide into a life of prostitution. And certainly I believed the scene more representative of our show than the hated freak scene.

"If I only win one fight," I told Barbara, "this is the one I guarantee you I'll win. I'll kill that freak-show scene if I have to resort to assassination."

Next came a squabble about publicity, and the unequal division thereof. Carol Hall long had fumed that I received more attention in the press than did my collaborators: "It is *not* 'Larry King's musical,' " she said again and again.

Though Pete Masterson never said anything directly, I was amused to find letters in the *Texas Monthly* and the *Texas Observer*—signed by his friends—making similar protests. I thought I knew enough about ego, vanity, and human nature to conclude that Pete was not entirely unaware such letters were being posted. "Look," I ultimately said to my collaborators, "I haven't hired a publicity agent. I've worked in the print medium most of my adult life. A lot of my friends are newspaper and magazine people. They know me, they don't know you. It's only natural they come to me, or call me, when they're writing about our project." My speech drew no applause.

Carol Hall was incensed by some of my quotes. Typical was one in *The New York Times:* "If somebody on stage is breathing hard, I prefer for it to be because of internal turmoil rather than because they've just sung and hoofed an uphill swordfight." Her response: "It's ridiculous for you to knock musicals! I'm sick and tired of reading how you can't stand singing and dancing. That's undermining our show!"

I didn't agree. On any given day, any number of dreamers in New York are hustling a show, a book, a drama, a dance recital—whatever—in a very competitive market. I figured that by advertising my ignorance of musicals and by exaggerating my natural antipathy for them, I might capture newspaper ink and air time that otherwise might not be available. And that could do nothing, as I saw it, but call attention to *Whorehouse.* So I went on "grabbing the glory," as others saw it. Perhaps, had I troubled to explain my reasoning, this would not have been a point of irritation. I did not, however. Neither, apparently, did Stevie Phillips explain that she selected me for most TV and radio interviews because my collaborators were busier in rehearsals than I.

Miss Edna proved a distinct disappointment as a publicity vehicle. Oh, to be sure, she faithfully showed up for interviews. But she came on so staid and proper one might have thought she was running for Congress or auditioning to teach Sunday school. Not once did she unleash a colorful expression or opinion that would have guaranteed above-average newspaper or television exposure. In a typical interview she talked about her sweet old mama, how much she liked New York, and how being in *Whorehouse* reminded her of when she had performed in "school and church plays" as a child. Dullsville.

I knew Edna was capable of more candid and colorful interviews—she'd done well while hostessing the Dallas restaurant when newsmen came around—and so I coaxed her to insert a little more piss and vinegar into her press sessions. Apparently, however, the small-town madam thirsted for respectability in the big city: "I don't want everbody thinking I'm some kind of freak or criminal." Soon the press was staying away from Miss Edna in droves.

A day or so before we would open to preview audiences, however, Miss Edna threatened to break the publicity barriers. My son sought me out wild-eyed and excited: "Dad! Dad! Miss Edna's throwing a fit backstage!"

"What the hell is it about this time?"

"Everything!" Brad said. "She's mad at the way Carlin is playing her. She's upset because she doesn't have any lines. She says she's being ignored and just kinda pissed on in general. You know what she's threatening?"

"To quit, I hope."

"No! She says on opening night, or maybe the night of the first preview, when she's pushed out on stage in that wheelchair? Well, she's gonna rip off all her clothes, go down to the stage mikes at the footlights, and denounce the whole show as a fake! Says she's gonna tell the audience the Chicken Ranch wasn't anything like the show shows it!"

I broke into loud guffaws; Brad looked at me as if perhaps I'd finally cracked under pressure. "Keep your ear to the ground, Brad," I said. "We need to know the exact night—so we can have the gossip columnists and photographers in here ass deep!"

Alas, Miss Edna remained publicly docile.

We originally had been scheduled to play our first preview performance on March 31st. That, too, had been pushed back, along with our official opening. We couldn't stall much longer, however. We were in early April and the time to show our wares was all too rapidly approaching.

Preview performances serve a number of purposes. They acclimate the players to audience reaction and responses, permitting them to make early boo-boos or shake off the worst of their jitters before the stakes are high. They permit the director, producer, and author to see what works and what fails to work under battlefield conditions—or, at bottom, what *might* work and what is simply impossible. In short, previews are a vital help in making decisions to tune, prune, or tighten a show. Scenes that look good on paper—for instance, our original Aggie scene at Actors Studio—may be revealed as flat, lifeless, or hopelessly convoluted once exposed to an audience. Conversely, a scene that has limped along during rehearsals and has all but been designated for the scrap heap may mysteriously and magically strike a spark with the audience. Another advantage of previews is that critics are not present to whittle on dreams, carve on gizzards, and otherwise pass on harsh judgments. Theoretically anyway, the bugs and kinks can be eliminated before these cultural advisors to the public come running with their sharp pencils or knives.

Though previews are afforded a certain protection—no critics, an audience mindful that the show is still in a formative stage—they are not wholly without risks. Oh, no. Let a show drift or plod, without a certain degree of discipline or promise, let it appear a shade too muddled or chaotic, and you may be certain that word somehow will get around. The gossip columnists will sing of disaster, somebody telephones Aunt Matilda to tell her not to bother coming in from Jersey for the matinee, Alex Cohen chortles to David Merrick that he hears it's a piece of shit, Frank Rich of *The New York Times,* Clive Barnes of the *New York Post,* and Douglas Watt of the *Daily News* feel the future in their critical bones before they have their morning coffee; it won't be twenty-four hours until the show's failure is being celebrated in the Australian outback—I have seen it happen to *King of Hearts, Got Tu Go Disco, Charlie and Algernon,* any number of turkeys that once had high hopes of being the next *My Fair Lady.* Once the bad word goes out, box-office people kill idle time by playing cards with tickets never to be sold. Everyone from the producer down to the smallest walk-on player is likely to panic, ripping and tearing at the show and trying to put it together again. But, as was the case when Humpty-Dumpty took his great fall, it can't be done by all the king's horses or men. Result: another show shot down so quickly that decent numbers failed to see it crash.

On the eve of our first Off Broadway preview, I stayed away from the theatre during a dress rehearsal to which friends and relatives of the cast and company had been invited. Brad was in the show, so I had my apartment to myself. My purpose was to try to get some distance, some perspective on our efforts, and to assay where we stood. I honestly didn't know if we had a chance to eclipse the run of *Damn Yankees,* or might fold after three performances, or might land somewhere in the nervous middle ground. No one ever knows for certain, of course; else millions would not be lost each season in the theatre. I had reached a point, however, where I didn't have the slightest clue, suspicion, or inkling. This was a new experience: in politics I never had been truly surprised by the results of any election I was involved in; with experience, I could tell you almost to the critic or publication how each of my books would be received; on meeting a desirable lady I had not often guessed wrong as to how the adventure might turn out. For *Whorehouse,* however, I now had no feel. Oh, certainly, there had been moments when I felt we couldn't miss. There had been many more when my gut told me we were on the way to Flopsville in a fast wagon. But these were fleeting impressions, usually influenced by sweet intoxication on the one hand and bone-deep fatigue on the other.

I decided I would approach my private evaluation in much the manner Nick the Greek makes his pro football selections: by examining each component of the show. As Nick the Greek did, I would ask—in effect—how is our kicking game, special teams play, pass defense, running game? In order to insure against unreasonable euphoria, I mixed my Scotch and waters at half strength or less and vowed to imbibe slowly. Here is what I found:

CHOREOGRAPHY: Tommy Tune had worked a miracle in cleaning up our ragged, hopeless Aggie scene. He began with the Aggie footballers celebrating in their locker room after the Thanksgiving victory over the Texas Longhorns. Dressed in football uniforms and cowboy boots, they began a dance and song—"The Aggie Song," celebrating how they intended to break training at the Chicken Ranch—and as the number progressed they changed, onstage, into cowboy clothes. Then came a rollicking, boot-stomping hoedown dance, featuring a spectacular solo bit by Tom Cashin. The song continued, bringing the Aggies closer and closer to the Chicken Ranch in its lyrics; the long number ended in a rousing, hand-clapping finale. *Best number in the show,* I penned.

"The Angelette March," featuring a parody on halftime drill teams, was almost as good. Tune had devised a number featuring eight dancers wearing blond wigs and blank smiles, each strapped to two dummies costumed and painted to look exactly like the real girls; the breasts and buttocks of the dummies were well-filled red balloons.

The whore-girls' dance to "Twenty-four Hours of Loving," sung by the energetic Delores Hall as Jewel, was less spectacular but certainly not bad. "Two Blocks from the Capitol Building" I so detested—both concept and music—that I didn't really know or care how the dancing was. Tune's first two numbers, however, were so good and unusual we probably didn't need to worry about the rest. Score the choreography good-to-excellent. Tardily, I wished we had more of it.

MUSICAL SCORE: I very much liked "Twenty Fans," "No Lies," "Hard-Candy Christmas," "Bus from Amarillo," and "The Aggie Song." Though I was not wild about "Twenty-four Hours of Loving," I figured Delores Hall would sell it well; much the same might be said of Susan Mansur and her solo, "Doatsey Mae." I was lukewarm toward "Girl, You're a Woman" and "Good Old Girl." These I rated only slightly ahead of what I thought to be mediocre entries: "Pissant Country Place," "The Watchdog Theme," "Texas Has a Whorehouse in It," and "The Sidestep." As for "Two Blocks from the Capitol Building," Carol Hall could stick it up her nose.

On balance, using a win/tie/lose formula, as in football, I saw a record of five wins, two ties, and seven losses. Not a record to land a team in the playoffs. *Final verdict:* spotty. Could have a few good moments, but don't expect the audience to leave the theatre whistling and humming many new hits. In time, I would more generously judge "Good Old Girl," "Doatsey Mae," and "The Sidestep."

BOOK: Could be an unmitigated disaster. It had been so chopped and fragmented, I wondered if it would make sense to the audience. As I had long feared, the story now seemed to exist as a clothesline upon which to hang songs and dances. The script contained what I felt were many funny lines—but the humor was rough and chock full of colloquialisms; the language was profane. I couldn't predict how a New York audience would receive a Texas approach. If the humor worked pretty well, we might survive. If it failed, it would fail spectacularly.

As to book specifics, the opening scene with Mona and her girls—originally intended to reveal the hard facts of whorehouse life—had, with the aid of "Pissant Country Place," turned into a cutesy-poo bit of fluff that made me wince each time I saw it. The confrontation between Mona and her girls against a mob demanding that the whorehouse be closed had read well but played terribly; only a good song, "No Lies," saved the scene. I was satisfied only with the café scene, the sheriff's office scene, and the final good-bye scene between Mona and Ed Earl. I wrote myself a painful note: *Weakest part of the show.*

LEADING PLAYERS: Henderson Forsythe, Carlin Glynn, and Joan Ellis I expected to be excellent in their acting. Forsythe probably would be passable doing his lone song. The big question mark was Carlin's singing. If she came through, we might—just *might*—overcome our other weaknesses. If she faltered as a vocalist or was no better than mediocre, it could be bye-bye *Whorehouse* very early. In my bones, I felt that Carlin would come through. But who knew?

OTHER PRINCIPALS: I expected strong performances from Susan Mansur (Doatsey Mae), Delores Hall (Jewel), Pamela Blair (Amber), Jay Garner (Governor of Texas and C. J. Scruggs), and J. Frank Lucas (Mayor Poindexter and Senator Wingwoah). Clint Allmon's singing as Melvin P. Thorpe was worrisome and, indeed, I still hated the cartoon concept—all that barking and growling—Pete Masterson had superimposed. The character, I felt, might fall flat and the fault would lie in the direction. The role, the concept, and the player needed to be stronger than I felt them to be.

REMAINDER OF CAST: Among the whores, I particularly liked the work of Becky Gelke (Ruby Rae) and Louise Quick-Bowen (Ginger). Don Crabtree did good work as the newspaper editor, Edsel. The Aggie dancers were superb. The remainder of the players I rated fair to mediocre, except for a couple of young, inexperienced whores, whom I rated poor because they delivered lines without much style and had trouble projecting. Overall, however, a good cast which should supply some excellent-to-superlative individual moments.

PACE: After a brisk and funny prologue featuring "Twenty Fans," the show got off to a slow start. Scenes were too talky, too cutesy; the mediocre songs seemed to be bunched, as if we had decided to get them out of the way as quickly as possible. One of them, "Pissant," went on interminably, lasting only thirty seconds short of infinity. Not much happened, really, until a good half hour into the show, when Delores Hall began waking up witnesses with "Twenty-four Hours of Loving." Maybe we should tie patrons to their seats during the first half hour and send the ushers scuttling up and down the aisles with assurances that things were due to get better. After that slow beginning, I felt, momentum gathered all the way to the first-act curtain and we finished strong. (Masterson and I long had disagreed about the opening pace: he wanted to hit them fast with a strong prologue, relax the pace, and then slowly build to a first-act climax.)

The second act was shorter and better paced. In my opinion, two of our three strong dialogue scenes were in it, and a couple of the better songs ("No Lies" and "Hard-Candy Christmas"); and I truly liked the slow-motion tableau of the politicians and Melvin Thorpe that Masterson had fashioned for the curtain, roughly along the lines of the ending I had thought of in Nantucket so long ago. Tommy Tune had solved the problem of a sad ending by inventing a foot-stomping, hat-waving, gun-shooting, lariat-twirling, exhilarating finale featuring the entire cast during the curtain call.

PERSONAL DISLIKES AND DISAPPOINTMENTS: I was astonished, after all the snorting and hell-raising and cursing I had done, to find that I now objected to very little. Oh, the cut book bugged me, "Two Blocks" remained an irritant, as did the barking and growling. But what the hell had I been fighting mad at for so long? My minor disappointments were that Henderson Forsythe still stubbornly refused to say "nigger" and occasionally camped it up a bit as Sheriff Ed Earl Dodd, using more "musical comedy" techniques than he'd employed during his fine performances at Actors Studio; while these might please the audience, I felt he had diminished the menace I had been careful to write into the character.

"By God," I mumbled, looking down on the winos and bag ladies of Second Avenue, "we might have a shot at this thing!" I drank a couple of strong ones to that, and then three or four more, by which time the magic potion had done its work: now I knew we would run longer than *Fiddler on the Roof* and *Life with Father* added up and multiplied by *Oklahoma!* I was on the verge of calling friends to see if they needed to borrow money when Brad, returning from the dress rehearsal, pushed into the apartment with his head on his chest. He darted a furtive look from under his western hat as if he'd been caught at sodomy with a cow.

"What's the matter?" I asked.

"*Every*-goddamn-thing," he snorted. "Nothing went right. People blew lines and fell down and sang off key. Shit, Dad, it was embarrassing! Nobody laughed at the lines except when they were not supposed to." He grabbed a beer in each hand and escaped, slamming the bedroom door.

I medicated myself with additional doses of Cutty Sark and tumbled to bed.

The morning of our first preview we sat in the basement lobby of the Entermedia with faces longer than a Baptist prayer: Stevie Phillips, Tommy Tune, Pete Masterson, Carol Hall, your present hero. Masterson was attempting to refurbish and polish the history of the night before.

"I didn't think it was so bad for a dress rehearsal," he said. "I told the cast not to exert themselves, to play it low key. Save something for tonight."

"I wish I'd known that beforehand," Stevie said. "I had a couple of people from California here. Frankly, I didn't know what to say to them."

"Dammit," Pete said, "a dress rehearsal is like the last practice before a football game. You don't scrimmage your team at full speed the night before the big game!"

"Negative, negative," Tommy Tune sighed in his wispy way. He fluttered his long hands. "I wish just once I could see a positive face on some of you people."

"We've got to cut this show," Stevie said.

"We *will* cut it, Stevie," Masterson said. "For God's sake, you don't cut a show until you've seen it play several times before a paying audience. That's what previews are for!"

"I'm trying to be realistic," Stevie said. "Do you know how much our advance sales have totaled to date?"

A long silence.

"Four hundred dollars," she said. "A big, fat four hundred dollars."

"Ah, you mean for tonight?" I asked.

"No, my dear. That is for *tonight and forever.* I have four hundred thousand dollars in this show. And right now in the box-office till we have a *total* of a big, fat four hundred dollars for advance sales."

"That much, huh?" I said.

"That much," Stevie said, trying a poor laugh. We sat and stared at each other.

"My God," I said. "I wonder what the record for that is? Money spent to advance tickets sold?"

"We've broken it, I'm sure," Stevie said.

"This is getting us *nowhere,*" Tommy Tune said.

"Shit, let's go get drunk," I said. "Let's take that big, fat four hundred dollars out of the box office and go tie one on. We ought to get something out of this fucking mess."

*"It is not a fucking mess,"* Tommy Tune said, with such force that for a moment the shoe was on the other foot: I thought he might strike me.

Tommy ought not to have hollered at me, my head hurting the way it was and my spirits being down there playing tag with my shoe soles. I flared at him: "Well, if you prove wrong, I want you and everybody else here to remember that we brought in a pretty damn good play from Actors Studio. And it's been tinkered with, danced on, sang at, barked and snarled at, chopped up, tricked up, and camped up until I can hardly recognize the goddamn thing! Look at your watches, goddammit, and remember the hour and the date. I want you bastards to know *for the record* exactly when it was that I told you you'd messed up my play!"

Tommy Tune jumped to his feet and rushed from the room.

First preview night. Half hour to curtain. I stand in front of the Entermedia Theatre, delighted beyond words. People are jamming the lobby. There is a line at the box office. Buses pull up—three, four—disgorging middle-aged people and older. Son of a gun!

I go inside, stand at the back of the house, and grin at strangers. Patty Newburger, Girl Friday to Stevie Phillips, approaches. I grab her and hug her a crusher; she reacts in some surprise. "Look at this crowd!" I babble. "Son of a bitch! Praise Jesus! We're gonna have a full house! All the Equity laws allow, anyhow!" (By definition, an Off Broadway play is one permitted, under union rules, to sell a maximum of 499 seats per performance.)

Patty Newburger looks at me as if perhaps I should be certified. I babble on. "Did you see those buses? Whole goddamn *busloads* of people coming to this sumbitch! Who said we wouldn't make it?"

"Larry," Patty says, "you mean you don't know?"

"What? Don't know what?"

She leans close and whispers, "Stevie has papered the house!"

I stare at her, not comprehending: "Say what?"

"She's papered the house! Given away tickets!"

*"Given away tickets?* Goddammit, why?"

*"Shhhh!"* Patty says, and whispers: "We can't let the show play to empty seats! The cast might crater. And word would get around we're not drawing."

"But . . . all those buses . . . ?"

"Hospitals. Old folks' homes. We made the tickets available. Freebies."

"Shit," I say, feeling foolish and empty. *"Shit!"*

## CHAPTER

# 11

Odd, but these years later I remember nothing at all about how our first couple of previews played; nor did I make any notes as to how they went. Brad says he has no recollection, either. This probably means that we felt the show was so-so; neither very good nor very bad. It was, I recall, much too long and soon we set about whittling it with a vengeance.

"Two Blocks from the Capitol Building" was among the early expendables, and while this met with my approval, there were consequences I had not reckoned with. The night the number was cut, I found myself at a bar holding the hand of a crushed Marta Sanders, Carol Hall's friend, who had invited a number of friends to opening night and now would have no solo to perform for them. I drank a lot of whiskey that night, but not enough to confess to Marta my aggressive villain's role in killing her big number. This encounter caused me to marvel anew at the hard knocks actors let themselves in for, and at their ability to bounce back—for, within a couple of days, Marta was of good cheer again and did a most professional job of playing her various minor roles.

Pamela Blair, too, took it on the chin. After she had performed "Bus from Amarillo" a half dozen times, the number was shifted to Carlin Glynn. (Carlin, by the way, made a bad prophet of me by having absolutely no trouble handling the number.) Brad and others in the cast told me that the first time or two Carlin sang the number, poor Pam sobbed in the wings. Before long she would leave the show because of that disappointment, for a lead role in the ill-fated *King of Hearts.*

There was dissatisfaction in my own household, when the Shy-Leroy Sliney scene was eliminated on the eve of our official opening. Son Brad was chagrined that his sister Cheryl would not see him in a significant acting role and would have to settle for watching her "little brother" sing and dance. Long afterward, Pete Masterson said: "I kept that scene through the last preview because I loved it and wanted everyone else to. I mean, it actually made me cry. I thought Joan and Brad did super jobs in it. But the audience—I don't know, the people sat on their hands or coughed or whispered or went to the rest rooms. So finally there was nothing to do but cut it."

None of the cuts, once one saw the hurt of the players involved, proved to be without personal pain. After my evening with Marta Sanders I told Barbara, "Funny how you can get your way about something after a long, bitter fight and still wind up feeling miserable."

Though Stevie Phillips continued to advertise the show heavily, patrons could not be accused of knocking down the Entermedia's doors. "I'm still spreading paper around," she admitted as we stood in the lobby of the theatre one morning about midway through the week of previews. "If tickets fail to start moving in three or four more days . . . well, what can I say?" We regarded each other glumly. I wandered away.

Later in the day Stevie would relate an incident—a vital incident, perhaps—that had occurred only moments after I left her. She had heard a girl in the box office speak to another person approximately as follows: "Ya wanta hear the nerve of some people, huh? You wanta hear? Awright, this woman just calls and says she's Jackie O's secretary. Ya know? *Yeah! Jackie O!* And she says ta me, she says, 'Mrs. Onassis would like two tickets for tomorrow night.' And I says to her, 'A pleasure,' ya know? *Then* she says to me, she says, 'Can we get them at half price?' Can ya *believe* it? So I says to her, 'No, we're not selling her tickets at half price.' And she says to me, 'Most shows send her comps.' Imagine!"

That, apparently, was when Stevie began screaming. She frantically telephoned her office with instructions that Mrs. Onassis should be located, apologies made, and two tickets offered, compliments of the house. This was quickly done. Stevie then telephoned Jeffrey Richards, handling the publicity for *Whorehouse,* and confided that Jackie Kennedy Onassis would be in the theatre the following night; this confidence, she directed, should be widely shared among media people: TV, radio, theatre editors, gossip columnists, photographers; any and all.

A decision was made not to inform the cast that Jackie O would be present. The purpose was to keep the news from Henderson Forsythe and Carlin Glynn because of the play's final scene: that long good-bye in which Sheriff Dodd filibusters Mona's recollections of JFK's inaugural speech and—more to the point—his meandering speech about what he'd been doing when John F. Kennedy was assassinated and how he'd "assled around" and missed the satisfaction of seeing Jack Ruby kill Lee Harvey Oswald.

I was nervously pacing at the rear of the house when Jackie O and her date came in, photographers shoving each other to get pictures, to which she graciously consented. Jeffrey Richards approached and asked me to have my picture made with her.

"No," I said.

"But the publicity—"

"No," I said.

Richards, not knowing me well, took my recalcitrancy for genuine modesty. He tried to bait the hook: "Don't you want to meet the woman?"

"I've met her," I said.

"Oh," he said, "then if you know her, all the more reason—"

"I didn't say I *know* her. I've *met* her. She's being bothered enough and I'm tired of you bothering me. Say no more." He went off, grumbling. It was true I might have felt an interloper in pushing my way into a picture, but the larger truth was that I couldn't face the lady, knowing what she was going to hear about her late husband's death. Oh, certainly, I knew that in the intervening fifteen years she had seen, heard, and probably read much worse—but I felt a bit shoddy about the deal, and didn't wish to face her.

As we approached the final scene, I wasn't sure I could stand the suspense of awaiting the reaction of Jackie Kennedy Onassis. Let *New York* magazine tell it from there:

> During the recent preview of . . . *The Best Little Whorehouse in Texas,* the drama moved from the stage to a member of the audience—Jacqueline Onassis. It happened during an exchange between a character named Ed Earl, a sheriff, and another named Miss Mona, the whorehouse madam. "But I recollect where I was when ol' Oswald shot him," Ed Earl said, and explained that he had been in the process of arresting several youngsters for stealing a goat. "I had just slapped the cuffs on them little peckerwoods and marched 'em in lockstep back to the car, when it come across the *po*-lice radio that old Kennedy had been shot, up in Dallas. I 'member it all clear as a bell. . . . Funny, but you don't forget certain thangs.' Afterward, Jackie told friends that the gasps from the audience, which had been well aware of her presence, were a source of consolation to her.

I, too, heard those gasps and saw one woman bolt from her seat to rush by me, crying. Friends in the house later told me that any number of people were crying. I did not look at Mrs. Onassis during that moment and have talked to no one who did. A few moments later, however, I was aware that Jacqueline Kennedy Onassis graciously rose to her feet to lead a standing ovation during the curtain call. *Now that's class,* I thought. *She's doing it for the audience as much as for the cast.* Mrs. Onassis passed me as she left the theatre, smiling, and I mumbled that we were glad to have had her.

The cast was all atwitter. Some players had spotted Jackie O in the theatre early on but—fortunately—had kept the news away from Henderson Forsythe. "I knew she was out there," Carlin Glynn admitted, "but I told everyone not to breathe a word to Hank. He had the tough lines, and I didn't want him to suffer that pressure."

As Brad and I shared a beer before bedtime he said, "Did you see the fight?"

"What fight?'

"The one about Mrs. Onassis."

"*What?*"

"You didn't see it? Yeah, it was at intermission. Somebody got angry at the photographers for bothering her and kicked or hit a couple of 'em."

"Oh, Christ," I said. "It wasn't bad enough the poor woman had to hear about her husband's brains being blown out. Somebody starts a fuckin' *fight* . . ."

The telephone woke me early the next morning. A former lady friend said, "Still up to your old tricks, I see."

"What?"

"Don't tell me you didn't arrange that fight over Jackie O!"

"How in hell did you hear about it?"

"Come on! Don't tell me you don't know it's all over the papers! What did that cost you?"

It was, indeed, all over the papers—and radio, and television. The *New York Post* ran a huge picture of Jackie and her escort, investment banker Skip Stein, with a headline in large type, "THE AUDIENCE RAN INTERFERENCE," and told readers to check Earl Wilson's column on page 22 for the details. The gossip columnist led with it:

> Jackie Onassis and escort Skip Stein innocently touched off a shoving-and-yelling battle between the audience and photographers when they went to a preview of the controversial musical, "The Best Little Whorehouse in Texas," at the Entermedia Theatre at 12th St. and 2nd Ave.
>
> "Leave Jackie and her boy friend alone or I'll jam my hand in your camera," one plump patron threatened, and proceeded to push the camera, while another customer, a young fellow, tried to get a stranglehold on *Post* photographer Robert Kalfus.
>
> "Throw the photographers out!" yelled some patrons upstairs.
>
> Jackie and her escort hadn't objected . . . in fact, she'd been very cooperative posing for them . . . and sat quietly when the yelling broke out.
>
> Jackie's visit to the theatre was a surprise and one scene in the

show (about efforts to close down a famous brothel) depicts a sheriff and madam affectionately discussing the good times of the Kennedy years.

The pushing and yelling ended without bloodshed when the show's publicist persuaded the photographers to leave.

The *Daily News* had a story and short comments by Liz Smith. Just about every outlet in the New York area used something—including the suburban papers, from whence spring all good blue-haired ladies who support matinees—except the dignified *New York Times*.

"Son of a bitch," I remarked to Brad, beaming. "Do you realize we couldn't have bought this coverage for a half million dollars?"

"How in hell did you miss all that?" he asked.

"I was out on the sidewalk," I said, "eavesdropping on the smokers to see what they thought of the show. But all they did was ask each other whether they'd seen Jackie."

When I got to the Entermedia that night, I was momentarily startled to see a long line at the box office and people shelling out cash. No freebies, these. *Of course! Jackie! Lord love her!* One of the guys in the box office beckoned me over. "We're sold out for tonight," he said with a grin, "and booking heavy for the next two weeks. These phones just won't stop ringing!"

On opening my eyes I thought, *This is it! Opening night!* Monday, April 17, 1978. "This is the one we've been waiting for," I said to Brad and Barbara over morning coffee. "Up to now it's just been a bunch of swings and seesaws. This one is the real roller-coaster ride." My daughter Cheryl King McGetrick soon arrived on Amtrak from Washington. Throughout the day friends telephoned to offer good wishes; some made me nervous by offering premature congratulations. I really didn't want to talk to anyone but felt some obligation to take the calls.

I took one too many. It came from a man whom I must call Mr. Pluperfect Asshole, it being the only name that can adequately or fairly describe him. The first time I had heard from Mr. Asshole, who lived in Austin, was when he mailed me a print of a movie he had made from a magazine story of mine. He had not bothered to request permission to use the material and, on screening it, I found he had used my property badly. I wired the gentleman that I was about to sue his fanny off unless he immediately withdrew the film from circulation. He hastened to assure me he would. I later learned he continued to circulate a couple of prints. This time I had a lawyer threaten him. I then received a call from a woman in Austin who somehow claimed both me and Mr. Asshole as friends, and who begged mercy for him. He was just a kid—she said—and, more, a country kid who wasn't very sophisticated and hadn't known any better. On the lady's word that she would see to it he quit circulating my misappropriated story, I agreed not to take legal action.

Now it is my opening day and I am so uptight that when I comb my hair it feels as if I am stroking a bongo drum. And when I answer the phone, a cheerful voice says: "Larry? This is Pluperfect Asshole. From Austin. Say, I'm up here to see about distributing a new film I've made and—"

"I'm busy today," I snap.

"Well, I don't know any distributors in the East and I'd like to meet with you—"

"Goddammit, Asshole, my show opens tonight! I've got guests, and other things on my mind."

"Wouldn't take but a few minutes, if you'd—"

"No! I'm busy!"

"I'll talk to you at the theatre tonight," he says.

"Asshole," I say, "if you come to the theatre tonight I'll hit you in the goddamn mouth. I will *not* talk about your fucking film tonight!" And I bang up the telephone.

I arrive at the theatre early, nervous, awaiting guests, who include Dan and June Jenkins, David Halberstam, Frank Rich—not yet, I remind you, a theatre critic—and who looms in the gloom but a strapping, supertall dude about thirty years old who grins, thrusts out a big hand, introduces himself as Pluperfect Asshole, and starts trying to talk to me about film distributors!

"Goddamn you," I snarl, "I told you to leave me the fuck alone tonight! Don't come near me again, you son of a bitch!" And I whirl and go backstage, where the cast members are juking and jittery and it is too much to bear. I seek out the theatre manager's office and hide in it.

"Telegrams for you," the theatre manager says, and pushes a

stack of them across his desk. The thought flashes: *Mama's dead!* Terrible and irrational thought, I know, but when I was a kid in Texas telegrams portended death and other disasters. I calm myself by remembering that I'm a big boy now, and open the Western Union offerings.

The first contains a play on a line from *Whorehouse:* YOU MAY BE A COUNTRY DOG BUT IN THIS CITY I PREDICT YOU'LL RUN AND RUN. ALL THE VERY BEST. MIKE NICHOLS. I grin inanely at the telegram. *Mike Nichols!* Goddamn, pal, this is the Big League sure enough! I rip open another: THANKS LARRY FOR GIVING US ALL SUCH A GOOD TIME. I LIKE YOUR PEOPLE. BEST WISHES FOR A DESERVED SUCCESS. ROBERT REDFORD. *Well, howdy-do!* One from old friend Peter Gent, the ex–Dallas Cowboys football player and author of *North Dallas Forty*: HERE IS TO GOOD LUCK AND A LONG RUN. SEND MONEY. Wonder what else is in that sweet pile? I discover good wishes from Carol Hall (!), writer Bill Goldman and wife Ilene Jones, my agent, my daughter Kerri Lee Grandey from Texas, and a dozen assorted friends. All are warm and hopeful. I feel good, so much so that I momentarily forget that Mr. Pluperfect Asshole lurks about the premises.

I join Barbara and our guests in the lobby; we make for our orchestra seats, front and center. A row ahead of me I spot John Corry, who writes a Broadway column for *The New York Times;* though Corry and I worked together at *Harper's* magazine for a number of years and have many times shared the cup and midnight confidences, I decide against conversing with him because he is sitting beside the working critic for his newspaper, Richard Eder. I am uncertain of the protocol, and so content myself with a friendly nod and a smile toward Corry.

I am fidgety through the show's slow start, but relax a bit as momentum builds as it is supposed to; the house whoops, whistles, and applauds when the Aggies conclude their boot-stomping dance. Dan Jenkins leans toward me and bellows above the noise, "That's the single best goddamn piece of theatrical work I've ever seen." The audience laughs and applauds when my singing ditty signals the first-act curtain. I hug Barbara.

I rise to grab a smoke, and bump into John Corry, who also has reached the aisle. I hesitate a moment, the better to give old buddy Corry his opportunity to congratulate me. "I could have helped you with your book," he says. I stare at him, nonplussed. *Of all the things he might have said,* I think. *And the bastard says that in front of Richard Eder. That's gotta have an effect on Eder!* "Well, Corry," I say, "I guess it's a little bit late for that." I turn to plod up the aisle, feeling as if each foot weighs a thousand pounds. Goddamn him! *Goddamn* him!

As I near the back of the theatre a big hand grabs my shoulder and twirls me around. Pluperfect Asshole, a huge cigar in his mouth, says, "What happened, did they gut your book? I think this thing is misdirected. I know as much about directing as my old daddy down in Texas knows about horses and–"

"FUCK YOU!" Patrons near me grab their ears and look amazed. "JUST FUCK YOU, PLUPERFECT ASSHOLE. GET OUT OF MY SIGHT, YOU BASTARD!" I am pushing the big dude, kicking at his shins; he moves rapidly backward, bumping into people, blinking his eyes as if he has no idea what might be wrong. David Halberstam, who knows nothing of what the commotion is about, reflexively takes my side and begins to mutter and walk menacingly toward ol' Pluperfect. Asshole soon is gone, and has been seen no more.

Halberstam leads me outside to smoke and to calm me, while I explain the one-two combination delivered by old friend John Corry and a goddamned audacious stranger. He mumbles soothing words, pats my arm, and herds me back into the theatre when he thinks I am marginally under control. I am still mad enough, however, to fight a bear.

We approach Barbara and our guests, grouped in the lobby. Dan Jenkins grins and says the perfect healing line: "Start spending it!"

There are two cast parties. We go first to the Lone Star Café, the best country-western club in Gotham, improbably located in the Village at Fifth Avenue and 13th Street. It is a mad, noisy crush and there is a little air in all the smoke. I wave to Liz Smith, Nora Ephron, and Carl Bernstein and attempt to join their table but am blocked by our public-relations man, Jeffrey Richards. "Earl Wilson wants you to sit at his table so he can write down some of those Texas colloquialisms for his column," Richards says.

"Hell, didn't he see the show? Why didn't he write them down then?"

"Be a good fellow and help me," the P.R. man pleads.

I groan, push my way through masses of sweaty bodies, and plop down at the gossip columnist's table.

"Hi, Earl," I say.

He looks at me blankly. "Who are you?"

"I'm still the same playwright you met at the Entermedia fifteen minutes ago," I say.

Earl's Best Wife—"My B.W.," in the parlance of his column—is embarrassed and assures Earl that he remembers me.

I begin to feed the gossiper printable lines. Earl writes oh-so-slowly and requests that I say everything about three times. I am desperate to escape to the bar. I spot Henderson Forsythe at an adjoining table and wave him over, whereupon I do a cowardly thing. "Earl," I say, "the old sheriff himself knows these lines better than I do. He'll tell you anything you want to know." I give Forsythe a big grin and a wave and desert him.

Carol Hall is all smiles, telling a reporter of an unusual occurrence in her hometown, Abilene, Texas. "My daddy telephoned tonight," she gushes, "and told me that the entire congregation of his Episcopal church prayed for our success last night. It must be the first time in the history of Texas that a church has prayed for a whorehouse." I wink at her and move on, thinking that she obviously knows what will play in the newspapers, even if Miss Edna does not.

"Too early for the reviews," someone shouts in my ear. It is Peter Masterson. We must converse by gestures over the music and general hubbub. We move out onto the street. "Did you get any reading on what Eder of the *Times* thought?" Pete asks. No, I say, but tell him that John Corry probably hasn't helped us a lot. Masterson shakes his head. "I heard John Simon of *New York* magazine left at intermission. Told somebody he hated it." We shrug. I gather the family and guests and we head for the second party, at a disco called New York New York. Discos you can have. I stand in the flashing lights and the throbbing music, and relate to Dan Jenkins that John Simon apparently left *Whorehouse* at intermission, after putting the bad-mouth on it. "Fuck him,"

Jenkins says. "Simon hasn't ever liked anything unless it was in the original Czechoslovakian and had a lot of rain in it."

Masterson seeks me out. "Doug Watt liked us," he says. "We got the *Daily News.*" I look around for a newsboy, and ask Masterson how he knows that. "Stevie's in her office getting reports. I call her every little bit." We shuffle awhile and go to a pay phone to call her again. Masterson claps a hand over one ear to shut out the disco roar. "She's got the *Times* review," he says in an aside and listens. And listens. I do not like what I see in his face. When he hangs up, Masterson says: "Well, it's not too bad. It's kinda, you know, wishy-washy. At least he didn't kill us."

"But we needed the *Times* bad, didn't we?"

"You'd like to have it, sure," Pete says, scratching his nose. "It's not as important as it once was, though. Television can help you now, and Clive Barnes of the *Post* still has a big following. If we get him we're probably in business." I have the feeling, however, that Masterson is trying to paper over his true concern. For one thing, I can't get him to quote a word of what Richard Eder has written: "I don't recall the specifics; it wasn't really bad." (The next morning I will learn that the *New York Times* critic has written that our show is "a musical comedy on a milk diet. It takes a small, bright, wry idea and expands and dilutes it at the same time. . . . There is some fun in the idea, some sharply written dialogue that catches a local Texas flavor, and some agreeable songs. It is all put together too loosely and blandly, though." While Eder had praise for Henderson Forsythe, Carlin Glynn, J. Frank Lucas, Don Crabtree, Delores Hall, and Susan Mansur, he concluded, "There is a great deal that, if it does not come out badly, does not come out at all. It is a show that marks a lot of time: one fitted for compliments rather than for enthusiasm.")

Word comes that we have broken even on two TV reviews to the moment—Pia Lindstrom has liked us on NBC; Stewart Klein has knocked us on an independent channel. Everyone quotes Lindstrom: "I never had a better time! This is a show that's Broadway bound." No one will admit knowing what Klein has said. "He never likes anything," Masterson says; I have the notion Pete is whistling past the graveyard. (What Stewart Klein had said was, "Almost all the characters are caricatures and worse, and the fifteen country-rock songs are so bland they are forgettable. A musical is not in good shape when you walk out remembering the dialogue and not the songs. . . . Overall, *The Best Little Whorehouse in Texas* left me unsatisfied.")

Two or three more calls to Stevie Phillips fail to reveal what Clive Barnes has written for the *Post.* I become convinced she knows he has killed us and doesn't want to spoil the cast party by passing it on. Though our producer directly denies this accusation, I am firm in my faith that such is the truth. I decide that Mr. Barnes has written the most brutal review in the history of the theatre, else Stevie would not be so protective of our thin and nervous skins. Probably he has called us "no-talent idiots," or worse.

I seek out Barbara Blaine, weaving through the disco crush and the flashing lights, to request that we go home. Barbara is startled: I normally cannot be dislodged from a party until the sun comes up, unless winch-trucks and firehoses are brought into play. "I can't stand seeing the cast hugging and carrying on like some underdog cow college fresh from upsetting Notre Dame," I say, "when in my bones I know it's all over. We lost. The game's done. Finished." I cite in evidence the bad reviews I've heard of—Eder and Klein—and, more ominously, the Clive Barnes review I have *not* heard about; the last, of course, constitutes in my mind the most damning evidence of all. Barbara cannot persuade me that I may be prematurely throwing in the towel. We leave the cast kiddies singing and dancing behind us, unknowing leprechauns capering on a slippery ledge, and I think, *Poor, poor little fools.*

It is not a night for sleeping. I thresh around in the dark and use its cover for a private examination of problems that cannot be faced in the harsh glare of day. Now, I know, I must at last confess to Barbara that I am the biggest pauper to come down the pike since Erskine Caldwell permitted the pitiful old couple to be hauled off to the poorhouse in the final scene of *Tobacco Road.* I begin to add in my head the sums of money I owe for taxes, to credit-card companies, to friends, but quit when I reach $26,000 because the weight is too much on the brain. My assets, above and beyond furniture and personal items, consist of a checking account holding about $1,300 if I have not forgotten to subtract a couple of large checks written when drunk—and I probably have. I had not realized, until this moment, how desperately and deeply I had counted on *Whorehouse* to pull me out of the economic ditch. Not that I had expected, or even seriously hoped, to reap dazzling sums. The hope had been that we might enjoy a respectable run of six months, say, and that my percentage of the gross might be enough to retire half my debts by judicious saltings and permit me maybe to squirrel away $5,000 nobody knew about—seed money to carry me through while I wrote another book. There had been no alternative plan.

Now it appeared that my only choice was to forgo marriage, live under a tree in some lost valley where taxmen and creditors couldn't find me, and eat wild berries and roots of the fields. Certainly I could no longer skate by in Manhattan, spending myself poorer as I got drunk-rich, watching the debts pyramid while creeping around barefoot in my apartment, the better to fool process-servers. I began thinking of small, lost towns in Texas where I might hide for a couple of years while again trying to write myself out of trouble. Perhaps Brad might find occasional work in some local shitkicker's club; maybe we could raise vegetables, invest in a cow; whatever.

It did not once occur to me that my mother's family blood—Clark blood—was doing its deadly and melancholy work in my veins. The Clarks, of Scotch-Irish-English ancestry, clinch-saddled with the work ethic and a fundamentalist religious obligation to assume the dread burden of Original Sin, were known to have been bred and born to worry, to nurture worry, to bring worry to harvest, and to pass on its fruits to their descendents. Few Clarks, in memory or to be found in the yellowed and crackling pages of the family Bible, had failed to live at least eighty years; many had extended their spans far beyond that. Each robust member of that long-lived clan, remarkably enough, had, by his or her own testimony, been eaten up with cancer since early childhood; each Clark was destined to drown the next time it rained, was marked as the target of a fatal bolt of lightning, had been singled out to be kicked by a mule or hit by a runaway train. None of them expected to live through any day they woke to. If they did, of course, it was only because fate had it in mind to kill them slowly—probably by starvation. Though all Clarks professed a willingness—nay, an *eagerness*—to meet sweet Jesus face to face and dwell with Him forever in the land of milk and honey, they seemed to have an abiding fear of how, and when, He would choose to arrange their transport. I had never met a Clark who was not dying by swift degrees, who did not have one foot in the grave and the other at the mortuary, and I have known Clarks as old as ninety-seven. A blacker-minded clan never has breathed God's air.

Certainly, fretting about the future and planning dubious escapes that April night in 1978 in my sleepless bed, I was confirming my pedigree. Mother would have been proud.

I woke with the sun, red grit in my eyes and sores on my bones, listening to the rumble and clanging of Second Avenue traffic while I gathered courage to face the day. And Barbara. Damn, what would I say to her? *Ah, baby, 'bout this marriage thang—you mind honeymooning down at the Welfare office? Then we'll take a neat side trip over to Bankruptcy Court, see, and . . .* Shit! Wonder if I could get by with confessing only ten cents on the dollar when it came to my debts?

My son, daughter, and other houseguests snored on all available couches and beds; I tiptoed by their inert forms, went down to the street, and dodged dogshit mountains on the way to the corner newsstand. Back in my apartment with all three New York dailies tucked under my arm, I mixed a Bloody Mary and locked myself in my writing room to read the bad news. There might have been stories of plagues and famines on page one; I turned directly to the theatre sections.

I first read Richard Eder's evaluation, that we had presented a "musical comedy on a milk diet"; I muttered pox on all *Times*-men, and investigated whether Douglas Watt of the *Daily News* had come down on our side as advertised. He had, but I didn't read his verdict as predicting we would run *Annie* or *A Chorus Line* out of town. Though Watt had written things like "A whale of a good time . . . a lively, genial unassuming musical . . . a smartly tailored book . . . bright dance routines, delightfully staged . . . funny and sunny," I had the notion that in his soul he felt lukewarm. His review just had some . . . *tepid* . . . quality about it.

Perversely, perhaps, I had saved the Clive Barnes judgment for last. Everyone kept telling me that Barnes, once the second gun at *The New York Times* behind Walter Kerr, retained a huge personal following and was influential beyond the normal range of the *New York Post:* "It's no longer fatal to lose *The New York Times,* provided you get the nod from Clive Barnes."

I thus turned to Mr. Barnes's offering with some dread—and was surprised by the headline: "WHOREHOUSE IS LOTS OF FUN." I quickly scanned the accompanying story:

> If all the tarts with hearts of gold currently at the Entermedia Theatre down on Second Avenue banded together they could buy out Fort Knox. Seriously, *The Best Little Whorehouse in Texas,* which is where all those tarts are situated, is a fun new musical. . . . Considering the subject matter, the show is beautifully clear-eyed and totally free of the gooey sentimentality you might have feared. It calls a spade a spade with a frankness that is exhilaratingly delicate . . . a refreshing, tough honesty . . . music with a bustle . . . bubbling, delightful performances . . . It already looks pleasingly slick—a Busby Berkeley production number for six girls and twelve dummies is a riot—and if the show were to move to Broadway, where it is presumably aimed, it could be made even smoother with time and experience.

There was much more, including praise for Carlin Glynn, Hank Forsythe, Joan Ellis, Susan Mansur, Delores Hall, Jay Garner—all the people, just about, whom I considered to be strong. Why, then, did I feel a dissatisfaction—even a *disappointment*—when I had been convinced in my mind, going in, that Barnes would use a stiletto on us?

A bit later in the morning a messenger delivered copies of reviews from suburban papers, radio stations, and TV outlets. I read them, feeling at once strangely detached from them and increasingly depressed by them. When the household stirred, I handed over the packet to Barbara and glumly retired to my writing room. Occasionally I heard her, my children, and other houseguests exclaiming over one review or another, though their words were indistinct. In time I came out of hibernation, mixed another bracing Bloody Mary, and said, "Well, hell, we gave it our best shot, I guess. A break here and there and it might have happened, who knows?"

Everyone looked at me as if I was weird. "Are you *serious*?" Cheryl asked. Damn sure was. They all began to babble their protests: the critics had liked us, we had done well, very well. "Hell, Dad," Cheryl said, "I see it that you've got *a hit*!"

"No, no," I said. "No, some of them are pretty good. They say nice things here and there. But they don't seem to add up to much. There's not a review in the bunch that would cause me to go galumphing down to the theatre to buy a ticket."

"Larry, I'm much more optimistic," Barbara said. "I've seen shows run with much worse reviews than these."

"Oh," I said, "I don't think we'll close tonight. I mean, we might do three or four months Off Broadway. But it was Broadway itself I had my sights on."

Cheryl picked a review from the stack, read a quote, and cited the source. Others began to do the same. It went something like this:

*Cheryl:* " 'Down at the Entermedia Theatre tonight a hit was born! The Lone Star State got the treatment in a livewire, sassy, classy, full-of-spirit fun musical. . . .' That's by Virginia Woodruff, Channel Ten television."

*Brad:* " 'This is a comedy that has all the look of a show that is Broadway bound, so get down to the Chicken Ranch while prices are low.' Pia Lindstrom, NBC-TV."

*Barbara:* " 'An arousing, and rousing, musical with a great deal to boast about.' William A. Raidy, Associated Press."

"Ya'll just picking out the best ones," I said.

*"Dad!"* Cheryl said. "There's something good in just about all of them! Everything from *Newsday* to plugs by Liz Smith. She's crazy about the dancing!"

"I really don't know what more you want, Larry," Barbara said.

"He wants a life-sized statue of himself in Times Square," Brad said.

By this time everyone was laughing at me, and I managed a sour-apples grin. "I guess," I said, "that the country boy part of me wants a rave review in *The New York Times*. I guess that says to me, 'You've made it. You arrived.' It's . . . some sort of affirmation to my mind. Maybe Clive Barnes has a big paddle and a large stroke, like everyone says. But I'm nervous because we didn't get the big one."

"Wait for Sunday," Barbara said. "You still have a chance to get Walter Kerr."

At the Entermedia that night everyone was grinning like thieves who'd holed up to split the diamonds. Pete hugs Tommy. Tommy hugs me. I hug Carol. We all hug Stevie. Quite a lovefest among people who, only days or even hours before, had been convinced they had the misfortune to be associated with the most impossible group of collaborators ever assembled under one roof.

"You know when I knew we would be a hit?" Carol Hall asks.

Jeers and hoots as we scoff at Carol as a Monday-morning quarterback, though the laughter is good-natured and warm.

"No, I'm serious." Carol smiles. "It was early in the previews, and we still had problems. But the audience was reacting well that night—hissing Melvin Thorpe, clapping in time with the Aggie dance, laughing at the Angelettes. At intermission a friend said, 'Carol, it's Tuesday, it's raining, it's Twelfth Street and Second Avenue, you have no stars in your show, and nobody has ever heard of any of you. Look at this crowd and how it's responding! You have a chance.' I knew he was right—just *knew* it—and my heart stopped."

"You sure could have saved the rest of us some worry," Pete said, laughing, "if you'd let us in on the secret."

"And Larry King wouldn't have felt it necessary to charge us with ruining his play," Tommy Tune said.

"I categorically deny any such thing ever happened," I said, to catcalls and friendly boos.

I got Stevie Phillips aside and said, "Am I dreaming? Are we really gonna run? Are we moving to Broadway?"

"We're certainly going to try," she said. "Of course, success is not automatic. Playing to four hundred and ninety-nine people at nine or ten dollars each is one thing. Filling a theatre every night that seats twelve hundred to fifteen hundred or more is another—at seventeen or eighteen dollars a pop. The economics are such that we *must* move to Broadway as quickly as we can—say a couple of months, if we obtain the proper theatre. I lose money every time I open the doors down here."

"I wish I hadn't asked," I said.

"Don't worry." She smiled. "Relax and enjoy it. I feel a thousand percent better about our prospects than I did twenty-four hours ago."

Backstage, in the wings and in their dressing rooms, the players greeted each other with glad cries, hugs, and fraternal clasps. I thought I detected a change in the bearing of some cast members—those who had been singled out in the reviews seemed to walk a little taller, to sparkle a bit more. It would be interesting to watch a pecking order develop. (This never happened: Carlin Glynn and Hank Forsythe, aware that it could, took pains not to act like stars. Consequently, the cast never really split into cliques according to pecking order.)

Jay Garner told me, "You know, at half hour last night Tommy Tune got the entire case on stage in a circle—just before they opened the house to patrons. We held hands and stood there a couple of minutes. Now, I never really had put much stock in that stuff. But I swear to you I felt *electricity*! The same as if I'd grabbed a hot wire. And I have never been in a show where the energy level in the entire cast was as high as we had last night. I swear, call it magic or superstition or what you will, but I'm convinced that electric circle did it!"

Caught up in the effusive and cheerful celebrations of the moment, I did not notice the mood of Clint Allmon—Melvin P. Thorpe—as he stood in the wings, garbed for his role in an electric-blue suit with sequins, an outlandish silver wig, red-white-and-blue cowboy boots, and carrying an outsized flashlight.

I greeted him: "Hey, Clint! How you doin'?"

"Not worth a shit," he said.

That got my attention, and I reappraised him. Allmon was of such grim and sour visage he might have just finished a vinegar cocktail with a green persimmon chaser.

"Uh, what's the problem, Clint?"

"I wasn't going to say anything until you asked," he said, "but I'm really pissed. Every newspaper in this town ignored me today! Shut me out! I'm the lead figure in this show. *This show is about me!* And I wasn't even mentioned. They buried me! So how do you think I feel? How would *you* feel?"

"Uh, well. Pretty shitty, I guess."

"You called it," he said.

I did a little shuffle and ineffectually pawed at his shoulder. "I'm real sorry, Clint."

"I think it's the concept," he said. "You were right all along. They've made me a goddamn stick figure. They've made me look silly."

I was not about to get into that old argument again, though I had originally birthed it, since it appeared our show was afloat and might sail on to Broadway. I merely mumbled some brief condolence and walked away from Clint, leaving him as a small island of sorrow isolated in a sea of good cheer.

## CHAPTER 12

The heavy voice with the careful, workingman's accent said, "Meet me at dat the-atar tonight and I'll make ya a big man."

"Damn, Jimmy," I said into the telephone, "where were you when I needed you?"

"Dey tell me I got three million readers in da *Daily News,*" he said. "You can't use dat kinduh help?"

The caller was Jimmy Breslin, who sometimes can make his typewriter sing like a nightingale, and who often is the best free show in town when you are out drinking with him.

Breslin is a passionate man. He went to the land of his roots, Ireland, a few years ago to write a book. I never got the straight of it as to details, but he got into some sort of jam with the government for poking his nose into the terrible war in Northern Ireland. With all the troubled history of the Emerald Isle beating in his blood, Jimmy could no more have remained placid about the political convolutions over there than have refused his turn at the whiskey jug.

I liked Jimmy, liked him a lot. He reminded me of lines Kris

Kristofferson once wrote: "He's a walkin' contradiction/partly truth and partly fiction." I thought it amusing that Breslin, who cavorted with the powerful elite when he wished, took such pains to advertise that he lived in Queens and frequented workingmen's bars. Though he was then a heavy drinker, he became incensed when writer Midge Decter dismissed him in print as "a barroom journalist," and he referred to her ever after as "Podhoretz's Wife." Perhaps not everyone in the lumpen wastelands of Jimmy's beloved Queens got the joke, but it was funny to those who knew that the proud and independent Ms. Decter was married to the self-esteemed editor of *Commentary,* Norman Podhoretz. Breslin kept a shitlist of everyone who had made him angry during the year; at year's end, he wrote a column entitled "People I'm Not Speaking To This Year"—complete with the reasons why. It was sort of a left-handed honor to make that column. Breslin's personality is something like mercury: quick to heat, quick to change. One never knows what might send him off into a beautiful, artistic tirade. Jimmy can throw fits that are things of wonder. In his better exhibitions he stomps, jumps in place, invents new cusswords, kicks, and generally resembles a steam calliope in explosion.

We met at dusk in front of the Entermedia and by unspoken agreement adjourned to the nearest bar. We each ordered beers. Then I remembered: at Lawyer Blaine's behest, I had been tested for liver damage and had scored no better than a gentlemanly C. I had vowed on a stack of Bibles and the Texas flag to cool it awhile. All this had happened less than twenty-four hours earlier. And now I sat with a beer in my hand. What the hell, it might offend the bartender to return it.

"Ah, Jimmy," I said, "don't be writing in your damn column I'm drinking tonight. My doctor told me to cool it, see."

Breslin spreads his hands, helplessly. "Ya know I can't do dat! Ya know ya just wrote my lead, don't ya? I got no choice now!"

"Aw, bullshit! Come on, Jimmy!"

"Look, you been a big drink-ah all ya life. All the time ya starved and worried ya drink like *two* drunks, right? Now ya getting rich ovahnight and the bastids won't let ya enjoy it, ya know?"

I groaned. Jimmy in full sail is unstoppable.

"Ya know a story when ya see one! I gotta write it, right?"

"Just say I had a couple of small beers," I sighed.

I gave Breslin the background of how *Whorehouse* happened to be written. He asked where the three collaborators originally met, and I responded—not really thinking it out—that we met at Carol Hall's apartment, and gave her Park Avenue address. The columnist asked more questions, we quaffed a few more beers, talked politics, and returned to the theatre near show time.

As we approached, Breslin said: "Look dere! Dat's Wal-tah Kerr on da sidewalk! Ya want I should introduce ya?"

"No, no, Jimmy. It might be . . . awkward."

"I know da guy, from da old *Herald-Tribune*!"

"Yeah, but it might get sticky. He's here to review my show. It—it just wouldn't *feel* right."

Breslin, however, was born a dictator. Without a word he propels my bulk with his even greater weight toward the distinguished *Times*man, as if giving me the bum's rush from a saloon. He forces us to shake hands much as a referee might order two pugnacious fighters to touch gloves. All the while Jimmy is instructing Walter Kerr that I am his buddy and have authored *Whorehouse* and he likes to see his friends get along. Kerr and I circle and dance in some confusion. "Ya be good to my pal, ya hear?" Breslin says.

*Oh, shit, Jimmy!* I walk rapidly away with a weak wave at New York's number-one theatre critic. Breslin follows me. "Ya goddamn fool," he rasps, "all ya life ya been in politics and ya turn down a shot to get da man's vote!"

"This is a whole different game," I protest. "You don't win a critic by shaking his goddamn hand!"

"Damn fool," Breslin grumbles, and wanders off to spy on me during the show and jot down notes on a small pad.

I see in the *Daily News* two days later that Breslin's nightingale had been in his typewriter when he wrote the piece. It is warm, funny, and perhaps more dramatic than the circumstances warrant—"It looks like another writer has come out of the loneliness and made it"—but certainly a plus for me and the show. The only jarring note is that the story will reveal to Lawyer Blaine and my doctor that I have quickly trampled my temperance oath, though I suspect they will not be horribly surprised. "Good show, Brez," I mutter as the telephone rings.

Understand, now, that as a former police reporter I have stood by wailing mothers as they viewed the battered or mutilated remains of their children; I have monitored the caterwaulings of the dispossessed when Texas tornadoes swooped down to smash their homes to smithereens; I have seen and heard grief, rage, and its kindred emotions in many lands and tongues. But I have never—*never*—heard such anguish and pain as reaches me over Ma Bell's wires on that April morning.

It is, of course, Carol Hall at her peak.

*"You have ruined us,"* she is screaming. *"My children will be kidnapped! Murdered!"* Long wails and tremulous sobs, building to a crescendo that could not be equaled by Beverly Sills accompanied by a rock band and the Mormon Tabernacle Choir.

"Wait a minute, Carol. Wha—"

*"My address is printed in Jimmy Breslin's column! He gets letters from Son of Sam! We'll be murdered in our beds!"* Boo-hoo. Sob-sob. Wail-wail. Scream-scream.

"Jesus, Carol—"

*"Every thug and thief and rapist in New York will be here! Leonard and I were to leave today for the Caribbean and now we don't dare! My children would be murdered!"* Much more caterwauling and ungodly racket.

I attempt to tell Carol that probably a squad of Marines would have difficulty getting at her children in the rich, well-posted high-rise where she lives. After all, no apartment number has been mentioned; she lives high in the ozone behind guards and multiple locks. This is like trying to tell a president that "Hail to the Chief" was not written for him as a personal anthem, or that not everyone loves and admires him. I am talking against screams, curses, multiple mentions of Son of Sam, the deranged .44 caliber killer who specialized in random killings of young women.

"Carol, I'm truly sorry. I just wasn't thinking."

*"Give me Jimmy Breslin's telephone number!"*

"Ah, Carol, I don't see the purpose. The paper has been printed and distributed. He can't call it back."

*"I want him to know what he has done to us! What the two of*

*you have done to us! We'll be living in terror!"*

"Come on, Carol! This getting a bit ridiculous."

*"Give me that number!"*

"No, I'm sorry. I'm not going to do that."

*"I'll get it! I'll find him! And when I do—"* There is a climactic concert of snorts, sniffles, shouts, and screams; I hang up the telephone very much shaken and mutter the name of my Savior.

Now I face a decision: whether to punish my liver slightly or perhaps to expire of nervous exhaustion. Soon I have uncapped the Cutty Sark and am taking medication at full strength. As I debate repeating the treatment, my telephone rings. I make the mistake of answering it.

"WHA? WHA? WHA? DA FUCKIN' WOMAN'S CRAZY! WHY'D YA GIVE MY NUMB-AH TO A WILD WOMAN?"

"Jesus, Jimmy, I didn't!"

"I SET YA UP WITH WAL-TAH KERR. I MAKE YA A BIG MAN. AND YA GIVE DAT SCREAMING WOMAN MY NUMB-AH. SHE CALLS ME WEEPING AND CARRYING ON CRAZY. WHA? WHA?"

"Goddammit, Jimmy, I didn't give it to—"

"SHE TELLS ME ME AND SON OF SAM GONNA KILL HER AND HER KIDS. DA FUCKIN' BROAD'S NUTS! SHE TELLS ME I'M A TERRIBLE PERSON!"

"Sometimes she's a little excitable," I say.

"HYSTERICAL, YA MEAN! JESUS! DA BROAD SCREAMS AT EVERYBODY IN MY FAMILY! I INTERPRET IT AS J-E-A-O-L-O-U-S-Y!"

"You mean J-e-a-*l*-*o*-u-s-y, Jimmy."

"FUCK YA! DIS IS DA LAST TIME I WRITE ANYTHING ABOUT ANY-BODY IN DAT FUCKIN' CHILD'S WORLD, DAT FUCKIN' TOY WORLD. EVEN IF MY OWN KID IS IN IT! FUCK IT!" And a most aroused Irishman bangs down the telephone.

I do believe ol' Brez meant it: I have not caught him writing anything more about that "child's world," that "toy world" of the theatre—nor have I again heard from him personally. As for how he "set me up" with Walter Kerr—well, it took the critic more than five hundred words in the Sunday *New York Times* to express his enthusiastic apathy toward *Whorehouse.*

Though my colleagues seemed to assume we would move on to Broadway through a path of roses, my Clark blood knew that unless critical praise continued to be heaped on *Whorehouse* the Entermedia soon would be padlocked. We would arrive at the theatre one night to find the cast playing only to the ushers—half of whom would be asleep. Almost furtively, so as not to show an unbecoming interest in my own future, I sneaked around buying every magazine, neighborhood or suburban newspaper, and trade publication even remotely likely to contain a review. Too often, it seemed, the reports were mixed.

One would beam at *Variety*'s verdict—"For sheer entertainment, *Whorehouse* is one of the most enjoyable musicals of the current season"—and then frown when the *Village Voice* reported, "The show is half-terrible, half-wonderful. Unfortunately, since the two are woven together, you pays your money but you can't take your choice." *Time* magazine's judgment sent my spirits soaring: "Looks suspiciously like a migrant entertainment giant. Should it move north to Broadway there will be many more eyes than those of Texas on it. . . . This is the best new musical of the season." Then right behind that accolade would come *After Dark* with the spartan comment that "*Whorehouse* lacks focus," and Liz Carpenter's wordy review, syndicated in many newspapers, charging that our show reinforced eastern stereotypes of Texas and should have its mouth washed out with soap.

I kept a careful chart listing publications with positive reviews, especially those worded in a way that might encourage the sale of tickets: *Newsweek, Women's Wear Daily, Texas Monthly, The New Yorker, Soho News, The Wall Street Journal,* Dallas *Times-Herald, Hollywood Reporter;* any number of small daily or weekly papers in suburban New York, New Jersey, and Connecticut. Some of this may have been vanity, yes, but it also reflected a real concern about the dirty matter of money. In short, the plot line of my personal drama ran: "Will the out-at-elbows writer find fame and, more important, fortune enough in the theatre to permit him to take as his wife the fair lady lawyer?" I was constantly revising my estimates, hoping a kind word in this or that publication might sell X or Y number of tickets—and then computing my percentage of the gross.

Shortly after our Off Broadway opening, I sought out the writer William Goldman. Knowing he had been around the theatre and the movie business for years, I bluntly asked what a successful musical might earn me.

"I don't know your percentage of the gross," he said, "but if it's in the normal range and you have a big hit you could make . . . oh, say, ten thousand dollars a week."

"Aw, shit, Bill. Quit pulling my leg."

"I'm serious. It wouldn't be at all unusual."

"Well, damn. Hell. I mean, how do we get there?"

"Say you run a good year on Broadway, and then a touring company does good business around the country, and you also have a bus-and-truck tour for the smaller cities, you could easily make ten thousand a week for your share. And probably a great deal more."

I staggered away, fervently wanting to believe but not really believing. My private, secret goal was to make $50,000, total, for my end. That would pay my debts and back taxes, finance a honeymoon in Europe, and perhaps leave $10,000 as a nest egg while I fashioned a new book. If I could get even with the world and go $10,000 ahead, it would constitute a personal record.

I telephoned Pete Masterson that night to ask whether he thought we might last six months on Broadway. Probably, he said. A year? Well, maybe, but he wouldn't count on it. Would there be a touring company? He thought so, provided we'd done respectable business on Broadway.

I then reexamined all the reviews I'd squirreled away in my desk and concluded that perhaps—just perhaps—my $50,000 goal was in sight. Muttering a prayer that I might be doing the right thing, I slightly abused my liver in celebration and then telephoned Barbara in Washington to say I thought it was time we seriously negotiated a wedding date. The negotations went thusly:

BLAINE: Okay. May sixth.

KING: Ah . . . *this* year?

BLAINE: Of course.

KING: Uh, isn't that a little . . . soon?

BLAINE: No.

KING: Oh.

So the die was cast.

Shortly after I had made my commitment to matrimony, my eyes fell on a review by John Simon in *New York* magazine. It was no surprise that Mr. Simon did not like our show, he being the self-appointed guardian of high standards and rather inclined to look down his nose even in the presence of Shakespeare. Indeed, he seemed to think we had staged the show as part of a vendetta against himself and all who hold Culture dear. Only a Texan—he sneered—could love *Whorehouse.* Joan Ellis and Delores Hall were "gross," Clint Allmon and Don Crabtree "dull"; Henderson Forsythe was so pitiful a singer "that you wish he had appointed a deputy to sing." The book, the songs, the dancing—all left our most acerbic critic happily unhappy.

Mr. Simon was even more appalled by the audience than by the show itself. This should have been no surprise, either, from a critic who seems to delight in punishing actors for their big noses, buck teeth, and other physical characteristics, rather than in judging their acting, singing, and dancing talents. Perhaps Mr. Simon's mother was once frightened by a circus freak, and that's why he is so hung up about physical appearances; at any rate, an actress who did not appreciate his comments about her long neck and complexion once quite publicly dumped a plate of spaghetti on his head in retaliation. She will forever remain popular among those who work in the theatre.

"It was an audience"—Mr. Simon wrote—"such as I had never seen at a Broadway opening night before." (Never mind that it was an *Off* Broadway opening; Mr. Simon has small appreciation for the facts.) "There were ten-gallon hats galore, outlandish garb beggaring description, and faces that seemed never to have seen the inside of a theatre before. . . . Well, this audience responded with hoots and hollers to every G-rated naughtiness and Z-grade joke that threatened to make the Entermedia collapse like the Mercer Arts Center."

Bluntly put, Mr. Simon was and presumably remains full of

shit. Perhaps in that audience he found so offensive were forty to fifty Texans out of a total of 499 people. Maybe a dozen of these had "dressed western" as a lark in keeping with the show's theme, and I had because I've always dressed that way. Obviously, Mr. Simon had gone to the Entermedia with his mind set on the notion that the audience would comprise several bus loads of Baptists, yahooing oil men, and riverboat gamblers shipped up from Texas—and he wasn't about to permit the facts to mess up his preconceptions.

One night I go to the theatre feeling better than usual, more confident that we have beaten the odds. I am standing at the back of the house, tapping my foot to the Rio Grande Band's warm-up music, as near to happy as my nature permits.

A patron and his lady take their seats in front of me as I lean on the back rail. The man hands me two *Whorehouse* programs and says something I cannot hear above the band's rendition of "Bluebonnet Lady." I smile, nod, and when the fellow sits down I scrawl on each of the programs, "Thanks and Best Wishes, Larry L. King." Then I tap the dude on the shoulder, smile winningly, and hand the programs back to him. He looks puzzled and says, "You can keep 'em, fellow. I picked up a couple of extras by mistake."

I made the error of confiding this story to Brad. He spread it through the company, and I took a terrible ragging. A couple of nights later, when I enter a restaurant where many in the cast eat their snacks before the show, I am approached by the owner—an obsequious and mild-mannered old fellow—who says, "Mr. King, I saw your show last night and enjoyed it so much. Would it be asking too much to get you to autograph my program?"

I look around and see in a nearby booth several of the band members—Ben Brogdon, Ernie Reed, Lynn Frazier—and I am, of course, pluperfectly certain they have badgered the old gentleman into this act and intend some great joke when I sign. I ain't gonna bite, naturally. So I say to the nice old man, "Sure, and as soon as I do you can go piss up a rope." A look of genuine horror crosses his face. "But I don't understand," he stammers. "Is that improper of me to ask? I beg your pardon, I—"

"No, no," I say, lamely, feeling much the ass. "It is a joke, a bad one. I didn't really mean it." I sign his program, but the old man is so upset I lay two free tickets on him and flee without any supper.

In late April I divided my furniture between Brad and Goodwill Industries, packed my meager wardrobe and thousands of books with the help of daughter Cheryl, and delivered myself to Washington and the custody of Barbara Blaine. There, in the home of transplanted Texans Lynn Coleman and Sylvia deLeon, we exchanged vows as scheduled in the company of three hundred intimate friends and relatives.

There followed a honeymoon containing scenes that might more properly have been played by Peter Sellers and Carol Burnett. In Ireland, the travel agent had responded to our request for "a leisurely motor tour" of the countryside by booking us, each of four nights, in a town more than three hundred miles from the previous one. I went lickety-splitting down the narrow Irish lanes, scattering sheep herds and cows while driving on what seemed to be the wrong side of the road, while Barbara periodically shrieked that I was scraping stone fences at high speeds. Although we had asked to be put up in quaint "bed and breakfast" accommodations, the better to absorb local flavors, we somehow had been placed in Holiday Inns. "We are rushing past castles, thatched houses, and all the historic points," I grumbled, "to get to Holiday Inns and spend our evenings among a bunch of goddamned idiots from Indianapolis, all of whom sit in the lounges singing 'When Irish Eyes Are Smiling.' "

Nothing smiled in Paris, however, including yours truly. Everything I had heard about French arrogance had been understated. I enjoyed three Franco-American scuffles in five days (gendarmes attended the best of these at the request of a haughty restaurant manager), and I thirsted for more; only the talents of fast-talking Lawyer Blaine kept me out of the Bastille. I left Paris vowing to return only at the head of a conquering army. "Is this your first time in Europe?" someone asked my bride. "It's my first time in the company of a petulant five-year-old," she said. Only the civilities of London salvaged the trip.

Shortly after our return, *Whorehouse* won a number of Off Broadway awards. Carlin Glynn, who grew stronger and more confident with each performance, won a Theatre World award as best actress and was nominated for a Drama Desk Award. Pete Masterson and Tommy Tune won Drama Desk awards as best directors of an Off Broadway production, and Carol Hall won two Drama Desk awards, for best lyrics and best musical score. I was happy for them and for the show but, frankly, my nose was out of joint; all of my collaborators had won something, while I had gone unmentioned. Tommy Tune soothed my ego with a thoughtful note saying none of it would have been possible without me, though I would have preferred a bauble I could have shown to strangers ambushed at bus stops.

With all that going for us, you might have thought things were running smoothly back at the theatre. Not so. Joan Ellis, who from the time she'd begun at Actors Studio two years earlier had given sensitive and touching performances, suddenly began to play Shy as a broad caricature. She ad-libbed lines that interrupted other players, took the focus away from where it was supposed to be in a number of scenes, and generally became so undisciplined I grumbled to Pete that her name should be changed from Shy to Monkey. One evening, astonishingly, she appeared in a scene wearing two red balloons for breasts—infuriating Tommy Tune, as this took away the surprise of the Angelette dummies in a later scene with their balloon breasts and buttocks—and loudly popped one to obliterate a line by Carlin Glynn. It was weeks before the young actress settled down and again began to play the role as written and directed.

The more plaudits Carlin Glynn received, the more Miss Edna Milton resented her. Miss Edna began waving and winking to the audience when pushed on stage in her wheelchair each night. "She won't listen to me because I'm married to Carlin," Pete chuckled. "Why don't you say something to her?"

I went backstage that night and after effusive compliments to Miss Edna suggested that perhaps the illusion of her scene might be better preserved if she would not take such public notice, in a 1930s setting, of a 1970s crowd.

"You can kiss my ass," Miss Edna invited. "Lots of people are paying to see my story and to see me. Hell, they wouldn't even know who I *was* if I didn't wave and wink, the way you bastards has cut down my part." I beat a swift retreat; Miss Edna kept winking and waving until the day she left the show. Meanwhile, however, she continued to grab the other players backstage and rail against the way Carlin Glynn was allegedly "misplaying me." It got so when Miss Edna walked into the theatre, the other players scurried to hide in their warrens and hutches.

The tensions and undercurrents among players in a show were illustrated to near perfection by what happened between Modine and Harriet. Modine was the live chicken used in the opening prologue number, and Harriet—after a few weeks—was brought in as her understudy in case Modine should be incapacitated some night. Modine had long been kept in a bathtub in a room shared by members of the Rio Grande Band. When Harriet joined the show she, too, was put in the bathtub.

Ernie Reed, the fiddler, came to the theatre for a matinee and was the first bandsman to go into the dressing room. He shortly returned looking a little green. "There ain't nothing left of that new chicken but feathers and guts," he said. Sure enough, "star" Modine had pecked her understudy to death—an event that made *Variety* and even the staid *New York Times*. These items came to the attention of the Society for the Prevention of Cruelty to Animals, a rather humorless outfit. Their representatives came around to determine how we treated our chickens and to threaten injunctions should another one be mutilated. Modine, a few weeks later, expired from presumably natural causes and was remembered by *Variety* in her obituary as a murderess. She was replaced by a more docile fowl the cast dubbed Cluck Gable.

We discovered that after a few weeks of pampering and regular eating, our show chickens got so fat and lethargic they wouldn't properly flap and cluck as the script demanded. So we began retiring them early to poultry farms, and bringing in replacements who had that lean and hungry look.

Our search for a suitable Broadway theatre brought me into conflict with such conscience as I have. We wanted the 46th Street Theatre, located between Broadway and Eighth Avenue. It was the right size (1,388 seats), in excellent repair, and had a good history as the home of successful musicals. "*Guys and Dolls* started here, for God's sake," Pete Masterson commented, grinning, the afternoon we went to inspect it.

The problem was that we couldn't get the 46th Street Theatre unless another show failed. *Working* was based on material by an old friend, Studs Terkel, whom I both liked and admired. I really wasn't rooting for Studs's show to go under, you understand, but . . . well, I truly coveted that theatre. I must admit I did not cry when we heard that *Working* was folding after playing less than thirty performances. I forgave myself such selfishness by rejoicing that Studs's show at least was going out on tour.

The day we learned we would open in the 46th Street Theatre on June 19, 1978, a number of us went over for a closer inspection. I shall never forget standing on the stage with my son and looking out into the plush red seats of that Broadway house. I lightened the moment by kidding Brad that the parents of the youngsters in *Annie* could truly be proud of their progeny for making Broadway at an early age, while I'd had to wait until my son had reached the ripe old age of twenty.

Members of the cast, especially those who would be making their Broadway debuts, wandered around the stage, the dressing rooms, and the theatre proper, wearing beatific smiles. Stage manager Paul Phillips was equally euphoric: he had spent almost three years at the 46th Street Theatre with *Chicago* and felt he would be "returning home." Pete Masterson recalled that only eight months earlier, while posing for pictures for the Houston *Post* on West 44th Street in front of Actors Studio, we had joked of wanting to move east about four blocks. "We were only two streets off." He grinned.

I thought I had never been in the 46th Street Theatre before—until the journalist in me got the upper hand and I investigated its history. To my surprise, I found that *Finian's Rainbow*—one of the few musicals I'd seen in my youth—had played there for 725 performances in 1947–48; I obviously had been among the customers. In the early 1960s the theatre had hosted *How to Succeed in Business Without Really Trying,* starring Rudy Vallee and Robert Morse; I had been dragged to it by a determined wife, but quit at intermission in favor of a handy bar. That may tell you something of my ability to evaluate musicals—*How to Succeed* merely set the house record, with 1,417 performances. The theatre also had offered *Damn Yankees, Hellzapoppin', DuBarry Was a Lady, Panama Hattie, 1776, The Bad Seed* (one of its few non-musicals), *I Do! I Do!, Raisin,* and the aforementioned *Guys and*

*Dolls* and *Chicago*—not a bad history of hits. I attempted to stir or move the cast with this knowledge, seeking in some way, perhaps, to inspire them to greater heights. I even threw in the names of show-biz greats who had trod the 46th Street Theatre stage or composed works performed there: Fanny Brice, Jack Haley, Joe E. Lewis, Ole Olsen, Chic Johnson, Cole Porter, Henry Fonda, Ethel Merman, Betty Grable, Bert Lahr, Frank Loesser, Damon Runyon, Mary Martin, Gwen Verdon—but this only produced puzzled looks, and steel guitar player Lynn Frazier's economical "No shit?" Actors and musicians, I concluded, basically were not historians.

Stevie Phillips and I continued to be the show's worrywarts, fretting over whether we would prosper on Broadway as we had Off Broadway. We debated whether we should reinvite the critics when we moved uptown from the Entermedia. "Oh, hell, no," Pete Masterson said. "Suppose the ones who liked us Off Broadway changed their minds?"

Jules Feiffer, the triple-threat cartoonist-author-playwright, didn't help my confidence when he paused at my table at Elaine's on the eve of our move. "Don't think your success is predestined," he warned. "My play *Knock-Knock* was doing terrific business off Broadway. We got ambitious and moved it and—*pffffft!*"

"Thanks a lot, Jules, ol' buddy," I said. "You have a nice evening, too."

I missed the spectacle Stevie Phillips arranged on June 19th, transporting members of the cast from the Entermedia to the 46th Street Theatre by horse-drawn carriages. This, presumably, was to call Gotham's attention to our move to Broadway, but Gotham is difficult to impress. "We sat there waving our cowboy hats and grinning like jackasses," Brad reported, "but the only people who noticed cussed us for backing up traffic."

A goodly bunch of celebrities—whose names were carefully fed to gossip columnists—were attracted to our Broadway opening: O. J. Simpson, Carol Channing, Liv Ullmann, Steve Allen, Jayne Meadows, Ann Miller. We exploited the "real" Melvin P. Thorpe—Marvin Zindler—by bringing him up from Houston, providing a limousine, and posing him with his stage counterpart, Clint Allmon. Zindler, amazingly enough, saw himself as the hero of the show—no matter that the audience hissed and booed the character he represented. There was another big cast party at the disco New York New York, which had been Texanized insofar as possible by a few bales of hay scattered on the sidewalk in front, and in general things ran according to plan.

Feeling much the big man, I returned to Washington and Barbara, who had remained behind because of a legal commitment. No sooner had I walked in our door than Jim Fallows, then a speech writer for Jimmy Carter, telephoned. The President was going to Texas soon, he said, and would be pleased should I submit a few one-liners he might use in my native state. By this time I was feeling as smug and satisfied as the deep-dip Baptist who, once he has been totally immersed, knows that he is doctrinally incapable of working his way into hell. As I opened my mail—requests for interviews and personal appearances included—this wonderful feeling multiplied itself. Until, suddenly, I heard again from my old buddies at the Internal Revenue Service.

The I.R.S. boys said, in effect, that my unpaid tax bill now topped $13,000 and they had given up on my doing the honorable thing. This was to inform me that as of this minute they had garnisheed all my box-office receipts save $50 per week until the debt was settled. Very truly yours.

I knew that Barbara no longer fully believed in the fiction of my wealth, since I had borrowed $500 from her to be certain we wouldn't be stranded on our honeymoon, but I somehow had not gotten around to mentioning the size of my debts to others, Uncle Sam included. I telephoned her office to confess this perfidy and to snort that here I was, a near-war veteran who had earned the Good Conduct Medal, being shabbily reduced to $50 per week by an ungrateful nation. My bride laughed and said, "Well, I'll be as good to you as Uncle Sam is. I'll let you have fifty dollars a week so long as he does."

## CHAPTER 13

For a few weeks it appears that Stevie Phillips and I were right to fret; that Jules Feiffer was a true prophet in warning that not all shows transfer to Broadway with happy results.

Our first week on the Great White Way grosses a disappointing $96,973—slightly more than the average weekly take during our two-month Off Broadway run. "People haven't discovered that we've moved yet," we reassure each other. Well, if not . . . why not? Certainly Stevie is spending a small fortune on radio, television, and newspaper ads *telling* people we have moved. In our second week we are only slightly better, at $99,430 and play to only sixty percent of seating capacity. By comparison, down the street or around the corner, *Chorus Line* is topping $169,000; *Annie* does more than $164,000; *Dancin'* comes in at $163,000-plus, and *On the 20th Century* scores $158,000 and change. Indeed, of all the musicals on Broadway we finish ahead only of *Runaways* at the box office.

"We would do well to pick up soon," Stevie says. "California won't let me lose money forever." Ominously, she inquires whether the show's creators will agree to take deferred royalties should business get worse or fail to improve. We are reluctant, hem and haw, finally say we will consent only as a last resort to prevent closing.

Slowly, ever so slowly, our weekly gross grows: $104,000 . . . $108,000 . . . $119,000 . . . $123,000 . . . $130,000. When we hit $142,000 there is general rejoicing and a feeling that we are over the hump. "Don't cheer too quickly," Stevie warns. "September usually brings a seasonal slump. The tourists leave town." Sure enough, we skid to $118,000 and then abruptly to $101,000. "The newspapers call us a hit," Stevie says. "At best we are a nervous hit. I'm worried." We inch upward again; in late October we have our best week to that point, at $148,000. I think, *Surely, now, them good times gonna roll!* But by the middle of December, we have fallen back to $119,000. Bill Goldman's projected $10,000 per week for my cut now seems a cruel jest.

About this time, after an evening performance, Carlin Glynn is told that two stage-door johnnies have asked to see her and that one is carrying a huge bouquet of roses. Our leading lady graciously receives her admirers in her dressing room. One of the men has a camera and asks whether he may take a photograph of Carlin and his companion holding the roses. She consents. The man posing with her plops a borrowed cowboy hat on his head, and holds the roses so that almost all his face is hidden behind them. "I didn't notice it at the time," Carlin later said, "because I was naturally looking into the camera."

The rose man compliments Carlin on her acting, tells her he is aware of her good work in conservation and ecology causes. Peter Masterson walks in the door and is introduced.

The camera-shy guy sticks out his hand and says, "Hi! I'm Abbie Hoffman."

Well, Jesus! Pete and Carlin freeze. Hoffman is only the most wanted fugitive in America since they've bagged Patty Hearst. Pete laughs nervously and cracks that he is Bernardine Dohrn.

"No, I'm Abbie Hoffman," the man insists.

"Close that door, Carlin darlin'," Pete says.

"I didn't know what the hell to do," Masterson later said, laughing, "so I asked if they wanted to join us at Joe Allen's for dinner. And damn if they didn't accept!"

Actors buzz the Masterson-Glynn table, congratulating them on their hit and probably hoping to be later remembered for possible work. Hoffman, seeing his host's discomfort, clues Pete to the ways of Underground survival: "Just introduce Buddy here as *your* friend and me as *his* friend, see. Say 'This is Buddy and his friend.' Let your voice trail off." Pete has not been an actor for nothing, and does his work well.

Hoffman warms to him. He asks whether Masterson also directs or produces movies. Yes, Pete says, he is buying the movie rights to a novel, *Panic on Page One,* and has a deal in the works to produce it as a network TV movie. "How'd you like to make a movie of a book I'm writing?" the nation's number-one fugitive asks. Though astonished, Masterson says he thinks he would like that very much. Hoffman promises to get the manuscript to him the next day, and is as good as his word. The new friends embrace like old friends at evening's end.

Pete and Carlin replay the unexpected adventure late into the night, wondering how much to believe, considering the complications and the risks. They decide to do nothing until Pete can confide in a lawyer to determine his legal responsibilities and rights, and they vow to keep the matter strictly hush-hush even among their close friends.

They have reckoned without Abbie Hoffman's fierce love of publicity, however. Forty-eight hours later they are astonished when Associated Press sends out on its national wire the photograph of Carlin and Abbie, he crouching behind the roses so that only his eyebrows, eyes, and the bridge of his nose show. Their telephone begins ringing. Among the first to call are the vexed and embarrassed gentlemen of the F.B.I. Pete scurries off in search of his lawyer. At the theatre, Carlin is greeted by the cast: "Who was that masked man, Carlin darlin'?" She fibs a bit and claims she had no idea who the man was until the picture hit the newspapers.

At the same time the Mastersons' phone is ringing, so are those in the box office of the 46th Street Theatre—prompted by publication of the picture coast to coast, including in the New York newspapers. "Jesus," I say to Barbara, "it's the Jackie Onassis thing all over again." *Whorehouse* box-office receipts take a $38,000 leap in a single week.

Two weeks later, when we reap the highest weekly gross to that time in the fifty-one-year history of the 46th Street Theatre—$172,666.24—I am certain that inflation, and a special New Year's Eve preview at an inflated one-time price, made their contributions. But so, I am equally certain, did Abbie Hoffman. I owe the dude one. Had I been able to worm my way onto his jury, he never would have served a day.

Along in there somewhere, as our show became a solid hit, a lady from my agent's office called to say that we needed to sit down and discuss merchandising offers.

"What the hell is merchandising?"

"Oh, the spin-off items from the show."

"Like the cast album and souvenir programs?"

"Oh, no, those are taken care of. I'm talking about the offers we've received to merchandise T-shirts, key chains, book bags, buttons, ashtrays. All that marvelous junk! Some chap is thinking of issuing *Whorehouse* dollhouses if we'll grant permission. You know: the madam and her cute little girls in miniature with skimpy little outfits, and presumably rooms full of tiny beds." She laughed.

"Jesus, what decadence have we wrought? Where will all this end?"

"We very much hope," she said in her British accent, "that it will end at one of the larger vaults at Chase Manhattan."

One of the young ladies in the show was excited that her eighty-six-year-old grandmother was flying in from the Midwest to see *Whorehouse.* "Actually, she's coming to see Henderson Forsythe more than to see me." She laughed. "She watches him on the soap opera and she thinks Dr. David Stewart hung the moon."

"How'd Granny like the show?" I later asked.

"Oh, God! I thought I would have to bury her!"

"She didn't like seeing her granddaughter flounce around like a little chippie?"

"Oh, it wasn't that! She couldn't care less about me! She was shocked at Henderson's cussing. What she said was, 'I just wouldn't have thought Dr. Stewart would have talked so ugly.' She really took it hard!"

I mentioned this to Forsythe. He grinned and shook his head, ruefully. "Oh, yeah, I get a lot of that. Especially on matinee days. Those nice little old ladies stop me at the stage door or on the street and say, 'Dr. Stewart, I am so disappointed in you. Such language!' They write me that, too. And they're not kidding."

"What do you tell them?"

"I say, 'Look, I'm an actor! I'm neither Dr. David Stewart nor Sheriff Ed Earl Dodd. I'm *Henderson Forsythe.* As an actor it's my job to say the lines the show calls for.' But, I don't know, they seem unable to understand that. It's a little scary."

On a December morn as I idle in our Washington apartment, trying to coax back decent writing habits after the hoopla of the past months, Stevie Phillips telephones to say that Henderson Forsythe is due a two-week vacation beginning January 15th. "I'm worried about his understudy," she says. "We've rehearsed him for a week and he just gets worse. Would you consider going in the show as Sheriff Dodd for those two weeks?"

"Would a starving fish strike a worm?" I ask. I do not pause to think it out. What author could resist the opportunity to know the satisfaction of speaking his own lines from a Broadway stage as the leading man? Not this one, I assure you. It is soon arranged that I shall report to New York on January 2, 1979, to begin rehearsals.

Brad, temporarily out of the show due to a swollen soccer knee, comes down to Washington to work with me on the sheriff's song, "Good Old Girl." I have prepped by singing along with the cast album while Barbara is at her law office. Frankly, I judge myself pretty good. When Brad hauls out his guitar and we start running through the number for the first time, I am not through the first verse before my wife and my son break into fits of giggles. I pout and steam. Only after they apologize and claim they were laughing not at my singing but at how I looked do I consent to continue working.

An obviously worried Bob Billig, our musical director, puts me through the song while he plays piano on my first day of rehearsal. When I finish he grins and says, "Not bad! You'll be okay with a little work. After what Brad said, I expected you to be hopeless."

"Oh? Exactly what did Brad say?"

"Something about foghorns, chalk grating on a blackboard, and a sick cow." Billig smiles. "But you'll be fine. Let's run it again."

Billig's mild praise has made me dizzy and, worse, ambitious. I decide to give "Good Old Girl" an operatic treatment the likes of which it never has known. I rear back and reach for my best notes, adding trills and warbles and throat vibrations. Bob Billig stops the music. "Uh, Larry," he says, "don't try to sing it *pretty*. The main thing to remember is stay in key and tempo. That's all I expect and *more* than some do."

Now when I speak to you, dear reader, of being "in rehearsal" for a Broadway show you probably conjure up visions of me up there on that glittering Broadway stage surrounded by the entire cast, everyone in costume, the band on hand to provide music cues, the lighting cues coming in just as during a paid performance. Probably you see the director sitting in the third row barking brisk instructions while his gofers scurry off to bring him coffee, cigars, or wine. At the end of my rehearsal you see me climbing into a limousine, perhaps, while lackeys throw robes and capes over me to keep the precious body warm and drive me the two blocks to Sardi's, where caviar and champagne await. Would to God that such were so; it is how I might have envisioned the scene a year earlier, though I am savvy enough by the time I report to rehearsal to understand how bare-bones the operation will be.

Because everyone has a union—musicians, actors, stagehands, electricians, prop men, costume department—they insist on being paid special rates for any extra work they do. And because Universal, like all management, is parsimonious in such matters, no matter how extravagantly it may throw money around in other ways, I must rehearse without costumes, props, lighting cues, music cues, the set, or other actors. There is nothing but the bare stage, one "work light"—a naked bulb on a tall pole, at center stage by the footlights—and one other person, Jay S. Cohen, the assistant stage manager. For two weeks I will work eight to ten hours under those conditions each day except matinee days—Wednesdays and Saturdays—when use of the theatre cuts my time down to the morning hours.

Since most of Sheriff Dodd's scenes are played opposite Miss Mona, I find my imagination taxed in working those scenes with Jay S. Cohen. Jay is a nice fellow, but Carlin Glynn he ain't. It is hot and airless in the darkened theatre; after several hours of work, neither Jay nor your present hero exudes fragrances you would think to bottle and sell. Jay's five-o'clock shadow fails to remind me of Carlin. Though he attempts to bat his eyes coyly when the script requires, or to imitate Carlin's slinky walk or soft touch, he does not possess the equipment to make me believe.

In short, I am up there on a bare stage playing semi-love scenes with a hairy-legged man, pointing my finger and saying "Bang! Bang!" when Ed Earl is required to fire his six-gun. And somehow, neighbors, it just don't seem like Broadway. Not until the afternoon of the very night that I am to make my big-time debut will I be entitled to a "put in" rehearsal complete with cast, props, costumes, sets, music, lighting, et al. You ask me, it's a shoddy way to do business. Rehearsals have all the glamour of mining coal.

Nor did one always receive consistent instructions. Stage manager Paul Phillips suggested that I follow Henderson Forsythe around backstage for a few performances, to familiarize myself with when and where his entrances were made, and ask him technical questions. Jay Cohen, during the first week of rehearsals, corrected everything I did that wasn't exactly as Henderson Forsythe did it. Then Peter Masterson dropped by, watched me for ten minutes, halted the proceedings, and said, "Damn, King, you're just imitating Hank Forsythe! Forget him! Go back to *your* way—the way you played it at Actors Studio." So I have to unlearn my Forsythisms and start over.

My agent, in a misguided burst of goodwill, informed me that he had arranged the traditional party at Sardi's following my opening-night performance; many of my friends would join us after having watched my big debut.

While I sincerely appreciated the gesture, it only added to my internal stress. Who would want some of his best pals as witnesses in the better seats should he freeze, break down and cry, forget the entire first act? Now I know that any disaster will be witnessed by David Halberstam, Jean Sandness Butler, Russell and Mimi Baker, Lynn Coleman and Sylvia deLeon, Bud and Doatsey Shrake, Dan and June Jenkins, Sander and Virginia Vanocur, Alan D. Williams, and John Daniel Reaves. Had I been able to remember one of the prayers of my youth, I might have offered it.

In the late afternoon, at my "put in" rehearsal, I blow lines I know as well as my own name. Carlin Glynn, the cast earth mother, takes me aside and soothingly tells me to relax and have fun. "We're all with you," she says. "We know you can do it, because a lot of us remember how well you did it at Actors Studio."

"Carlin," I say, "this ain't Actors Studio. This is *Broadway* and I can't sing and what am I doing here? I had to be crazy to agree to this! I'm terrified of that song, Carlin! I can't sing it! I can't!" Carlin clucks and soothes and gently shoves me on stage to work on "Good Old Girl" with the Rio Grande Band for the first time. We run the number again, and again, and again, and I flub it differently every time. I notice that the house ushers, bartenders, and box-office personnel have gathered in the back of the theatre to see how badly the amateur actor may botch things. I ask Ernie Reed, the fiddler, whether it might be proper to ask them to leave. "Shit, I don't know," he says, "but in about forty minutes you're gonna be singing to about a thousand more people than that." I walk off the stage and, in the wings, bend over and enjoy three or four minutes of the dry heaves.

Members of the cast have left encouraging notes in my dressing room; there are telegrams from my daughter Kerri, cousins Lanvil and Glenda Gilbert, Stevie Phillips, Frank Rich and Gail Winston. The most appreciated gift is a bottle of bourbon, left behind by Henderson Forsythe with a note saying "Keep ol' Ed Earl cussin', Ed Earl. Best, Ed Earl." Though I am a Scotch man I rapidly convert to bourbon on the spot. Clint Allmon and Lynn Frazier join me. "I don't think we're supposed to be doing this," Clint says. "It's against all sorts of rules." I tell him what can be done with the rules, that in my case the liquor is a medical necessity.

I am led off to have my hair grayed. A swish hairdresser sprays goop on it and says, "Who in the *world* cuts your hair? Or should I say who *butchers* it?" I growl that the sheriff of a tiny Texas town likely would not show up in a hairstyle fashioned by Mister Cecil, and he sniffs. I am led back to my dressing room like a blind man and costumed and made up in greasepaint. I hear the warm-up music starting and the cast being told to take their places. *Don't think about it,* I think. I try to indulge in sports fantasies, in which I kayo Muhammad Ali; return a punt eighty-one yards for the Washington Redskins to defeat the Dallas Cowboys. There is little in it of satisfaction. I switch fantasies, but even making love to Dyan Cannon is no fun; I am too nervous to give her my full attention

The show moves inexorably on. My cue cannot be put off. I move out of my dressing room and start the long walk to the ramp running into the audience, from which I will make my entrance. The other players shout or murmur encouragement. I nod, attempt to grin; I feel nervous tics jumping in the corners of my mouth, which itself is as dry as a sand pie. Passing the concessions bar, I grab a pitcher of water and toss off a neat pint. Immediately, I have to pee. There is no time.

I rush up the ramp and begin my line: "Goddammit, Mona, I gotta—"

My friends unexpectedly burst into applause, and the audience follows. I am thrown off, and do not know whether to begin the line again or to complete it at the point of interruption. Nor do I know how to conduct myself during the applause. The insane notion strikes me that perhaps I should wink and wave to the audience, like Miss Edna. My temples throb, I seem to have a fever, and I am out of breath. I move as if walking in water or through plowed ground. When I regain my voice I sound strangled.

Two minutes onstage, and I sit down in accordance with the script. My goddamn six-gun falls out of my holster and dribbles across stage like an iron basketball . . . *clunk . . . clunk . . . clunk!* I mumble something inaudible about it being my first night to carry this gun, while the audience goes into hysterics. Carlin Glynn covers by ad-libbing, "Watch it, Ed Earl, don't shoot yourself!" Two minutes more and Carlin is scheduled to remove my cowboy hat as she says, "Ed Earl! Come sit over here! You've got to learn to relax!" When she removes the hat, my head seems to explode in a mushroom cloud of white powder: that damned spray to gray my hair has disastrously dried. Again, the audience enjoys a burst of unscheduled mirth. I feel like the last-place jackass at the county fair.

The rest of the evening is a hot walking nightmare. I do not recall much of what occurred onstage because of worrying about my song. The best I can say is that I did not break down and cry. When I go off stage in the final scene, I begin an impromptu dance of celebration that the damned show is over, and almost forget to join the cast for the curtain call. Carlin Glynn grabs me and propels me into place. I must do a simple cowboy shuffle to music during the curtain call; my friends in witness later report that I have watched my feet during this ordeal, as if afraid someone might steal my boots. They also tell me that from the moment I dropped my gun, I went through the remainder of the performance holding it in place and bent over like the Hunchback of Notre Dame. (The next day it is discovered that the gun problem occurred because no one had thought to tell me of the heavy brass clip used by Henderson Forsythe to nestle the gun belt snugly against his regular belt.)

My loyal friends are in place at Sardi's when I rather sheepishly walk in; they stand and break into friendly applause. Sardi's customers are accustomed to this theatrical bit, and automatically join in—up to a point. I see Liv Ullmann of *I Remember Mama* and Stacy Keach of *Deathtrap,* dining together, flash bright smiles and begin to applaud. I nod at my fellow thespians, smile, wave. Their smiles disappear, their applause falters; they turn to each other mouthing, "Who is it?" Dan Jenkins has not missed that bit of byplay, and laughs: "King's the only person who ever got a standing ovation in Sardi's without anyone knowing who they were cheering."

Later, after I unwind a bit, Russ Baker says, "You know, what you did tonight takes a particular kind of courage."

"Yes," I say, "it is the kind of courage that causes soldiers to charge machine-gun nests. There is not any reason in it, and probably it should never be done."

* *

Here is what goes on backstage, while you, as a theatre patron, are getting caught up in the lights, the music, the costumes, the sets: all the trappings used to make magic, create illusion.

Begin at the stage door. A bored doorman sits in a cubbyhole office, usually watching a tiny black-and-white television set. Fred Astaire may be dancing onstage, or Richard Burton emoting, but the doorman's eyes will in most cases be glued to a *M*A*S*H* rerun or *Monday Night Football.* During the show the doorman has little to do other than occasionally answer the backstage telephone and perhaps post a message on a nearby blackboard for some cast member. His main work comes immediately after the show, when patrons want to meet the stars, or friends of cast members show up with notions of getting a glimpse backstage. The primary function of the stage doorman is to be a security guard. Now and again, someone eludes him—and then money, jewelry, or purses disappear. (During our run at the Entermedia, a young dude slipped backstage, dressed himself in three costumes belonging to the stage whores, and attempted to sneak down a fire escape. Someone sounded the alarm. Henderson Forsythe appeared in his sheriff's duds and wearing his gun and held the thief at bay. Not until the real police arrived did the young man understand he had been apprehended by a make-believe sheriff.)

In wardrobe, even as the show plays, are several women washing and ironing costumes, polishing boots or shoes, seeing that each costume is ready when needed and then put in good repair before being placed back where it belongs after use. Every hat, boot, dress, belt, gown—whatever—has a particular place. Except when in use or being groomed, that costume is never to be anywhere else. When you have a cast of around thirty, doubling and tripling in roles, this turns into a huge operation. People known as dressers stand by to assist the players who must make quick changes. Sometimes an actor may leave a scene in one costume and be required to appear back onstage within seconds in another costume. Where possible, the actor "underdresses"—which is the opposite of what it sounds like to the layman. That is, he wears the costume for the second scene under the costume for the first; when the first scene is over, he or she steps off stage, quickly strips off the top costume, and lets it fall in a heap before bounding back on stage; a dresser swoops up the abandoned clothes and heads with them to wardrobe. Underdressing is not always possible, however. It can be comic to witness an actor come off stage and immediately be set upon by two or three pairs of hands ripping off his clothes down to his skivvies, and just as quickly stuffing him into a new outfit. Here one stubborn button or one jabbing miss of an arm aimed toward a flapping sleeve can bring on a crisis. These quick changes are invariably accompanied by sweating, cursing, and a frantic tension.

The busiest person backstage is the assistant stage manager—Jay Cohen in our show. Though just a few feet from the stage behind a curtain at stage left, he watches the action on a closed-circuit TV set with a script in his hand. It is his job to call all cues—for lights, sound, "flying in" flags or cowboy hats or whatever the moment calls for. Though Jay had literally hundreds of cues to call each show, I know of his making only one major booboo. Naturally, it occurred while I was playing Sheriff Dodd. In a scene where Jay was to have called for a spotlight to single me out as the rest of the stage went dark, he called the wrong cue; suddenly, a huge Texas flag dropped down from the ceiling between the sheriff and the audience. I don't know whether I was more startled than Jay, or vice versa.

Downstairs, in a huge basement room at the 46th Street Theatre, the majority of the cast members—those who do not have private dressing rooms—must disrobe and change in quite public circumstances. Oh, there are a couple of big blankets hanging to separate the girls from the boys but no one pays much attention to the boundaries. The unwary can get a surprise when a near-nude girl or boy suddenly looms up for a kiss or a handshake.

In one corner of this communal room are couches and throw-pillows where players may rest for a few moments when offstage; understudy players and swing dancers—that is, understudy dancers—read, chat, strum guitars, or otherwise kill time. Prop men and stagehands are at their posts, going through routines so familiar they can talk or joke on any number of subjects without missing a beat. Some have timed their routines so accurately they know when they can skip out the stage door for a quick drink at the Golden Gate Bar across the street and whisk back, with no one the wiser.

Through this seeming confusion moves Paul Phillips, the stage manager, keeping a wary eye on everything—pausing to encourage or admonish a player, listening to a complaint. At key points backstage and in the dressing rooms are sound boxes piping the show so that players know when to ready themselves for their entrances. No one overtly listens to these "bitch boxes"—players stand talking, joking, laughing, griping, whatever, until seconds before they must be onstage—but suddenly, they hear their cues and rush off in time to bounce on stage dancing, singing, or speaking their lines. The casual observer, seeing all this, will be puzzled indeed at how order emerges from such chaos. Somehow, though, it does.

Shortly before my two-week run ended, Stevie Phillips inquired whether I might be available as the regular sub for Henderson Forsythe when he took his vacation each six months. I was as quick to turn her down as I had been to accept the first time she called.

This was not because I felt inadequate in the role. Once I got over the opening jitters, I think I did a pretty good job, and I even enjoyed some moments of fun. I learned from the other actors, especially Carlin Glynn, and it was satisfying to grow. Overall, however, I found the sport not worth the candle: the work was difficult, tedious, too confining, too repetitious. I simply don't understand what enables actors to repeat themselves in a role time and time again. I began to get bored before my sixteen performances were done and, indeed, counted off the last half dozen in the manner of a prisoner approaching the end of a long jail stretch.

The notion that it would be a double kick to mouth my own lines proved to be false. This surprised me. As the author, I had enjoyed sitting in the theatre or pacing in the back of the house while hearing an audience laugh, grow silent and attentive, or whatever the moment was designed to make an audience do. It seemed logical this satisfaction should be increased by my participation.

In actuality, I felt distant and remote from my own material while onstage. Laughter from the audience was nothing more than a noise causing a technical hold in the dialogue, and one listened carefully to time the next line—not to bask in the reaction. One was busier onstage than a one-armed paperhanger. As an example, in the sheriff's office scene, where Ed Earl telephones Mona to inform her he must padlock her place, I had to listen for several music cues and give one myself in a matter of a couple of minutes. It was vital that I start dialing her in the moment the cowboy chorus begins to sing, that I not speak into the receiver until a given word in their song—else the audience would see me talking to her before she had picked up the telephone on *her* music cue—and it was just as vital that I hang up the telephone on yet another music cue. At the end of the scene, the music was to end and the lights go down *exactly* at the moment I clapped my hat on my head and started my exit down a set of stairs leading into the theatre's basement. With all those sound cues to concentrate on, I had no time for considerations other than the technical. Similar conditions prevailed in almost every scene.

(I had asked Henderson Forsythe whether, when he supposedly talked to Miss Mona on the telephone, he just mouthed words or actually said something. "Oh," he said, "I have a regular little spiel. I tell her I'm sorry that the thing has come about, that I'll make it as easy for her as I can, and so on. I have it memorized, just like I do my script." I tried that approach, felt silly, got confused, and almost missed a music cue. Thereafter, I just moved my lips or said things like "Oh, I'll be glad when this shit's over" or "I'm gonna drank me a *batch* of that ol' Cutty Sark tonight." It worked for me better than Henderson's way.)

I had problems, too, when the stage went totally dark and I had to get off in a hurry before the lights came back up. I've always been "night blind"—it takes forever to accustom my eyeballs to sudden changes—and one night, rushing pell-mell from the second-level stage during a blackout, I smacked into a solid brass pole with such force I both grunted and farted. I knew that the pole was on the edge of a gaping hole and that if I fell, it was a ten-foot blind drop. Consequently, I grabbed the pole for dear life. When the lights came up for the next scene, there I was, disastrously onstage, blinking at the audience in dazed confusion, wrapped around the brass pole like a monkey trying to climb it. Brad claims I set a world record for shimmying down a pole and rushing off stage—but I wasn't quick enough to avoid the titters that swept the house. The next day we marked my exit route with reflector tape, and though I had no more collisions, I remained forever apprehensive.

I developed a great deal of respect for actors—so many of them did effortlessly or automatically (or so it seemed) what I had to struggle to do. This was because they worked at it rather than because they were born accomplished, I believe. Indeed, I came to the theory that no one should be permitted to direct, produce, stage-manage, or otherwise ramrod a show until he or she had stood in an actor's shoes at least as long as I did. Before appearing in *Whorehouse* I sometimes thought the players petty or querulous when they complained of six-guns that occasionally misfired, or flashlights held together by tape, or wigs that didn't quite fit. I thought they were too concerned with small details. Lemme tell ya, laymen: small details are ignored in a show only at everyone's peril. Put an actor out there with a job to do and pressures on him, and he's got to feel that everything is right, looks right, and will work right, or you are going to see erratic performances that will throw off timing, reduce the energy level, and otherwise bollix up the show. I've had some mule-work jobs—farming, the oil fields, long days in politics—but nowhere have I found the work and the pressures any tougher than onstage. Don't set out to be an actor unless you're willing to *give* to exhaustion and work in rough conditions where surprises lurk at every turn.

If I came to respect actors more, I was appalled by the rude or thoughtless conduct of many in the audience. I don't know why people come to the theatre if they want to talk, rustle shopping bags, or wander around in the aisles. Two of my entrances required me to go through the theatre's main lobby to reach a small corridor leading to a ramp running to the stage. Though the show was in progress, there always were people going to or coming from the rest rooms or the concessions stand—and they insisted on talking to me or asking questions. "Hey, Sheriff, come here a minute . . ."

"Sorry," I would say, "I've got to go on stage."

"Well, just a minute, I wanted to ask you . . ."

Several actually followed me almost to the ramp, rattling and gabbling so that I could hardly hear my cue, and got in a huff when I wouldn't pause to chew the fat. Other players repeatedly had the same experience.

Carlin Glynn and I had to go back up that ramp for the finale and our curtain call. Invariably, as the finale music began, a surge of twenty or thirty people would rush toward us—pushing aside a couple of ushers—and *literally* try to run over us on their ways, presumably, to beat the crowd to cabs. I mean, they could *see* us standing there—holding hands, waiting to skip up the ramp in time to the music when we heard our cue—and yet they would actually run *through* our hands even as we, and the ushers, begged them to wait just a few seconds. Or some few fools insisted that we then and there sign their programs or talk to them. I called several such patrons idiots, clods, sons of bitches, and the like, and even swung on one guy, but—thank the Lord—I missed him, and avoided a lawsuit.

I suppose the patron I longest shall remember attended my third performance—a Wednesday matinee. Before that show Carlin Glynn came to my dressing room, bestowed a warm hug, and said, "Listen, darling, you've got past the tough part so now's the time to have fun out there. Make this a happy experience! Don't worry about the song or anything—just relax, go out and do your thing and take away warm memories you can relate to your grandchildren." Soon she was comparing me to a cross between Tony Bennett and Orson Welles, and her flattery did its work. I *did* have fun, I *didn't* dread the song, and when it came time for "Good Old Girl" I planted my feet confidently and prepared to thrill them in the farther reaches of the second balcony.

The music-under intro began and I spoke the first word of the lead-in: "Well . . ."

Then, from third row center, came a woman's piercing laugh and a comment they probably heard over in Hoboken: *"Oh, my God! He's gonna try to sing!"*

My daughter Kerri flew in from Texas to see Daddy do his stuff on Broadway. She and her husband, John, were guests at the fine penthouse apartment of Dan and June Jenkins on Park Avenue and she soon was dazzled by the New York experience. "This being a Broadway star must be so exciting!" she said.

"Baby," I said, "let me tell you what it's *really* like." I told her then much as I am telling you now:

During rehearsals, I worked so long and hard that all I wanted to do at night was eat a room service cheeseburger and tumble into bed. Once my run in the show began I had—save for matinee days—the entire long day on my hands and couldn't do much with it. I didn't dare drink to excess, which meant in my case that I hardly dared drink at all, for fear of showing up at curtain time singing "Hinky Dinky Parlay Voo." I couldn't take long walks because I might exhaust myself—I'd done that one day, and barely got through that evening's show. Movies or over-eating made me drowsy. I really couldn't concentrate enough to read, let alone write.

Barbara and I had rented a kitchenette apartment in a formerly fine old hotel gone considerably to seed, and spent our time eating cheeseburgers and playing dominoes. I came down with a bad throat and had to suck cough drops; caught a cold and smelled constantly of Vicks Vaporub; got leg cramps and had to be massaged. "Oh, this glamorous Broadway life," Barbara said one day as we sat around, bored out of our gourds, and it became our private byword.

On matinee days, my free time, such as there was of it, was chopped up, so that one didn't know what to do with it. Typically, I arrived at the theatre at 1:00 p.m. to prepare for the two o'clock curtain. I got out of the theatre around 4:50 p.m. There was time for a quick, light dinner and then it was back into harness for the 8:00 p.m. show. I got out of the theatre around 11:45 each night, too wired to sleep and too tired to risk heavy play of the type I preferred because of the tax of the next day's show. So it was back to the dominoes and the cheeseburgers. It was a life for monks, and that certainly was a factor when I told Stevie Phillips, "Thanks, hon, but I think I've enjoyed just about all of this stardom I can stand."

*Poor ol' Stevie Phillips,* I sometimes thought. *Poor Universal Pictures.* Our producer was so good at poor-mouthing it about expenses, problems, and disappointing ventures that I often felt guilty about taking my percentage from the show. I came close a couple of times to asking whether it might help Lew Wasserman's morale should I make a personal loan of a few bucks to the parent Music Corporation of America. Just to tide those poor people over until things got better.

*Variety* blew Stevie's poorhouse image in February 1979 by announcing that Universal had recouped its $800,000 *Whorehouse* investment exactly one year from the time we began rehearsals—only ten months from the time we'd opened off Broadway—and was sailing along with a $40,000 weekly profit. Thereafter, I could eat each meal without fearing I might be taking bread out of Lew Wasserman's mouth.

# CHAPTER 14

In February 1979, *Whorehouse* made show-biz history in Texas. This, admittedly, was not difficult, since not much such history had been made there. Texas cities had no facilities adequate to host big-cast, first-class musical productions. Universal Pictures made a deal with Pace Management to share the cost of remodeling an old movie theatre in Houston, the Tower, at a cost of about $250,000. When our show moved in on February 25th, it became the first big musical ever to book an open-ended run in the Lone Star State.

Stevie Phillips, as always, was worried. "They don't have the theatre habit down here," she complained. "Advance sales seem a mystery to these people. They just show up at curtain time and demand six tickets in the orchestra." It bugged our producer that she could not get across the concept of an open-ended run. People would call the box office and say, "How long's that show gonna be in town?" Told the run was open-ended they might say, "Yeah, but I mean, how long's it gonna *be* here?" Stevie finally threw up her hands and advertised tickets in three-month lots with ads saying "Tickets on sale through May 15th" and then

"Tickets on sale through August 15th." That seemed to satisfy everyone. Not many who called the Tower Theatre would say the word *whorehouse.* They referred to "that show" or "your present attraction" or maybe "that play about Texas." This was a pattern that held throughout the South and the Midwest.

*Whorehouse* ran exactly one year in Houston, almost always at capacity in a thousand-seat theatre, before going on the road—with some cast changes—for ten months as our second national company. In early 1981 it returned to Houston for another open-ended run and after another six months started touring again. Shortly after the first Houston opening, one of the box-office people on Broadway said, "Opening that company in Texas has cost us money here. We used to get calls from Texas every day. Someone would say, 'You got four tickets for your show tonight? Well, good, put me down for 'em. We'll be flying in there this afternoon.' "

Never before had a first-class production of a Broadway show been cast wholly with Texas talent. Players from all across Texas spilled into Houston to audition. The leading lady, Marietta Marich, had appeared in many productions at Houston's fine regional theatre, the Alley, and owned her own dinner theatre in the area; she later was replaced by June Terry, another Alley veteran and nightclub singer. William Hardy, a Houston stockbroker, was cast as Sheriff Ed Earl Dodd. Hardy was no amateur, however: he had acted in or directed more than eighty productions at the Alley. Pete Masterson persuaded an old friend and fellow Texan, Larry Hovis, to leave his California home for the role of Melvin P. Thorpe. Hovis was best known as the ineffectual demolition expert in the TV sit-com *Hogan's Heroes.* Both Bill Hardy and Larry Hovis later would leave the Houston company to tour with Alexis Smith in our first national company.

Sociologists might have fun with the fact that our opening-night performance in Houston was bought out by Planned Parenthood, and the second night was taken by the Texas Home Builders Association. Barbara and I flew down for the opening along with the other creators for a big Texas homecoming. As we awaited the curtain she nudged me and said, "Look at that." I followed her gesture to discover Marvin Zindler, tuxedoed and in the usual silver wig, shaking hands in the aisles and signing *Playbills*. Though Zindler had again accepted our hospitality, he kept his hand in as a crusading TV newsman by rushing back to his Houston studio to announce that our theatre was in violation of the fire laws.

(A year later, Zindler would attend the opening of our first national company's Washington run—again as our guest—and appear at a cast party hosted by Texas Congressman Charles [Good Time Charlie] Wilson, which was held in the National Archives Building. This was an arrangement perfectly legal and permissible, so long as the congressman paid the expenses of the personnel required to keep the building open—which he did. As soon as Zindler got back home, he blasted Wilson for throwing a whiskey-drink in a public building and castigated him, and other Texas congressmen, for missing President Carter's State of the Union address in order to attend *Whorehouse* and the cast party. As our show says, "Watchdog never sleeps."

It was during the Washington run that I finally asked Zindler, face to face, why he had crusaded to close down the Chicken Ranch when Houston was full of whorehouses that didn't seem to bother him. Marvin said the state's attorney general and the local district attorney had urged him to act, because of alleged organized-crime influences and payoffs. He seemed a bit defensive. "You don't have to apologize to me, Marvin," I said. "I thank God for you three times a day, and if I had any decency I'd do it more." Marvin humorlessly said that he was not apologizing: "I removed a cancer from that little town, and I would do it again.")

One night eighty-three people jammed into a chartered bus and motored from LaGrange to Houston to see what Broadway had wrought and brought home. They made a good, lively audience, though one man complained that the show had been written "by somebody that ain't from LaGrange and didn't get everything right." Another, however, claimed the show was right on the money: "Why, there's not a person in LaGrange couldn't recognize somebody in that play. In fact, you could find a few of them characters right here on this bus!"

An enterprising reporter telephoned Sheriff Flournoy to ask why he had not come along to the Houston performance. "The worst mistake I ever made," he said, "was lettin' them people put on that show and stir everthang up again. I wouldn't walk acrost the street to see the goddamn thang."

In Houston, we had even more problems with censorship than we had originally faced in New York. Television and radio outlets were squeamish about letting us use the killer word *whorehouse* on the air. Our arrival in town provided good pulpit fodder for fundamentalist parsons, who warned their parishioners in such doomsday terms about the root-rot their souls might contract should they visit the show that I am certain they sold a goodly number of tickets.

About the same time, our first foreign company opened in South Africa and ran into a passel of no-noes. The government's Directorate of Publications decreed that we must bill the show as *The Best Little Blank in Texas* on the theatre marquee, the theatre programs, and in all advertising. He also struck from the script the words *fuck, screwing, shit, bullshit, apeshit, shitass, piss, pussy, tallywhacker,* and "any word or combination of words making use of the name of the Deity save when in a reverential manner."

We won back at an appeals hearing the use of the word *whorehouse* in our title, but the ban on the dirty words was upheld. We got around that by honking a bicycle horn when the forbidden words were uttered onstage, and South African audiences found that terribly funny. The irony of the whole farce is that the South African company presented the sexiest, raunchiest "whores" dressed in the skimpiest costumes I have seen to date—and no one complained.

Stevie Phillips contracted with the New York Transit Authority to place twenty-seven-foot banners on eighty city buses (at a cost of $1,333 per week plus production expenses) for a period of three months. These giant streamers said HAVE FUN AT THE WHOREHOUSE! In smaller letters appeared the title of our show and the location of our theatre. After several days, a reporter for the *Daily News* telephoned the office of Cardinal Terence Cooke, Catholic Archbishop of New York, to obtain the reaction of His Eminence. He had one, of course, and it was predictably pious and disapproving. I mean, did the reporter expect the good cardinal to say, "Gee whiz, I think that's real peachy keen"? The Transit Authority immediately "reconsidered" and very publicly canceled our contract while issuing utterances that equaled the cardinal's in piety.

(I don't know why censors fail to understand they can never win. Not really, not in the long run. Censorship of any sort is *news* and serves to give wider circulation to the offensive material. We won the publicity battle at every turn.

In Houston, the *Post* ran a huge headline: "BEST LITTLE WHAT IN TEXAS?" A second story resulted when one of the censor's spokesmen mistakenly referred to me as the author of *Confessions of a White Rapist* rather than *White Racist.*

Associated Press carried worldwide the story of the South African attempts at censorship—and of how we got around the law by using the bicycle horns. This was printed in many countries, including South Africa, and doubtless sold tickets there.)

After Cardinal Cooke's denouncement, Stevie Phillips telephoned to ask me to concoct a rebuttal, which was issued in the name of Warren Knowlton, one of the show's publicists: "Cardinal Cooke and various old ladies who don't know what is going on on Eighth Avenue complain about the word 'whorehouse.' If they, theatregoers, and the gentlemen of the Transit Authority want to see something terrible, let them get on the buses and look out rather than standing outside looking in." This rebuttal caused two New York television stations to go into the streets with their cameras, interview people getting on or off our bannered buses, and ask them to make a moral judgment. A lesson in advertising: most bus riders hadn't noticed the signs! Both A.P. and U.P. moved bus-censorship stories; A.P. also dispatched a wirephoto of one of the *Whorehouse* buses—stopped on Fifth Avenue directly in front of Saint Patrick's Cathedral!

Perhaps a month later, visiting Manhattan, I was surprised to see several buses still bearing our signs. When I asked Stevie Phillips about this she winked and said, "There's more than one way to skin a cat in New York. The Transit Authority didn't say *how fast* those signs had to come down." Yes, business can be done in Gotham if you know whom to deal with.

I got the giggles when the shoe was on on the other foot: some Universal executives got exercised when a real whorehouse used our show logo without authorization in advertisements in *Screw* magazine! Using our lariat script, television screen, and a sexy pair of legs protruding from it, the ad proclaimed "The Best Little Whorehouse in New York"—featuring Miss Gail and friends—might be reached by telephoning a certain number. Some silly lawyer suggested suing, but Stevie Phillips decided it wasn't worth the trouble. Pete and I conjectured about collecting our damages in trade, but our sterling characters won out.

I could never quite understand the hostility of some patrons, who came to see *Whorehouse* and then complained about its being a "dirty show." Given the title, and the photos outside the theatre of the Chicken Ranch girls in their skimpy costumes, you'd think anyone buying a ticket would know not to expect *Peter Pan* or *Annie*. Some people even brought small children, in the seven-to-eleven age range, and after a couple of scenes stormed out to the box office to demand their money back. Such actions reinforced my conviction that a great number of stupid people wander free in our society.

The hostility most overtly expressed toward our show came from real-life street hookers in New York. Periodically, it would be discovered that overnight someone, or several someones, had written hostile and obscene messages in lipstick on the glass covering the photos of our stage whores outside the theatre. A stage doorman caught a couple of hookers doing this one night and inquired about their actions. "You mother-fuckers exploitin' us working girls," one of them said, and cursed the doorman with such fervor he retreated into the theatre. After perhaps a year of defacing our show pictures and posters, the prostitutes abruptly ceased—as if, somehow, we had finally been accepted along with other Times Square sleaze.

Good news arrived in May, when *Whorehouse* received seven Tony nominations, which are to the legitimate theatre what the Oscar is to the movie business.

We were in contention for:

1. Best Musical (against *Sweeney Todd, Ballroom,* and *They're Playing Our Song*).

2. Best Book of a Musical: myself and Pete Masterson.
3. Best Direction of a Musical: Masterson and Tommy Tune.
4. Best Choreography: Tommy Tune.
5. Best Featured Actor in a Musical: Henderson Forsythe, as Sheriff Ed Earl Dodd.

6-7. Best Featured Actress in a Musical: Carlin Glynn, as Miss Mona,* and Joan Ellis, as Shy. (This pitting of two of our stars against each other gave rise to certain tensions.)

Now, friends, when nominated for high honors I try never to get excited about my prospects. This is because I have been nominated for about fourteen things and have won only twice. Anyone batting .142 in the Nomination League ought not to dream of hitting the big home run. Invariably, however, I am beguiled. My daydreams take on an alarming reality. I start composing acceptance speeches and rehearsing them in front of mirrors. It was no different this time.

The way I figured it, all Pete Masterson and I had to do was beat out Neil Simon and two other guys. That gave us a twenty-five percent shot at the thing from scratch, right? And should Neil Simon and only one of the two other guys happen to die, our chances would immediately double. Any fool could see that.

My main hope was that Neil Simon had won so many, many Tonys everybody was bored with voting for him. Then I learned that although he had been nominated for eleven Tonys—yes, *eleven*—he had never won one. Naturally, this gave me new hope: I now rationalized that obviously God did not want Neil Simon to have a Tony.

They told all the nominees to be at the Shubert Theatre ninety minutes before telecast time, so they could light our faces for the camera and teach us to bow or curtsy. Hundreds of fans stood in the rain, behind police barricades, squealing and jumping and waving when such people as Angela Lansbury, Henry Fonda, Jack Lemmon, Tom Conti, and Len Cariou leaped, grinning, from their limousines into the stammer and stutter of strobe lights. I had a limousine, too. When I leaped out, that action had a curiously calming effect on the crowd.

Inside the Shubert I left my wife, on the excuse of grabbing a last smoke. Seeking a private corner, I walked up on what appeared to be a group of well-dressed winos, mumbling to themselves and making broad gestures. All were smiling, though some had tears in their eyes. As I recognized the faces—Vincent Gardenia, Tommy Tune, Dorothy Loudon—I realized it was my fellow nominees practicing their acceptance speeches. Not wanting anyone to hear mine until the nation did, I repaired to a booth in the gents' room.

Nervous, yes. But I felt good. Along about my sixth pre-Tony Cutty-and-water, I had even begun to dream of a *Whorehouse* sweep—*seven* Tonys! Had any show won that many before? There I was, in a tuxedo for only the third time in my life and imagining myself just short of lean, rubbing shoulders with the Big Boys of Broadway the first time out. If you ain't gonna dream then, you ain't gonna ever.

And then I saw my seat in the Shubert Theatre.

See, they had sent all nominees a friendly letter saying we would be placed in aisle seats so that when they sang out our famous, winning names we could reach the stage quickly. Naturally, I assumed the ticket that came along with these instructions was for an aisle seat. Wouldn't you?

"You don't have an aisle seat," Barbara hissed. Her legal training came to the fore and straightaway she began threatening to sue. About the time I got her marginally shushed the Tony show's producer, one Mr. Alexander Cohen, said my name over a microphone from center stage in a tone usually reserved for errant children. Whereupon he added, "You somehow have managed to get in the wrong seat. Will you please correct yourself?" I tried to shout that my location, by God, exactly matched the ticket he'd sent me. But I don't think he could hear me over the scornful laughter.

They found me an aisle seat, all right. Lemme tell you about that booger:

It was in the third row, extreme stage right, very near the prop department's broom closet. And *in front*—somehow—of the first four or five steps leading up to the stage, where the winners would go. I was damn near *under* the steps. It became apparent that should I win, I could reach the stage by (A) climbing on the shoulders of the TV technicians so that (B) I could boost myself to the top of the camera and then (C) leap from there down to the stage. Or, alternatively, I could turn hard left and dash to the back of the huge theatre, shoot only two more hard lefts, and thence race two hundred yards down the center aisle to the steps leading up to the winners' circle.

Barbara turned to me and said, "If you want to belch that acceptance speech tonight, you'd better whisper it in my ear."

I said, "What?" Smiling in case the cameras were on us.

She said, "Those effing TV people are lighting only the nominees on the two inner aisles."

I said she should quit making trouble.

"No! They're not even pretending to light the two outer aisles! And you, chum, you're on an outer aisle."

"Excuse me," I said to a TV technician who at that exact moment stepped on my rented tuxedo shoes. He said, "Sure, Bub, but try to keep your dogs off them coils and cables. We got work to do here."

Barbara issued a word her mother surely never taught her and added, "I thought the winners were supposed to be kept such a big dark secret."

"It was a secret to me," I said, "until just a moment ago."

Mr. Alexander Cohen was by now scolding everybody not to make acceptance speeches longer than thirty seconds, though he added we should be witty. He called attention to a huge, blood-red clock, which would tick off time in the speaker's face, and hinted that the long-winded might get the gong. Once the telecast started, however, he divested himself of many long speeches, despite the fact that he had not won anything. Perhaps he was merely doing his job, just reading off the cue-cards. It makes me suspicious, however, to know that his wife, Hildy Parks, wrote the Tony show.

I am not kidding you about that. Nor am I kidding you that the longest musical number shown on the national telecast was not from *Whorehouse* or one of the three other shows nominated for Best Musical. No, it was from *I Remember Mama.* Mr. Alexander Cohen not only produced the Tony show, see, he also produced . . . three guesses. Right: *I Remember Mama.* Them show-biz folk is sneaky rascals.

Censors laboring for good old CBS-TV butchered our *Whore-*

*house* song on the telecast by bleeping—with a xylophone band, yet—such horribly offensive words as *laid* and *made*. Though the singers were dressed as football players, the network do-gooders even bleeped the expression "Right between the goal posts." This in effect reduced Carol Hall's funny "Aggie Song" to coast-to-coast gibberish. Later on, I hugged her while she sobbed in our shared limousine. (We had quit having such long, interesting fights once we'd started helping to make each other about half rich.)

After a while I commenced thumbing through the *Playbill* while a lot of people who lisped and walked funny pranced up to claim their Tonys. I noted that all nominees—not only actors, directors, and lordly producers, but the lighting technicians and set designers and costume makers as well—had their pictures beaming from the *Playbill* pages alongside several paragraphs bragging on themselves. Well, everybody except the stagehands . . . and the writers. There was one page in the *Playbill* upon which they dumped the bare names of all the writer nominees and said not another mumbling word about us. I might have been a Korean orphan, or blind, or a blond transvestite for all the *Playbill* knew. I looked up from this perusal when Mr. Alexander Cohen had the audacity to say, "Before it can get to the stage, it must be on the page." I sat there and wondered why, if the son of a bitch insisted on treating writers as second-class citizens, he had troubled to marry one. Maybe it was his way of punishing her, I dunno.

Carlin Glynn won a Tony for her excellence as Miss Mona, first crack out of the box, and I got a little teary-eyed thinking of this Cinderella housewife and mother who had not been on a professional stage in a dozen years until *Whorehouse* and who *never* had sung in public before. Henderson Forsythe immediately won a Tony as cussin' old Ed Earl Dodd, and the *Whorehouse* contingent was going crazy: two-for-two! We cheered our winners out of the Shubert as they disappeared across the street to Sardi's, where they were met by the press and photographers and waiters bearing champagne. As for me and the rest of the *Whorehouse* gang, it was all a bumpy downhill ride from there.

Two long, dry hours later Jane Fonda presented her daddy a special Tony for years of excellence in the acting business. They hugged each other with tears in their eyes. Down there in our wretched seats, Barbara and I did the same. We had to do it surreptitiously, because you aren't allowed to cry in public unless you win.

A footnote: God again did not permit Neil Simon to win. One of the other two guys won in our category. I damn sure don't intend to call his name, nobody having called mine.

It appeared that ten thousand people pushed and shoved into the Grand Ballroom of the Waldorf-Astoria for the Tony Supper Ball after the telecast. I doubt whether old man Jim Beam himself could have obtained a decent glass of whiskey in the sweaty crush.

I was out of snuff and had a headache and a mad on at those squealing, hugging, kissing finks from *Sweeny Todd* who had beat us out for Best Musical and, overall, had out-Tonyed us seven to two. "*Todd* is a goddamn tuneless opera," I grumbled. "It has no book, and everyone in it's so afflicted with fake cockney accents I couldn't understand a word." Lawyer Blaine said, "Gee, sport, you're a lot of fun tonight. You must drop in more often."

We found Delores Hall of the *Whorehouse* cast and lamented Carol Hall's not having been nominated for her score and Tommy Tune losing the Tony for choreography to Michael Bennett and Bob Avian of *Ballroom,* which had been a Broadway flop. "It's a weird year," Dee-Dee said. "I'm glad I was up for my Tony last year . . . when the *real talent* won," and she broke into delightful laughter. Carlin Glynn joined us; we hugged, I offering congratulations and she returning condolences. "Hank and I waited in Sardi's for the rest of our *Whorehouse* family to join us," she said, "but every time a new winner walked in the door it was some stranger." She sniffled. Delores said, "Now, enough of that jazz, Carlin darlin'. You go on and enjoy the Tony *you* won. I know what it is to sweat out all that opening-of-the-envelope hocus-pocus. And you better believe that when *I* won, honey, I didn't waste tears on no also-rans!"

At dinner, around one of hundreds of round tables seating a dozen persons, I found Joan Ellis on my immediate right. I did the polite thing and mumbled that I was sorry she hadn't won.

"If I *had* won," she said, "I intended to denounce the whole

Tony process. I think it's destructive and ridiculous to put artists in competition with each other."

"In which case," I said, "I am glad you did *not* win."

"Why? Why should artists be in competition with each other?"

"Why do some 'artists' try to steal scenes?" I asked, thinking of her undisciplined performances during the six weeks she'd almost driven us nuts. "Look, these awards create interest in the theatre. They're good for business, they help meet the payrolls, and they boost careers." And all the time a little voice in my head is saying, *My God, King, you sound like a Republican banker.*

"Well, anyway, I'm leaving the show and all this phoniness behind," Joan said heatedly. "I'm going to Hawaii and live with *real* people and pick pineapples."

"*What?*" I said, laughing in spite of myself. "Have you ever done any work like that?"

"No, but I'm not afraid of it."

"Just remember that scene you had with Brad," I said. "The one where you talked of picking cotton, remember? About how you stay on your knees until they rub raw, then bend over until your back breaks, and you go back on your knees again? If you're looking for *real,* Shy, you'll damn sure find it in the pineapple patch! And you'll probably find that kind of 'real' is worth about a nickel a bushel." We said no more. Everyone concentrated on the Chilled Cream of Avocado en Tasse. (I may have been a bit hard on the young lady. Eighteen months later I heard that Joan Ellis was back in New York, resuming her acting career, and telling friends that sudden Broadway stardom had freaked her out and she hadn't known how to handle it.)

As Barbara and I reached our bed at a late hour I said, "No more. I ain't going to hang around no more of these Tony dos. Too depressing."

"I imagine you'll stick to your guns," she said, "until you're nominated again."

I turned over, punched my pillow as a substitute, and went to sleep. If there's anything I can't stand it's a smartass who's probably right.

Those who run stage shows—the producer and the various company managers—come to know that actors have at least as many human problems as the rest of us. Each company—players and crew—of *Whorehouse* numbers about forty-five to fifty people and few of them are perfect. Not a company is formed but what the range of tribulations may include love spats of both heterosexual and homosexual nature, a secret drunk or two, someone who's always being garnisheed for debts or taxes, a chronic tardy-ass whom the other players must sweat out each night, a thief, infrequently, and even an occasional attempted suicide.

There are constant replacement problems. People are fired or quit over contract disputes, misunderstandings, for reasons of fatigue, or because they can't stand a given colleague. Though much is made of each company's being a family—and there *is* a great deal of warmth and a generally supportive attitude—families have their disputes, too. Sometimes the fighting goes public.

In mid-1979, Marietta Marich—Miss Mona in the Houston company—let fly with her complaints to the press. She blasted "out of tune instruments in the orchestra, amplification problems, ad-libs by other actors, and a general sloppiness in day-to-day performances." She had complained to management without results, she said, so it was time to go public. Stevie Phillips fired her forthwith, blaming the dismissal on "personal and personality problems on the part of Miss Marich." Marietta shot back that she was fired "for being a perfectionist who made demands for perfection." No matter who shot John, June Terry came in as the new Miss Mona.

Soon Miss Edna Milton came to Paul Phillips, our Broadway manager, to announce she'd had it with show biz and was going on her merry way immediately.

"Your contract calls for two weeks' notice, Miss Edna," Paul said in his gentlemanly way. Miss Edna suggested where her contract might be stuck. "I'm just thinking of you, Edna," Paul said. "If you walk out on a contract you can get your business in bad shape with Actors' Equity."

"Piss on them people," Edna said. "All they done was take dues from me. What do I need them for? I ain't likely to be back on Broadway again." Paul Phillips found that pretty difficult to argue with, and wished her Godspeed.

Edna left forthwith for Dallas, where she opened a small bar—Miss Edna's Chicken Ranch—featuring country-western bands. I am afraid she inflicted her singing on her customers a few times, which may or may not account for the fact that her club shut its doors after a couple of months. She disappeared, reportedly to a farm in East Texas, and I know of no one who has heard from her since.

One evening I was in New York, dropped by the 46th Street Theatre during intermission to greet friends, and discovered Pete Masterson there. We had not seen each other for a spell, and we strolled up to Joe Allen's for beers.

I brought up the name of a cast member whom I shall disguise by calling him Joe-Joe. I had never been truly enamored of Joe-Joe's work and, indeed, thought he got worse all the time. "We really should replace that dude," I said. "We're permitting him to limit what that role could be. The right guy in it—well, Jesus, he could liven up the scenes by thirty or forty percent."

"I agree," Pete said.

I was startled. Never before had he flatly made that admission. Oh, sure, he had muttered a sort of general accord but he always ended by saying he felt sorry for the fellow and couldn't bring himself to fire him. The last time Pete had said that, I had berated him for permitting his personal feelings to interfere with the good of the show. So now I said, "Well, shit, that's it then! Go fire the dude."

"No," Pete said, "I'm gonna let you do that."

"Uh . . . what?"

"I'm giving you authority," Pete said, "to fire him. I want it done tonight."

"Well, now, shit. I mean, wait a minute—"

"Naw, I've heard for six months or a year how Joe-Joe ought to be out on his ass. I agree with you wholeheartedly, and I think the time has come. You go up there and fire his ass, and I'll be there to watch."

"Aw, shit, Pete. I, uh . . ."

"Come on," Pete said. "We're going back to the theatre and you do your duty. I'm tired of hearing about this."

We stood in the back of the house and I heard not a line, not a song. I was rehearsing how to fire Joe-Joe and getting worse at it by the minute. Maybe Pete was funning me. *Sure! That was it!* He wouldn't actually go through with this charade.

But when the finale was over and as the audience filed out, Pete grasped me firmly by one arm and said, "Okay, let's get this Joe-Joe deal over with."

"There are too many people around, Pete. How about I call him tomorrow and—"

"Hell, no. Tonight's the night. This is what you've always wanted."

We seek out Joe-Joe and I scuff my feet awhile and whistle and sigh and Pete stands by patiently while Joe-Joe mouths inane pleasantries. When it can be stalled no longer I say, "Uh, Joe-Joe . . ."

He looks at me expectantly.

"Uh, Joe-Joe . . ."

"Yeah, Larry?"

"Uh, Joe-Joe. There's something I got to tell you."

"Yeah? What?"

"Uh, Joe-Joe." I glance at Pete, who is standing arms akimbo and looking innocent.

"Uh, Joe-Joe," I say. I reach out and paw at his shoulder. "Joe-Joe, you doing one hell of a job in this show. Keep up the good work."

The life of a publicist handling a Broadway show cannot be an easy one. Like his political counterpart, who must always present the boss as a competent and patriotic statesman while hiding his warts, the show-business publicity man must deal with large egos and present his charges in the best possible light. No matter how many talk-show bookings or newspaper interviews he arranges, it is never enough. If he too prominently promotes one player, another feels neglected and complains. Sometimes it is the publicist's job to prevent news of cast feuds or worse from getting into the newspapers; on the other hand, he must think of ingenious schemes to keep the show's name before the public long after the news has worn off. It is a competitive field—every show on Broadway, every prominent actor or actress or movie star or author expects to receive more attention than is statistically possible.

When I was not as understanding of these facts as I later became, I received a call from some dude in the office of Jeffrey Richards, our publicist, who wanted to "check an item" with me. He then read: "Larry L. King, coauthor of *BLWIT*, will commute from New York to Houston once a week next semester to teach Mexican culinary arts at Rice University." While I sat stunned he said, "Okay to feed that item to gossip columnists?"

"Why, hell no," I snorted. "That's silly. I can't fry a goddamn egg. When it comes to cooking I don't know the difference between a tortilla and refried beans. Where'd you get such a bullshit item?"

"Well, ah, I invented it," he admitted.

"Uninvent it," I said.

Rice University apparently stayed on the fellow's mind. A year later I picked up the *New York Post* to read: "The 'must' course at Houston's Rice University this year is 'Living Texas,' with lectures to new arrivals to the Lone Star State on eveything from chicken-fried steak to talkin' Texas. Larry L. King, coauthor of *The Best Little Whorehouse in Texas* (which marks its 1,000th Broadway performance on September 13th), will lecture on the famed Chicken Ranch which inspired the play."

This time, I just shook my head at such hogwash. At least I understood the game better: the purpose of the item was to get the name of our show in print and to call attention to our having passed the 1,000-performance milestone—which only sixty-odd shows have managed in the history of Broadway. Somehow, though, the rules of the publicity game will not permit a straightforward one-liner saying, "Hey, gang, *BLWIT* will play its 1,000th performance on September 13th." You have got to jazz it up.

Henderson Forsythe, while being interviewed by Martin Burden of the *New York Post,* said, "I bet you didn't know that I am the mayor of West 46th Street."

"No," the gossip columnist said.

"It's a high honor," our sheriff said wryly. "Nobody knows it but me and the publicity man who created the title—and now you."

Everyone knew it, of course, who read Mr. Burden's subsequent column—and a couple of other columnists promptly picked up the sobriquet. Which leads me to believe that ol' Hank Forsythe ain't a bad publicity agent in his own right. I've even wondered if *he* invented the story of the publicity agent's having invented it.

The more attention *Whorehouse* attracted, the more it seemed to upset the good people back in LaGrange. Newsmen from all over the country, facing a slow news day, dropped by the little town so they could tell their readers what life was like in the place that spawned one of the nation's most famous cathouses.

Increasingly, the quotes from the locals in such stories took on a more acrimonious tone. Sheriff T. J. Flournoy got so he was almost as hostile as during the days when the Chicken Ranch was shut down. Of talk that the movie version would be shot in LaGrange—which we really never had considered—he said, "We don't want 'em, we won't have 'em and that's it." When the old sheriff announced his upcoming retirement from office at the end of 1980—by now he was almost an octogenarian—he told the Associated Press, "I don't want to hear 'Chicken Ranch' or the name of that show again as long as I live. My wife is sick of hearing about it and so am I." I strongly suspect the A.P. reporter thoroughly fumigated the quote before using it.

Edwin (Bud) Shrake, my writing buddy from Austin, paused at a beer joint in LaGrange one day and asked the bartender how he felt about all the publicity *Whorehouse* had generated. The barkeep said, "I tell ya, friend, I can near about put it in words I seen wrote in the crapper in a bus station one time: *I wish the man that started in/a-writin' in this place/would have to sit/where all the shit/could dribble in his face.*"

In mid-1979 we began casting for the first national company. Three experienced actresses were in the running for the role of Miss Mona: Alexis Smith, Fannie Flagg, and Kathryn Grant Crosby. I happened to be on hand the day Ms. Crosby swooped into City Center for her interview and audition.

She was attended by enough lackeys and gofers to have impressed the late Nizam of Hyderabad, who is mourned by three wives, forty-two concubines, two hundred children, and three hundred retainers; Ms. Crosby's lackeys sprang ahead, opening doors, holding coats, and so on, until I thought they might get around to sprinkling rose petals in her path.

Ms. Crosby took a seat in the production office while one attendant hovered about, occasionally fluffing her hair, and a second whisked at her clothing with a small brush as if grooming a show dog. In the opening pleasantries she managed to inform us early on that she was Bing Crosby's widow—which, as far as I'm concerned, is the very thing she is best known as—and thereafter almost every utterance was preceded with "Bing thought" or "Bing said" or "Bing did." Soon she made some reference to the possible need to clean up Miss Mona's language should she play the role—I think Mona uses one cuss word in the entire show—and I raised my eyebrows to Pete Masterson.

Shortly, I prepared to light a cigarette. "Oh, you mustn't smoke in my presence," Ms. Crosby said.

"I mustn't? Why?"

"I'm terribly allergic to it," she said. "No one may smoke in my presence."

"Lady," I said, "you are going to be in a hell of a shape on the road with a bunch of actors who puff everything from cheap cigars to Mexican Boo-Smoke."

"Not in my presence," she said.

I asked Pete to step outside while I smoked. Once we were in the hall I said, "Pete, I want you to audition that woman's ass off. Sing her, dance her, read her. And then, by God, if you hire her I'm coming after you with a gun."

He laughed and said, "Don't you want her to stick around so you can learn more about Bing?"

"No wonder he died," I said. "I bet it was a great relief to him."

I am happy to announce that Alexis Smith got the role.

Although Fannie Flagg lost out to Miss Smith, she later replaced Carlin Glynn when our original Miss Mona quit to play painter Mary Cassatt in a seven-character workshop drama, *Cassatt,* which had Broadway ambitions, never realized. When Carlin left *Whorehouse* she told *The New York Times,* "I'll return to this show someday. When you create a role that becomes a phenomenon, you always want to do it again." True to her word, she opened as Miss Mona in the London company in early 1981—

opposite the original sheriff, Henderson Forsythe, who had given way on Broadway to Gil Rogers.

Alexis Smith proved to be a great lady. There was no haughty "star" quality about her, no phoniness, no looking down her nose. Cast members loved her because she treated them as equals and was not afraid to cut loose with a hearty, earthy laugh even if the joke was on her. I several times had dinner with Alexis and her husband, Craig Stevens (best known for his title role in the old television series *Peter Gunn*), and found him as nice as she is.

Which made it all the more lamentable that I said an awful thing about Alexis that got published in *Women's Wear Daily*. My excuse is that it occurred during my drinking days and that I had been led into the quote by a presumed friend, who I didn't think would print it.

Lois Romano, whom I had known since she worked for a small newspaper on Capitol Hill, *Roll Call,* came to my home to interview me for *WWD* and kept pestering me to compare the different stars in the various companies—especially the leading ladies. I begged the question, backtracked, equivocated. Finally she said, "Oh, come on, are you satisfied with Alexis Smith as a singer?" My injudicious answer, which was typical of my hyperbole, ran: "Well, she was the best one who auditioned for the national company. You and I know she can't carry a tune in a goddamn sack, but I don't want to get into artistic criticism. She's a great draw on the road and she's making a lot of money for the show." Almost immediately I said, "Lois, now, goddammit! Don't you quote that!" I foolishly believed she would not, though as a journalist I'm certain I would have. And, of course, Lois Romano did, too. Quoted me exactly.

Stevie Phillips telephoned from New York: "Larry, you blabbermouth, what in the world shall I tell Alexis Smith?"

"Oh, shit! Has she read that mess?"

"If she hasn't she certainly will! It's been picked up by *W*, the national edition of *Women's Wear*. And unless I miss my guess, every gossip columnist that sees it will pick it up."

"Then I'm gonna lie," I said.

*"Lie?* 'You and I know she can't carry a tune in a goddamn sack.' That quote *is* you. It *can't* have been faked."

"Then I'll tell a bigger lie," I said. "I'll claim I was talking about my own lack of singing ability when I played the show—and the chickenshit reporter misapplied the quote for her own sensational purposes. I'd a hell of a lot rather have Lois Romano mad at me than Alexis Smith."

"What I think is priceless," Stevie said, laughing, "is that *after* blasting her you say you don't want to get into 'artistic criticism.' "

"Well, shit. Hell. Goddamn. I feel terrible. I *like* ol' Alexis, like her a lot. And actually, I don't think she sings all that bad. She ain't no Peggy Lee, but who is?"

I telephoned my son Brad in Detroit. His bad knee had driven him from the Broadway production as a dancing Aggie, and he became the lead singer-narrator of the Texas Tally Wackers, the show band playing with the Alexis Smith company.

"Jesus, Dad," Brad said immediately, "why'd you say that about Alexis? She's a real fine lady!"

"That's why I'm calling. Is she upset?"

"Well, we don't know if she's seen it. Everybody in the show is tearing up every copy of that damned article they run across. I've tipped off her dresser and driver to keep her away from it. But I don't know how long we can hold the fort."

"Try," I said. "Fight fiercely. And in return, Daddy promises hereafter to be a good boy."

## CHAPTER

# 15

There is something about the thought of being in the movies that makes the average American turn to Silly Putty and go daft. Somewhere—in some wretched Appalachian hollow or Back Bay drawing room—there must be someone—a black-lunged coal miner, a gentle dowager—who does not wish to be in pictures. I have yet to meet them, however. And, if I should, and they somehow learned I was even remotely connected with a movie scheduled for production, they doubtless would change their minds.

From the moment it was indicated there just *might* be a *Whorehouse* movie off in the distant future, I was besieged by friends, relatives, and strangers wanting to be in it. I don't know why this should be so. Not many people seriously consider themselves or their protégés as ripe prospects to sing and dance on Broadway, but transfer the same story to film and suddenly everybody's an actor. "I'll take a small part," people would volunteer, as if we might otherwise draft them for the leading roles, "or I'll even be an extra. But I've *got* to be in that movie." People I had not heard from since the Truman administration wrote or telephoned or looked me up to tout this old girl friend or that cousin or somebody's in-law as "exactly right" for roles that did not yet exist because no screenplay had been written. Never mind that the would-be new stars were by trade milkmen or computer programmers and had not acted since their fourth-grade Christmas pageants. The amateurs, indeed, were more insistent than the professionals—and, Lord knows, they were bad enough.

It goes without saying that almost every player in all of the *Whorehouse* stage versions campaigned for screen tests to one degree or another; just about every other actor I know, and many I did not know, mailed résumés and pictures or begged for personal appointments. It did not do one smidgen of good to tell either the amateur or professional hopefuls truthfully that I would not be involved in casting, had no authority to cast, had no qualifications to cast, and did not wish to cast the movie. Nor did it help to say—again, truthfully—"Listen, if I could get anyone a part in that movie I would get *myself* a part in that movie." These truths were seen as clever evasions or heartless disclaimers and were received in disbelief, anger, or an accusing silence. Though I had no idea who would actually do the casting for Universal, I ultimately adopted the tactic of siccing people on Pete Masterson or Bonnie Champion in Stevie Phillips's office. On days I felt playful I solemnly assured the aspirants, "Don't take no for an answer. He (she) can do it if he (she) really wants to." The recipients of such assurances were almost pathetically grateful.

The earliest and most persistent campaigner, I suspect, was the actress Shirley MacLaine, seeking the role of Miss Mona. Not that Miss MacLaine ever got in touch with me, no. I don't know that she once got in touch with anyone from Universal for that matter. But if one read the gossip columns, everyone from Liz Smith to Robin Adams Sloan, one could not help but suspect that Miss MacLaine wanted the role badly. She was forever being reported as "having the inside track," or being "favored" to play the *Whorehouse* madam. I had learned enough of press agentry to suspect that Miss MacLaine had not ordered her flack to cease and desist. Actually, I was rather enamored of the idea. I liked Shirley MacLaine's acting, considered her a bright talent, and thought we'd be lucky to have her. When I mentioned this to Universal bigwigs, however, I was told she was not big enough box office. I got the same answer when I plumped for Jill Clayburgh, Carlin Glynn, and Dyan Cannon.

Early on, it turned out, Universal had Dolly Parton in mind. "Jesus," I said on hearing the news. "Too obvious. She *looks* like she might run a whorehouse or work in one." Some Universal nabob, however, had become enchanted with the idea of Dolly Parton and I don't believe anyone else ever was seriously considered. She is the only actress I know of who was squired to the play by Stevie Phillips and a half ton of assorted Universal brass. The night Ms. Parton was at the 46th Street Theatre, by the way, our irrepressible steel guitar man, Lynn Frazier, leaned over during the warm-up music and said to fiddler Ernie Reed, "Hey, man, you see Dolly's tits?" Frazier did not realize, until it was too late, that a microphone had shared his question with much of the audience—including Stevie Phillips, who was furious. Fortunately, Ms. Parton thought it funny and so Lynn Frazier did not get handed a sandwich and a road map.

I wanted old Texas outlaw Willie Nelson to play Sheriff Ed Earl Dodd. Though this suggestion was made long before Nelson had filmed either *The Electric Horseman,* with Robert Redford and Jane Fonda, or *Honeysuckle Rose,* in which he played the starring role, Universal officials seemed more than ordinarily interested. Willie was flown up from Texas to see the stage play. Stevie Phillips called me to come up to New York for that event, on the grounds I was the only one connected with making the show who knew Nelson.

When I walked into a swanky hotel suite in midtown Manhattan that night, I could not believe my eyes. On one side of the room sat Universal's mafiosi, in tuxedos and black ties; on the other side of the room stood Willie Nelson, songwriter Hank Cochran, harmonica player Mickey Raphael, and the rest of Willie's outlaws wearing bandanas around their heads, scuffed boots, and ragged blue jeans. Everybody was sipping white wine. *White wine,* now! It was as quiet and tense in there as a funeral parlor where two exwives have shown up to outmourn each other, and each has brought her own claque.

"God's sakes, Stevie," I said. "Send somebody out to get these boys a decent drink of whiskey." Cheers from the raggedy-ass side of the room. Soon the party was in full sway.

Willie was allowed to drink in his box seat during the show. At intermission, we repaired to a limousine Universal had rented for him, which was parked directly in front of the 46th Street Theatre. We smoked a bit and ate some stuff I guess was baking powder.

"How much you reckon I can get from these sumbitches?" Willie asked.

"Ask for two million," I said. "You probably won't get it, but you might get a million or more."

"That right?"

"Damn sure is."

"Shit," Willie said, "that sure beats playing in beer joints."

We began talking music and trash and such. Suddenly I looked up to notice the intermission sidewalk was bare of folk. Inside the theatre lobby, Stevie and a dozen tuxes stood peering anxiously at the limo. "Oh shit, Willie," I said, "we've missed ten or fifteen minutes of the second act."

Afterward, they took us to Sardi's. The maître d' originally looked askance at Willie—hair in braids, bib-and-gallus overalls, a red bandana wrapped around his forehead, tennis shoes—but decided he must be a V.I.P. when he saw a dozen tuxes bowing and scraping and opening doors for him. Lynn Frazier had joined us from the band at Willie's request—they had played together in the old days, when each was a mite hungry. By the time all the tuxes sat at the long dinner table prepared for Stevie's party, we were a chair short. "That's okay," Frazier said. "I'll go upstairs to the bar."

"I'll go with you, Frazier," I said, thinking Willie would stay behind to talk business.

But as Lynn and I walked up the stairs and approached the bar, we turned to find Willie Nelson trailing behind us. "I'd druther be up here with ya'll," he said. We drank beer and bullshitted, three old Texas boys invading Broadway.

"Ya'll like it up here?" Willie asked.

"It's a living," Frazier said.

"Hell, I love it," I said. "If you've got enough money, it's the greatest city in the world."

"If you got enough money," Willie said through a grin, "you could probably say that about Waco." A moment later he said, "Who are all those penguins down there with Stevie?"

"Only one I know is Thom Mount," I said. "He's some big injun with Universal. I think the rest are just Hollywood finks they flew in to carry your jock tonight."

"I wish some of 'em would go home," he said. "I don't care to have to talk to 'em."

We shortly were approached by a tuxedo, who told me Ms. Phillips very much wished for us to join her party.

"You go pull her aside," I instructed, "and tell her Willie says all them penguins making him nervous. Tell her to send some of 'em home. We'll be along directly."

When we ultimately joined Stevie's party, the crowd was down to manageable size. Stevie got the drift, however, and whispered that Willie looked as if he'd rather be elsewhere. "You got it," I said. She told me to take him where he wanted to go, do what he wanted to do, and send her the bill.

Lynn Frazier and I took the country-music superstar to the ratty old Golden Gate Bar, across the street from the stage door of the 46th Street Theatre—which Lynn frequented so often he called it "my office"—and drank beer long into the night.

A few weeks later, when negotiations with Willie Nelson's agent didn't seem to be getting far, Stevie asked me to go to Austin to heat Nelson up. I checked into the Driskill Hotel, where Willie, his band, and others in the cast of *Honeysuckle Rose* were staying to begin rehearsing the music for that movie. When Willie was not busy, I hustled him at all hours. A week later I returned East, and telephoned Stevie Phillips in hot excitement to say that I had extracted from Willie his promise that he would be in *Whorehouse*. All she had to do was make the money right.

"Willie?" she said. "Oh, didn't anybody tell you?"

What, tell me?

"Dolly Parton's decided it would be bad for her image to play a whorehouse madam. And if we can't get Dolly, we're really not interested in Willie. We wanted them as a team."

I wrote Willie Nelson a note of apology and explanation, saying I felt I had been led down the primrose path. I heard nothing in return.

One day Stevie Phillips called to announce with pride that negotiations were underway with Burt Reynolds for the role of Sheriff Dodd.

"I don't know, Stevie," I said. "I've never seen Burt Reynolds play anything but Burt Reynolds. I'm not sure he can play anything else."

"Well, remember this," she said. "He *is* the number-one movie box-office draw in the world and he could make you big bucks. And he could make an exciting pairing with Dolly."

*Dolly?* What, Dolly?

"Oh, didn't anyone tell you?" Stevie said. "Burt Reynolds talked to Dolly personally and she's changed her mind. We're in negotiations with her, too."

I didn't write Willie Nelson another note saying the bastards had clotheslined me again. By then, I figured, he would never believe another word I told him.

Peter Masterson and Tommy Tune were to codirect the *Whorehouse* movie, and Pete and I would script it. We wrote three drafts before we got it where we wanted it, which is about par for the movie course. I foolishly figured that was it. Despite all I had read about movie stars demanding changes and rewrites, I didn't give much thought to that possibility: how could they improve on perfection?

Meanwhile, negotiations with Burt and Dolly had hit a snag. Burt wanted $5 million in front and a piece of the gross and Dolly wanted $2 million and a piece of the gross. After the haggling had gone on for weeks, I picked up the newspaper one morning to find Universal president Ned Tanen dithyrambing. "They are trying to hold us up for seven million between them, and they're using as a club that one won't do the film without the other. Well, you can only be pushed so far." Mr. Tanen went on to say that courageous executives must put their feet down or draw the line or some such, and that "we will do the film without them." I didn't believe a word of it. "It's a ploy," I told Barbara, "to get them back to the negotiation table. Like Lyndon tried to get the North Vietnamese to negotiate by bombing 'em."

Sure enough, it shortly was announced that Burt Reynolds had signed for $3.5 million in front and an unannounced percentage of the gross, and that Dolly Parton had signed for $1.5 million and ditto. Not bad for about five weeks' work each. I do believe they can winter on it.

Pete Masterson met with each of our stars, individually, and pronounced the discussions satisfactory. "Dolly's nice and down home," he said. "Burt's a little uptight but I think he may come around."

"What does he say about playing a sixty-two-year-old man?"

"Well, ah, I wanted to mention that. He wants to play him a little younger."

"No shit?" I said dryly. "How young, twenty-eight?"

"Naw, naw. He'll sail for about fifty. I don't think that will cause too many problems in the script. He does want a few changes, but they aren't really major."

When I next talked to Stevie Phillips she told a different story. "Burt says he doesn't want to play the sheriff as 'an old fart.' And he wants another car chase and two more fistfights."

"You tell the son of a bitch I know where he can get his first fistfight," I said.

"Now, Larry, please! Let's don't get everyone in an uproar right off. Give us a little time to work things out."

Next it seemed that Burt Reynolds thirsted to sing. *Oh, my God! Not the Battle of the Singing Sheriff again! I've fought that fight more times than John Wayne defended the Alamo.*

Have any of you kiddies ever heard Uncle Burt sing? Huh? Uncle Larry heard him sing. It was in a film where Uncle Burt and Cybill Shepherd both tried to sing *and* dance, kiddies, and you know what? Can you guess? It was *muy malo, compadres.* El Stinkaroo. El Floppo. Bet your sweet bibbies Uncle Burt didn't smash the worldwide box-office record *that* year. Not with *At Long Last, Love* like an albatross around his macho neck.

"He wants a solo," Masterson said gloomily, "and a couple of duets with Dolly."

"Our best defense," I said, "is to screen for Dolly that awful musical he made. Make her see it three or four times. Do that, and I'll bet Dolly tries to get it in her contract the sumbitch isn't even allowed to hum in her presence."

I ran into my friend Bud Shrake, who'd just returned from Hollywood after completing what proved to be the next-to-last screenplay for Steve McQueen, called *Tom Horn.*

"Who's directing your movie?" he asked.

"Pete Masterson and Tommy Tune."

"That's not what they're saying out on the Left Coast."

"Oh? What did you hear?"

"Just that Universal is putting too much money into the film to let it be directed by a couple of guys who've never directed a film before."

"Who told you that?"

Shrake named a Universal official I won't name here, so as not to cause Shrake grief. It was a name big enough to impress me.

The next time I talked to Masterson I said, "Ah, Pete, are things going well with you and the Universal big shots?"

"Oh yeah," he said. "We're off in a few days to scout locations in Texas. Got a half dozen little towns to look at. Right now we're leaning toward Lockhart. It's got this great old courthouse and the town looks kind of shabby. Made to order!" Pete seemed in such high spirits I decided not to mention Bud Shrake's report. Perhaps Shrake was wrong.

I asked Pete what was the latest from our stars. "Well," he said, "Dolly's not entirely satisfied with the music. She wants to write several new songs."

"She's good at it," I admitted, "but what will that do to our screenplay?"

"I've asked her to try to write songs that won't disturb it too much. Of course, if she writes a real whiz we'll just have to make adjustments."

Soon it developed that Dolly Parton was unhappy with more than the songs. To *People* magazine she said, "In the play, the madam and the sheriff don't even touch each other. That's got to be changed. Ya don't think I'm gonna miss my big chance with Burt Reynolds, do ya?" Variations of this theme appeared in gossip columns and show-biz stories all over the country. "She's never said a word like that to me," Masterson said. "I think Reynolds is putting her up to that. He's the one who's been bitching about no hot love scenes."

In early July 1980, I enrolled in a school where they teach you not to drink whiskey once you've become too proficient at it. Should this confession embarrass my loved ones, may they be consoled by the knowledge that William Faulkner—among other writers—took the same course several times, and others might have lived longer if they had. "King's matriculating at Whiskey A&M," my Texas pals joked.

Whiskey school was deep in the scenic Maryland countryside. Though well appointed, it was isolated and lonely and not a nickel's work of fun. About the eighth day I am there, battling my conscience to keep from running away, Stevie Phillips tracks me down.

"Larry," she says, "you must fly to California immediately. You, Pete, and I must meet tomorrow with the studio honchos on script changes."

"You don't understand," I say. "I'm not even allowed to go to the mailbox out here. Isolation is part of the program."

"Well, we've got to make some changes Burt Reynolds wants. Ned Tanen, our president, is going along with Reynolds. What shall we do?"

"I'll talk with Pete after you guys meet with the Universal biggies. We'll work it out."

Pete reports back that Burt Reynolds is being as difficult as a spoiled child: "He wants to play it real macho. The sheriff can't be older than about thirty-five, and all the whores must be in love with him."

"Jesus Christ! I thought Lyndon Johnson had an overgrown ego. Ol' Lyndon was a bashful country boy compared to this Reynolds asshole."

For several evenings, after my rehabilitation classes, I work far into the night writing scenes to give Miss Mona and Ed Earl a warmer relationship. I even go against my high principles and permit a scene where a couple of whores flirt with Burt and he gets to leer at them and slap one smartly on the backside. Each night, at midnight or after, I telephone the new scenes to a secretary in California whom Stevie Phillips has standing by to type them up for examination by Universal big shots the next day.

After each such exercise, Hollywood's pooh-bahs proclaim themselves pleased beyond any singing of it. Then, when all the scenes are done, Pete telephones to say that the Hollywood hotshots have decided they will not do. All have been vetoed.

"I don't understand," I tell him, "how the scenes can be so marvelous individually—and yet so absolutely unsatisfactory in the aggregate. What are those bastards smoking out there?"

Pete sighs. "This goddamn industry runs on two fuels: money and fear. Let's face it, Burt Reynolds has the economic power. So he has fear working on his side."

"Buncha goddamn rabbits," I mutter. "Well, screw 'em. I ain't rewriting another scene or writing another new one. If Burt Reynolds wants to write them himself, or bring in somebody else to write his drivel, tell him to go on ahead."

"That's probably what they'll do," Pete says.

"Fine. I'm sick of this whole mess and wash my hands of it. You know, I'm out here in this sanatorium or rich man's nut farm or whatever you want to call it, and those Hollywood fools are running free. So who's the crazy one?"

A couple of mornings later, as my whiskey-school classmates and I watch television in our rec room while awaiting the breakfast bell, still photos of Pete Masterson and Tommy Tune flash on the screen. Rona Barrett, the Hollywood gossiper, informs America approximately as follows: "Universal Picture sources say that Peter Masterson and Tommy Tune, who codirected the hit Broadway play *The Best Little Whorehouse in Texas,* will *not* direct the big-budget movie of the tuner to be shot on location in Texas. The search is on for a replacement director. A Universal spokesman says that the movie company is simply not willing to entrust the twenty-million-dollar picture to directors who have no track record."

A few days later, Universal prexy Ned Tanen is quoted in the newspapers as saying that Colin Higgins—then shooting a movie called *9 to 5*, starring Dolly Parton, Jane Fonda, and Lily Tomlin—will direct the *Whorehouse* film. Taking the picture away from the two men who made it a stage smash signals "nothing against the abilities of Tommy Tune or Peter Masterson," Tanen adds. Sure, Ned. Sure. Like the Japs didn't mean it to be taken personally when they bombed Pearl Harbor.

"I don't think they ever intended to let us direct it," Masterson later said. "They used us to get the basic script, to scout locations, and do all the shit work, and then kicked us out." These months later, no one from Universal has officially notified Masterson or Tune that they are off the project. Plans are simply going forward without them. No person connected with the stage show—and no person with any Texas roots or Texas history—will be in any way involved with the movie.

Even after all that, I continued to see stories with headlines like BURT WANTS A SPICIER WHOREHOUSE or DOLLY SAYS SCRIPT WON'T LET HER HUG BURT'S NECK.

One morning Maxine Cheshire, who writes the V.I.P. column for *The Washington Post,* telephoned to ask me what was going on. I gave her the movie history and added, "I think Burt Reynolds wants to make *Smokey and the Bandit Go to a Whorehouse.* Apparently they don't intend to follow our script at all, and Dolly's said to be writing her own songs. I see only a tenuous connection between *Whorehouse* as we did it and the mess they're concocting in Hollywood. I doubt whether I'll even go see the film version of the sonovabitch, though I may send my lawyer so she can take my name off if it's as bad as its potential."

"Will Dolly wear her outlandish wigs?" Maxine asked.

"I suppose she will," I said, "and probably Burt will wear his, too. I understand they're both bald."

Wellsir, kiddies, that little jest stirred 'em up out in Lotusland to a fare-thee-well. Someone who wouldn't give his right name but hid behind the sobriquet of "a Universal Studio spokesman" sniffed that "Burt Reynolds is a much more important element in the deal than Larry King."

Reynolds himself, issuing a statement through his agent, David Gershenson, said, "I knew I would be made the heavy, and I'm not going to be." Burt went on to claim that he "loved the challenge of playing an older man" and was "thrilled about it until *the studio* decided to make him thirty-five."

Here's my reaction to that, Burt, old buddy and pal—and it's taken directly from the mouth of Sheriff Ed Earl Dodd: "I got me a purty good bullshit detector, boys, and I can damn sure tell when somebody's pissin' on my boots and tellin' me it's a rainstorm." Reynolds later wrote me, maintaining that Universal had, indeed, insisted on a young, macho sheriff, and hotly threatening to take me out behind the barn if I didn't quit bad-mouthing him. At this point I wouldn't know whom to believe if everyone took polygraph tests.

Aw, shucks, I guess I ought not get so worked up at those movie folks. They're just a bunch of business types, selling their product the best they can for maximum profit, the same as the guy who manufactures widgets or toilet-bowl covers. Somebody's got to run pawnshops; can't everybody be Cartier's or Tiffany's.

And though I was fond of the screenplay Pete Masterson and I put together, let's face it: even if the Universal nabobs and Burt and Dolly come up with a movie I hardly recognize, they can't justly be accused of having tampered with Shakespeare or having done violence to Art. *Whorehouse* is an entertainment, pure and simple. Perhaps we set out to do more than that, but we did not. There are no great messages in our show, or philosophy, or high-minded preachments, or any of that junk. It is a show that's fun for most people who see it, that's all, and as I said in the beginning it happened quite by accident. Perhaps we should all kneel at our bedsides each night and thank the Great Whoever that it turned out as well as it has.

As of November 10, 1981, *Whorehouse* had played on Broadway for forty-one months and, with 1,418 performances, had set a new house record, surpassing *How to Succeed in Business Without Really Trying* to become the twentieth-longest-running show in Broadway history—and it was still going strong. I have to pinch myself to realize it has lasted longer on Broadway than such old hits as *Damn Yankees, Carousel, A Streetcar Named Desire, Teahouse of the August Moon, The Pajama Game, Can Can, Annie Get Your Gun, Mister Roberts, The King and I, Funny Girl, The Music Man, Cabaret,* and *Guys and Dolls.* Our three national companies and the Broadway company had grossed $67 million to November 1981—to round it off to the nearest million. We have had foreign companies in South Africa, Australia, and England. Later will come all those summer-stock companies, dinner-theatre versions, and amateur productions. Not bad for a bunch of first-timers who started out in a funky old church building.

A number of people have gotten fat—or fatter—off *Whorehouse.* No way of saying how much Universal has made, them all time crying the blues and poor-mouthing it, but bet your ass they have cleared meeny, meeny million pesos. Even Carl Schaeffer's "soup kitchen" got a goodly bone: Universal paid back the $11,000 Actors Studio put into our showcase, and honored the one-eighth of one percent of the gross we had signed over. Some weeks, that "fraction" means $1,000 or better for Actors Studio. Pete, Carol, and I got about two-thirds rich and Tommy Tune, who joined us later and has a lesser percentage, at least half rich.

Several magazine editors have asked me to write an article about how the success of *Whorehouse* has changed my life. I still carry such scars from so many years of magazine journalism that I haven't been tempted to write that piece. For the curious, however, I suppose this is as good a place as any to ponder the question briefly.

As you might suspect, the changes have largely been for the good. I live better; I no longer have to hide from creditors or stall the tax man. These considerations are worth a great deal in peace of mind. I can be more independent in my career, not having to approach editors like a blind beggar rattling a cup in his hand. I can say no, after years of not daring to or feeling uncomfortable when I did.

A whole new world has opened up for me—the theatre—and I intend to work more in it. In the summer of 1979, at New Playwright's Theatre in Washington, Barbara Blaine produced with some success a one-man show, *The Kingfish* (which I had co-authored with Ben Z. Grant), based loosely on the life of the late Huey Long of Louisiana. The show was well received, too, in Texas—starring John Daniel Reaves—when it toured a half dozen cities to raise funds for liberal political candidates I favored. We are starting now to work on turning that show into a full-scale musical and, of course, we have that Broadway gleam in our eyes. Despite the many fights I had with Carol Hall during *Whorehouse,* I wanted her for the music and lyrics but we couldn't agree on percentages. So what else is new?

I now have the pleasure of working with my wife in an allied field. Barbara, eager to add to her knowledge in the many fields of law, and wanting to strike out by herself, has her own operation as an entertainment lawyer and literary agent. She started with me and has added numerous other writers to her stable. One day I hope to retire and live off her earnings.

There have been certain drawbacks, of course. As the late Father Divine once reared back and remarked from his heaven on earth in Detroit, "Bein' God ain't no bed of roses." (Yes, I know that line first appeared in the play *Green Pastures*, but I liked old Daddy Divine's reading.) There is business to attend to, for example, and I have always hated business more than any member of the Communist Workers party; indeed, I am inclined to agree with the late Louis Armstrong, who once opined that "business has killed more men than war." Yet, despite the fact that Barbara sees after the lion's share of such transactions, it seems I now spend an extraordinary amount of time satisfying accountants, tax lawyers, and investment advisors. And me not able to remember if it's better for the price of gold to go up or down.

No one throws a charity ball, sets out to save the whale, or runs for public office without soliciting me for their cause. I am besieged by people who want me to invest in their perpetual-motion machines or instant cancer-cures. Hopeless playscripts arrive in the mail from strangers, along with letters curtly instructing me to whip the plays into shape, get them on Broadway, and split the profits with the authors; these letters usually order me to report back by a week from Thursday. Everybody who has a breakfast club, a luncheon group, or an annual banquet seems to think I want to come to Wichita, Kansas, or Fat Mountain, Georgia, to speechify to them.

Once I could roam the streets unrecognized by all save the most dogged of my creditors; now that is not always so. I am tired of strangers who stop me in midpassage—at bookstores, the supermarket, on the street—to ask what I am working on now, will I get them four orchestra seats for tomorrow night, and how about coming over here to say hello to Aunt Millie or Uncle Oscar. I think they should work it out that us celebrities can go to a central throne and sit on it, while attendants fan us and serve chocolates and cheese tidbits, on days when we want our feet kissed; the rest of the time they will have to leave us the hell alone. The telephone, which I always have hated as an instrument of intrusion, is a larger risk than formerly; your chances of getting me to answer it are about one in two thousand.

I have noted a certain hostility in the past couple of years, not from old friends but from people I hardly knew in the long ago and who now imagine that we once were close. These are made furious when I don't recognize them on sight or agree to cosign their notes or invite them to our occasional parties. I have had a couple tell me what a stuck-up chickenshit I have become; I can no longer pop 'em in the mouth because they might sue and collect, me no longer being judgment-proof. So yes, in certain ways I have given up a bit of freedom.

A couple of hot young journalistic guns have come after me. One, a Dallas reporter, followed me around Texas a couple of days in the spring of 1980 while I was on a book-promotion tour. Though he matched me drink for drink, he wrote a great deal about my misuse of alcohol. While I cannot fault him from the standpoint of accuracy, I think he might have made less of it in pre-*Whorehouse* days. The same dude badgered me to name my close friends and associates in New York, Washington, and Texas. After I did, he made it sound as if I had rushed through Texas dropping names at all pit stops; I mean, I suppose I *could* have named him a plumber or a ribbon-clerk or two—but then, that might have spoiled his game. The fellow also took me to task for wearing an accent and blue jeans, habits I first acquired in Putnam, Texas, around a half century ago. Somehow he made it sound as if I had gone to some cowboy school in Manhattan and had visited Texas to take my final exams.

I have recently read a couple of pieces lamenting that I have been "beguiled" or "enraptured" by the theatre—implying that this is something like the acquisition of an incurable social disease—and therefore may have been lost to "serious" writing. If some of that fluff I wrote for quick-pay, easy-read magazines—how to dodge the draft, sex fantasies of truck drivers, comparing the charms of northern women with southern ones, mail received by congressmen—was "serious" writing, no one noticed at the time.

It is true that one of the attractions of making money was the prospect of being able to write what I wanted. After so many years with nose to the typewriter, it developed that I temporarily wanted to write nothing. I put together a nonfiction collection of previously published material, which required about three days of writing bridging materials plus a lot of pasting-up, and I spent a few weeks on the Huey Long play with Ben Z. Grant. Otherwise, I lay around wallowing in prosperity and whiskey. Largely dry these several months now—yes, I've stumbled a time or three—I do want to get back to an abandoned novel and the old LBJ book. I am not, however, tempted to try my hand at poetry or agonize over philosophies or discover new plateaus of introspection. I have never done any of that, really, though to hear or see laments about how I've been spoilt and ruint by Broadway, one might think so.

All my grumbles are in a minor key, to be sure. I ain't about to trade the new problems in to get back the old ones. Neither am I thinking of giving the money back, to somehow purify my poet's soul. I'll do that only when two beefy dudes knock on my door, flash their badges and the arrest warrant, and say, "Okay, King, you walking fraud! Come with us! And you better bring your lunch, buddy, 'cause you're in such a heap of trouble you're gonna be away a long, long time."

My Clark blood about half expects that to happen any day now.

## APPENDIX

Original casts, listed in alphabetical order, of the various companies of *The Best Little Whorehouse in Texas:*

ORIGINAL CAST (Off Off Broadway). An Actors Studio production. Opened October 27, 1977, at the Actors Studio, 432 West 44th Street, New York, N.Y.

Clint Allmon
Barbara Burge
Eric Cowley
Lorrie Davis
Christopher Duncan
Joan Ellis
Henderson Forsythe
Tex Gibbons
Carlin Glynn
Gayle Greene
Jane Ives
Mallory Jones
John Kegley
K. C. Kelly
Elizabeth Kemp
Bradley Clayton King
Larry L. King
Thom Kuhl
Bonnie Leaders
Susan Mansur
Marci Maullar
Patrick McCord
Jay McCormack
J. J. Quinn
Pamela Reed
Elaine Rinehart
Gil Rogers
Marta Sanders
Ed Setrakian
Elliott Swift
Beverly Wallace

*The Pick-up Quartet:* George Schneider, piano; Bradley Clayton King, guitar and harmonica; Curtis Fields, reeds; Bruce Smith, bass.

OFF BROADWAY CAST. Opened April 17, 1978, at the Entermedia Theatre, Second Avenue and 12th Street, New York, N.Y.

Clint Allmon
Pamela Blair
Lisa Brown
Cameron Burke
Gerry Burkhardt
Jay Bursky
Tom Cashin
Carol Chambers
Don Crabtree
Joan Ellis
Henderson Forsythe
Jay Garner
Becky Gelke
Carlin Glynn
Delores Hall
Bradley Clayton King
Donna King
J. Frank Lucas
Susan Mansur
Jan Merchant
Edna Milton
Louise Quick-Bowen
James Rich
Marta Sanders
Michael Scott
Paul Ukena, Jr.
Debra Zalkind

*The Rio Grande Band:* Craig Chambers, guitar and lead vocalist; Pete Blue, piano; Ben Brogdon, bass; Lynn Frazier, steel guitar; Chris Laird, drums; Ernie Reed, fiddle.

BROADWAY CAST. Opened June 19, 1978, at the 46th Street Theatre, 226 West 46th Street, New York, N.Y.

Clint Allmon
Lisa Brown
Gerry Burkhardt
Jay Bursky
Tom Cashin
Carol Chambers
Don Crabtree
Joan Ellis
Henderson Forsythe
Jay Garner
Becky Gelke
Carlin Glynn
Delores Hall
K. C. Kelly
Bradley Clayton King
Donna King
J. Frank Lucas
Susan Mansur
Jan Merchant
Edna Milton
Louise Quick-Bowen
Gena Ramsel
James Rich
Marta Sanders
Michael Scott
Paul Ukena, Jr.
Debra Zalkind

*The Rio Grande Band:* Craig Chambers, guitar and lead vocalist; Pete Blue, piano; Ben Brogdon, bass; Lynn Frazier, steel guitar; Michael Holleman, drums; Ernie Reed, fiddle.

HOUSTON COMPANY. Opened February 25, 1979, at the Tower Theatre, Houston, Texas.

Jan Alford
David Ray Bartee
Peggy Byers
Connie Cooper
Larry Earl-Lane
Ann Faulkner
Clare Fields
Cecil Fulfer
Ed Geldart
Jim Goode
Pat Hamilton
William (Bill) Hardy
Glenn Holtzman
Larry Hovis
Tommy Hulsey
Steve Leatherwood
Allison Marich
Marietta Marich
Yvonne McCord
Francie Mendenhall
Mitch Mitchell
Tommy Rogers
Susan Shofner
Jackie Teamer
Nick Walker
Cynthia Watts
Angie Wheeler
Pamela Whitten
Art Yelton

*The Average Country Band:* Mike Boyd, guitar and lead vocalist; Kerry Demeria, drums; Don Dempsey, bass; Eddie Nation, guitar; Bob Paulsen, piano; Jim Powell, steel guitar; Bob White, fiddle.

FIRST NATIONAL TOURING COMPANY. Opened October 2, 1979, at the Shubert Theatre, Boston, Massachusetts.

Beau Allen
Valerie Austyn
Tom Avera
Don Bernhardt
Mimi Bessette
Valerie Leigh Bixler
Jeff Calhoun
Dolly Colby
David Gaines
Jeffry George
Joe Gillie
Ruth Gottschall
William Hardy
Joe Hart
Robert R. Hendrickson
Larry Hovis
Marilyn J. Johnson
Roxie Lucas
Deborah Magid
Amy Miller
Robert Moyer
Barbara Marineau
Andy Parker
Pamela Pilkenton
Rebecca Ann Seay
Alexis Smith
Karen Tamburrelli
Joseph Warren

*The Texas Tally Wackers:* Bradley Clayton King, guitar and lead vocalist; Greg DeBelles, drums; Mark Hummel, piano; Lynn Frazier, steel guitar; Jeremy C. Cohen, fiddle.

SECOND NATIONAL TOURING COMPANY. Opened March 15, 1980, at The Theatre in Orlando, Florida.

Roy Alan
Jan Alford
Neil Badders
David Ray Bartee
Peggy Byers
Kevin Cooney
David Doty
Ann Faulkner
Clare Fields
Ed Geldart
Jim Goode
Sylvia Greene
Glenn Holtzman
Thomas Hulsey
Michel Kaye-Alan
William Larsen
Steve Leatherwood
Allison Marich
Steve Marland
Yvonne McCord
Francie Mendenhall
Mitch Mitchell
Theresa Nelson
T. Jay Rogers
Sidney Rojo
Susan Shofner
Jackie Teamer
June Terry
J. Nick Walker
Angie Wheeler
Pamela Whitten
Richard Wyatt

*Six Easy Pieces:* Tony Booth, bass guitar and lead vocalist; Jimmy Powell, steel guitar; Kerry Demeria, drums; Eddie Nation, lead guitar; Bob White, fiddle; Art Yelton, piano.

THIRD NATIONAL TOURING COMPANY. Opened November 17, 1980, at the Playhouse Theatre, Wilmington, Delaware.

Eric Aaron
Joel Anderson
Susan Beaubian
Alan Bruun
Jan Buttram
Charmion Clark
Marcia Ann Dobres
Steve Earl Edwards
Martha Gehman
Kristie Hannum
Susan Hartley
Page Johnson
Wendy Laws
Francie Mendenhall
Joey Morris
Ernie Reed
Marian Reed
Mark Reina
William Ryall
Gena Scriva
Guy Strobel
Vincent Vogt
Jenny Lee Wax
Robert Weil
Christopher Wynkoop

*The Bandera Regulars:* Ernie Reed, fiddler and lead vocalist; Jim Loessberg, steel guitar; James Hines, bass; Ed Payton, drums; George Groehls, piano.